SHADOW PEOPLE

HELEN DesERMIA

JD
A JAN
DENNIS
BOOK

THOMAS NELSON PUBLISHERS
Nashville • Atlanta • London • Vancouver

Published in Nashville, Tennessee, by Thomas Nelson, Inc., Publishers, and distributed in Canada by Word Communications, Ltd., Richmond, British Columbia.

Scripture quotations are from the NEW KING JAMES VERSION of the Bible, Copyright © 1979, 1980, 1982, Thomas Nelson, Inc., Publishers.

Library of Congress Cataloging-in-Publication Data

DesErmia, Helen.
    Shadow people : a novel / Helen DesErmia.
        p. cm.
    ISBN 0-7852-7920-2
    I. Title.
PS354.E83535S48 1995
813'.54—dc20   94-39272
                                                    CIP

Published in the United States of America

2 3 4 5 6 — 00 99 98 97 96

DEDICATION

To Michael

Pax, Mike; Pax Aeterna

ACKNOWLEDGMENTS

Special thanks to my husband Bob, whose patience and forebearance allowed me to finish this book; to daughter Jeannette for her suggestions; to Raymond Dann, M.D., whose medical information made several scenes come alive; to Kenyon Baird, Ph.D., leader of the Vista group of the San Diego County Christian Writers' Guild; all the members, too many to mention although they deserve to be named, who helped me through difficult passages and situations; and to Sherwood E. Wirt, Ph.D., whose encouragement was invaluable. Warm thanks also to Jan Dennis, for being so patient with me, and the staff at Thomas Nelson Publishers, who were always ready to answer questions and help in any way they could.

But most of all, to our Lord Jesus Christ, without Whom none of this would be possible.

ONE

Wednesday, October 16, 12:50 P.M.

Susan pushed her soup bowl away and sat back, staring out the restaurant window. Gulls, stark white against the dark gray clouds gathering over the distant horizon, swooped around a small fishing boat coming in toward the pier. A jet heading west over the ocean pencilled twin white lines against the cobalt sky above the sunlit cloud tops. Bronzed young people played volleyball on one of San Diego County's finest beaches. Youngsters carried their boogie boards into the sun-sparkled water pretending they were riding the waves as the surfers did farther out.

"What's the matter? Isn't the soup any good?" Lacey's fork, loaded with crab salad, was halfway to her mouth.

"Oh, it's fine. Actually, it's great." Susan glanced back at Lacey, looked out the window again. "I guess I lost my appetite." She looked back at her friend. "A grisly story came in at the paper this morning, and I can't get it off my mind." Nothing in her journalism classes at San Diego State had prepared her for the personal shock of her first real-life, appalling news story.

"What's it about?" Lacey asked, probing around her plate for chunks of crab.

Susan shrugged, ran her fingers through her tawny hair. "Nothing big. Just some cats all cut up and mutilated and put back on the owners' lawns. Every one of them drained of blood. Up in the Seaview Heights area. You know—where the CEOs live."

Lacey slid her dishes to one side, stared at Susan. "Wow. How can anyone be so mean?"

Susan shook her head. "It's another sign of the times."

Lacey's mouth tightened. "Don't give me that nonsense again," she said. "Some psycho just went off his nut and—ugh," she shivered lightly, "cut up some neighborhood cats."

"Think what you like, but it seems as if things like this are happening more and more often." She looked out at the sky. "At one house, a little girl came out to find the feet, head, and tail of her pet placed so she'd see them the minute she came out. That poor little girl—" The clouds were moving slowly inshore, driven by a northwest wind.

"Poor kid."

"Sorry. I didn't mean to—well, you know." She continued, "And I set up another story about a new store in the Atterbury District that will sell occult supplies—newts' eyes and bats' tongues and wings. That sort of stuff. They can order anything else anyone wants. Sounds like a store to supply witches, satanists."

"Satanists in Playa Linda? Oh, don't be silly! Your imagination's working overtime."

Susan's eyes flashed blue fire momentarily. "Not imagination. I think the two items are connected."

"How?"

"Satanists use animals as sacrifices in their rituals, some of which use the supplies these people are selling. I've heard satanists also sometimes sacrifice humans."

Lacey smothered a laugh. "That was in Salem hundreds of years ago. You're letting your fundamentalist background run away with your imagination. People don't do such things anymore." She glanced at her watch. "Oops. Gotta go. Dad'll be on my case if I'm not at my desk in seven minutes! Lunch is on me this time."

They pushed back their chairs, Lacey signed the tab, and the two wound their way among the tables to the exit.

Lacey got into her red Corvette and watched as Susan started up her Ford Escort. She sighed. Susan was such a ninny sometimes, but so good-hearted. Ever since kindergarten, they had been best friends, even though they disagreed on a number of things. Mostly matters having to do with church. *I'm glad she's not tiresome like some of them*, she thought, *always quoting chapter and verse every time you say something they don't like*. She started her own engine and sped off to the tower where her father, Jerrod Robinson, headed Robinson, Beckman, and Stolt, Attorneys-at-Law. The most influential law firm in town. She decided it was all right to feel a bit smug about her family's position in the community, and smiled with satisfaction as she pulled into her parking slot in the garage.

1:37 P.M.

Susan walked into the lobby at *The Playa Linda Register* and greeted the receptionist. "Hi, Alison." Sounds of bustle—muted voices, clatter of keyboards, chattering whine of printers, and ringing of phones—came to the lobby from the various offices.

"Jackson's waiting to see you," Alison said, pointing a pen over her shoulder at the editor's office door, and reached for the phone.

Susan raised her eyebrows and nodded thanks as she walked to the door and knocked.

"C'mon in!" a masculine voice roared. Susan looked back at Alison, winced, and opened the door.

"You're late!" Hobart Jackson was a large bony man, about fifty-five, bald, with wild, bushy eyebrows and a wilder mustache. He looked far more formidable than he was. "Sit down." He waved a pencil toward the one chair in the cluttered little office.

Susan sat and made a scared little face.

"Oh, don't be silly," roared Jackson. He looked mock sternly at her, drawing his brows down over eyes sparkling with humor. "Just get back from lunch on time." He stirred the papers on his desk until he found what he was looking for. "Here. Another story came in after you left. I want you to find out all you can about it." He handed her the fax.

Susan read it and looked up wide-eyed. "More?"

"Yeah. The other end of town. Just like the first. Except it was a couple of puppies and more cats."

Silence. Susan put the paper down in her lap and looked at Jackson. "Who would do a thing like that?"

"That's what I want you to find out. Talk to the police, the people concerned, the humane society, and anyone else you can think of. Find out if it's connected in any way with any group or just one poor devil who's out of his mind." He thought a moment. "Can't be just one wacko."

Susan looked through the release again. "Do you think it has anything to do with the occult store story?"

Jackson shrugged again. "Who knows? Find out." He pointed a finger at her. "But be careful! I don't want to find parts of my rookie reporter scattered all over town."

"Me, too," she said in a small voice. "Mind if I talk to Matt and get him to help me?"

"Your computer wiz boyfriend? Guess not. Matter of fact, it's a good idea. He might be able to find out stuff you can't." Jackson levered his bony mass up from his seat. "Call me any time you need help. You have my home phone?"

Susan nodded and rose from the chair.

"Remember," he warned, "be careful. Don't work yourself into a corner. I don't want the story that badly. But do what you can." He turned back to the papers on his desk, looked up again. "If you get the whole story, there's a bonus in it for you."

Susan's eyes sparkled. "Thanks, boss," she said and walked out. Alison grinned as she went outside again.

Susan parked in a space directly in front of the entrance to the store Matt called The Computer Warehouse and locked the car door behind her. Ragged strands of gray clouds had begun to invade the blue sky overhead. A strong wind blew at her as she hurried to the door with her story research files in hand.

Inside, fluorescent lights brightened the many sample machines and highlighted the covers of numberless programs, books, and games Matt had for sale. Ricky Martinez, Matt's salesman, smiled broadly as she came in.

"Matt's back in the office. Did you want to see him?"

Susan nodded. "If he's not too busy."

"Never. Not where you're concerned." He led the way to the glassed cubicle where Matt kept the store on an even financial keel.

"Look what the wind blew in," said Ricky, opening the door, ushering her in and excusing himself in the same breath.

Matt looked up and turned away from his spreadsheet. A broad grin spread over his good-looking freckled face. Not handsome as movie stars are supposed to be, but wholesome and likeable.

"Well, hi. What brings you here in the middle of the day? Paper run out of news already?"

Susan bent to kiss him lightly. "No such luck." She perched on the edge of the massive desk. "No, I'm here to ask a favor. How about going across the street for a cup of coffee? I'd like some, and we can talk there."

"Sure." Matt punched a key to save his work and piled papers off to one side. "I'm tired of this anyway. I need a break."

A chill wind blasted them as they stepped outside. "Wish I had brought a sweater," Susan mumbled, clutching her file. "Come on!" she said, noting a break in the moderate traffic that let them race across the street.

Inside the warm little coffee shop, they sat at a table by the window. A few people walked past, leaning into the wind, some holding bundles close. Dust skittered down the street as a gust hit dirt, and an advertising flyer fluttered behind. Susan looked out with dismay. "It was such a nice morning when I came to work. Now look at it. I hope it won't rain."

"'It's too early for rain," said Matt, looking over the menu. "It's only October. I'm hungry. Haven't eaten yet."

"I already had lunch with Lacey. All I want is coffee."

A middle-aged woman in a tight brown dress and ruffled apron came to the table, poised a pencil over her order book, and smiled a welcome. "Hi, Matt, Susan. What will it be today?"

Matt looked up. "Hi, Connie. Hot beef sandwich and coffee. Coffee for Sue—did you want anything with it?" he asked her.

Susan paused a moment, thought of Lacey's slim figure, and shook her head. "Just coffee, black."

Connie scribbled, stuck her pencil into her Clairol Blonde bun, smiled again, and went off.

Matt leaned back. "Okay. What's the problem?"

Susan told him about the stories she'd worked on. He was still listening when Connie brought the coffee. His eyes were hard.

Susan sipped the scalding liquid. "That's what Jackson wants me to investigate," said Susan. "I don't even know where to begin. He said it would be okay for you to help me."

"He expects me to help you?" Matt stared at her. "All I know is computers. How can I help?"

"You'll find a way. You always do." Susan put her cup down and leaned a little toward Matt. "For one thing, if there is a group of satanists here, what are the chances they'll buy a computer?"

Matt shrugged. "Everyone who has to keep records eventually winds up with a computer. Wouldn't they have a list of members, addresses, that sort of thing?"

"I dunno. I guess. And I wonder if they keep in touch with other covens?" She paused. "If so, it might be by modem." She looked at Matt. "You have the largest selection and best prices in town, so maybe they'd come to you."

"Maybe. But they might have another source. Besides, maybe they don't operate that way. It's not a sure thing."

Connie set a steaming plate of mashed potatoes, sliced beef, and gravy in front of Matt, nodded, and left. Another couple came in, bringing a gust of chill wind, and sat at a table nearer the back of the cafe.

Susan sipped. "Nothing's a sure thing. Well, the computer angle was kind of a shot in the dark. I thought you might have some way of getting information that I don't. Don't you hear about purchases at other stores?"

"Only sometimes," he said around a mouthful of mashed potatoes. He swallowed. "The only thing I can think of is to go to the police and find out what they know."

Susan nodded. "That's next. Want to come with me?"

"Can't." He swallowed some coffee and cut off a chunk of meat with his fork. "Gotta do my accounts. Tomorrow I'll have more time, and in the meantime, I'll try to figure some way to get information. Okay?" He slipped more meat into his mouth and chewed.

Susan sipped more coffee. "What about the dismembered cats and puppies? Any ideas about that?"

Matt choked, coughed, and looked daggers at Susan. "Hey, I'm trying to eat lunch!" He shook his head. "Okay," he said and put down his fork, reaching back in his memory. "Remember the story awhile back of some ranchers in Indiana who found cattle with all the blood drained out of them? Sorta weird, like this deal."

Susan nodded. "And where was it—Kansas?—they found sheep 'surgically dismembered,' if I remember right," she said. "They never found out anything about that, either. Tabloids blamed it on UFOs." She shuddered. "And the time they found howling dogs that had been tortured half to death on a beach north of here. Ugh!" She shook her head. "That story just kind of disappeared. I never saw a follow-up." She sipped her coffee. "And last week I heard that cats had been killed and left on the owners' lawns at Laguna Grande Country Club, too. Scary. Not my story, though." She swallowed the last of her coffee. "Well, that shows this isn't an isolated incident. I'd better get to the police station to find out what they know. Then, the animal shelter. But you will help, won't you?" Her eyes implored as she leaned toward Matt.

"Honey, the Lord knows I can't say no when you look at me like that. Of course, I'll help, but I don't know what I can do."

Susan smiled. "You'll think of something. Maybe that's why I love you so much." She reached out and laid her hand on his.

"G'wan with you!" Matt grinned at her. "You going now?"

Susan nodded, stood, and set her purse strap on her shoulder. "Thanks, Matt. See you tomorrow."

Matt watched her as she looked both ways, timed it just right, and ran across to her car. She unlocked the door, slipped in, and with a wave of her hand, drove off.

What's she got herself into now? he wondered. With a sigh, he picked up his fork again to finish his lunch.

TWO

Wednesday, October 16, 1:38 P.M.

Lacey couldn't help admiring her father as she walked into his wood-paneled office. Jerrod Robinson was tall, handsome, and trim. His dark hair was showing a bit of silver at the temples, adding to the impression he gave of strength and integrity. He was leafing through a law book he had just taken from one of the shelves, absently fingering his dark mustache.

With its rich appointments, deep carpeting, paintings, and other *objets d'art* scattered among the books lining two walls, the fifth floor room looked as if it belonged in a castle somewhere. The difference was that behind the teak desk the wall was glass, over-looking a seaside park, now nearly empty except for palms and eucalypti tossed by the rising wind. Lacey looked at the ocean, still sparkling but turning dark near the horizon, white combers breaking on sunlit golden sands.

Robinson looked up, saw Lacey, and put the heavy book back on the shelf. He kissed his daughter on the cheek and ruffled her short dark hair, so like her mother's. "Did you finish the research on the Carleton-Swift merger papers yet?" he asked.

"Started. It's pretty complex, you know."

"We're on a deadline. Check with Frances. She knows where all the bodies are buried." He put his hand under her chin and smiled grimly, as if a whip hid in the background. "Get busy on that merger. I want the papers on my desk before you leave this evening. Okay?"

Lacey sighed. "Okay. If you say so. But you're a bully." She made a face and left the office. Her father grinned as she paused at the door and pretended to stagger under a load.

"Outta here!" he said, and she disappeared.

By the time Lacey had finished with the papers, laid them on her father's desk in his empty office, and gone down to the parking basement for her car, the wind was blowing a misting rain around corners, behind eyeglasses, up sleeves, and down necklines. The evening was definitely miserable.

She drove up the ramp and shuddered as wind wailed mournfully into the exit. Streetlights wore halos and the pedestrians still out bent their heads into the wind, holding their collars tight. Headlights shimmered in the streets, and Lacey adjusted her wipers to clear the accumulating mist. Turning carefully onto the boulevard, she headed toward home in the prestigious residential district called Tres Encinos, so named for the three ancient oaks at the entrance, remnants of a coastal live oak forest cut down in favor of expensive executive homes.

On impulse she decided to visit Susan, to ask if there was any more news about cat-killings, then remembered that Susan had said she was having dinner at her folks' home. She wondered if they would mind if she showed up. Lacey was practically a regular at the Walkers'. Surely they wouldn't.

She drove a short distance along the boulevard and made the right turn onto Washington Avenue, one of the city's original streets through the old, deteriorating Atterbury district of once-impressive homes. Washington was her shortcut to the Walkers' home, although it was narrow and winding in the manner of older streets everywhere.

Lacey had never before driven the street after dark and was surprised at how gloomy it was. Some of the streetlights were shattered; some burned out. Only a few of the houses had light glowing through one or another window. Strong winds hurled the unseasonable rain at her windshield. Vague figures appeared and seemed to melt wetly into wells of darkness among trees between the old houses, and in her imagination, unknown dangers waited around every curve in the road. She became nervous to the point of fear.

Suddenly, an unearthly shriek ripped the air. Startled, Lacey swerved to miss a shadowy figure running across the road. She regained control of the car, and, thoroughly terrified, stopped momentarily to look back. She heard an eerie keening and wailing, and, more scared than she had ever been before, floored the gas pedal, slipping and skidding as she pulled away. Driving fast as she dared, dazzled by rain-shattered light and barely missing oncoming traffic, she finally turned on Cutler Way, stopped under a bright streetlight, and put her head down on the wheel, shaking, striving for self-control.

When her heart had quieted down to a beat slower than her wipers, she looked around at the tranquility of Susan's neighborhood, quiet and respectable, safe and comfortable. The lights of a convenience store illumined the gleaming wet street halfway down the block. Drawing a shuddery breath, she drove to the store.

Still shaking, she ran through light rain and entered the store. The fragrance of fresh-brewed coffee enveloped her. A large gray-haired man behind the counter wearing a badge labeled "Joe" looked up from counting change.

His smile changed to concern. "Is something the matter?" he asked. "Are you sick or something?"

Lacey tried a smile, but it went crooked. "No. I just had a scare. I drove down Washington Avenue and heard some noises. They startled me."

Joe shook his head. "Washington Avenue ain't no place for a lady like you, miss, 'specially on a night like this. What can I get for you?"

"Coffee! Just coffee. One sugar and cream."

She stood by the counter, huddled within herself, her hands wrapped around the styrofoam cup, sipping gratefully, drawing strength from watching big, solid Joe put pennies, nickels, dimes, and quarters into rolls. Three energetic teenage boys burst in and, chattering noisily, examined all the magazines. Finally, each chose one, got a six-pack of colas, paid, and left. Such a contrast—so normal.

Feeling better, Lacey threw away her empty cup, thanked Joe, and went back to her car. She sat for a minute with the doors locked and convinced herself that now she really could drive to the Walkers' house and talk with Susan awhile. No one else would believe what had just happened. And something about Susan and her family always made her feel—what was the word she wanted?—secure. Warm. Loved. Perhaps even more than she did at her own home. Then she would drive back to the boulevard—the long way! Not by Washington. Straight home. Remembering the screams made her shudder. Again, a touch of fear crept up the back of her neck.

The lights were on in the living room at the Walkers' modest two-story house. Mrs. Walker met her at the door, but her smile turned to concern when she saw her expression.

"Is Susan here?" Lacey asked, fighting to keep her voice steady.

"Of course. Come on in. What—never mind. Just come in!" Mrs. Walker led her to the living room, where Susan sat on the couch beside Matt. Susan got up and went to Lacey, looking questions at her. "What happened?" she asked. Lacey just shook her head.

Matt stood up and extended his hand. "Hi, Lacey. It's been awhile." Concern showed in his face. Lacey took his hand but was unable to say a word.

Susan put her arm around Lacey's shoulders. "Migosh, you look awful. What's the matter?" Susan's fifteen-year-old brother Raymond stopped on his way down the stairs to watch.

Lacey crumpled into a chair, her self-control fragmented, and burst into tears. "I've never been so scared," she stammered. Matt, Susan, and the Walkers all put questions at once. Susan dropped to her knees beside her and hugged her. Raymond came down the rest of the way and watched. Soon, Lacey lifted her head.

"All right, now, Lacey," said Susan, holding her at arm's length, "tell us. What happened?"

Lacey took a tissue from Matt, wiped her eyes and blew her nose. She told of taking her spooky Washington Avenue shortcut, her fright at the shriek, the dark figure running across the street, and the unearthly screams. Mrs. Walker went to the kitchen to make tea.

"It was probably nothing more than a catfight and people trying to stop it," said Lacey, "but it really scared me." She dabbed at her eyes and looked at Susan. "I've never been on Washington Avenue after dark, and it's—I dunno, it was weird."

Raymond stared wide-eyed at her and Matt nodded. "It's an old district, a lot different from where you live. The people who live there don't have much, can't afford to keep up their houses, but they're just folks, like anyone else."

Mrs. Walker put the tray with steaming teapot, cups, saucers, and cookies on the coffee table and started pouring. "Here," she said, handing a cup to Lacey. "Have some cookies, too." Raymond came over, helped himself to a couple of cookies, excused himself, and went upstairs. Sounds of a rock band floated down from his CD player.

Lacey smiled as she took the tea. "You're all so kind," she said, and looking embarrassed, went on. "It was silly of me to get so upset and disturb you like this. I apologize."

"Not a bit," said Mr. Walker. "I'm glad we were here."

Lacey sipped at the tea and reached for a cookie. "Actually, I came over to ask if you'd heard anything else about—" she looked around at the older Walkers and back at Susan, "—you know—the story?"

"I've told everyone," said Susan. "And yes, there is more."

While they drank tea and ate cookies, Susan told Lacey about the other dismembered pets, and that Matt was going to help them find out what was going on. "And that's about it for now. I've been to the police, but they don't know anything more than we do. At least, they didn't say much. I got the impression they were trying to get rid of me."

By the time the last cookie crumb was picked up, Lacey was back to normal. She set her cup down on the tray, stood up, picked up her purse, and smiled her thanks at everyone.

"I'd better get home now, or Mom and Dad will think I've run off with someone. I can't thank you enough," she said to Mrs. Walker.

"Any time," she said, and Lacey knew she meant it.

Saying good night at the door, Lacey had all but forgotten her fright. The rain had stopped, so she rolled down her windows to enjoy the fresh smells left by the evening storm. Once behind the wheel, she fancied she could hear that unearthly shriek again and shuddered as she turned the key. The engine purred like a large cat. *Now why did I think of that?* she scolded, seeing in her mind a huge dismembered panther. She shivered as the car moved off smoothly.

The familiar surroundings of exclusive Tres Encinos flooded her with relief. She pulled into the garage as the door swung up and closed quietly behind her.

In the house, her parents were entertaining an old family acquaintance, John Merkel. He was charming them with stories of business triumphs. He was darkly good-looking, but there was something slippery in a beguiling, theatrical way about him that set Lacey's teeth on edge.

"Ah! Here she is!" he said and, with a flourish, bowed from the waist.

"Where in the world have you been?" asked her mother, an older version of Lacey, who was seated gracefully on a Louis XIV armchair.

"Indeed! Where have you been?" her father demanded from the matching settee, his pipe clenched between his teeth.

"I stopped at Susan's on the way home," she said casually. "By the way, Dad, the papers are on your desk. You weren't in the office when I left them."

Mr. Robinson cleared his throat. "Ah. Yes, I found them. I was in conference with some associates." He knocked the ashes out of his pipe, looking a bit distracted. "Thanks, honey, you did a good job." His eyes met Lacey's. He changed the subject. "John said the two of you had a date tonight."

John looked ostentatiously at his watch. "Lacey, we were going to the Lyceum tonight," he said. "It's too late, now."

"Oh, I'm sorry. I forgot." Lacey looked wearily at John. "Another time?"

John took her hand and sighed. "Ah, well. You've bewitched me. How about tomorrow?" He nibbled at her fingers.

Lacey snatched her hand away. "Stop that! I'm busy tomorrow night. Call me Friday, and we'll work something out. But I'm tired. I'm going to bed now." She yawned elaborately and kissed her parents good night. She started up the stairs, and waved to John, who spread his arms imploringly.

"Good *night*, John," she said sweetly, continuing up the stairs. He sighed, blew her a kiss, and saying good night to all, went out into the darkness. A light rain was still falling.

Lacey was not tired. She closed her bedroom door behind her. *That shriek was not a catfight*, she thought, struggling with the idea that something evil had happened just as she drove by. *Those screams afterward—whoever screamed was even more scared than I was. What's going on?* A chill spread through her, and she had a premonition that this was not all over.

She undressed, put on a nightgown, and slipped between the satin sheets. She lay there for a long time, thinking. Shortly after she heard the old grandfather clock in the downstairs hall chime two she fell asleep.

Back on Washington Avenue, shadowy figures gathered near where Lacey had been startled by the shriek, and one after the other, disappeared into a boarded-up house set well back on its lot. A flickering light appeared through the chinks in the boards, and a soft chanting might have been heard if one had been close by.

THREE

Thursday, October 17, 7:30 A.M.

Lacey reached groggily for the clock radio to turn it off, stretched, yawned, and luxuriated in well-being.

The storm had passed and sunlight streamed through the sheer curtains at her windows. *What a beautiful day,* she thought. Water droplets still clung to leaves in the jacaranda tree near her window, scattering tiny rainbows as sunlight glittered on them. She showered, chose a lightweight emerald green suit that complemented her eyes and skin, and not until then did she remember the events of the past evening.

She was suddenly embarrassed. What an idiot she had been. Washington Avenue was just a normal, old, low-rent residential district, and people scream at lots of things. She had blown the whole thing entirely out of proportion. Maybe it had even been a loud TV. And someone running across the road—people do that all the time. The Walkers must have thought she was looney.

Downstairs, she found breakfast set up out on the patio. She drank her glass of orange juice and helped herself to scrambled eggs and bacon. Margaret, the housekeeper, brought out a pot of fresh coffee.

"Where's Mom?" asked Lacey, noticing her mother's plate was untouched.

Margaret looked troubled. "In bed, Miss Lacey. Her stomach's all upset. Woke up during the night and had to throw up. I've called the doctor. He said he'd be over after awhile."

Lacey put down her fork. "It's about time she saw the doctor. She's complained about pain for awhile now."

Margaret nodded and poured Lacey's coffee. "Your father said for you not to be late for work, Miss Lacey," she said. "He left early for Los Angeles. Said there was a lot for you to do."

Lacey made a mouth. "Great." She bit into her toast. "Did he say what it was about?"

"No. Only that he'd be late getting back." She turned and disappeared into the shadowy depths of the house.

Lacey watched her go, feeling uneasy. She and her father had been urging her mother to see Dr. Damron for a long time, but Mom always made excuses, saying it was nothing. She ate quickly and hurried to work.

Everything went smoothly at the office all morning, the extra workload notwithstanding. When Lacey finally looked at the clock, it was nearly one.

She came out of her office and paused at the secretary's desk. "Frances, I'm going for lunch," she said, and walked across to push the button for the elevator. When it dinged and the doors slid open, a perfect man—like one who stepped out of a cologne advertisement—walked out.

"Lacey!" he said. He smiled and held out his hand. "You're lovelier than before." Lacey looked blank. "Oh. Maybe you don't remember me. I'm Gilbert Crozier."

His grip was firm and warm. Memory tugged at Lacey, and she was suddenly extremely aware of his wavy chestnut hair, his well-shaped skull, his six-feet-plus height. His light blue eyes seemed to penetrate to her very thoughts, and she blushed. She pulled her hand away.

Placing him suddenly, she regained her composure, smiled brightly, and looked back up at him. "Thank you. So. We meet again. After all this time."

Her mind shot back years to when they had both been in junior high school. This Adonis had then been painfully shy, plain, almost homely, and always wore long-sleeved striped shirts, even in the summer. She'd hardly even known him.

"It has been a few years." Gilbert smiled.

"Ah—Dad's not here. He mentioned that he would be in Los Angeles today."

"Yes, I know. We've been working together on a financial project, and he mentioned his trip yesterday. Actually, I was wondering if you've had lunch yet. If not, would you like to join me at Le Petit Pécheur?"

Lacey's eyes widened momentarily. "Well," she said, glancing at Frances, "if it won't take too long. With Daddy out, I'd planned to eat in. But I'll say yes if I can get back early."

"Whatever you say." Gilbert ushered her into the elevator and pushed the button for the lobby floor, looking appreciatively at Lacey.

"You've changed a lot," said Lacey, uncomfortably aware of his scrutiny. "You were so shy when we were in junior high."

He nodded. "I got over that." The doors slid open, and they stepped through the small knot of people waiting to get on. He took her arm, and they went out onto the sunlit sidewalk to a silver Jaguar parked close by.

"Mmm. Whatever it is you do, you seem to be doing well," Lacey said as he seated her.

Gilbert nodded, got in, and started the engine. It purred like its namesake as they edged easily into traffic. They were silent as he drove the short distance to the restaurant. Lacey felt awkward. She had never been alone with him before.

A string quartet was playing Vivaldi as they entered. The sounds of silver on china and muted conversation complemented the rich fragrances of French cuisine. Lacey was suddenly ravenous.

The maitre d' greeted Gilbert by name. He seated them beside a glass wall at a table covered with snowy linen. Behind the wall was a patio planted with exotic foliage and flowers. When the waiter brought a menu, Gilbert ordered for them both. He asked about her work.

"So you work with your father in the firm, then?"

Lacey nodded. "Dad wanted me to be a lawyer," she said, "but I had enough first year pre-law at USC to know I didn't want that. I graduated with a BA in fine arts." Gilbert nodded as she continued on. "Dad put me on as a law clerk anyway. It's okay, I guess. I don't mind doing the research. It's the rest I can do without."

Gilbert raised a perfectly shaped eyebrow. *How devastatingly handsome he is,* thought Lacey. She toyed with her fork. "For right now, I'm just drifting. Maybe something will open up somewhere, and I'll find out who I am and what I'm supposed to be doing."

Gilbert smiled, his perfect teeth gleaming. "I'm sure you will. Oh. By the way, your father has invited me for dinner Wednesday evening. Will you be there?"

Lacey was silent a moment. It troubled her that he was coming to her home. "Yes, I'll be there." She avoided looking straight at him. Strange. He looked so handsome, so smooth, yet there was something about him—she stopped pursuing the thought. She couldn't sort out her thoughts now.

Lacey was enjoying the broiled halibut and light conversation when the waiter brought a phone to the table. "A call for you, Mam'selle," he said, and handed her the instrument.

"Miss Lacey, your mother started feeling worse today." Margaret sounded as if she were trying to keep worry out of her voice. "Now don't you get all upset," she said, "but the doctor ordered your mother to the hospital just after noon. He thinks it's food poisoning, of all things. As if it could be, me being so careful and all."

Lacey, startled, looked at Gilbert and spoke into the mouthpiece. "What happened?"

She listened, dismayed. "Where did they take her?" she asked. Then, "All right. You try to get hold of my father, and I'll see Mother at the hospital. All right?" She listened a moment more. "Okay. G'bye."

She handed the phone back to the waiter. Gilbert looked the question at her.

Lacey summoned calm from somewhere within. "My mother seems to have food poisoning. She's at Richmond General. Will you take me there, please?"

Gilbert touched his mouth with a napkin and stood up. "Of course." The waiter handed him the check, he paid it, and extended his hand to Lacey. "Ready?"

In a short time they burst through the door to Mrs. Robinson's room. "Doctor! What's the matter with my mother?" Lacey demanded, striding in.

Dr. Damron was standing by her bed, holding Mrs. Robinson's wrist. He put a finger to his lips. Her mother lay still, pale, on the narrow hospital bed, sleeping. He put the limp wrist down and came to Lacey, gently urging them both out into the hall.

"Your mother is very lucky," he said, closing the door behind him. "She ate hollandaise sauce last night?" he asked.

"I don't know. I wasn't home for supper."

"The lab reports egg contaminated with salmonella."

Lacey closed her eyes and sighed in relief. "I'm glad that's all it is!" she said.

The doctor looked tight-lipped. "The reason I say she's lucky is that we did some tests and found there could be another problem."

Lacey looked at him sharply. "Is it serious?"

Dr. Damron was silent a moment. "Tell me, has your mother complained about abdominal pain previously?"

"Yes, occasionally. Why?"

"I wish she had told me when it first started." He paused. "I won't lie to you, Lacey. It looks as if she has ovarian cancer. But thanks to the hollandaise, we're aware of it now."

Lacey stared at him, dread of the disease in her eyes.

The doctor put a hand on her shoulder. "It looks as if we may have caught it in time, but we're keeping her overnight for further tests." Lacey started to interrupt but he went on. "You can't do anything here, so go home. Your mother will be asleep for hours. I'll call you if we learn anything new."

Gilbert took Lacey by the arm and guided her down the hall toward the elevator. Lacey's eyes never left the doctor as she stumbled along beside Gilbert.

At the Robinson's neo-classic white mansion, Gilbert helped her out of the car and to the door. "Would you like me to come in for awhile?" he asked as Margaret opened the door.

Lacey nodded. They went into the living room and sank down into the couch. Lacey, too tense to sit still, got up and paced. She glanced at her watch and groaned. "I'm supposed to be back at the office!" Her stomach was a tight, quivery knot, and the last thing she wanted to do was to face a desk loaded with work.

"I'll take you back there, if you like," Gilbert offered.

She shook her head. "I'm too nervous." She resumed pacing. "I'd never be able to concentrate, not knowing just how bad it is with Mom. I hate to let Dad down—" She paced again then stopped. "I know," she said. "Mom has some tranquilizers. They'll untie the knots in my stomach." She stood up, went to her mother's small desk, opened a drawer, took the cap off a prescription bottle, and shook three tablets into her hand.

"Margaret," she called. "Please bring me a glass of water," she said. Margaret came in and looked dubiously at the prescription bottle and the pills in her hand. "Oh, Margaret," Lacey protested, "these are just Mom's tranquilizers. They won't hurt me."

Margaret sniffed but went toward the kitchen.

Gilbert raised an eyebrow. "Are you sure you want three?"

Lacey nodded impatiently. "My stomach's in knots."

Margaret came back with water in a crystal goblet. Lacey swallowed the tablets, drained the water, and handed the goblet back to Margaret. "Call the office and tell them Mom is sick and that I won't be back this afternoon."

Margaret looked at her disapprovingly, but nodded and left. Lacey continued her rounds of the living room. She chewed her lower lip and twisted her fingers. Images of her mother caring for her through measles, taking her to ballet class, bidding her good-bye when she left for USC flitted through her mind. Her eyes fogged with tears. Gilbert watched her in silence.

"Come," he said finally. "Sit down here by me."

She looked at him, sat, and he put an arm around her shoulders. "This has got to be hard on you," he murmured into her hair. She nodded. He put his finger under her chin and lifted her face toward his. "You're too beautiful to be worried about anything," he whispered as his lips gently touched hers.

Automatically she wound her arms around his neck, he held her close, and they sat there for a minute. She was beginning to feel light-headed. "I'm beginning to feel a little funny," she said. "I think I'd like to go to bed."

"Here. I'll help you," he said. She nodded, he looked around, saw no one, picked her up, and carried her upstairs. "Which is your room?" he asked softly.

She pointed with a limp arm, and he opened the door. He laid her gently on her bed. "My poor mother," she said.

"Shhhh. It's going to be all right," he murmured. "Your mother's going to be fine." He stood there a moment, looking at her, her eyes half closed as she relaxed, at the sweet curve of her cheek—he tugged at his tie.

Later, he pulled a light cover over her and looked at his watch. It was just after four. After looking at Lacey once more, he left the room and closed the door softly. He heard the distant sound of a vacuum cleaner. Looking all around, he saw no one, and he went soundlessly down the stairs and let himself out.

FOUR

Thursday, October 17, 3:15 P.M.

Susan read over what she had written. It didn't say enough. But as a reporter, she was obliged to tell only the facts, even when she didn't feel completely objective about the situation. She set the monitor on slow scroll, and read it over again. Best she could do under the circumstances. She punched "print" instead of "send," picked up the pages, and headed for Jackson's office. She needed his opinion.

The editor was reading a news release, his expression somber. When he heard the knock, he grunted. "It's open."

Susan entered. Jackson looked up, scowled. "I was just about to call you in," he said.

Susan stiffened. "Not another one?"

"Dunno for sure. Look." He handed her the fax.

She read the first paragraph and sat down suddenly. "So that's what it was!" She set the fax on the desk, looking pale.

"What was what? You know something about this?"

Susan tightened her hand, crumpling her story in her fist. "I dunno. Maybe." She paused to organize her thoughts. "I had dinner with my folks last night, and Lacey Robinson came over. She had turned off the boulevard and drove down Washington Avenue on her way to my folks' house. She said she heard a shriek and some terrible screaming. She said someone—couldn't tell whether it was a man or a woman—ran in front of her car just as she heard the screech. Scared the bejeebers out of her. Said she almost hit him—or her." She scowled. "You know, it's really dark on Washington at night. When's the city going to fix those lights?"

Jackson grunted. "What I'd like to know is what's going on?"

"Mmmmh. Me, too." She looked at the fax. "But this is awful. A body badly mutilated just like the cats—they haven't even identified it yet. And left out in the yard like that—sort of like a warning—"

"Has your boyfriend found out anything yet?"

"He's working on a lead. Wouldn't tell me about it."

Jackson gestured at the fax. "Add this to your cat story. I presume that's what you've got crumpled up in your hand there."

Susan took the paper reluctantly. "I hate this." She went back to her desk, dropped the crumpled copy in her wastebasket, called up her story, erased it, and started over again with a different lead. Just as well she hadn't sent it to makeup, where it would be pasted up into its proper spot in the paper. It was turning out to be a bigger story than it had seemed at first.

Thursday, 4:06 P.M.

Just as Gilbert closed the door quietly behind him and turned to walk to his car, he was startled to see Lacey's father get out of his limousine. Instantly quenching a rare momentary panic and assuming an expression of sympathetic concern, he stepped forward to the older man, his hand extended.

"I'm sorry to hear about Mrs. Robinson," he said.

"Thanks for your concern. I got a call from the doctor during the meeting. He mentioned food poisoning."

"Yes, that's what we heard, too," Gilbert said. He thought it would be better not to tell Mr. Robinson about the doctor's tentative diagnosis of cancer.

"Lacey and I were having a late lunch when she received the news. We went to the hospital, and I brought her home."

"Well, thank you, my boy," said Robinson, gripping Gilbert's hand. "Where is she? Lacey, I mean?"

"She's upstairs, sleeping. She was upset and took a tranquilizer."

Robinson nodded. "I'm grateful you were with Lacey. She and her mother are very close." He let Gilbert's hand go. "I just got back from Los Angeles, so I haven't been to the hospital yet. How is Amelia?"

"Asleep. The doctor gave her a sedative. She'll be there overnight for more tests," said Gilbert. "If you'll excuse me, I must go. By the way, may I ask how things went in Los Angeles?"

Robinson's face became blank. "I can't say. The call from the doctor came before anything was settled, and I left right away. I need to call the Chairman anyway, and when I find out, I'll let you know, if you're interested."

Gilbert nodded. "Thank you, sir. I'd appreciate that." He sketched a vague salute and walked briskly to his Jaguar.

Robinson watched him, thinking what a nice, polite young man he was. He opened the door and called, "Margaret, I'm home," to find that she was already on her way to the entry, wringing her hands nervously.

"Yessir. I see you are. How's the Missus?"

He shook his head. "Gilbert said it's food poisoning. She'll be at the hospital overnight for more testing." He went up the stairs leaving Margaret standing there watching him, mouth and eyes wide open.

"Food poisoning? No way! Not from my cookin', it ain't!" she muttered, and stalked back to the kitchen.

Robinson opened Lacey's bedroom door quietly. She was sleeping, a light cover tucked around her. Reassured, he closed the door silently.

Back downstairs in his office, he sat and wondered if he should go to the hospital. Perhaps he'd do just as well to call the doctor and talk to him.

But first, he thought back to Los Angeles. Things were not going well at all there. From what he had heard that morning, the Corporation was heading in the wrong direction. He had not had a chance to make his presentation, a strong one, which should have persuaded them that his plan was not only the better one, but the only one worth considering.

The worst of it was that in his anxiety he had forgotten his briefcase. If the wrong people were to get hold of the sketchy information in it without him to explain it in greater detail, the whole structure could come falling down on him. It would mean complete disaster for him.

Chilled with apprehension, he picked up his phone and punched in a long number, waiting impatiently as it rang. Finally, his party answered.

"Yes. This is Robinson. She's in the hospital. Probably food poisoning. No, I haven't seen her yet. Well, thank you. But what happened after I left? They did? I would have thought Kruger or Mishima. Then who's going to take over? Hmmmm. By the way, I left my briefcase there. Oh, you did? Thank you. Fine. Will you express it to me ASAP? Thanks. Yes. The next meeting."

He hung up the phone and sat, musing. It wasn't as bad as it might have been. He suddenly stared ahead wide-eyed. Or was it? Come to think of it, he didn't actually know what the Chairman thought about the situation. Robinson reviewed the conversation. With a touch of alarm, he realized the Chairman's comments could be taken either way. Whose side was he actually on? After all this, the only thing he knew for sure was that he still didn't know if his briefcase was in friendly or hostile hands.

He looked at his clock. Nearly quarter to five. If he was going to talk to the doctor, he'd better place the call right now. Then he'd call Gilbert.

Thursday, 5:05 P.M.

When the story ran that evening, it wore a bold twenty-four-point headline in a double column box just below the fold on the first page. "Mystery Killings, Mutilations Citywide," it said above Susan's byline. She had stated the facts without speculating. Her story about alleged satanic activity in Playa Linda, evidenced in part by the establishment of a new occult supplies store in the Atterbury district and satanic symbols painted on fences and sidewalks, was on page seven. It ended, "Police suspect a connection with the murder and animal mutilations (see photos, page 1)."

Susan's mother, coming home from teaching at a nearby Christian school, picked up the paper from the lawn and brought it into the house, reading headlines from the top as she walked. Raymond was home, judging from the mess on the kitchen counter and the sounds of rock music from upstairs. She unfolded the paper, noticed with shock the headline on the box, set down her books and papers, and read the whole item.

She was putting down the phone when Mr. Walker came in after locking up his bookstore for the night.

"Don, look at this!" She handed him the folded paper.

Donovan Walker took it and read a few words. He looked up at his wife and read the rest. "So it wasn't just a catfight, was it?" he said, putting the paper down.

Elizabeth Walker shook her head. "Guess not. Oh. Matt just phoned. He saw it, too, and he's worried. Said he found out something that might fit in."

"Good." He paused. "I'm not sure I want my daughter mixed up with this story," he said. "Maybe she and Matt and the rest of the Reileys should come for supper tonight. We need to talk about this," he said. "Do you know if Matt has talked to them about it?"

Elizabeth shook her head. "They'll know tonight anyway. And I'll call Susan now. She may still be at the office."

Donovan nodded, took the paper, and went to sit in his favorite easy chair to read.

Some time later, Susan came in, looking tired. Setting her purse down, she smiled wanly at her father, who was doing the crossword puzzle. "Hi, Dad. Mom getting supper?"

Her father nodded. "Good to see you, Hon. What's a five-letter word for 'dybbuk'?" he asked as she dropped a kiss on his cheek.

Susan narrowed her eyes, thinking. "Try 'demon.'" She watched as he put it down triumphantly. *How in the world had she come up with that one?* she wondered. A light shiver went through her.

She went to the kitchen where her mother was scrubbing carrots. "Hi, Mom," she said, with a hug and a kiss. "Thanks for asking me to supper again. Can I help?"

"You can make the salad. By the way, the Reileys will be here, too."

"That's great," she said, setting lettuce, celery, tomatoes, sweet onions, and green peppers on the counter. "We need to talk. This whole thing has me spooked."

Mrs. Walker rinsed the carrots and moved away from the sink to slice them into a pot. "Me, too. And your father is getting antsy about your being involved with the story. I don't like it, either."

Susan rinsed the vegetables, and proceeded to tear and cut them to bite-sized pieces. "Someone has to do it."

Her mother set the pan on the stove and turned up the heat. She faced Susan. "Why does it have to be you?"

Susan shrugged and put a bit of green pepper in her mouth. "Jackson put me on it. At first, it was just a small story," she said. "Just a couple of cats. You know, like the stories from Los Angeles. Only, it's grown. But it's still my story." She added ripe olives and grated cheddar. "It has to be in the paper. Christians need to be aware of this kind of thing so they can pray for help. Someone has to do something about it." She paused a moment, and set down the salad spoon and fork. "I honestly don't think it's a purely human thing that's happening."

Her mother tightened her mouth. "You're right, of course, but still—seeing Lacey last night—so frightened—" She looked at Susan. "It makes me wonder how much worse it's going to get."

Susan took a deep breath, nodded, and got out the dressing.

As the two families sat down at the table that evening, Don Walker bowed his head to ask the blessing. After the "Amen," he said, "You all saw in the paper about the body on Washington and the dead pets?"

A chorus of "Sure did," "Isn't it awful?" "Uh-huh" went around the table. Sean Reiley gestured with his fork. "That's what comes from all this permissiveness and 'If it feels good, do it' philosophy they're teaching in the schools these days!" He stabbed a piece of potato and put it in his mouth.

Meg Reiley looked sharply at her husband. "There has to be more to it than that," she said. "And look at all the fine young people coming out of our schools. It isn't only the schools' fault."

Elizabeth nodded. "That's what we've been thinking. There's something really evil going on."

Donovan looked around the table. "Right here at our table are the people I love best in the world—my family and our best friends. And our children are caught in the middle of it."

"It looks like satanism to me," said Elizabeth quietly, stirring her salad with her fork. "People just don't do things like that unless—well, you know."

The others murmured agreement as they applied themselves to Elizabeth's good cooking. "Let's talk about that after supper. This food's too good to mix up with deviltry," Sean Reiley said, shoving a forkful of potatoes and gravy into his mouth.

"All right, now, Matt," said Susan after a few moments, "what's the lead you wouldn't tell me about?"

Matt swallowed salad and sipped water. "I was calling up computer sales centers to get listings of prospective customers," he said. "In the process, I noticed a phone number, 555-0666." The rest looked uneasily at each other.

"Now, wait a minute," he said. "It could be just a coincidence, you know. Anyway, I had never seen it listed before, but right then the store got so busy I could only copy it down. Later, just before I left, I picked up the phone, dialed it, and some woman answered. 'Welcome to Belial's Lair,' she said. She had a really raspy, almost sensual voice."

Some gasped. Raymond muttered, "Wow! Just like Demon Crypt!" He retreated into his pot roast and potatoes when his mother glared at him.

"I was so startled I just reacted," said Matt. "I slammed the phone down. I've been kicking myself ever since. If I'd had my wits about me, I could probably have found out something."

"So could they," said Susan, wide-eyed. "Did she really say 'Belial's Lair'?"

Matt nodded. "It sure sounded like it. I'm going to do some more digging if their number isn't unlisted now. Apparently it wasn't then, but they might have done it since, depending."

"On what, son?" asked Meg Reiley.

"On whether or not it really has something to do with Belial," Matt answered.

Sean Reiley looked at Matt. "Better take care, son," he said. "You're mixin' in with the Enemy. I've half a notion to forbid you to go on with it."

"Would you give them a free hand, then, to spread their corruption all over and through Playa Linda and who knows how much farther?"

Reiley looked at his son in silence. "No," he said at last. "We can't do that. You're right. They have to be stopped, but—" his voice rose a couple of decibels, "why does it have to be the two of you?" He looked anxiously from Matt to Susan and back.

"As Susan said, 'Someone's got to do it,'" Mrs. Walker said. "Since she got the assignment, I'm sure it's meant to be that way. Maybe it's because Susan and Matt have the perfect jobs for it. How better to learn and get information out?" She shook her head. "Not that I care much for it either. But come on. Eat. We can talk after supper."

After the berry pie, they trooped into the living room. "You know who we need to get in on this?" asked Meg Reiley. "Dorothy Webb, that's who."

Susan leaned forward. "That's a wonderful idea, Meg!"

"It doesn't matter that she's wheelchair-bound," said Don Walker. "She can fill the heavens with her petitions, as you well know, Sean." Reiley nodded. "And the pastor, too, of course. As a matter of fact, the whole congregation should be in on it."

Matt was already at the telephone, dialing. A broad grin spread over his face as Dorothy Webb responded enthusiastically.

Coming back to his seat, he told them that Dorothy had felt something was going on but couldn't pinpoint it. "She doesn't get the *Register*, you know," he said, looking apologetically at Susan.

"I know. She's been subscribing to the *L.A. Times* ever since—oh, ever since. We're new in town, you know, only twenty-one years." The brief ripple of laughter gave way to more solemn topics as they wrestled with the problem.

It was late before the Reileys said good night. Susan yawned as the door closed behind them.

"I've got to get back to my apartment and go to bed, too," she said. "Fridays are always busy at the *Register*—there's always late stuff coming in for the weekend issues."

Susan left, the rest of the family climbed the stairs, lights went out, and soon the house was at peace.

Not so halfway across town. In spite of little lights glittering through the slats in the boarded up windows, an unnatural darkness seemed to surround a house in the Atterbury district, of which Washington Avenue was the main artery. Mutterings, chantings, wailing and groans, and a short, sharp scream could be heard, if one were near enough.

FIVE

Friday, October 18, 6:30 A.M.

Lacey yawned and stretched, feeling contented. She glanced at the window. It was barely dawn. She turned on the light by her bed.

All at once recollection shocked her. Gilbert! She looked around hastily, but saw no trace of him. She tried to remember the details, although she was rather fuzzy about everything, especially Gilbert. Just exactly what had happened? Was it a dream? She honestly didn't know. Misgiving grew as she showered.

True, they had been in junior high together, but she didn't know him then even to speak to. He was just the class oddball. But now—he seems so rich. And so smooth. How did he get that way? What does he do for a living?

She paused in her scrubbing, suds running off her hair down her shoulders and back. A tiny alarm tickled at the back of her mind. *He never said what he did for a living, either,* she mused. *I gave him an opening when I said something about his Jaguar, but—he said nothing. As a matter of fact, he told me nothing about himself, and I told him so much about me! I don't really know him at all!* Misgiving became consternation. She shook her head uneasily, and scrubbed some more, feeling strangely unclean. Finally she rinsed, toweled, picked up the scattered heaps of clothing from the day before, threw them into the hamper, and selected clean underthings and a blue tailored dress to wear. She checked her appearance, and to her surprise, saw she looked very much as usual.

With another shock, she remembered that her mother was still in the hospital. Forgetting Gilbert, she reached for the phone book on the shelf of the bedside table, looked up the number, and called the hospital.

When she identified herself, the female voice finally said her mother's condition was satisfactory.

Lacey gritted her teeth together. *A lot that tells me*, she thought. "Is Dr. Damron there? May I speak to him?"

"I think so. Just a moment. I'll have him paged."

Lacey tapped her foot impatiently. A male voice came on. "Dr. Damron."

"Doctor, this is Lacey Robinson. How's my mother? Have you found out anything? When can she come home?"

The doctor chuckled. "Pretty well, some, and this afternoon. We'll know more when we get the results of the tests, probably Monday. In the meantime, she may come home."

Lacey sighed with relief. "Oh, thank you, Doctor! I've been so worried. When should we come for her?"

"Noon will be fine. I have to finish my rounds now. If you need anything else, call my office."

Lacey put down the phone and looked at the clock. It was just after seven, so she reached behind it to turn off the alarm. It was off. Of course. She had not set it. But her fingers touched something on the table behind the clock. She picked it up. An onyx cuff link.

Embarrassment flooded her again. It had to be Gilbert's. She looked at the strange design carved into the onyx. Studying it, she made out an ornamental capital "B," the carving hypnotically unsettling somehow, but fascinating. "B"? for Gilbert Crozier? His middle initial, maybe? She stared at it, wrenched her attention away, and inhaling sharply, shook her head to clear it. Deliberately turning her thoughts away from Gilbert, she wondered if breakfast was ready. As she opened her bedroom door, she smelled coffee. Her father was probably home, too. She glanced down the hall toward her parents' room, but the door remained closed, and there was not so much as the shuffle of a slipper to suggest that her father was awake.

Margaret looked up, startled, as Lacey came into the kitchen. "Miss Lacey! You're up early. I didn't expect—"

Lacey nodded. "It's all right, Margaret. I—ah—fell asleep early yesterday afternoon. I've had more than a good night's sleep. Is the coffee ready?"

Margaret poured a cupful and handed it to her. "There are croissants and preserves, if you like," she said, her voice cool. "They don't any of them have any food poisoning." She sniffed and turned away.

"It's not your fault," said Lacey, taking a croissant and reaching for the blackberry preserves. "The store or the egg rancher goofed. Not you."

Margaret huffed, but looked placated. "I threw out all the rest of them eggs," she said. "We'll have to get more."

Lacey, her mouth full, nodded.

Friday, 12:00 Noon

Precisely at noon, the chauffeur parked Jerrod and Lacey Robinson in front of the hospital lobby. Lacey got out of the car, and the glass doors swished open at her approach. *Come on, Dad!* she urged mentally. *Hurry!*

Up in the hospital room, her mother, still pale, smiled hello from the compulsory wheelchair. Several ladies from their church surrounded her: Mary Westmoreland, Genevieve Stuart, that flutterbrain Sylvia Cushman, and a couple whose names escaped her. The minister—rosy, substantial Rev. Harvey Drane—stood beaming by the wheelchair.

With a chorus of "She's going to be just fine," "We heard she was sick, so we came right over," "How nice you look, Lacey," and the Rev. Drane's baritone, "We're sure your mother's going to be fine," there wasn't much left for Lacey to do but bend down and kiss her mother on the cheek, being careful not to crush the mounds of bouquets in her lap.

The doctor came into the little private room and drew Jerrod aside to talk to him. One of the ladies picked up two potted flowering plants, and another the two basket arrangements. Jerrod took a slip of paper from the doctor and thanked the ladies and Rev. Drane for coming. A nurse pushed the wheelchair out into the hall, down the elevator and out, where the little contingent of well-wishers handed the plants and flowers into the car and waved and chirped their good-byes and see-you-laters.

At home, Amelia insisted on staying on the lounge in the morning room. Margaret arranged the flowers in a half dozen or so vases and hurried to get some fruit juice.

"Listen!" her mother said, urging both Lacey and Jerrod to come close. "I know the doctor said I might have cancer, but wait 'til you hear what Sylvia Cushman told me!"

"Sylvia?" Lacey was surprised. It continued to amaze her that the woman could put a coherent sentence together.

Her mother nodded. "She heard from her cousin about a man who can remove cancers and tumors without surgery! He healed her cousin's husband after the doctor told him there was nothing more he could do and that he'd die in six months."

"Oh, Amy, surely you don't believe that!" Robinson said.

"Jerry, it's true! Sylvia saw him only two weeks ago, and that was almost a year after the doctors gave him up. Doesn't that prove something?"

"Only that there's one born every second. Amy, it's a sucker deal. Don't you remember the films of that fake healer in the Philippines? He just pretended to pull out a tumor. The stuff in his hand was really the insides of some chicken or pig or something he had hidden under the table. Don't you remember?"

"But this man's different! He's a Christian and a real doctor, an M.D., not one of those witch doctors like in the Philippines. Anyway, Sylvia said he would examine a patient for free, and then if there was a tumor or a cancer, he'd make an appointment to remove it. Jerry, can't we give it a chance?"

She looked appealing, fragile and beautiful. Robinson was irritated. "Oh, for heaven's sake, Amelia, don't be stupid! The whole thing is a fake."

"Please?" Amelia begged.

He hesitated and yielded. "Oh, all right! If you insist on being idiotic, let her make an appointment for an examination," he said crossly. "Only I insist that Dr. Damron go along."

"Oh, I'm sorry, Jerry, but this healer doesn't want unbelievers with his patients. He wouldn't let the doctor into his treatment room. At least, that's what Sylvia said."

Lacey groaned. "Oh, Mom, doesn't that tell you something? A doctor could spot a fake. He's afraid of being exposed."

Amelia's delight crumpled, and she looked down, her expression mournful. "You're both against me."

"Oh, no!" Lacey protested. "It's just that we want the very best for you. We love you." She reached down to hug her.

Robinson stared balefully at his wife. He mumbled something unintelligible.

Lacey dropped to her knees in front of her mother, taking both her hands. "Besides, I've read that the only effective treatments for cancer are surgery, chemotherapy, and radiation."

Her mother shuddered. "I don't want surgery. And chemotherapy—my hair would fall out, and I'd be so sick. And I'm afraid of radiation—" Tears brimmed in her eyes. "Please, Jerry, can't we give it a try? Then if it doesn't work, we can let the doctor do his surgery or whatever. Please?" A large tear plopped on her forearm as she leaned toward her husband.

Robinson squirmed. "Oh, all right, Amy, while we're waiting for test results. But then, promise you'll do just exactly what Dr. Damron says. Promise?"

Amelia smiled radiantly. "Of course! I promise! But now, get me the phone, please. I want to call Sylvia."

Friday, 10:20 A.M.

As Susan had predicted, the newsroom at the *Register* was a zoo and it wasn't even eleven yet. Much of the copy scheduled for the Friday edition had to be postponed until Saturday, and some had even been put off to go into the Sunday edition. Late items were still coming in, and typesetters were racing frantically through their work. Reporters were hurrying to get their stories written, phoning for details, out searching archives or interviewing people.

Susan was setting up a story about a liquor store robbery that had taken place the previous evening when Peter Benson, one of the associate editors, placed another news release on her desk. He always reminded Susan of Red Buttons.

"Oh, no, Pete," she wailed. "I can't possibly take on another story today! Look at this stack." She waved a hand at her IN basket.

"Okay, okay," said Pete, "but I thought this kind of thing was your big deal this week."

Susan picked up the fax and read it. She sagged back into her chair. "All right, Pete," she sighed. "Has Jackson seen this?"

"Not yet. It just came in. You going to take it?"

Susan nodded, and Pete went back to his own office. She set the fax aside while she finished and sent the story about the holdup.

Jackson took the fax from her hand, read it, set it down, and looked up at her. His beetling eyebrows and mustache seemed to wilt a little. "Did you check to see if there is room for this today?"

"If we pull something else. Want me to dig into it?"

Jackson thought a moment, picked up the intercom, told makeup to take out the water dowser story and include it in the Sunday edition instead. Then, to Susan, "Go ahead. But be careful." He dismissed her with a wave of his hand.

Susan stopped at Pete's office, picked up the girls' addresses, went out to her car, and sped off.

Strange, she thought, dodging through heavy Friday traffic. Three girls from various parts of town, attending two different high schools, vanished on the same day. What sort of a connection was between them?

She pulled up in front of the weatherbeaten duplex where Ellen Rodzinsky lived. When she knocked on the door, she saw a window curtain pulled back slightly, an eye looking at her.

The door opened only as far as the chain allowed. "What you want?" the man asked. She could see only a portion of his face.

She displayed her press card. "I'm Susan Walker from the *Register*. My editor told me your daughter was missing. I hope you'll tell me about it."

"Why should I tell you?"

"Maybe someone saw something involving her, and if the story is in the paper, we might get some information to help find her."

The door closed, then she heard the chain being taken off. The door opened all the way. The man was of middle height, middle-aged, stocky, florid, and worried. He waved a hand toward a plump woman in an overstuffed chair, leaning forward slightly. Her brown hair was brushed back into a bun. She had been crocheting medallions, which she set on the table beside her. Her hands seemed to have a life of their own, fidgeting with her apron, the arms of the chair, picking off bits of lint. "This is my wife, Rose. Sit down, please." He indicated a chair.

Susan took a notebook and pen from her purse and asked the usual questions. They told her Ellen was seventeen, a junior at Roosevelt High, and she played clarinet in the band. Well, she used to, but quit for some reason. She had gone to school Wednesday morning as usual, but no one had seen her at all after lunch that day. "This is her picture," said her father, handing her a snapshot of a girl with short, curly brown hair, a pretty face, stocky build, in a Roosevelt High School T-shirt and shorts. "Bring it back, please, if you use it in paper."

Susan looked up from the photo. "Did you notice anything unusual before she disappeared? Was she worried, or different in any way?" Susan looked from the father to the mother.

Mrs. Rodzinsky got up and went to her husband's side. "She was excited about something," she said in her light Polish accent. "Something about a new church, but she didn't say much."

"Yah," said Ellen's father. "She carry strange book with her all the time. She won't let us see, but it was black and—" He looked at his wife. "We think maybe it is not real church at all."

Mrs. Rodzinsky nodded. "Tuesday night she was saying words in her room, words I couldn't understand. I went in, ask her what she talk about, but she shut the book quick and say it was nothing. Just some stuff for school. I don't think so."

Susan kept her expression neutral as she scribbled. "Can you tell me anything else?"

The Rodzinskys looked at each other, and their expressions closed. "No," said Ellen's father. "Only, like my wife say, she was excited when she leave for school. And she not come back." His eyes reddened, and Mrs. Rodzinsky took a tissue from her apron pocket and dabbed at her eyes. "Can you help find my Ellen?" she asked, her voice wistful.

Susan looked at her, not daring to let emotion show in her face. "I hope so. That's why I'm here. Have the police come to talk to you yet?"

"Yes. But they say they have nothing to go on."

Susan nodded sympathetically. "Before I forget, may I have your phone number, just in case there are more questions?"

Mrs. Rodzinsky nodded, went to a small table and wrote it on a piece of paper. "Here. Call if you hear anything."

Susan took the paper, and put it with her pen, notebook, and the photo in her purse. "I hope someone who knows something will see the article and tell us about it."

Mr. Rodzinsky stuck his big hand toward Susan. "Thank you, lady," he said. "We hope, too." Mrs. Rodzinsky shook hands and darted away, a tissue to her eyes.

The other two interviews yielded very much the same information. Both were juniors at Playa Linda High School. One of them, Sandy Parkhurst, had disappeared late Wednesday, and the other, Karen Garcia, Wednesday noon. All three were seventeen, but the Garcia girl was short and slim with long, wavy dark hair and the Parkhurst girl was about five feet six and blonde.

It was nearly 2:30 when Susan came back to the office.

"There you are!" cried Pete as she came into the newsroom. "We'd almost given up. Get your story?"

Susan nodded and sat down at her work station. "Gotta get it down while it's still fresh. Go away."

Pete grinned and went away.

She reached for her phone and called the schools the girls attended, but even though she promised the information would be confidential and never written down—she simply wanted to understand the reason for their disappearances—the records offices refused to talk to her. She called the parents, learned the names of some of their friends, and called them. Putting bits and pieces together, she learned that all the girls' grades had gone down in the past few months, they "got to be sorta different, not like they used to be," and they had been absent quite a lot recently.

From a "best friend," Susan learned that Sandy Parkhurst seemed to have changed even more than the others. She had been very popular, an A student involved in several sports and clubs. She quit her sports and clubs, and her grades dropped "way down," the girl said. "She'd hardly even talk to me any more," the friend said. "She was like, sorta, a loner. And a lot different from what she used to be, y'know?"

Susan didn't like what she was hearing from the friends. Why hadn't she heard it from the parents?

Susan's fingers flew as she wrote the story and sent it to makeup. She finished with the few articles left in the IN basket, turned off the computer, picked up her purse, said good night, and left.

As she drove home to her apartment, the story churned through her mind. Surely, if they were just joining a church, they'd have come home, wouldn't they? But then she remembered that in some of the Eastern-religion-related cults, young people cut themselves off entirely from their families and friends to live in a sort of commune. Was that what had happened here?

And what about the changes in their grades? Why hadn't any of the parents said anything about that? Had there been other personality changes they might not have noticed that someone should have mentioned?

Was it a simple case of kids running away from a difficult parental situation? Or might each have run off with a boyfriend? No. Too coincidental. She couldn't overlook a more obvious possibility. Were they getting involved with drugs? Or was there something going on, more strange, even more sinister, more dangerous, that drugs could lead to? She refused to consider the implications of the mutilated body found on Washington Avenue.

Well, she had done all she could. The rest was up to the police. She pulled into her parking slot and let herself into the comfort and sanity of her apartment.

SIX

Saturday, October 19, 11:45 A.M.

The phone rang as Susan put her dusting tools away.

"Susan, I've got to talk to you!" Lacey sounded troubled. Susan had just finished her Saturday routine of cleaning the apartment. She sank into a chair, ready for a long conversation.

"Sure. What's the matter?"

Lacey caught her breath. "A couple of things. First off, I saw your write-up in the paper." She paused; Susan waited. "That business on Washington Avenue the other night—it was really a killing, wasn't it, not just my imagination." It was not a question.

"No, not your imagination," Susan said. "It was real enough. But I don't know any more than what's in the paper. It's just as well you got out of there when you did. But you said there was something else?"

"It's my mother—" Her voice seemed to give out.

Susan sat up straight. "She's all right, isn't she?"

"For now," Lacey said. "But she's got this crazy idea—" She broke off. Susan heard her blow her nose.

Susan sat silent a moment. "I think we'd better meet somewhere we can really talk." She looked at the clock. 12:50. "How about lunch? Barron's?"

Lacey hesitated. "No. Somewhere no one knows us. That Mexican place on Market Street, you know, El Rancho. Okay?"

"Fine with me. Half an hour?"

"Good. I'll be there. 'Bye."

Susan sat looking at the phone in its cradle. *That's all I need,* she thought. *Ritual sacrifice of animals, a mutilated body, an occult supplies store, disappearing teenage girls, and now a panicky friend.* She shook her head and changed out of her Levi's and T-shirt into pants and a blouse.

The restaurant was colorfully decorated in Mexican style, and the aromas of good Mexican food made nearly impossible promises. Susan sat waiting near the entrance, getting hungrier by the minute, watching the brightly dressed waitresses bustling back and forth carrying trays, drinks, dishes of tortilla chips and salsa. Just as she wondered what was keeping Lacey, she arrived. Her face was drawn with worry.

The hostess looked up from her notes as Susan stood up. "This is your friend?" she asked. Susan nodded. The hostess took a pair of menus and led them to a quiet isolated table in the inner courtyard. Ancient bougainvilleas wound around the pillars supporting the balconies, their red and purple bracts trailing from the railings and hibiscus bushes blooming in huge planters.

Lacey waited until they were alone. "Thanks for coming."

Susan nodded. "It's okay. But what's the matter? You said something about your mother?"

Lacey nodded. "You remember Sylvia Cushman? That bubble-headed birdbrain who would believe anything?"

"You've mentioned her, but I haven't met her."

"She's made an appointment for Mom with a witch doctor!"

Susan's jaw dropped.

"Well, maybe not exactly a witch doctor, but he's one of those frauds who pretends to remove cancers and such without surgery."

"Cancer? What's that got to do with your mother? I thought you said she had food poisoning."

"Well, that was what Dr. Damron thought at first, but when they took some more tests and X-rays, they saw something that might be cancerous and kept her overnight for tests. Now she's panicked and insists on going to this—fraud!"

Susan stared at Lacey.

"And that nitwit Sylvia Cushman went right ahead and made an appointment for Mom on Monday with this—this—Brother Justin," Lacey continued. "Mom absolutely refuses to even consider what the doctor said. What can we do?"

Susan sighed. Didn't she have enough troubles of her own? Lacey looked at her with the appeal of a spaniel puppy. How could she not try to help?

Suddenly, Susan realized something else. This type of fraud also came under the heading of the occult. A chill rippled through her. Did this fit in with the cats, the body, the disappearances?

Lacey continued to look at Susan, waiting for an answer. Susan took a breath. "Lacey, I don't know what to say, except it worries me. I don't know anything about these faith healers, fake or not. All I know is that Jesus is the one who really heals."

Just then, a pert brunette waitress in a short red flouncy skirt over snowy petticoats arrived with a bowl of tortilla chips and a dish of salsa and set them down, smiling brightly. "Are you ready to order?"

"I am," Susan said. "I'll have the chimichanga Acapulco and iced tea. What about you, Lacey?"

Lacey looked up blankly from the menu. "The same, I guess."

Red Skirt scribbled, nodded, smiled, and left.

Lacey looked helpless, frightened. Susan drew a deep breath and sat back, trying to find the best approach. She picked up a chip, dipped it in the salsa, and crunched.

"Tell you what," she said after a moment. "Matt's working on something that might or might not have some bearing on this. Suppose I talk to him, and maybe he can find out about this—what did you say his name was?"

"Brother Justin." Lacey helped herself to chips and salsa.

"Right. Brother Justin. If he's a fake, maybe Matt can get some information, and we'll take it to your mother." She sat quietly a moment, thinking, dipping more chips in the salsa.

Lacey nodded absently. "What about the library?" she asked. "They have a whole lot of papers on microfiche." They were interrupted for a minute when the waitress arrived with their drinks.

Susan picked up on Lacey's last thought, "Good idea. That way I won't have to bother anyone at the paper today to dig in the morgue. After lunch, why don't you see what you can find out? I'll check with Matt and see what he can do."

Red Skirt came back bearing fragrant, steaming plates loaded with chimichangas draped in guacamole and sour cream topped with a black olive, accompanied by the traditional beans and rice. "I'll bring more tea. Anything else?" she asked.

Susan shook her head. Red Skirt smiled and disappeared.

They picked at the food in silence. When Susan put her fork down, neither had finished what was on her plate. Ordinarily, Lacey's appetite was equal even to El Rancho's largesse.

Back out on the street, Susan watched Lacey drive off toward the library, and she headed for the Computer Warehouse. Ricky, talking to a couple of customers, waved hello at her and pointed toward the back of the store. She found Matt moving used equipment around, apparently looking for something.

"Hi, honey," he said, turning around when she approached. "What brings you here?"

"You know. What have you found out, if anything?"

Matt leaned back against the shelves and dusted his hands. "That number, 555-0666? I tried it again this morning and got a recording saying that it had been changed. Then I tried directory assistance and the new number is unpublished."

Susan raised her left eyebrow. "Mmm. Unlisted now. You must've really jolted them. But isn't there some way to get hold of unlisted numbers?"

"I think so. A friend of mine did it once, but I haven't had a chance to call him yet." He looked at the used computer beside him. "A customer called asking if there was a used IBM at a reasonable price, so I dug this out. Among others. But this ought to do it."

Susan looked at it and nodded absently. "Well, get in touch when you can. But there's something else." Matt looked at her. "It turns out Lacey's mother might have a cancer, and somehow she got mixed up with a quack—you know, one of these psychic healers who pretends to take out cancers and tumors without surgery?"

Matt pursed his lips in a low whistle. "Yeah. Saw a program once on TV about that. Don't tell me Mrs. Robinson has fallen for that scam?"

Susan nodded. "Lacey's worried. But what I'd like you to do is to find out everything possible about a Brother Justin. Lacey's gone to the files at the library, and I'll ask questions from a few people who might know. But what gets me is that all this occult garbage seems to be coming on all of a sudden. How come?"

"Beats me." Matt shook his head. He looked at Susan fondly and put his hands on her shoulders. "Hey, I've got to call my customer back, but right after that, I'll get on it. The phone number and—what's the name? Brother Justin. Got it." He kissed her and gave her a light shove toward the door. "Got a business to keep afloat."

Susan waved good-bye at Ricky, who was demonstrating a machine for his customers.

Back in her car, Susan sat a moment, wondering where to turn. The Philosophical Library, she remembered suddenly. They have all sorts of books about the occult in general. *Why didn't I think of that sooner?* she wondered. Making a U-turn at the next intersection, she headed for Citrus Avenue in the Atterbury district, where she once had noticed the sign above the entrance.

The "library" was nothing more than a narrow bookshop, its shelves filled with an unlikely assortment of books, some new, some used, and many that looked ancient. Coming into the shadowy store from bright sunlight, she stood still for a moment to let her eyes adjust. She became aware of a desk at the back, where a young woman with a headband over her long auburn hair sat reading paperback science fiction by the light of an overhead bulb.

Susan walked toward her, and the girl looked up. "Oh, hi," she said, smiling thinly. "Can I help you?"

"Yeah," said Susan. "I'm looking for stuff about Satan. Got anything?"

"Sure." She got up and headed for a section near the back. "Some of this stuff we keep here ain't for sale, y'know, but you can look at it. Some we lend out. The ones for sale, y'know, they're marked with a price. They're all marked different, y'know?"

Susan nodded. "Okay. Thanks."

The girl returned to her desk and her book. Susan read some of the titles and took down an ancient-looking black volume called Arcane Wisdom, thick as a dictionary, and opened it at random.

"In nomine dei Satanas, Lucifer excelsi! In the name of our great god Satan, Lucifer, the ruler of the mystic pits . . ." She closed it with a snap, shuddering, and replaced it. Was she really ready for this? She looked for something less frightening. When she left, it was with paperbacks called "The Baals of the New Age" and "Satan's Strategies." Her head spun with the thought of the mountains of witchcraft, New Age, occult, and satanic literature that was available in just the small area to which the salesgirl had led her. How much more was available in other such stores? Especially that new occult supplies store, which she should check out, also. And how many young people bought such books, unwittingly putting themselves at risk of eternal destruction? She looked at her watch and was surprised to see it was nearly five.

Hurrying across town, she entered the Computer Warehouse to see Ricky and Matt closing up shop. "Hi," she said unenthusiastically.

Ricky raised a hand in greeting. "Hi yourself," said Matt. "What's up? You look beat."

Susan told of her afternoon with demons in print. "I never realized it was so widespread, so—available," she said. "But what about you? Did you get in touch with your friend?"

"Yeah. He said he'd get right on it, but it might take some time." Matt shuffled through video games, putting them in their proper places. Ricky was already locking the front door and turning off lights.

While Matt and Ricky bustled, Susan picked up the phone and called her mother to assure her she was all right. She listened, nodded. "Okay, Mom, see you at church tomorrow. 'Bye."

Matt was still in the office, punching figures into his computer. Susan dialed Lacey's number. After a brief conversation, she put the phone down and turned to Matt. "Lacey didn't find much at the library. They don't publicize these psychic healers, I guess. I haven't seen anything myself."

Matt looked around at her. "Uh—yeah, I guess—just let me finish this—" and he turned back to his figures.

Susan leaned back against a counter, watching Matt. How lucky she was to know him, she thought. Darn few would put up with her and her crazy friends like Lacey.

Matt slipped disks out of his CPU and turned everything off. "Okay. Where do you want to go for supper?" He took her by the arm and they exited, arguing the merits of one restaurant over the other.

The sun was sliding into the sea, a breeze blew shreds of fog toward Playa Linda. As Susan and Matt headed for what was known locally as Restaurant Row, it seemed as if a subtle darkness settled down unnoticed around an impressive mainline church in the fashionable Tres Encinos district.

Lacey was changing into a clinging scarlet dress for her date with John Merkel. For some reason, she shivered as the silk slithered down her body. She remembered her grandmother saying when someone shivered for no apparent reason, "Must be someone walking across your grave." What an awful thought. Lacey dismissed it as she chose a matching lipstick, then brushed her cheeks lightly with color.

She glided down the stairs, nodded to John, sitting waiting near the door, and went to hug her mother on the deep, soft divan. "Be good, now, Mom, and go to bed early," she said. "I wish you'd forget this Brother Justin business and do what Dr. Damron says."

Amelia Robinson looked fondly at her daughter. "Stop fussing at me. I'll go to bed as soon as your father gets home from his meeting. And as for Dr. Damron, I'll see Brother Justin first, then we'll see Dr. Damron. All right?"

Lacey sighed. "Okay. We'll do it your way." She hugged her mother. "Good night, then. We may be late."

John came over and took Amelia's hand. "I'll take good care of her, Mrs. Robinson. You just rest," he said. He kissed her hand, and with a flourish, presented his arm to Lacey.

"Oh, John, for heaven's sake—" she protested, but put her hand lightly near his elbow.

Amelia watched as the two went out the door. *They're a good-looking couple,* she thought, *but there's something about that John Merkel— something that rubs me the wrong way. Well, he's Lacey's friend, not mine.* She took a deep breath, tightened her lips, and turned back to her book.

SEVEN

Sunday, October 20, 10:42 A.M.

"The church's one foundation," the congregation was singing as Susan slipped in late, "is Jesus Christ her Lord—"

Susan raised her sweet soprano voice to sing one of her favorite hymns. Joy flooded her being.

Friends nodded greeting as she looked around and sat down with her family. Being in this simple, open, sunlit church with her friends and family around her had always been a high point in her week.

After the Rev. Ernest Wayman's sermon, comparing the signs of the end times from Matthew 24 with current news, he asked for announcements. Don Walker stood to speak of the murder on Washington Avenue, the animal mutilations, and possible connections with the occult.

"And the worst is, my daughter and Matt Reiley have the dubious distinction of digging out the truth for the paper. We need prayer groups," he said, "especially to ask for protection for them. Anyone willing to take part, please meet with Pastor Wayman and me after the service."

A rustle and murmur of hasty conferences rippled through the congregation. Many heads nodded. Others sat silent.

Donovan sat down, and the pastor stepped forward, suggesting they pray right there for Susan and Matt. The congregation bowed their heads, and Pastor Wayman led them in a powerful prayer, asking the Lord to bind the devil and protect them all.

After dismissal, people gathered around Pastor Wayman and Don Walker. About two thirds of the congregation slid past the embryonic prayer groups with a nod. In her wheelchair, Dorothy Webb seemed to be everywhere, urging individuals to join. She was the sort of older woman who didn't seem to realize how many years had gone by, or that she was, by average standards, handicapped by injuries from an automobile accident that happened years ago.

After Susan had huddled with a group of young people, she thanked Pastor Wayman, kissed her mother and father, hugged her brother, got into her car, and started it up. She wondered why Matt hadn't been at church.

Sunday, 10:50 A.M.

Lacey had persuaded her mother and father to come to the Church of the Oaks that morning. The young oaks that had recently been planted around the neo-gothic stone building to replace the ancient trees had done well, and the manicured grounds were nicely, if sparsely, shaded.

The Rev. Harvey Drane stood splendidly attired in his robes at the ornate entrance. Stained glass windows of abstract design in varying sizes and thicknesses of glass to resemble masses of jewels were spaced generously in the tall walls. A large tile design over the altar set a lustrous cobalt blue cross in a sunburst of gold, orange, and scarlet. Contemporary-styled chandeliers hung from the vault of the ceiling, casting soft light on the carved oaken pews below.

As the Robinsons left their limousine, Sylvia Cushman waddled with a bright smile toward them from the little knot of fashionably dressed women surrounding the Rev. Drane.

"Amy, darling," she gushed, planting a smack on Amelia's cheek, "it's so good to see you! We've been talking about your appointment with Brother Justin," she said, as the rest of the women arrived to surround the Robinsons, chattering their hellos. Jerrod nodded toward each and escaped to greet Rev. Drane.

"Are you really going to see Brother Justin?" asked breathless Gladys Goodstone. "I've heard wonders about him!"

Mary Westmoreland sniffed. "I have no trust in these faith healers," she said. "Healing is the province of modern medicine. Faith has nothing whatever to do with it." She was tall and stately, the years apparently having added only to her bustline.

Genevieve Stuart said cheerfully, "Now, Mary, there's a lot we don't know. The Rev. Drane is always preaching about having faith in whatever we do, and you know how it is, we've had faith that we could prosper and get rich, and we have! So there might be something to this Brother Justin, after all. He works by faith, you know." She nodded as if to say "that's the end of that."

Lacey had heard enough. "Please excuse us," she said. "Mother is tired and would like to sit down. Wouldn't you, Mom?"

Amelia nodded. The women untangled to let them through, and stopping only to greet the pastor, they walked down the aisle to where Jerrod was waiting for them.

"I thought they'd never let you go," he hissed.

"Shhhh!" Amelia shushed him. "They're just being friendly."

The maroon-robed choir preceded by a gilded cross marched in, singing "Holy women, holy men, with affection's recollections greet we your return again." The organ was majestic in its power, playing to the half-empty church.

Lacey, struggling with her own thoughts, listened to the Scripture readings without hearing them and paid scant attention to the pastor's homily about how trust in God can make everything new and restore a blighted life, if only one has a strong positive attitude and can visualize it happening. "Don't worry," he chortled. "You're in good hands!" He held up his hands in imitation of a popular television commercial.

When the choir sang the offertory, Lacey was scarcely aware of the music. When the service finally ended with the postlude, Lacey still had not found any answers.

Lacey hung back as the small congregation filed out, congratulating the Rev. Drane for a "most inspiring sermon." Jerrod motioned for her to move up, but she shook her head. "I want to talk to the pastor," she said. "I'll walk home."

Her father half shrugged and took Amelia by the elbow.

"Pastor Drane," Lacey said when almost everyone had left, "I'd like to talk to you."

"Why, of course, my dear," he said, slipping into his coat. "Come into the office." The ushers were picking up programs and putting hymnals into their places. One of the deacons was counting up the offering.

In the quiet of the small office, Lacey sat down in the chair beside the pastor's littered desk.

"Well, Lacey, it's been some time since we've had a real talk. What's on your mind?"

Lacey's face tightened with her effort to put into words what she had been feeling. Finally, she said, "I'm scared. My mother is sick. The doctor thinks she has ovarian cancer. What's going to happen to her?"

He smiled and leaned forward on the arms of the chair. "Why, she'll get well, of course. You know we've all prayed for her."

"But she's decided to go to this Brother Justin who is supposed to be able to take out cancers without surgery. You know, a faith healer."

The minister spread his hands. "Some people say they've been helped greatly by faith healers. But isn't she going to see her own doctor, too?"

"She already did. Do you really think Brother Justin can help her?"

Drane leaned back, took off his glasses, and rubbed the bridge of his nose before he put them back on again. "To tell you the truth, I've never heard of Brother Justin. We do hear, however, that people have been healed by faith, but I must be honest. Personally, I've never seen it happen."

"Then shouldn't my mother forget all about Brother Justin and trust the doctor instead?"

"That's something she must decide for herself."

"Suppose my mother goes to Brother Justin, he fools her into thinking that she's cured, and she's not, then what?"

Pastor Drane shrugged. "If it's cancer—"

"But you preach faith! Won't faith make my mother well?"

Drane squirmed in his chair. "You mustn't try to second-guess God." He patted her hand. "It will all work out."

"But that's no answer!" Lacey looked at him angrily. "You're our pastor! You're supposed to know the answers and give them to us. Why can't you give me a straight answer?"

The Rev. Drane looked down at his hands, folded in his lap. "There are many things we don't know, Lacey. One of them is what is going to happen. If we could foretell the future, we could all be rich as Croesus." His eyes gleamed.

Impatient, Lacey ignored the remark and went on. "But you tell us that if we have faith in something, it will happen!"

"Yes, it does seem that when one has faith in something, one makes the extra effort to make things happen the way it's wanted. But when it comes to such things as cancer, there are no positive answers. But be assured, your doctor and medical science will do all they can."

Lacey stared at him, a touch of exasperation glinting in her eyes. "I remember when I was in Sunday school at the old church, we had stories from the Bible. We learned lots of things there that we don't hear from you. Like how Jesus would cure people who were sick."

Drane shook his head. "I'm sure the people who wrote the Bible meant well, but healing comes with modern medicine. There were terrible diseases in those times, and back then, they didn't know enough about medicine to cure them. Don't take those stories literally. They're written to give people hope."

"Then, how come they're in the Bible? Isn't the Bible true?"

"In a spiritual sense, yes, of course. But—"

Lacey interrupted. "But there's nothing spiritual about my mother's cancer! Nor—nor leprosy! What about the times Jesus cured leprosy in the Bible, and the promises that Jesus made to His disciples?"

The pastor looked at her blankly. "What promises?"

"You know!" She dug in her purse and took out a slip of paper. "I wrote it down. It's in John, chapter 14, verse 12. Jesus said, 'Most assuredly, I say to you, he who believes in Me, the works that I do he will do also; and greater *works* than these he will do, because I go to My Father.' All right. You say you have faith. So if Jesus healed people of leprosy, and even raised some from death, why can't you pray and heal my mother's cancer by faith in Jesus?"

Drane opened his mouth, hand upraised, but impatient. Lacey went on.

"He *promised*! 'Anyone who has faith in Me,' he said! If you really have faith, you should be able to help her!" She looked at him, her heart in her eyes.

Drane sighed. "My dear, I do have faith. But some people still die and, unfortunately, they stay dead. We pray for a spiritual event."

"But Jesus was so special—He was born of a virgin—and He promised—"

Drane put up a hand to interrupt. "Lacey, my dear! That's pure symbolism, of course," he said. "Medical science has proved that virgin birth is impossible. Scientists have cloned amphibians, but the offspring is always the same sex as the one the cells were taken from. Don't you see? If there had been some sort of cloning, which might come under 'virgin birth,' Jesus would have been a female. So you see, Mary must have become pregnant by Joseph or someone else before they were married. Jesus was only a man like any other man, but a better one, like Buddha or Mohammed."

"Are you saying that Jesus was not truly the Son of God? And because of that, faith in Jesus can't heal?"

Lacey paused for breath and Pastor Drane sputtered. She paid no attention. "And suppose my mother does die? What will happen to her?"

"Why, just what the Bible promises. She will be at peace."

"But how? If Jesus is not the Son of God, and consequently there is no resurrection, no heaven, what is there?"

Drane sighed. "Lacey, there are many great religions in the world, and they all lead to God. We've learned from others that our spirits join the great oversoul with all the rest of humanity. Others believe we move on into some other dimension where we have new problems to solve. And some very sincere people believe that we come back in another body." He shrugged. "And others think it all adds up to oblivion. And isn't that peace?"

Lacey stared at him, and after a long moment, stood up, frustrated, dissatisfied, empty. "I'm sorry I bothered you, Pastor Drane." she said. "I thought you might be able to help me. Thank you for your time." She strode out.

The pastor stared after her. He shook his head. *Poor girl*, he thought, *she has no faith. Too bad.*

3:20 P.M.

When Susan arrived at the Computer Warehouse, she rapped at the door. Matt turned, saw her, and went to let her in. Sitting at one of the computer consoles was a studious-looking young man with twinkly gray eyes. His unruly brown hair was held down by the pair of headphones he was wearing. He set them back off his ears as Susan came in.

"Susan, this is my friend Andy Bergstrom, the one who located an unlisted number," said Matt.

Andy grinned with delight at meeting Susan.

"Hi, Andy," she said, taking his hand. His grip was firm and warm, like his smile. She liked him immediately. "I'm happy to meet you. Were you trying to find that number again?" She turned to Matt. "Was that why you weren't in church?"

Matt nodded and straddled his chair. "We've found a lot of numbers, but they've all been wrong ones. We'll hit on it yet, though. Andy's a genius."

Andy grinned again. "I've had him fooled for a long time."

"Don't listen to him," Matt said. "Anything special happen at church?"

"We formed some prayer groups. Dorothy Webb is in charge, of course. What about you guys? Any progress?"

Andy glanced at Matt. "Not yet. What's with this guy? He keeps asking for the impossible all the time!"

Matt chuckled. "With you, that only takes a little longer."

Susan grinned, and looked at the papers covered with numbers and squiggles littering the desk. "Well, don't let me keep you from your work. I'd better be on my way." She held out her hand to Andy. "It was a real pleasure to meet you," she said. "I hope we'll see a lot of you."

Andy reddened. "Me, too," he said, obviously embarrassed but pleased.

Matt walked Susan to the door. "He's one of the best," he said. "Not just in what he does, but he's a real Christian and as nice a guy as one could hope to meet." He squeezed Susan's shoulders and dropped a light kiss on the top of her head. "I'll let you know as soon as we have anything."

Susan looked up with a smile. "Okay. See you later, then."

When she arrived at her apartment, her phone was ringing.

"Susan," said Lacey without preliminaries, "is there any way you could come with us to Brother Justin's tomorrow? Mother's determined to go through with it." Her voice was tight.

Susan thought. "What time is your appointment?"

"Ten in the morning."

"Tell you what. I'll try to get the boss on the phone. This could be a good story, and he might go for it." Susan heard a sniffle. "Lacey, are you all right?"

"Yeah, I guess so," Lacey said. "I went to talk to our minister after the service. I'd hoped he could help, but he didn't. And I'm so worried—"

"Listen," said Susan, realizing Lacey's church was not as Bible-oriented as was hers, "would you like me to come over there and talk to you? Matt's busy at the Warehouse."

"Would you? Please! My folks went out, so I'm alone."

"I'll be there in half an hour. Just relax. And get out your Bible, the one I gave you." When she hung up the phone, she called Jackson at his home. He agreed it would be a good story, but to not name the Robinsons. "Jerrod Robinson cuts a wide swath in this town," he warned. She set down the phone, picked up her worn Bible, and headed for the Tres Encinos district.

Upstairs in Lacey's room, the friends opened their Bibles, and Susan picked out her favorite passages and promises. By the time the sun was low in the west, they had reviewed many pertinent truths that applied to Amelia and her situation.

"I really want to believe," said Lacey, when Susan asked. "It's hard. Pastor Drane and so many others tell me that most of the Bible isn't really true, but just spiritual encouragement. Or that it was written for illiterate shepherds and doesn't have anything to do with us. Or that it's purely a myth."

"Unfortunately, that's a pretty common opinion. Most of the

people who think that have never read, much less studied the Bible and don't really know what's in it. It's too big a subject to get into right now. But can you believe what we just read?"

Lacey looked at some of the passages. "I think so. At least, I can try."

"Then hang on to them. Especially Isaiah 41:10, where it says, 'Fear not, for I *am* with you; Be not dismayed, for I *am* your God. I will strengthen you, Yes, I will help you, I will uphold you with My righteous right hand.' And remember, too, that Jesus is the Great Physician. Talk directly to Him about this."

Lacey sighed. "It sounds so wonderful. I want to believe. I'll read this all again tonight."

They hugged, and Susan started for the door. "By the way," she said, her hand on the doorknob, "I called Jackson and he told me to get the story. I'll be there at Brother Justin's."

Lacey sighed with relief. "Wonderful! I dreaded going, but with you there, it'll be better."

"And about the story, don't worry. There won't be any publicity about the Robinsons."

"That would be all we'd need, wouldn't it!" said Lacey, making a wry face. "So I'll see you tomorrow morning?"

"Uh-huh. What time are you leaving?"

"Nine thirty. Would you like to ride with us?"

Susan grinned. "I was hoping you'd ask me. Thanks. I'll see you here, then, about twenty after nine." She walked to her car, turned, waved, and was gone.

Lacey leaned back against the door jamb. *This whole thing*, she thought, *it's just too weird. I'd go out of my skull if it weren't for Susan.* She closed the door behind her, saying quietly to herself, 'Fear not, for I am with you; Be not dismayed . . .'

As she walked into her bedroom, she snapped on the television and sat down to watch. A popular talk show host was interviewing a New Age teacher. ". . . so I walked along the beach," she was saying with a blissful expression on her face, "more free than I had ever felt before, and shouted, 'I am god! I am god! I am god!' And you know, everything else all of a sudden just came into focus. My problems vanished. I was truly free!"

The host encouraged her to go on. Lacey sat down, enthralled, as the teacher went on to describe how her trance channeller increased her knowledge of herself, of her oneness with the universe, of life on other planets, and of reincarnation.

EIGHT

Monday, October 21, 9:55 A.M.

Brother Justin's quarters were on the fringes of the Atterbury district on Logan Street. The flat, smoggy sunlight did not flatter the house, which was set well back on the lot and in much need of paint and repair. The lawn, if such it could be called, had been neglected. What had been rose bushes were straggly with long, curving suckers and small, undistinguished blossoms of the rootstock. A few misshapen blooms struggled for life. It was not very different from the rest of the neighbors. Only a little more so.

The limousine drew up to the curb slowly and parked with the motley collection of vehicles presumably driven by other patients. No one got out.

Inside the limo, Jerrod argued that anyone who lived in such squalor could not possibly be qualified to practice any sort of medicine, whether it be conventional, psychic, faith, magic—black or white—or whatever. Amelia insisted that outward appearances really didn't mean everything. Susan and Lacey looked out in dismay.

"Well, I don't care what *you're* going to do," Amelia said finally. "I'm going in. I have an appointment, and I intend to keep it." She opened the door and stepped out, walking along the broken concrete blocks that led to the entrance. Jerrod groaned and followed. Susan looked at Lacey and shrugged. They got out of the car and stepped carefully on the cracked slabs. As they walked toward the house, two excited women came out the door. Speaking nonstop at each other, they scarcely noticed the Robinsons, who stepped aside to let them by. Jerrod looked after them, annoyed.

Inside the entry, a pale, thin woman asked Amelia's name. She nodded, then made sure Jerrod, Lacey, and Susan were not medical practitioners. Satisfied, she led them through a curtain of long strings of colorful beads into the half-light of an interior waiting room. The Robinsons found seats together. The wraith went behind a counter to rearrange the items for sale there—herbs, beaded or crocheted necklaces, brooches and pendants of strange mystical and occult designs, incense and burners, statues and prints, fetishes, little prayer books, and other occultic supplies. Susan wrinkled her nose in distaste at the sickly sweet odor of incense combined with the smell of dust and human sweat.

Several people sat in chairs along the walls in various states of health. Some had bandaged arms or legs; the left side of one's face was swollen; some were thin, others fat, and most, although not all, appeared to be what sociologists call economically disadvantaged. Quite a few wore necklaces or brooches similar to the ones in the case.

A large silvery crucifix hung over the entrance to what was apparently the treatment room. The walls were covered with framed pictures that might have been taken from a child's illustrated Bible. Large candles on ornamental iron stands wreathed with artificial flowers stood beneath the pictures, some burning brightly, others smoking, guttering in melted wax. Here and there were framed Bible quotations such as "Blessed are ye who are poor, for yours is the kingdom of God." A large artificial dieffenbachia stood dusty in a corner, festooned with plastic roses, lilies, and several unidentifiable silk flowers.

Jerrod sat uneasily beside Amelia, looking around in consternation. Amelia nudged him. "See?" she whispered. "This man is a Christian. He has the power of God. He will make me well!"

Jerrod looked at his wife, but said nothing. Susan and Lacey exchanged glances.

A sudden cry of "Hallelujah!" from behind the door to the treatment room caused all heads to turn in that direction. Presently, a man came out crying "I'm cured! I'm cured!" He left a handful of currency with the pallid woman, and went away still shouting that he was cured.

The colorless woman looked around, her gaze stopping at the Robinson entourage. "You're next," she said in a thin voice, ignoring the protests of several who had been sitting there longer than the Robinsons.

Amelia stood up, took Jerrod's hand, and followed through the door into the shadowy treatment room. Lacey and Susan trailed behind.

A single shaded light bulb hung over the table, leaving the rest of the room in comparative darkness. Two women assistants were cleaning up a bloody mess and putting down a clean sheet on the examining table. Brother Justin, clad in the brown robe of some unidentifiable brotherhood, stood at a sink, scrubbing his hands free of blood. Although the treatment room was more austere than the waiting room, a trio of crosses was centered on the wall opposite the door. Beneath it, groups of votive candles surrounded by artificial flowers clustered under small statues of Jesus and Mary, prints of St. Luke, St. Jude, and others Susan could not identify. Several looked Oriental. Pictures of Hopi kachinas, a Tlingit sea wolf, and the Haida raven were hung on an adjoining wall. A Tibetan prayer wheel stood on its handle in a vase.

"Mrs. Robinson, is it?" Brother Justin turned away from the sink, drying his hands on a clean towel. "Mrs. Cushman has told me a good deal about you. She said that yours is a particularly urgent problem."

As he came into the light, Susan saw him clearly. He was clean shaven, of medium height, slight of build, with thinning dark hair and intense dark brown eyes. His voice was gentle, with a slight accent Susan could not place.

With a gesture, he indicated chairs for the others to sit in as he led Amelia behind a curtain where she could disrobe and put on a hospital gown.

"What we're going to do here," he said to Jerrod, "is find out how serious the problem is, and go from there. If it can wait, we'll make an appointment for next week, but if it's urgent, I will help her today." Jerrod nodded, studying Brother Justin.

Susan felt extremely uncomfortable, wishing she were out of there. Something—she could not pinpoint the cause—was causing shivers to run up and down her back. The man himself, this Brother Justin, looked harmless enough. The assistants appeared competent in their duties.

Then she noticed a dark-haired woman sitting slumped in a chair in a dark corner across the room, her lips moving silently. She seemed to be large, although it was hard to tell with the excess of shawls and scarves which surrounded her in a disharmony of colors and patterns. Her hands moved under the fabric, and peering carefully, Susan saw she was scribbling on a small pad of paper. She nudged Lacey, sitting beside her, and indicated the woman. Lacey looked, her eyes widened, and she touched her father's arm. "Over there in the corner," she whispered, identifying with a nod. Jerrod looked, raised his eyebrows, and shrugged.

The woman lifted her head and held up a sheet of paper she had torn off the pad. Brother Justin went to her, took it, and read. As soon as he headed back to the examining table, the woman began fingering something. Susan tried to see what it was, but it was too dark under the shawls.

Brother Justin raised his eyes from the paper and looked sharply at Susan. "You have a question, young lady?"

Susan was startled. "Oh. I, uh, was wondering about the lady in the corner. I'm sorry. I don't mean to pry."

Brother Justin nodded. "It's all right, miss. That is Deva, my friend and psychic. She prays for me, helps in the diagnosis, and brings down the power that helps me to help others." He smiled, but somehow, Susan was not reassured. On the contrary, she wished she hadn't come.

Amelia emerged from behind the curtain, holding the skimpy hospital gown around herself. Her face glowed with anticipation.

Unaccountably, Susan wanted to cry out to Mrs. Robinson to put her clothes back on and get out of there. Now the woman in the corner was mumbling, but Susan could make nothing of the words. They didn't sound like any language she had ever heard.

Amelia lay down on the table, settled herself. Brother Justin put his hand on her forehead and spoke a series of incomprehensible, eerie words. Her eyes drooped, her body went limp. Susan thought she saw a faint bluish haze surrounding her.

Brother Justin nodded to Deva and bent over Amelia. His lips moved, mumbling in concert with hers. His hands flitted lightly over the robe above her abdomen, and with a low cry, his right hand shot to the lower left quadrant of her abdomen. He suddenly became rigid, his face paled, lost all expression. For a moment he seemed frozen. Then he drew a sharp breath. "Here!" he cried, his hand pushing down hard. "It's here!" Sweat glistened on his forehead. He was tense, unreadable.

Jerrod stared. Lacey was openmouthed. Susan felt a heavy oppression in the room. She forced herself to sit still.

The woman in the corner swayed back and forth, back and forth, her eyes closed, continuing to mumble louder and louder in the enigmatic language that to Susan now sounded revolting. She felt rather than saw a sinister darkness emanate from the corner as the mumbling grew louder.

Brother Justin hesitated, fixed a penetrating gaze on Jerrod, his expression a mix of sorrow and blank endurance.

"Mr. Robinson, your wife is extremely ill," he said. "I must take care of it at once. Do I have your permission?"

Jerrod paled. "What must you do?" he asked.

Brother Justin closed his eyes for barely a moment. "You are no doubt familiar with the etheric body?"

Jerrod shook his head.

Brother Justin spoke rapidly, as if by rote. "Ether is the fifth element, after air, water, earth and fire. I don't have time to tell you much about it, except that each of us has an etheric body as well as the material body we see every day. It is exactly the same as the one you see here, occupies the same space, and what happens in the etheric body also happens in the material body. I will remove the tumor from the etheric body, and as it disappears from the etheric, it will manifest in the material. Do you understand?"

Jerrod looked at him blankly, not knowing what to say.

"I must remove the malignant tumor in her abdomen. Now. Otherwise, it might be too late." He seemed extremely tense.

The woman in the corner was weaving back and forth, groaning, wailing, keening. Lacey gripped Susan's hand.

Jerrod's lips parted, but he made no sound. His eyes darted around the room. What should he do? The wailing was piercing his skull like a rapier.

"Yes!" he cried, half-rising to his feet. "Yes," he said as he sat back. "Go ahead. Do whatever you have to do." He felt awkward, embarrassed, anxious.

The wailing subdued, trailed off into incoherent muttering. Brother Justin turned his back on Amelia. His hands were clasped at his chest, his head bowed, eyes closed, lips moving. The assistants took their positions, one at the head, her hands on Amelia's shoulders, and the other at her feet, holding her by the ankles. Each bowed her head, and their lips moved as if in silent prayer. Jerrod sat as if frozen. Lacey clung to Susan.

Suddenly, Brother Justin turned and raised his hands. His voice trembled. "Lord, I am your servant. These are your hands. Your will be done."

Susan shivered.

His hands dropped suddenly, seeming to disappear into Amelia's abdomen. Writhing, he bent from the waist, raised his right hand high, looked at it, and slipped it under her body approximately beneath the left hand. His face reflected effort, sweat appeared again on his lip, his brow. Amelia cried out softly in her stupor. The woman in the corner moaned with her.

"Just a little more, dear lady, and it will be done," Brother Justin wheezed, and then, with a cry, raised high his right hand, holding a mass of tissue. The woman in the corner held up her hands and shouted something unintelligible.

Susan looked quickly toward her but before she could be certain of what the woman held in her hands, they were down again and she resumed her swaying, muttering, and fingering. Cold shock rippled through Susan, for the momentary impression she had was that the woman held the severed feet of a chicken.

"Here it is!" cried Brother Justin. "It is done!" He handed it to the assistant who had been holding Amelia's shoulders. She took the tissue, hurried from the room, and Susan heard the sound of running water from what must have been a bathroom.

The haze around Amelia had faded, disappeared. She sighed, opened her eyes, looked around in confusion, and struggled to sit up. Brother Justin put his left hand on her shoulder. "It's too soon. Lie still. Give yourself a few minutes to recover. Your cancerous tumor has just been removed, and you need to relax for just a few minutes to regain your strength."

Amelia blinked at him, looked around, closed her eyes again and seemed to fall asleep. Brother Justin nodded and went to clean up.

Jerrod slumped in his chair and mopped at his face. Was what he had seen possible? He studied Amelia. She lay still, breathing softly. Her gown was bloody, but without a tear.

Susan watched Brother Justin as he scrubbed his hands again at the little sink. All his triumph and joy had vanished. He was distant, impenetrable. Had he really done what he appeared to do? Doubts pelted her.

Lacey disengaged herself from Susan and hesitantly got up to go to her mother. "Mom?" she said softly, standing beside the table. "Mom?" She touched her mother's arm. Amelia sighed, opened her eyes, looked at Lacey, looked around at the others.

"What happened? Where am I?" she asked, bewildered.

Jerrod hurried to her. "Don't you remember? You're at Brother Justin's. He just took out your tumor."

"He—" her eyes widened as she began to remember. She swallowed. "My tumor? He took it out? It's gone?"

Jerrod nodded and took her hand. "I saw it."

"It's really gone? I'm all well again?"

Jerrod beamed and nodded. "Yes. It's gone. And yes, you're all well again."

Amelia sat up, felt her side, pulled her hand away, and stared at the blood with disgust. "It's true!" she cried, and put her arms around his neck and laughed. "Oh, how wonderful!" She pulled back and looked at Jerrod. "Didn't I tell you? Sylvia was right!" She laughed again and hugged her husband, getting blood on his coat.

"Mother?" Lacey touched her arm. Amelia looked around and turned to face her daughter. "Mom, are you really all right now?"

Amelia took both of Lacey's hands in her own and nodded. "I feel completely healed, my darling! I'm so much better!"

Susan sighed, shook her head, and turned to watch the woman in the corner. She had stopped swaying, but she still muttered. For an instant, she opened her eyes and looked at Susan. Susan shrank back. Never had she seen eyes like those. They closed again immediately, but for that moment, Susan felt reaching out to her such hatred, such—evil—that she cringed. Only with tremendous effort did she manage to sit still.

She reached out for meaning in the muttering, and she could make out something that sounded like "mandragoras", and again, "buriel", and repeated, "etzah" or "itzah." Then—what was that she said? Had the woman said "Belial"?

She paled with the shock of recognition. And that look of pure evil—she had not only seen it, she had felt it. But why? She had nothing to do with this. She was here only as moral support for Lacey, and the story for the paper. Or was that enough in some way?

Suddenly, it began to make a horrid sort of sense. Her eyes narrowed as she studied Deva, still muttering. Belial, psychic healing, and mutilated bodies. She felt cold.

Susan looked toward Mrs. Robinson. She seemed so relaxed, so happy. Mr. Robinson, too. He was smiling at his wife, holding her hand, speaking soft endearments. Brother Justin was drying his hands again on another clean towel, walking toward the family.

"I'm sure this was an unusual experience for you," he said in his gentle voice. "You must have been shocked."

Jerrod nodded. "I had no idea. I had heard that in the Philippines, there was a psychic healer pretending to do what you've just done, but—this, now, this is different!"

"I have an M.D. and a Ph.D. in psychology from distinguished universities," said Brother Justin. "If you'd care to see, I have them on the wall in my office."

"Thank you," said Jerrod. "I'd enjoy talking with you."

Brother Justin turned to Amelia. "Rest, now, with your daughter and your friend, while Mr. Robinson and I have a little chat. I'll be back in a short time, and you'll be able to leave then." His small, tight smile did not reach his eyes, and the two men went through a door Susan had not noticed before. The silent assistants were still bustling around, putting the room to rights, and—what's her name?—Deva?—was still sitting slumped in her chair in the dark corner, silent now, fingering whatever it was she held. Her eyes were closed.

When finally they were seated in the limousine on their way back to the Robinsons' house, no one spoke. The experience had struck too deeply for words. Susan was thinking hard.

When the limousine stopped to let them out, Susan glanced at her watch. She was astonished to see it was just after noon.

"Oh, gosh," she stammered, "I'd almost forgotten. This is Monday, and I have to go to work. Would you please excuse me?"

Amelia shot a radiant smile at her. "Of course, dear. And I can't tell you how happy I am that you were with us. I'm sure Lacey is, too, aren't you, honey?"

Lacey nodded. "Thanks for coming. I'll never forget it!" She hugged Susan, and Jerrod put his arm around her shoulders. "I understand you will write this up, but please don't use our names. But be sure to give this wonderful man full credit for what he did for my Amy, won't you?"

Susan hardly knew what to say. She made the corners of her mouth go up and nodded. "And thank you for taking me."

She started up her engine. Winding her way toward the *Register*, she wondered how to write the story. She'd go talk to Matt right after she reported to Jackson. Maybe he and Andy would have something new on the phone number, something that would fit in with what she had seen at Brother Justin's.

She turned off the boulevard toward the *Register* offices. An ordinary-looking neutral gray sedan followed her at a distance, but Susan didn't see it.

NINE

Monday, October 21, 12:30 P.M.

Lacey had decided to stay home with her mother rather than go to the office for the rest of the day. For once, the whole family was together for lunch. She had never seen her mother so happy.

Amelia had called Dr. Damron right after they had come back from Brother Justin's and told him she was cured and that she would not need to see him again. The doctor had sputtered and objected, saying the tests had been positive and that he had scheduled her for surgery Wednesday morning. Amelia dismissed the whole idea with a laugh. "You'll see. I'm absolutely well!" she said and hung up.

Lacey put down her fork and looked at her father. "Are you sure you won't need me this afternoon?"

"I'm sure, honey. You stay here and enjoy the afternoon with your mother. Dave can handle some of your more urgent stuff." Jerrod poured another cup of coffee.

Lacey looked with delight at her mother. "Let's go for a swim."

Amelia looked back fondly. "You swim. I'll read."

Lacey looked with regret at her mother. "Okay. I guess you've had enough for the day." She excused herself and went upstairs to get into her swimsuit.

After Lacey disappeared and Amelia went to lounge by the pool, Jerrod entered his office and picked up the package that had arrived early that morning. It had to be the briefcase he had left in Los Angeles.

Pulling away the wrappings, he sighed with relief, and keyed his code to open the case. The papers appeared to be in order, but he shuffled through them anyway.

He looked sharply at two of the pages, comparing them carefully. Blood drained from his face. The one that outlined the main points of his presentation was a copy! To be sure, an excellent one, but nonetheless, a copy. Someone had replaced his original with a copy. Accidentally? Deliberately? Had all the papers been copied? By whom? The Chairman?

He sat down hard. How? Only he knew the combination to his briefcase. So far as he knew, only the Chairman had handled it after he left Los Angeles. It had to have been the Chairman. What did this mean?

He had to know. He went to a bookcase, pushed on a portion of the carved facing, swinging the bookshelf around to expose a bar. He took down a bottle of Scotch, poured, and tossed it off in a single swallow.

He sat down, elbows on his desk, fingers tented, planning what to say. Would this be disaster or would he find an ally? He looked long at the phone, and finally picked it up.

12:40 P.M.

Lacey splashed in the pool. Amelia lounged under the shade of a jacaranda tree set in the lawn well away from the water, reading, sipping a long, cool drink.

"Mother! Are you sure you won't come in?" called Lacey from the middle of the pool.

Amelia shook her head. "I'm happy here. Just have fun."

"Ah, it's no fun alone." Lacey stroked to the coping and pulled herself up. "I'm going back in to change. I want to call Susan, see if the article will be in tonight's paper." She disappeared into the house wrapped in a towel.

She ran up the stairs to her room, and stripping off the swimsuit, showered, dried, and shrugged into a playsuit. She picked up the phone and was about to dial when she heard her father's voice.

"—did you know my combination?" He sounded outraged.

"I make it a point to know everything about my associates," a cold, emotionless voice replied.

"Even to such private things as—"

"Of course."

Her father was silent for a long moment. "You had no business opening that case!" His voice—was there a tinge of fear in it? "That presentation was planned carefully to make a substantial profit for all of us, and a large premium for the Corporation. Those bonds are a safe investment! None of that hit-and-run stuff we've been doing." He sounded angry.

Lacey was torn. She should put it down, but did this have something to do with why her father had been so upset recently? She knew she shouldn't listen, but she placed her hand over the mouthpiece and put the receiver to her ear again.

"You're treading on some very tender toes, Robinson," said the other voice, too precise, too glacially indifferent. "It's just as well you never got to present it last week."

"And what of my toes? I've put everything I could get my hands on to get this thing going. You let me down now and I'm ruined!" Robinson shouted.

"Your toes are of no concern. You haven't the faintest glimmer of what's going on down here or you'd never have conceived that presentation in the first place. Leave administration to the administrators, and you keep your position. Butt in, and you're history. And as far as the money is concerned, that's only what's expected of you." The connection broke off, and white-faced, Lacey put the phone down with exquisite care.

What's going on? she wondered, apprehensive. *What's Daddy got himself mixed up in?* She stood up and started down the stairs. Her father was just closing the door to his office, carrying his briefcase, his face a ruddy mix of rage, fear, and humiliation. She came down step by careful slow step, wondering what to say, when he looked up at her.

"Dad—" she said, "I didn't mean to eavesdrop—I was just going to call Susan—"

She had never seen such sudden fury in her father before. "You heard? You dared to listen in?" He stepped toward her, and she backed up two steps. "Dad—I didn't mean it—" she said, frightened.

"Don't you ever do that again," he roared, shaking his finger at her, his face purple with rage. "And don't you ever mention what you heard to anyone, hear me?"

Lacey shrank back. "Yes, Daddy," she stammered. "I'm sorry. I didn't mean—" Her eyes rounded with fright.

"I don't care what you meant. Just never do that again!"

Suddenly aware that his daughter was looking at him as if he were a complete stranger, he sighed and dropped the briefcase. He looked up at her, no longer the terrifying stranger, but her adoring father. He held out his arms to her. "Lacey, baby, I'm sorry. Come here."

She descended slowly to the bottom of the staircase. Then, in sudden affection, she rushed into his arms.

"Honey, that was unforgivable of me," he said, folding her close. "But you know how it is with lawyers."

Lacey nodded against his chest.

"You know I am sworn to keep our client's confidences. You can understand how I felt when I realized someone else was listening to a confidential conversation I was having. Forgive me?"

Lacey looked into his troubled dark eyes. "Of course, Daddy. I'm sorry. I know I shouldn't have listened in, but you've been so worried lately that I—well, I thought maybe—"

Robinson put his hands on her shoulders and pushed her off at arm's length. "Maybe nothing. This has nothing to do with you or anyone else. It's just—well, it's a difficult case, that's all."

Lacey drew a deep breath. "Okay. I never heard a thing. I never picked up the phone. I don't know anything at all. Right?"

Robinson almost grinned and ruffled her short, dark curly hair. "Right. And now I have work to do at the office." He picked up his case, turned, and went on out the door.

Lacey looked at the closed door and questions flew at her like crows at a cornfield. She shook her head, for any answers she could think of led only to more—and more difficult—questions.

1:20 P.M.

After a quick lunch, Susan went to the editor's office to let him know what had happened during the morning.

Jackson leaned back until Susan was afraid the swivel chair would topple. "You're telling me that this Brother Justin kneaded Mrs. Robinson's abdomen and came up with a bloody mess of some sort of stuff, and never sent any of it to a pathologist?"

Susan nodded. "From the sound of it, the assistant just flushed it away."

"Hmmmm." Jackson sat up and leaned his elbows on the desk. "Robinson's law firm is powerful. If we don't handle this exactly right, we could be facing a lawsuit we couldn't possibly win." He looked up at Susan. "We'd better hold off on this until someone can do some digging. We need plenty of solid evidence to back up what we print. But I don't have to tell you that."

"So what do you want me to do?"

Jackson stared at her, thinking. "You're on this crazy cat-killing, mutilated body, disappearing girls story. Stay with it. I'll get someone else on Brother Justin."

"The Robinsons are expecting to see something in the paper. And

Mr. Robinson wants full credit given to that charlatan. He really believes Mrs. Robinson is cured. They all do."

"If they ask, tell them there just wasn't room, and it'll be in soon." He looked sympathetic for once. "You know, I'm a little sorry I sent you with them. I should have known better."

Susan shrugged. "That's life. Especially in a newsroom."

"By the way," Jackson said, handing her a sheet of paper, "here's a story that just came in. Write it up."

She took it, read it over, and looked back. "Another shooting? This is ridiculous. There was one just last week. Well, okay. I'll get it out first." She stood up. "Then I'd better see what Matt's found out. I'll be back soon."

"Take all the time you want. Just be back in an hour," Jackson called as the door closed behind her. He shook his head. *She'll be a fine reporter if she lives long enough*, he thought.

1:42 P.M.

Business was heavy at the Computer Warehouse. Matt was demonstrating a computer to a customer; Ricky was on the phone, giving instructions for installing a program. Several people wandered around, looking at computer keyboards, game programs, various peripherals.

Susan saw it was hopeless for the moment, waved at Matt, mouthed "Later!" and went back to her car. She decided to double-check newspapers at the library microfiche. Maybe Lacey had missed something. Looking into the rearview mirror to make sure the street was clear, she saw a gray sedan in the block behind her pull out just as she did. Every now and again she glanced in the rearview mirror. To her growing alarm, she saw the gray sedan was staying either one or two cars behind her.

Pretending a calm she didn't feel, she circled the library parking lot until a car left a spot, and she took it. Looking around surreptitiously for the gray sedan, she saw it parked at the curb a block away. She turned off the engine and made sure both her car doors were locked before she entered the library.

Once inside the cavernous building, she stood for awhile behind a massive pillar where she watched the entrance. Evidently whoever followed her wasn't coming into the library.

Going to the bank of telephones at the rear of the lobby, she went to the one she hoped would be the least visible. Dialing the Computer Warehouse, she told Matt she had been followed, and that the gray sedan was probably still waiting for her.

"What's going on?" she asked. "So you think it's this cat-killing mutilated body bit, or is it Brother Justin?"

Matt was silent. "Look," he finally said, "Andy came across something—uh, is there a rear entrance that library patrons can use?"

Susan looked around. "No, I don't think so. There's a door that says 'Emergency Exit Only.' It would probably set off an alarm unless I were authorized to use it."

Matt was thinking so hard Susan could almost hear the wheels turning. "Tell you what. I'll send Ricky over in his pickup. He'll park as close as he can to the entrance, and come in for you. Try to stay behind him as you leave, and come here with him. We'll get your car later."

Susan closed her eyes in relief. "Thanks, Matt. You're wonderful! See you."

Susan went into the ladies' room, and with a wet comb, fought against waves to plaster her hair down on her skull. It was all she could think of to change her appearance. She took off her jacket, draped it over her arm, and went back to the pillar to wait for Ricky. In a few minutes he entered and looked around. She waved, and he came over. He looked at her hair and grinned, but said nothing.

"C'mon, Sue, I'm parked illegally. Gotta hurry." He led her by the arm to the door. The gray sedan was not visible from the entrance.

Susan kept Ricky between herself and the street, and slipped into the pickup. She twisted to look toward the block where she had seen the gray sedan. It was still parked where it had been, the shadowed figure behind the wheel, still apparently watching her Ford, ignoring the pickup.

Back at the Warehouse, Matt looked up from his work as the two came in. The customers had faded away. They were alone in the store.

He shook his head. "I hope you're not planning to keep that hairstyle," he said, waving her toward the washroom. "I like it loose."

Susan grinned and punched him playfully as she passed him on the way. In moments, her hair was combed out again. She joined him in his office.

"Better?" She posed provocatively, fluffing her hair. He threw a paper clip at her; she made a face. "Hey! I have a story for you." She perched on the edge of the desk to tell him about Brother Justin's "healing" practices, about Deva, the chicken feet, and the way she had felt when Deva looked at her.

"I don't for a moment believe that mess in his hand was her cancer, but the Robinsons do," she said. "And Jackson's taken me off that story. He wants me to stay with the cat-killings and missing girls. But how can I? Lacey's my best friend."

Matt leaned back, his lips pursed in a low whistle. He looked at her for a minute. "We did a little investigating on this Brother Justin fellow and found out a few things."

Susan cocked an eyebrow. "Such as?"

"He actually is a doctor, but had his license revoked. To begin with, his name isn't Justin. It's Isham Yadush. He studied medicine in Damascus, psychology at the Sorbonne in Paris, and started his practice in London. That's where he lost his license. A young duchess died in surgery while he was operating under the influence of Demerol. She bled to death. The file called it 'gross negligence.' Terrible scandal. Two or three years later, he managed to get to the States, and it's only within the last two or three years that he's been Brother Justin."

Susan thought about it a moment. "Fascinating. But we knew from the beginning that he's a fake. Just not that he's an M.D. He did say something about that to Mr. Robinson, I think."

Matt looked at her. "We also latched on to a piece of something else. A—well, I guess you'd have to call it a consortium of about half a dozen of the county's leading citizens together with a number of lesser-known lights. Anyway, they bought that enormous so-called Viking Castle out on Briggs Canyon Road before you get to old Highway 395, up in the hills, you know, and are refurbishing it. We got copies of work orders, purchase orders, permits—the works. And it's weird."

Susan looked at him, puzzled. "What's weird about buying and refurbishing an old building? They might be planning to—I dunno, make a bed-and-breakfast thing?"

"Not with the kind of hardware they've ordered. It's all sort of medieval. Even to materials that if they're put together in a certain way, would produce racks for torture, the Iron Maiden things—that sort of stuff. And the furnishings sound as if Dracula were the interior decorator."

Susan thought. "That's bizarre. But what does that have to do with what's going on?"

"Isham Yadush is one of the members of the consortium."

"Oh." Susan slipped down from the desk and paced. "Sort of fits in with the eerie atmosphere of the place where he does his thing." She looked puzzled. "But where does that take us?"

Matt shook his head. "I don't know for sure. But I get a funny feeling about it. It's spooky. Like all the rest of it. It's my guess that everything is somehow connected." He looked thoughtfully at Susan. "And now they're following you. I don't know what's going on, but you've managed to get in the middle of it."

Susan's face paled. "You mean, the cat-killings, the stuff Lacey went through on Washington Avenue, the mutilated body, the missing girls, Brother Justin, and that Castle are all parts of one big megillah?"

Matt nodded. "It's beginning to look that way. And there's more, but we don't have enough of a handle on it to say anything about it yet." He bit down on a fingernail. "I hope they don't catch on that Andy's trying to break into their computers. He's pretty slick, but I've an idea they're pretty smart, too."

"Wow." Susan perched on the desk again and swung her legs. She looked out the window. It was getting dark. "Ooops. I was supposed to be back at the paper hours ago. I think I'm late."

Matt raised his eyebrows. "Yeah. Better call your boss."

Susan reached for the phone and dialed. Matt chewed on a pencil while she argued and explained. When she put the phone down, he continued. "I don't know how much they know about what you know. The very fact that they're following you means that they think you know more than they want you to know." He paused a moment. "I mean—oh heck, you know what I mean!" He got up and walked around to the side of the desk where Susan perched. "I mean you better proceed with caution, as they say. Keep in touch with me. Don't do anything or go anywhere unless you let me know. Okay?" His eyes pleaded, warm with such love and concern that Susan had to smile. She slipped off the desk and stepped close to Matt.

"If you say so, master," she said softly, her eyes glowing.

"Aw, quit it!" he said, drawing her into a long, loving hug.

After a timeless moment, Susan pulled away. "Jackson said I might just as well call it a day." She glanced at her watch. Almost four-thirty. "How would you like to take me somewhere for dinner?"

"My thought exactly. I know just the place. But I gotta finish up something here. Ricky can handle the rest and lock up the shop. Grab a magazine or something, and I'll be ready in a jif." He stuck his head out of his cubicle, told Rick he was leaving early, and went to his computer. A few minutes later they were backing out of his parking spot. Matt drove inland to an Italian restaurant near Cromwell. There they entered Marco's Restaurant, already anticipating the rich spiciness of Lasagna Caruso.

9:52 P.M.

The small gray sedan was still parked near the now-deserted library, the driver listening to a squawking diatribe for being so stupid as to lose such an easy mark as that Walker girl. He put the car phone down on the seat where it continued to sputter, and disgusted, pulled away from the curb and turned toward Washington Avenue.

Susan's little Escort sat alone in the parking lot, all locked up. After awhile, another car drove close, Susan got out, waved to the driver, unlocked her door, and slipped in. Both cars drove away, leaving the silent lot empty but for glowing pools of light from the standards.

TEN

Tuesday, October 22, 8:35 A.M.

The first thing Susan did at the *Register* was to tell Jackson what Matt had learned about Brother Justin. "And I don't know if it means anything, but I was followed from the Computer Warehouse to the library. A gray sedan." Jackson's eyebrows shot north. Susan continued. "I called Matt. He sent Ricky over to pick me up. Lost the tail that way."

Jackson chewed a knuckle as he considered. "It isn't enough for a story. We don't know who or why. Leave it alone for now. Ken's investigating the Brother Justin thing. Give him the information. He'll check into it." He looked hard at her. "You're getting in pretty deep for a rookie. Don't get careless. Stay with the missing girls story."

"Okay. But Matt's got a friend who's working on it, too. Between the two of them, they'll dig up more. I'll let you know." He nodded and she left the office.

9 A.M.

Jerrod Robinson had said nothing during breakfast to Lacey about the phone call she had overheard. Downtown, he went directly to his own office with a quick "Good morning" to the staff. Lacey went back to work as usual.

Later, when Lacey brought in the files she had been working on, he was on the phone. With a wave of his hand, he indicated for her to put them on his desk, and he went on with his conversation. Lacey left the office with the feeling that something was wrong. He was too preoccupied, too intense.

9:20 A.M.

Susan went to the homes of the missing girls and met silence.

The nervous parents closed up, refusing to answer questions. *Why?* she wondered, as the third door closed in her face. They had been willing to talk before. And the few people on Washington Avenue who would even talk to her denied there had been any disturbance the previous Wednesday evening, but everyone seemed edgy. In the Seaview Heights area, the mother of the girl whose cat had been killed came to the door, paled, said, "I've nothing to say!" and slammed the door. *What's going on?* Susan wondered. *They're all frightened. Something or someone's scared them off.* She went to the police to ask if there had been any new developments, but it was the same there. Nothing but questions upon questions, and no answers anywhere.

Back at the paper with nothing new on her own stories, she wound up editing the police blotter—several burglaries, a holdup at one of the major markets, an embezzlement at a savings and loan. And another senseless drive-by shooting. This time the victim had died. Susan scowled. "It's getting to be more like L.A. all the time," she muttered as she blue-pencilled the copy.

Tuesday, 9:50 A.M.

Andy came into the Warehouse to talk to Matt. "Hi, guy," he said. Matt told him about the gray sedan following Susan the day before. Andy's eyes widened, but he nodded.

"I guess I'm not really surprised," he said. "That sort of thing seems to fit this pattern. No one trusts anyone."

Matt made a sour face and glanced at the clock. "Hey, it's almost time for a coffee break," Matt said. "Let's go across the street to Connie's." He turned to Ricky. "Want me to bring you some coffee? Anything?"

"Sure. Coffee and one of her big cinnamon rolls."

Nodding, Matt and Andy hustled across the busy street and entered into the warm fragrance of coffee and good food. Half a dozen customers scattered around the little cafe were enjoying a late breakfast or hurrying through a coffee break.

Seated by the window, Matt called out to Connie, "The usual. One for Ricky, too." She nodded and went to pour coffee.

Matt turned toward Andy. "Y'know, I've been wondering about how they got on to Susan. I don't think they could have picked her up here unless the phone was bugged."

Color drained from Andy's face. He took off his glasses and laid them on the table. "I've been using your modem," he said, alarm edging his voice.

"Yeah." Matt stared at Andy. Both fell silent for a moment. "Susan wondered if my apartment was bugged. I checked it out last night, but I couldn't find anything."

Connie brought them coffee, rolls, and a paper bag with Ricky's order in it together with the tab. Andy waved Matt off and dug into his pocket. "This is on me," he said. Connie took the money, flashed her customary smile, and left.

"Have you checked your store yet?"

"No. Figured you'd know more about it than I do. We can do that after we get back—that is, if you have the time."

"Sure," said Andy, sipping his coffee. "Got any real idea of what's going on?"

Matt shook his head. "No more than you do. Susan called. Said she'd gone around to all the people involved, but got nowhere with anybody. They just weren't talking anymore. Something or someone has probably scared them off."

"I put in a system for a friend late yesterday, so I haven't had a chance to do anything else, either. Just as well." He bit into his roll. "Wonder if I'm bugged," he said. He swallowed, and looked up at Matt, furious. "This is crazy! What the heck's going on? Here we've been minding our own business, and all of a sudden, it's like a James Bond movie!"

Matt shrugged. "Well, almost our own business. We're investigating for Susan. Someone must think it's not our business."

Back at the store, they kept their conversation general while they took phones apart, scanned everything they could, including the phone connection at the back of the building. Nothing. No bugs.

Still outside, Matt scowled, frustrated. "Maybe we missed something. You know how it is—every day someone's coming up with something new. I didn't see anything of the induction type, either. Did you?"

Andy shook his head. "Just the same, I think I'd better do my stuff somewhere else. I'll get in touch with some of my friends, see if they can let me use their equipment—you know, a little here, a little there—make it hard to trace anything. In case anyone is trying."

They went inside. The store was busy. Andy bought a new game program and went his way. Matt watched as he left, a puzzled frown creasing his brow. The store wasn't bugged. Nor his apartment. So how did they tie Susan into this thing, whatever it was?

4:47 P.M.

Matt called Susan at the paper. "Hi, honey," he said when she answered. "Are you doing anything special tonight?"

"Not unless you have something planned," Susan said, propping her phone on her shoulder while she finished her story and punched "send."

"Got anything you could feed a hungry businessman at your place?"

"Oooh! What nerve! Inviting yourself to dinner! Well, if you'll bring some ice cream, I guess I could put something together."

Matt grinned. "Thanks. Well, I'll see you about six, okay?"

"Sure. Just call me a pushover for a panhandler. Oh—make it chocolate fudge mousse. Light. The ice cream, I mean."

Matt hung up, his face somber. He didn't tell her he was planning to sweep her place for bugs, although, if they hadn't found any at the store, they probably wouldn't at her place. So how come she was followed? His eyes widened. She had gone with the Robinsons to Brother Justin's. Could that be the link?

Wednesday, October 23, 5:50 A.M.

Elizabeth and Don Walker had not slept. Raymond had not come home from his friend Alan's house. When they had phoned the Baxters after eleven, only his parents were there. The boys had left hours before, saying they were going out for more 7-Up, and had not come back. The Baxters were frantic, as were the Walkers. When they called, the police took descriptions, but said they could do nothing except keep their eyes open. Long after midnight, Don and Elizabeth had finally given up and gone to bed, but neither could rest.

Dawn was just breaking when the telephone shrilled, startling them.

Donovan reached for the phone. "Yeah?" He sat straight up, suddenly wide awake, listening. Elizabeth stirred and sat up, looking at her husband.

Don put down the phone and looked in disbelief at Elizabeth. "Raymond is at the police station!" he said.

Elizabeth rubbed her eyes. "Where? Police? What—"

Don got up and started dressing. "I'm going to get him."

"Not without me!" said Elizabeth, suddenly wide awake.

Don nosed their car through the gray chill of the fogbound city to the police station. There was nothing to say—just questions racing in their heads.

Five boys had been held in the same cell. Alan, who had been walking around in a circle, giggling, had been taken home by his angry parents. Two were sleeping. Raymond sprawled in a daze. The fifth tried unsuccessfully to count his fingers.

"They were playing Demon Crypt at the Baxter home," said the officer, "and one of them—we haven't yet found out which—got some marijuana and two six-packs of beer. We found them staggering down the middle of Cutler Way about two hours ago."

The Walkers claimed Raymond, led him to the car, and took him home in silence. As they turned into the driveway, Raymond seemed to come awake. He looked around and started mumbling. "I'm sorry. Dad, Mom, I'm sorry. I shouldn't have—"

"You've got that right!" said his father, his jaw clenched. "Get out. You're going to bed, and then we'll have a long talk!" He took Raymond by the arm and half dragged him into the house, mumbling all the way. Elizabeth followed.

The Walkers sat at the kitchen table while the coffee maker bubbled and dripped and wafted rich aroma around the room. Neither looked at the other.

"What gets into kids that they do such crazy things?" Don demanded finally. "A decent, Christian kid like Ray—What got into him?"

Elizabeth looked at her hands and shrugged. "He's at the age where he wants to try everything there is in life, I guess, and—well, you know how everyone talks about getting high, how great it is, how bad it is—I suppose he just had to find out for himself. And there's peer pressure. The rest of them were trying it, and I suppose he felt he had to go along or be considered a creep or a coward."

Don sighed. "I guess we were lucky the police caught them. This had better be his first—and only—time!"

Elizabeth nodded. "Maybe we'll be able to talk sense to him when he wakes up." She looked at the coffee maker and got up to put bread into the toaster. "This is not going to be easy," she said.

ELEVEN

Wednesday, October 23, 7:45 A.M.

Lacey awoke with a strange sense of foreboding. Then she realized—*it's Wednesday. Gilbert is coming for dinner. Why does he make me feel so uneasy?* she wondered.

Getting into the shower, she puzzled about her feelings. *He's handsome, obviously rich, polite and thoughtful—maybe too polite? Too smooth? Too—what?* She knew too little about him. He was a mystery. She turned off the water and grabbed a towel. Maybe there hadn't been enough time with him to get to know him. Well, perhaps tonight she'd get to know him better.

She had slept too late, taken too much time getting dressed. Breakfast was hurried, traffic was heavy, and when she arrived, the office seemed to be an oasis of calm. She sighed with relief as she sat down and leafed through the materials on her desk.

1:45 P.M.

Susan sat down at her work station, late again. Everyone else had come back from lunch and was hard at work. She smiled, reviewing the quiet lunch she and Matt had shared at Seaside Park. He had no news about the elusive phone number nor anything else, which left them nothing to talk about but each other and their future together. *Tough*, she thought with another contented smile.

She sighed, getting back into work mode and leafed through her IN basket. There was nothing new on the pet mutilations nor the disappearing girls, so she picked up a letter to the editor complaining about school board members who do nothing but argue about the condition of the teachers' lounge and the no smoking regulations. It needed considerable editing.

5:10 P.M.

None of the Walkers spoke as they ate supper. The talk with Raymond after he woke up late in the afternoon had not been pleasant, but Elizabeth hoped they had made an impression on him. She looked at her husband. Don's expression was grim as he tackled the stew. Raymond toyed with his food.

Raymond finally put one bite into his mouth and excused himself. Elizabeth watched him start upstairs. Why hadn't she realized how often Raymond played Demon Crypt at Alan's house? Friends had warned her it might be dangerous to get involved with that game.

"Don," she said, "we should get Susan in on this. Maybe she'll have some ideas about how to get Raymond away from Demon Crypt. I'll call her to see when she's free."

Her husband looked up from the stew and nodded.

Elizabeth scooped up a spoonful and put it down. Things like this never happened to decent Christian families, did they? She walked across the room, picked up the phone, dialed Susan's number, and left a message on her answering machine.

5:12 P.M.

The day had sped by too fast. Lacey called out good night to Frances, who nodded back, still putting files away, a pencil between her teeth.

Pulling her Corvette into the garage at Tres Encinos, Lacey noticed that the grounds looked exceptionally nice. Inside, the house looked as if photographers from *Good Housekeeping* were about to arrive. Her mother, unusually harried looking, was fussing at a strange girl in a traditional maid's uniform, stretching the short skirt down in the back.

"Cindy, remember not to bend over!" she said. "That skirt is too short."

The girl nodded. "I rented the uniform, and this was the longest skirt they had," she said, picking at the ruffles on the little white apron. "I guess I'm taller than most."

Amelia stood back and appraised her new maid. "Well, except for the short skirt, you look fine. You'll do." Cindy nodded and disappeared toward the kitchen.

"Hi, Mom," said Lacey. "What's the big deal?"

Amelia looked around and flashed a nervous smile. "Hi, honey. Your father wants to make a good impression on Gilbert," she said. "It's been hectic. The gardener has been here all day, I hired a girl to help Margaret and Cindy to serve dinner tonight, but even so, it was a race to get everything done." She hugged Lacey, and went into the kitchen to check progress there.

Lacey looked after her mother and shook her head. As she started up the stairs, Gilbert's forgotten cuff link came to mind, and a troubled feeling washed over her. In her room, she took it out of her jewelry case and peered at it. *Why should this make me feel so uneasy?* she wondered. *It's only onyx and gold. But—"B"? Why "B"?* She put it down on her vanity. *Maybe it was his father's cuff link. He might have been a Ben, or a Brian, or most anything beginning with B.* She tried to dismiss the thought, but uneasiness nagged at her.

Shortly before six, she heard door chimes announcing Gilbert's arrival. She wore her short black evening dress with the small pocket tucked into the waistline seam under the iridescent belt. She had put the cuff link there and at her first opportunity, would give it back to Gilbert.

She fastened a gold chain with a large opal and diamond pendant around her neck to relieve the plain scooped neckline, checked her appearance, and started downstairs. From the landing, she saw her mother, looking relaxed, seated on her favorite Louis XIV chair.

Amelia extended her hand gracefully to Gilbert, more handsome than ever in a dark gray silk suit. Amelia's lavender charmeuse gown flattered her, making her deep blue eyes look violet. Lacey continued down the stairs.

"It's impossible to believe that you have a daughter of Lacey's age," Gilbert was saying, taking Amelia's hand and raising it to his lips. "I'd have thought you her sister." Amelia smothered an embarrassed smile and thanked him.

"And Mr. Robinson," said Gilbert, as Jerrod rose from the settee. He extended his hand. "How good of you to invite me."

Jerrod touched his hand and nodded. "Would you care for a drink? We have almost anything you might want."

"Thank you, but no," said Gilbert, turning toward Lacey, who had just come into the living room. She sat down on a small chair upholstered in deep pink. "In the presence of such beauty, I'm already intoxicated." He walked over to Lacey and taking her hand, raised it to his lips. She pulled it away.

He looked at her appraisingly. "You've changed a lot since the ninth grade."

Lacey became aware she had been holding her breath. She let it out in a quiet sigh. No mention of what had happened on Friday. Maybe he wouldn't be a problem after all. "So have you. I'd hardly have known you," she said.

Conversation was general, polite, and unremarkable. Jerrod poured himself another drink, his eyes on Gilbert. Lacey saw the expression. What was it? Dislike? No, just questioning.

The dinner table resembled an illustration from *Gourmet* magazine. Conversation was polite, even amusing, but nobody said anything significant. Cindy was quiet, efficient, and unobtrusive.

"The evening is so lovely," said Amelia as Cindy removed the dinner plates. "Cindy, serve dessert out on the west patio." Amelia led the way to the patio, with its superb view of the coast. The sun had set, lighting cirrus clouds just above the horizon with gold, scarlet, and orange below a luminous turquoise sky, leaving the east clothed in night. A silver moon hung just above the treetops east of the house. The breeze from the ocean was cool.

The malls and homes of Playa Linda sparkled at the foot of the hill a short distance away. Head and taillights formed glittering bracelets of diamond and ruby along the streets, the coast road, and the freeway. The lights of a cruise ship slid southward on the dark waters, while overhead, a jet winked its way north.

The table had been moved from the center of the patio to one side, and seating had been arranged to take best advantage of the view. Amelia claimed the lounge and settled into the languorous mood of the evening. Lacey sat on a chair near her. Gilbert walked to the edge of the patio to enjoy the view. Jerrod paced.

Cindy brought out a tray filled with dishes of pineapple cream garnished with strawberries. She offered a dish to each, set the tray on the table, and disappeared.

Lacey noticed that Gilbert had sat down at the table and was spooning his dessert. She took hers and sat across from him. "This is good," she said, looking up at him.

"Mmmm. The best."

Lacey slipped a hand to her waist, retrieved the cuff link from the little pocket, and reached toward Gilbert, staring intently at him. He looked at her, reached toward her closed hand, slipped the link from her, and withdrew his hand. A few moments later Lacey noticed he touched his pocket lightly. He nodded slightly, a tiny cast of relief on his face.

Jerrod continued to stare at Gilbert. Now was the time. They had to talk.

"Gilbert, my boy," he said, putting down his glass, "I have a rather unusual collection of ancient coins. Would you like to see it?"

"Certainly. I'm something of a numismatist myself," he said. With a slight bow toward the ladies, he followed Jerrod.

"He's such a nice young man," Amelia said when they had left. "You should get to know him better."

"Oh, he's nice enough, I guess," Lacey said. "I haven't had much chance to get to know him, though."

"Mmmmm," said Amelia, sighing as she leaned back, looking at the lights of the ship, now quite far south. "How nice it would be to take a cruise somewhere," she said.

"If you like cruises. Trouble with them is you have to spend so much time on board the ship."

Amelia smiled. "But that's what makes it such fun!"

For awhile, neither spoke, enjoying the evening. The colors in the west had drained away with the light, and stars twinkled above the waves. Lacey became aware of voices in the house above the distant rumble of traffic, her father's and Gilbert's. Her father sounded angry. Gilbert's voice was scarcely discernible, calm and quiet, but cold. The evening had chilled, looked less lovely, somehow.

The men returned to the patio. Jerrod clapped Gilbert on the shoulder. "This young man knows coins! There wasn't much I was able to tell him," he said, forcing a cheerful manner.

"I must say it's an exceptional collection," said Gilbert. "I think there are more rare coins in your collection than I've seen in any other."

Jerrod went to the edge of the patio, as Gilbert went on. "You have one coin, sir, I've never seen anywhere else," he said, looking at Jerrod. "That oriental coin, the Tibetan one."

Jerrod cleared his throat. "Mmmm. Yes. That's an interesting one. A friend of mine who does a lot of traveling brought it to me. He picked it up in Lhassa."

Gilbert raised his eyebrows. Jerrod continued. "He had gone there to study Tibetan beliefs, and while there, used their coinage, of course. Gave me that one."

"Interesting. Have you looked into oriental religions?"

Jerrod shook his head. "No. I have trouble enough keeping up with my own."

"They're fascinating." Gilbert turned to include Amelia and Lacey. "For instance, Zen. It's similar to old Quaker beliefs. They believe truth is not to be found in any writings, because truth is greater than words. To find it, they meditate."

"That's Japanese, isn't it?" asked Lacey, not really interested, but trying to keep conversation flowing.

Gilbert nodded. "Then there's Hinduism, with their worship of

all living creatures, you know, like the sacred cow?" He looked at
Amelia, who nodded absently. Lacey stifled a yawn.

"And there are dozens of others—voodoo, spiritualism, Wicca,
and lots of others. But enough of comparative religions." He continued. "By the way, some friends of mine are having a séance
tonight about nine. Would you like to attend? I'm sure you'd be
welcome," he said, looking from one to the other.

"Oh, Jerry, what fun!" said Amelia, rising from the lounge and
going to her husband. She put her hand on his arm. "Let's go, shall
we?"

Jerrod threw a baleful look at Gilbert and turned back to Amelia.
"No, my dear, I can't. I have some work to do yet tonight. But you
go. You and Lacey. Have a good time."

"Couldn't you put it off, please?" Amelia begged.

"Sorry, sweetheart, but it's something that can't wait."

Amelia turned away in dainty defeat. "But you'll come, won't
you, Lacey?" she asked.

Lacey didn't really want to go, but her mother was eager. "All
right, Mom. I'll go."

Amelia smiled in triumph and put her hand on Gilbert's arm.
"Thank you for the invitation, Gilbert. I think I'll get a light wrap.
It will be chilly coming home." She took Lacey by the hand and
started back into the house.

As they climbed the stairs, Amelia asked, "Did you notice anything
about your father? Do you think he's upset about something?"

Lacey looked sharply at her mother. She must have heard them
quarreling inside the house after all. "We had a busy day at the
office," she said. "He's probably tired. I guess he didn't get everything finished and brought it home."

"You think so?"

"Sure. What else?"

"Nothing, I guess." Her mother still looked troubled as they
parted at the top of the stairs. Lacey scowled as she opened her
bedroom door. *Everything had been okay until they went to look at
Daddy's coins,* she thought. *Something got them angry at each other.
Wonder if it has anything to do with that phone call?*

Lacey picked up a light shawl to throw over her shoulders and
looked at her reflection, wondering what they were getting into. *A
séance,* she thought, *is nothing but a charlatan's trick. So why do I not
want to go?*

She shook her head, picked up her black beaded handbag, and
turned out the light as she closed the door behind her.

TWELVE

Wednesday, 8:50 P.M.

Gilbert drove inland for some distance, then turned off into a narrow drive that led nearly a quarter of a mile through an avocado grove. Branches arched above the car to form a dark tunnel. When it opened up, Lacey gasped at the beauty of the house nestled in the middle of a skillfully landscaped clearing. Moonlight silvered the tiles on the slanted roof; the small-paned windows glowed with golden light. Lamps placed a foot above the ground illuminated the parking area and the walkway to the door. *If the house were smaller,* Lacey thought, *it would resemble the fairy-tale cottages in the books I loved as a child.*

Gilbert parked his Jaguar by a rock retaining wall. Jasmine trailed from the top, scenting the air with its heady perfume. Several other cars were parked nearby. Judging by the number of vehicles, there would be a substantial gathering at the séance.

At Gilbert's suggestion, they walked to the edge of the clearing, where the land planted in avocado and citrus groves sloped down the hillsides. Lights shone at intervals where houses were tucked among the trees. A range of hills to the west blocked their view of the ocean. Behind them and above the hills to the east, a glow in the sky marked the location of an inland city. The air was fresh and cool, fragrant with scents of rich, moist soil and a hint of sweet alyssum.

Gilbert led them to the front step and touched the doorbell. Cathedral chimes sounding inside the house made Lacey feel she was in a dream world, a fantasy right out of storybooks.

The door opened, and a tall, silver-haired woman dressed in a clinging silver-gray gown greeted them. "Gilbert, my dear!" she said in a low, throaty voice, kissing him on the cheek. "And who are these lovelies with you?" She looked expectantly at Amelia and Lacey.

"My good friends Mrs. Jerrod Robinson, Amelia, and their daughter Lacey." He turned to Amelia. "This is our hostess, Laurelyn."

"I'm so happy you could come," Laurelyn said, extending her hand first to Amelia, then to Lacey. The touch was soft, her gray eyes questioning. "Do come in and meet the others. We're about to begin. Please be as quiet as possible."

The entry walls were hung with pictures of little beings in wooded groves. Their storybook appearance was enhanced by carved wood frames. A similarly carved small table and framed oval mirror faced the door.

Lacey was surprised to see the setup in the living room. Three rows of chairs upholstered in tapestry featuring forest motifs faced a cloth-covered table. All the wooden parts were deeply carved in leafy designs like the furniture and appointments in the entry. The carpet was patterned to resemble the floor of a forest. The light was soft, as in a dream.

Behind the table, tall, thick green candles in wooden stands carved to resemble knobby tree trunks bracketed a portrait of Laurelyn. Lacey stared, fascinated. While the silver-crowned head and bared shoulders and arms were exquisitely delineated, the rest of the body seemed to melt, dissolve, into a leafy torso which in turn faded into a background of living forest.

"Mother," Lacey whispered, "I don't think we're in Kansas anymore—" and suppressed a giggle. Amelia looked stern and shushed her. Lacey looked around.

She was unaccountably startled by the images of strange beings clustered on tables set against the wall at her left. They didn't fit the wooded fairy-tale ambiance everywhere else. African tribal masks stood next to Indian totems, Oriental dragons, Polynesian tikis, satyrs and fauns, and figures which could best be described as nightmarish gargoyles. Some were festooned with fresh flowers; all were surrounded with votive candles of various colors. Small gifts of food had been set before them as offerings and sacrifices. Gilbert excused himself and went to one of the tables, put something on a plate before one of the gargoyle figures, and bowed. He turned to another man nearby. They stood in hushed conversation for a few moments before returning.

Most of the seats were already filled. People acknowledged others with solemn nods or handshakes. Laurelyn beckoned to a young couple and in a quiet voice introduced them as Ann and Stuart. Gilbert's greeting suggested they were old friends. He embraced Ann lightly and held Stuart's handshake in both hands. They found chairs together in the third row, and sat down in silence.

A few more people arrived and were seated. Laurelyn stood off to one side, talking quietly with another woman. Lacey noted the contrast in style. Laurelyn was tall, stately, formal, and ethereal. The other woman was short and stocky, with an olive complexion and large dark eyes. She wore a white blouse over a multi-colored full skirt; long dark hair escaped a matching scarf around her head. To Lacey, she gave the impression of irrepressible, earthy energy.

Laurelyn glided to the front of the table. "My friends," she said, "we have a guest medium tonight to conduct the meeting. Sharleena is well known in the Caribbean area, and we are fortunate to have her here for her first West Coast meeting. Please welcome her."

A murmur of "Welcome, Sharleena" rippled softly through the group. Laurelyn sat down in the front row.

Lacey watched, fascinated, as Sharleena bowed her head in acknowledgment and walked behind the table. She beckoned, and a black-garbed assistant placed a crystal tumbler three-quarters full of water, a bowl of eggs, another bowl filled with herbs on the table, and what looked like a large baking pan on the floor beside her. Lacey choked back another giggle. It looked as if Sharleena was about to give a cooking demonstration.

Seated in the high-backed chair, the medium looked at each guest present individually. Lacey shrank back into the upholstery when their eyes met. Sharleena's eyes were like onyx marbles, unreadable, unflinching. An almost physical force seemed to emanate from her. The gaze moved on. Lacey breathed again and relaxed.

"In a moment," the medium said in a brisk voice, "I will go into a trance. You must all be very quiet, for my control, Nuna, an Incan, is very sensitive to disturbances. Please, all of you, concentrate on Nuna while I make contact."

The lights dimmed until the only illumination was from the many candles in the room. Lacey became aware of the scent of woodsy incense, increasing, thickening the air.

Sharleena's eyes closed as she began to moan softly. A period of silence passed, then she moaned again and began breathing heavily, writhing as if trying to find a comfortable position. She murmured something incomprehensible and slumped back into the chair. For a moment, there was a heavy silence. Lacey felt the hairs at the back of her neck prickle.

The medium's eyes opened. Lacey was startled. Someone else seemed to be looking out of them as Sharleena's body straightened. "I am pleased to greet you," said a dry, wispy voice, issuing from Sharleena. "I am happy to be here in this lovely setting. Now. Concentrate on your requests. I shall try to help you." Silence. "There is one here who has had a severe migraine for a week."

A woman in the second row stood up. "I think I'm the one you mean."

"Come near," said the dry voice.

The woman slid past others to the end of the row and went to the table, her face puckered with pain.

"No. Here beside me."

She walked around behind the table and stood facing Sharleena.

The medium stood, took an egg and rolled it up and around the woman's head. She moaned, rocked back and forth, and suddenly threw the egg into the pan on the floor, where it splattered noisily. "The evil is gone!" cried the medium in a wispy voice, and the woman with the migraine put her hands up to her head. She nodded her head, and smothered a laugh. "It is! It's gone!" she said. She went back to her seat, smiling and murmuring incredulously.

Lacey, skeptical, turned to look a question at Gilbert. He put a finger to his lips. She shrugged and turned back to look at Sharleena. She would ask him later.

"A man has had severe stomach pains recently," the old voice continued.

After a brief silence, a portly man stood. "You mean me?"

"Yes. Come here."

The man hesitated, but went to the table. The medium's hands fluttered around the man's stomach and abdomen, not quite touching, until they settled in the general area of the duodenum. After a moment, the hands reached for the man's body, appeared to dig in, and began drawing out what might have been a long, invisible rope. A bluish haze seemed to envelop Sharleena's hands. Suddenly she struck the glass of water with her right hand and immediately with her left. The bluish haze vanished and the water in the glass clouded briefly. "The evil is gone!" Nuna cried. The man returned to his seat, unbelieving, joyful.

A boy of about thirteen was called up, and was asked to remove his shirt. The medium took handfuls of herbs and rubbed him well around his chest and back. The herbs then were thrown into the pan. The assistant mixed them quickly with the broken egg mass. "It doesn't hurt any more!" the boy cried, rubbing his chest. He picked up his shirt and ran back to his mother, who shushed him, wrapping him in her arms.

"There is one here who is rejoicing, for she has just been healed," said Nuna's voice.

Amelia's eyes widened. She looked around to see who would respond. No one moved. Amazed, she said, "Me?"

"Yes. You."

"But I didn't say anything—"

"I hear your thoughts. Come near."

Amelia rose slowly.

Sharleena's hands flitted over Amelia's abdomen, again not quite touching. Finally she placed her hands firmly at the sides of Amelia's tiny waist. "This was done well. I congratulate your physician. You may go now."

Amelia stared, bewildered, and returned to her seat. She sat down beside Lacey, staring at Sharleena as much in perplexity as surprise.

Individuals with skin problems, arthritis, marital problems, and many other conditions were called for healing or for counseling. All seemed to be cured of illness or helped with difficulties in their lives.

After almost two hours, the voice of Nuna said, "That will be all for tonight. So may it be done." The medium's eyes closed and the body sagged back into the chair.

Silence. Sharleena's breathing slowed, became stronger. She sighed deeply, opened her eyes, and sat up. In her own strong voice, she said, "You may turn the lights back on now."

The lights came up, and a murmur rippled through the group. Laurelyn stood up, went to Sharleena, and took her hand.

"Friends," she said, "I know you will want to leave your donations in the bowl in the entryway, for Sharleena has done wonders here tonight. Thank you all for coming. Our next meeting will be here at this same time next week. Good night, all."

The two mediums turned to converse, and by twos and threes the group dispersed. Each dropped currency into the bowl as they went past on their way out. Gilbert dropped in a fifty-dollar bill, indicating to Amelia that it was for them, too. A few groups remained standing outside, deep in conversation. The air was sweet and fresh, a relief after the heavy incense inside.

Amelia turned to Gilbert, pulling her wrap around her shoulders. "I was really surprised. Tell me something. How did she know? About me, I mean?" she asked.

He glanced toward Laurelyn, standing at the door in conversation, and quickly back to Amelia. "My dear lady," he said, "how does anyone know anything?"

Amelia murmured, "Interesting," looking pensive.

Lacey asked her question. "Gil, what was all that with the headache and the egg?" They walked toward the Jaguar.

"Nuna, the spirit in Sharleena, extracted the evil spirit from the woman, transferred it to the egg, and threw it into the pan where it was destroyed when the egg broke. The rest was basically the same."

Lacey drew back and stared at Gilbert. He nodded. "And this was a séance?" she asked.

"Why, yes, of course. What did you think?"

Lacey shook her head. "I don't know exactly, but shouldn't we have sat around a table with a crystal ball and held hands or something?"

Gilbert chuckled, an almost musical sound. "That's done mostly in the movies. We've just been to a religious service—specifically a healing service—not a pretender's setup to get your money away from you."

"A religious service? You mean like a church?" asked Amelia.

"In a way. We were there to honor and serve our god."

Amelia stared at Gilbert. "You mean Laurelyn is the minister?" she asked.

"She is our priestess. Actually, I sometimes think she's more wood nymph than human," he mused. "My dear, perhaps you misunderstand. This was not a Christian service."

Lacey stiffened. "Then what was it?"

"Just what I said. A séance. A priestess goes into a trance, and a spirit enters her. The spirit is connected to our god, and through the spirit, our god comes into our presence. Understand?"

"No," said Lacey. "Who is your god?"

"Why, Belial, of course."

Cold shock shivered through Lacey like an icefall. "B." The cuff link. Belial. A name for Satan. She looked wide-eyed at Gilbert. "I don't understand."

"It's as simple as it sounds. We come here to worship our god Belial, and he gives us gifts of various sorts, only one of which is healing. There are many other gifts—wealth, power, all sorts of things."

"Belial is a name for Satan, isn't it?"

"Yes."

"But Satan is evil."

"Is he?"

Lacey looked long at him. "Yes." She stood still, puzzled. "But—I saw people being healed! People with big problems were helped. One man—his leg was crooked from being broken long ago, and right there, it straightened!"

"It's a matter of viewpoint. You have your God. Belial is our god. He does remarkable things for us. As I said, he gives us power—like the power Sharleena has to heal. Laurelyn is a prophet. I have a gift for finances. He gives many powers."

Lacey looked at her mother, back at Gilbert, and shook her head. "I don't understand any of this," she said. Her thoughts reeled. "I'd like to go home now."

Gilbert looked at Lacey with a wry little smile. "Anything you say," and opened the car door for her. She slipped into the small backseat.

The drive back to Playa Linda seemed to take forever. Her mother and Gilbert chatted all the way, but she scarcely heard them. Her thoughts were troubled. She felt soiled again. Now she knew why she had felt so violated. Gilbert worshiped the devil.

And yet, all this, the whole service, the healings, everything, all seemed so benign, so harmless, yet miraculous. So different from everything she had imagined went with devil worship. It was all so beautiful, so—gentle. Except for one thing. She remembered how hard Sharleena's eyes had looked and how stunned she'd been when they met hers. Somehow, that didn't fit the rest of the picture.

Pastor Drane had had no answers; yet, here it seemed as if everything—almost everything, anyway—was the way the Bible said it should be. But this god is Belial—Satan, the evil one! How can that be?

When they arrived at the Robinsons, Gilbert suggested to Amelia that they come to the meeting the following week.

"No," said Lacey on sudden impulse. She could not have said why, but all at once she feared going back. "I don't want to."

"Lacey! Why ever not?" asked Amelia. "Apologize to Gilbert. He's been a delightful host, and we've had such an interesting evening." She turned back to look at her daughter, waiting for the apology.

Lacey didn't know what to say. Her feelings were too mixed.

"Mother, please. I want to get out." She pushed at the back of the front seat to move her mother out of the car. Amelia looked at her crossly, but she stepped out, and Lacey followed quickly.

She took her mother's arm and dragged her toward the house. "Come on, Mother, we need to talk. Please! Now!"

Amelia stumbled a little as Lacey dragged her off. She smiled an apology over her shoulder at Gilbert as she was drawn toward the door. "I haven't a clue as to what's the matter with her," she said. "But thank you! We had a wonderful time!"

Gilbert grinned, saluted her, closed the car door, and drove away.

In the house, Amelia turned to Lacey. "I'm ashamed of you! That nice man took us to a very interesting meeting tonight, and we met some lovely people. Why did you refuse him so rudely?"

"Mother, I don't think you have any idea of what's happened. You know who Belial is." She stared, imploring, at Amelia.

"Oh, he must be some nature god or something. Everything in that house looked like something out of a great storybook forest. Maybe he's a god of some fairy-tale kind of magic?"

Lacey shook her head, scarcely believing her mother didn't know. "Belial is one of the names of Satan."

Amelia looked surprised. "But you know Satan is a figment of the imagination."

"Mother," said Lacey, struggling to be patient, "that was a service where they worship the devil!"

Amelia thought. "Well, suppose it was?" she said. "You know what Pastor Drane said. The idea of the devil is something made up by early Christian priests to frighten people into doing what they wanted them to do. There's no such thing as Satan."

Lacey shuddered. "I'm not so sure about that. Susan told me that just as there's God, there's Satan. He's a fallen angel. It's in the Bible. And Satan, or Belial, is the source of evil in the world." She looked confused. "But I can't understand the healings."

"Lacey, you're just being foolish. Sunday when we go to church, we'll talk to Pastor Drane and he'll explain it all to you."

Lacey sighed. Not Drane again. She was tired, and the only thing she wanted was to take a hot shower and go to bed. She didn't want to argue with her mother. But how could she convince her that evil really exists, and that the devil is responsible for evil? Or—is that true, after all?

"Mother, can we talk about this tomorrow? I'm tired."

Amelia put her arm around Lacey's shoulders. "I'm sorry,

Honey. Of course." She looked around at the tall grandfather clock. It was nearly midnight. "Your father is probably sound asleep already." She kissed Lacey on the cheek. "Good night, then. See you in the morning."

Lacey hugged her mother and turned to go upstairs. "But think about what I said, won't you, Mom?" she said, looking back.

Amelia pushed her fingers through her hair, massaging her scalp. "Yes, dear, I'll think about it. Get a good night's sleep. I'm going to have a cup of cocoa." She headed for the kitchen.

Lacey went on upstairs. She was disgusted with the whole thing. *Why did Gilbert have to come back? Why couldn't he have disappeared forever after the ninth grade?* Everything he did and said just mixed her up.

And Daddy? What's going on between him and Gilbert? Whatever it is, it seems to be bad news. She opened her bedroom door and, taking off her clothes, left a trail of them behind her, entered her bathroom, and turned on the shower.

THIRTEEN

Wednesday, October 23, 11:57 P.M.

The developer on his way home from the meeting was pleased with the possibilities opening before him. He decided to drive his BMW down the dirt road north and east of Playa Linda past the old tomato farm on which he had just arranged to build luxury homes. As he approached the ninety-acre parcel, he noticed a fiery glow on the horizon.

"What's going on now?" He wondered. He turned to drive across the field toward the glow, and the glow separated into bonfires. Pausing, he counted them. Nine, in a circle. And they seemed to be connected by people, hands clasped like folded paper cutouts, going round and round the circle. In the center he saw an upside-down cross. On *his* property! Suddenly angered, he tromped on the gas pedal. Dirt flew from his rear tires, and the car roared, bucking over the uneven ground toward the group.

Almost at once the people saw the headlights and heard the engine. They scattered, vanished, in all directions. One, a woman, ran to a hole near the foot of the cross, bent down and appeared to try to retrieve something. She looked up, and, seeing the car bearing down on her, gave up and fled. The developer stopped, undecided whether to run after the woman or examine the hole. The woman had disappeared into darkness, so he drove between two bonfires and stopped near what looked like a grave near a burning cross.

"What is that?" he muttered as he opened the car door. Someone was in the hole, crying! Shocked, he walked over and looked down at a struggling, terrified child. "Oh my!" he breathed, staring in loathing at the rest of what lay there. Shakily, he made the sign of the cross.

Thursday, October 24, 8:30 A.M.

The moment Susan walked into the staff meeting at the paper, everyone fell silent, all eyes on her. Suddenly apprehensive, she sat down.

"Hi, guys. What's up besides the surf, prices, and hemlines? Or what are you trying not to tell me?"

"Oh, nothing much," said Pete, handing her a paper, his face sour. "This was on the fax when we got here."

Susan read rapidly and turned pale. She looked up at her editor, her eyes bleak.

"It might be tied to your story," said Jackson. "Maybe by now they have an ID on the kid. Find out all you can. And get your wiz of a boyfriend on it. See what connections it might have with the rest. Anything else—? No, I guess that's enough for you for the morning." His expression as he looked at her was unreadable.

Susan took a deep breath, picked up the paper, and read it again as the others discussed their own assignments. She felt as if she were isolated. None of their voices reached her. All she was aware of was the facts on the paper.

The report told that Jack Alvarado, a local developer, had found a grave at the foot of a burning upside-down cross. Inside, he had found the mutilated body of a man and a little girl, who was alive. A number of dead kittens were also in the grave. Alvarado had called the police from his car.

The bonfires were still burning when the police arrived. Even these hardened officers were shocked by what they saw. One of them extricated the hysterical girl, screaming, pulling to get away. She appeared to be six or seven years old. The other officer ran to the patrol car, grabbed the radio, and called an ambulance.

When he returned he draped a spare jacket around the shrieking child. As soon as the ambulance arrived, medics took her to a hospital. The officers combed the area for any others who might not have escaped. Some distance off, they found a teenage girl lying in a drug-induced stupor. They put her in the backseat of the patrol car and took her away. She was later identified as Karen Garcia, one of three girls who had disappeared two weeks before. End of report.

Susan was aware that everyone had stopped talking. She looked around. "Is this all they have?" she asked, trying to speak normally.

Jackson nodded. "At least, nothing else has come in. Start at the police station."

Susan was anxious to get out of there. "Gotcha." Her throat closed. She folded the fax, put it in her purse, and left.

She got into her car and leaned her head on the steering wheel. "Lord," she whispered, "why?" She sat in silence for a few moments, wiped away the tears, took a deep breath, and started the engine. She felt as if the whole world had taken on a darkness she had never known before.

At the police station, she asked her usual questions: where had the girls been taken? City Hospital. What was the little girl's condition? Unknown. Had she been identified? No. What about the Garcia girl? What was her condition? No comment. Has the man's body been identified? Not yet.

When she called the hospital and identified herself, she was told only that the little girl was in good condition. Police had ordered no visitors. The Garcia girl was in critical but stable condition. No visitors. No further information.

For a moment, she hesitated. Distasteful as it might be, her job was to get all the news possible. Gritting her teeth, she looked up the Garcias' phone number, called it, and let it ring until she tired of listening to it.

At the hospital, she found reporters, cameramen, and photographers from several TV stations, the San Diego paper, and several smaller local papers. She shoved her way to the information desk, asked her questions, was refused permission to interview the parents, received the official handout. She listened without appearing to do so to the older, more experienced reporters, made notes, and looked around to see if she could find anyone with whom she was acquainted, someone who might talk to her. None came into sight.

She went outdoors and leaned against the sunny wall, eyes closed, trying to adjust to the loathing the story aroused in her. Matt. She had to see Matt. She went to the public phone just outside the door. Matt answered.

"Matt, I've got to talk to you. Can we meet at Connie's?"

"Uh—" In her mind's eye, Susan saw him looking around the store. "Sure. Are you at the paper?"

"At City Hospital. I can be at Connie's in twenty minutes."

When she arrived at the coffee shop, Connie indicated the corner booth in the back. Susan hurried to sit down. Two cups of coffee steamed on the table.

Matt sat facing the back wall. One look at her face told him she was more distressed than he had ever seen her. "What's happened?"

Her lips tight, she took the crumpled fax and the hospital hand-out from her purse and gave them to Matt.

"Oh, dear Lord Jesus, have mercy!" Matt breathed, as he read. He put the paper down, his face white. "How can sane people do this?"

"They're not sane. They can't be."

"Drink some coffee," said Matt. He began praying for her silently.

She picked up the cup and sipped. The scalding liquid was comforting. She sipped again. And again.

Her hand was steady as she put the cup down. A little of the color had come back into her face. "Andy needs to know about this, too. He might have some ideas. Seems like a sharp guy."

"Only a genius. But he'll do. I'll meet him for lunch and talk to him then." He shoved the papers away from him angrily. "This is getting to me. Things are going on we wouldn't imagine in our worst nightmares. It's got to stop!"

Susan drew a deep breath and let it out. "Sure. But how? What can we do? What is there we can take to the police? This fax *is* from the police. They say they don't have any evidence beyond the physical remains, and so far that's a zero. And nobody knows anything. Nobody will talk to me. They don't even know who the little girl is."

They sipped coffee in silence for a few minutes.

"What're you going to do now?" asked Matt.

Susan shrugged. "Go to the police anyway, I guess. See if they have an ID on the body and the girl yet. If so, I guess I'll try to talk to the parents." She shuddered. "I hate that."

Matt shook his head sympathetically. "Well, you wanted to be a reporter."

Susan looked up at him. "Thanks for reminding me." She inhaled. "Oh. And Mom called last night. Raymond was picked up by the police the other night. One of his friends has a D.C. game. They said they were going out to get more soft drinks, but the drinks turned out to be beer, and marijuana to boot. Police found them staggering around on Cutler Way."

"Oh, Lord," Matt sighed. "As if we didn't have enough on our minds. Well, if there's anything I can do, just let me know."

"Thanks. I will. And thanks for the coffee, and thanks," she said softly, getting up as he rose, "for being you." They embraced briefly, and Susan left, the papers back in her purse.

Matt went to the door and watched her start up her car. He stood there for awhile, making sure no one was following, his lips moving in silent prayer.

2:45 P.M.

Lacey had had a difficult morning, and the afternoon wasn't much better. She mislaid files, caught herself quoting the wrong precedents for the wrong cases, put books back on the wrong shelves in the wrong order.

Her mother had looked pale at breakfast and had eaten very little. Lacey thought about the séance where everyone was healed. Sharleena had said her mother's physician had done a wonderful job. But if that was so, why was her mother pale, and why did she not eat much? She usually had an excellent appetite.

And how could Belial heal? Susan had showed her many passages in the Bible saying it was Jesus who had the power to heal. Even if he didn't really believe the Bible, Pastor Drane prayed to Jesus to heal members of the congregation, and many of them did get better. But these healings were simple, like recovering from surgery, or cases of the flu, which got well anyway. No one was healed of heart disease or cancer, or even arthritis. She was confused. She needed to talk to Susan, but when she called the paper, they told her Susan was out on a story.

Frances came into her office. "Your father is not pleased," she said emphatically, putting down a file. She raised an eyebrow. "Your mind is definitely not on your work. What is it? That handsome young man you went to lunch with the other day?"

Lacey looked at the file, puzzled, and up at Frances. "Uh—oh, no. It's just something that happened last night. Something I don't understand." She forced a smile. "Thanks, Frances. I'll check it over and get it back to Dad." Frances nodded and left.

She looked over what she had done, and was astonished at the obvious errors she had made. *A walk-in off the street could have done better!* she thought, and dumped the file. With a sigh, she began again.

Finally the clock read four-thirty. None of her other files had come back. She wondered if she should try to call Susan again. But what could she tell her?

She picked up the phone anyway and punched the numbers.

"Register. Susan Walker."

"I'm so glad you're in," Lacey was surprised at how relieved she felt. "Susie, can we have dinner together tonight? Something happened last night—I don't know what to think. I need to talk to you."

Susan was silent a moment. "Okay. You want to come to my place, or a restaurant, or what?"

Lacey thought Susan's voice sounded a bit strained. "Your place. I'll bring Chinese. Is everything all right with you?"

"There was a hideous story today. It'll be in the paper tonight. But what's happening with you? You sound upset."

"I'll tell you all about it when I see you. Okay?"

"Sure. See you later, then. 'Bye."

Susan put down the phone. She had a feeling this would be a long evening, and she'd already had enough for one day. She sighed. The darkness had not gone away.

FOURTEEN

Thursday, October 24, 6:10 P.M.

Susan was home when Lacey arrived, carrying containers of China's finest fragrant cuisine. "And how was your day?" she asked, noticing Susan's grim expression.

"Rough. Here," she said, pushing aside a toaster, a blender, and several other appliances on the counter. "Set the food down here. We can help ourselves."

They filled their plates and sat down in the little dining area, which, like her living room, overlooked the beach. The sun had disappeared behind the sea. Gold-scarlet streaks danced on the waves toward the apartment building, reflecting the after-glow. The few mare's tails drifting high above the golden horizon glowed with inner fires beneath the deepening violet sky. They watched as the coral glow vanished.

"No wonder you love this place," said Lacey.

"You get pretty much the same at your house, only more so," said Susan, struggling with chopsticks. She managed to get a morsel of sweet-sour pork into her mouth. Frustrated, she put them down and picked up her fork.

"All right. Which of us goes first?" asked Lacey, demonstrating her skill with chopsticks.

"Me. I don't want to think about it while I'm eating." Susan put down her fork, got up and went to the table near her entry, picked up the paper, and handed it to Lacey.

"Oh, how awful—" Lacey put her chopsticks down. She read the rest. "Child unidentified—one of the missing girls found drugged on the scene—no other clues—" Her lipstick looked too bright against her pale face. "Who in the world would do a thing like that?"

Susan shrugged. "Evil people." She put the paper back, and sat down again. "Your turn." She was completely withdrawn.

Lacey twisted noodles on her plate, untwisted them, and looked up at Susan. Her own problem seemed like nothing beside what Susan was dealing with. "I hardly know where to begin."

"From the beginning. That's usually a pretty good place."

Lacey sighed. "You won't like it." Susan shrugged. Lacey told of having lunch with Gilbert, her mother at the hospital, and Gilbert coming home with her, putting her in bed, the cuff link.

She went on. "He came to dinner at our house last night, and I managed to get the cuff link back to him without my folks noticing." She described the carved onyx as well as she could, the "B" in the design, and his invitation to a séance.

"You should stay away from those, you know," said Susan, pouring tea. "They can be dangerous."

"But this was so different from anything I'd ever known. You know how in the movies and in books they sit around a table, hold hands, or use a Ouija board, and some strange woman goes into a trance and peculiar things happen? Well, it wasn't like that at all."

Susan looked up at her.

"No. It was at a beautiful house in the hills just this side of I-15 in the middle of an avocado grove, and the nicest lady lives there." She described the seating, the medium Sharleena, the healings, solving problems. "And she said Mom's physician had done a wonderful job," she added.

Susan tilted her head. "This was a séance?"

Lacey nodded. "That was my reaction, too. But when I asked Gilbert about it, he said it was a worship service." Lacey hesitated. "They worship—Belial."

Susan dropped her fork. "Are you sure he said Belial?"

Lacey nodded. "Belial. Mother thinks he's a nature god or something, because everything in the house looked as if it belonged deep in a fairy forest."

"Lacey, that's one of Satan's names! They were worshiping the devil! They're satanists!"

Lacey studied her plate. "That's what's got me so mixed up. Everything was so nice and gentle, and everyone was kind there, and people were healed, and it's not at all what I thought satanists would be like. I don't know what to believe." She looked at Susan, appeal in her eyes. "That's why I wanted to talk to you."

Susan stared, her mind racing through all that had happened since the cat-killings. Was this another piece in the puzzle?

"Lacey," she said, no longer withdrawn, "you've stumbled into something that might be mixed up with a story Matt and a friend of his and I are working on, something evil, maybe tied with the story tonight, and we don't know how much more. But I can't talk about it."

Lacey looked at Susan, confused. "I don't understand," she said. "What are you saying? What's going on that I don't know?"

Susan reached for Lacey's hand. "I can't tell you yet. Just trust me! But getting mixed up with satanism is really dangerous business. Leave the whole thing alone, and I'll explain when we know more. Promise?"

Lacey studied Susan and nodded. "Okay, if you say so," she said. She drew a deep breath. "But what about all the healings?"

"Oh, Lacey, there's so much you need to know about the Bible!" She paused to collect her thoughts. "Healings aren't always from Christ. Especially now. Satan is working overtime to deceive people."

Lacey looked at Susan dumbfounded. "Deceive? How?"

"How best to explain?" she muttered, mostly to herself.

"What's to explain?" Lacey asked, leaning back in her chair. "I saw it with my own eyes. And how can it be evil if it does so much good? Like healing?"

Susan leaned forward. "Look. Satan is jealous because Jesus is God, and he isn't. Jesus, being God, has powers that Satan does not. The best Satan can do is to arrange counterfeit miracles. Like this 'healing' service at the séance. But mostly it's just plain deception. And when Satan does heal—and apparently he can, to some extent—there's a monstrous price to pay—"

"Wait." Lacey interrupted her. "You said 'deception.' You mean if Satan healed my mother, she wouldn't really be healed?"

Susan looked sympathetic. "It isn't only that, Lacey. If the healing is real, that's wonderful. But then, the danger is that the person healed is grateful, and often, that person will think that whoever did it has to be God. If your mother was truly healed, might she begin to think that Brother Justin's god was really God?"

Lacey stared at her wide-eyed.

"If she did, she would be turning away from Jesus, from God, and would no longer be His child, but a child of the devil." She stared at Lacey. "Children of the devil share his fate. And he's going to hell."

Lacey looked at Susan, alarmed. Then she brushed it off with a half-laugh. "Oh, don't be silly. There's no such thing as a devil. Or hell. They're just fairy tales." She tried another laugh, but it didn't come off too well. "Aren't they?"

Susan shook her head. "No, not fairy tales. Satan and his demons are real, and so is hell. I thought you understood that."

Lacey tackled her noodles again half-heartedly and looked back at Susan. "I know you told me, but what I saw last night seemed so genuinely good, and so helpful—well, how can it be bad? I just don't understand. I thought everything good was from Jesus, and only bad things were from the devil. So wouldn't that make what happened last night be from Jesus, since they were good?"

Susan dug in with her fork, chewed, and swallowed. "Not necessarily. Remember the proverb? The one that says 'There is a way which seems right to a man, but its end is the way of death'?"

Lacey stared at Susan.

"For instance," Susan continued, "this awful story that came out today. It probably started with something that in some way *seemed* to be good. The way it ended, though, shows it's satanic, and everyone gets hurt."

Lacey ate silently for awhile. "But the two things are so different. No one was helped in that awful scene last night. It was pure horror."

"That's just it," Susan said mildly. "People get sucked in with some fantastic gimmick, maybe like the healings, and when they're in so deep they can't get out, they discover it was only a shiny, tinsel-topped counterfeit of the real thing. Then they have hell to pay, literally."

Lacey looked at Susan, her brow puckered in thought. "Then if what you say is true, Mom is in real trouble, right?"

"Not necessarily, but she could be. You could talk to her and save her from all sorts of trouble. I'll show you some stuff in the Bible to read with her."

They finished dinner in deep thought, heavy silence. When they were done, they packed what was left into containers and put them into the refrigerator.

Settled comfortably in the living room, Susan reached for her Bible and turned to the pages near the back of the volume. "Look," she said, pointing. "Right here in Second Thessalonians it says this 'man of sin'—and that can mean anyone who follows Satan instead of Christ—this man will come 'according to the working of Satan, with all power, signs, and lying wonders.' Like those healings. He will deceive those who have said 'no' to the truth of the gospel. And

Lacey, I believe those healings at the séance were done by a demon dominated by Satan."

The passage troubled Lacey, but how could she deny what she had seen? She squirmed. "But if real healing is from Jesus, I still don't see how the devil can heal—or even seem to."

"It's because Satan has a great deal of power. Not nearly as much as God does, but a lot. And so do his demons. Remember? Before they sinned by turning against God, they were angels, and angels are tremendously powerful. It took only two to destroy the cities of Sodom and Gomorrah."

Lacey's head swam. She was trying to assimilate what Susan was saying, putting it together with what she had seen at the séance, but it wasn't working. "I'm confused. Could we talk about it some other time?"

Susan was apologetic. "I'm sorry—I guess I poured it on pretty heavy," she said. "Sure. Anytime you're ready. But stay away from séances and even from Gilbert. From what you've told me, I don't trust him."

Lacey's eyes opened wide. "That's really funny. I don't, either!"

They both laughed, and some of the tension vanished. Lacey yawned and looked at her watch.

"Omigosh. It's late. Gotta get to bed. There will be a lot to do at the office tomorrow." She stood up, stretched, and picked up her purse. "Thanks for trying to explain things to me. We'll talk some more about this, okay? I mean, really talk? I honestly want to know." She looked wistfully at Susan.

"Of course. Whenever." She hugged her friend. "Call me when you're free. Anytime you want."

Lacey smiled. "Okay. Will do."

Susan closed the door. *When will this all be over?* she wondered, as she got ready for bed. Dismembered pets, mutilated bodies, disappearing girls, satanists in Playa Linda, psychic surgery, someone following her, a little girl in a satanic ritual, Lacey mixed up in a séance, her kid brother Raymond getting arrested—where does it end?

Friday, October 25, 2:50 A.M.

The telephone shrilled, startling Susan out of a deep sleep. She picked it up, cleared her throat, and half asleep, mumbled, "Hullo—"

The strange voice was muffled, husky. "Susan Walker?"

"Yes—"

"You wanna live, don't ask no more questions. Don't write no more articles. Leave it alone." The caller hung up.

Susan sat up, staring wide-eyed. "Hello—hello—" Only the dial tone answered. She put down the phone, pulling her hand away as if it had been burned. She looked at the clock. Nearly three. Her heart thudded, her hands shook. Who? Why? She looked around in the darkness of her bedroom, half afraid she'd find someone there. She turned on the light. No one in sight.

Terrified, she thought about calling Matt, her father, Jackson, the police. What could the police do? She couldn't even give them a name. The police can't act on a threat; they have to wait until someone does something illegal. Like murder. She shuddered.

It had to be because of that grisly story that had just come out in the paper. Otherwise, why call now?

Susan was more frightened than she had ever been before. Finally, she picked up the phone and called Matt.

His phone rang and rang, and finally, a sleepy "Yeah?"

That did it. Her voice caught. "Matt? Is that really you?"

She heard the sound of bedclothes rustling. "Susan? Are you all right?" She clutched her phone as if it were a lifeline and told him about the phone call, the muffled, disguised voice, the threat. "What should I do?" she begged, holding back tears.

Silence for a moment. "Just stay right where you are," said Matt. "Don't even get out of bed. I'm coming right over."

Susan sighed. "Thanks, Matt."

"Just be sure it's me. Don't let anyone else in."

Susan put the phone back in the cradle and lay down, pulling the covers up to her chin, and prayed. She looked at the clock. It was 2:57. Car headlights splashed in her window, and she jumped. She heard the vehicle go on down the street, and sighed in relief, squeezed her eyes shut, and prayed some more. She looked at the clock again. 2:59. Her heart beat a tattoo in her chest; breathing was difficult. *Where was Matt?* She looked at the clock again. 3:03. Taking a deep breath, she closed her eyes, determined to relax and be patient, and prayed. Tension mounted. She lay still as long as she could. A beam creaked, she jumped. Her eyes flew open and she looked at the clock. 3:08. She burrowed into the covers and squeezed her eyes shut.

Suddenly, a knock at the door! Startled, she swallowed a scream. The clock said 3:15. *Oh,* she thought, *it's got to be Matt.* She got up, hastily wrapped a robe around her, looked through the peephole, unchained, unbolted, unlocked, opened the door, and fell into his arms. He closed the door behind him and led her to the sofa, where she wept into his shoulder.

He kissed her forehead, her hair, patted her back. "It's all right now. There was no one outside. It's okay."

Susan sat up straight, took a tissue from a pocket and blew her nose. "I'm sorry. I guess I shouldn't have called you, but I was so scared. I don't get many calls in the middle of the night."

"Especially from people who threaten to kill you." Matt was not amused. "Sweetheart, it isn't safe for you to stay here. I'll take you to my place. I can look after you there."

Susan looked at him. "Thanks, but I don't think it's necessary." She sighed and snuggled. "I think I just needed to see you, to have you hold me." She sat up and wiped her nose. "Whoever called just wanted me off the story. But that's all. He won't try anything else tonight. Remember, all he said was not to ask any more questions, not to write anything more."

Matt looked hard at her. "But you're not going to quit on the story, are you." It was more a statement than a question.

She sat still for a moment, then shook her head. "No, I'm not. This has to stop." Her jaw was set, her eyes held a blue fire he had seldom seen.

"All right," he conceded. "But suppose I sleep on the couch for the rest of the night, then?" He yawned. "Do I really have to drive all the way across town to my own place?"

Susan almost smiled. "No. I'll get you a pillow and some covers." She went to a closet and came back with bedding. "If you hadn't offered to stay, I'd have had to ask you," she confessed, spreading half the sheet over the sofa, folding it over to form a top sheet under the blanket. She patted the pillow into place.

Matt looked at her, at the sofa, sighed, and grinned. "Okay. Well, get back to your bed, woman, or you'll be sorry."

Susan chuckled, kissed him lightly, and disappeared into her own room. Closing the door behind her, she looked around the bedroom. The terror brought by the phone call seemed to linger in the atmosphere, and she stiffened her back. *Come on, Susan,* she told herself, *shape up! That phone won't hurt you, Matt's in the other room, and everything's all right for the moment.* Snuggling back into bed, she was fully aware the situation was genuinely serious. *These people aren't just kidding around,* she mused. *There's something really scary going on.* Even under the down comforter, she felt cold.

She couldn't help thinking longingly of Matt, alone on the couch in the next room. It was awhile before she was asleep again.

FIFTEEN

Friday, October 25, 9:45 A.M.

Andy was taking a long chance. The clues from his previous exploration might have absolutely nothing to do with anything, but he keyed the code anyway. When the information came up on the screen, he involuntarily rolled the chair back, staring at the screen, unbelieving. Without really thinking what he was doing, he punched "print screen."

Still goggle-eyed, he tore off the two-page printout, abandoned the file, and called up one of his friend Roger's own files. Sprinting out of the house, he thanked Roger for allowing him to use his equipment and headed for the Warehouse.

Ricky was alone in the store, setting up newly arrived programs on the display shelves. "Where's Matt?" he asked without preliminaries.

"Went to the phone company about a phone call. Why?"

Matt waved the printout. "Important information. What's Susan's phone number? Oh, yeah, the paper. I'll get it."

He dialed the number, and Alison answered. "No, she just went out on an errand. Would you like to leave a message?"

Andy thought fast. "No. I'll probably see her later."

He sped to the phone company, was told that Matt had been there but had left about fifteen minutes before. No, he didn't say where he was going, nor did the receptionist know what he had been looking for.

Andy was stymied. He went to one of the public phones in the lobby and dialed the Warehouse. No, Matt wasn't back yet.

He climbed into his 4-wheel drive and just sat. *Where to go now? Back to the Warehouse to wait,* he decided. Matt would come back sooner or later, but the sooner the better.

10:20 A.M.

Susan picked up her blue pencil and took the top item from her IN basket. Two gangs on the south side of town had declared war on each other. Several of the youths had guns, and two had been critically injured. Asked what started the fight, one of the shooting victims shook his head, a sullen expression on his face. "Dunno. They just started shooting at us. We had to defend ourselves."

The phone call during the night still vivid in her mind, Susan was shaken. She edited, entered the story into the computer, shook her head, thinking such things had never happened before in Playa Linda as far back as she could remember, and sent it to makeup. Why were all these things happening now?

That done, she went back to the police station, but learned nothing new. She went to the hospital and rode the elevator to the fourth floor, hoping that a friend of hers, April, was on duty. She spotted April in the corridor near the nurses' station and called to her.

April turned, startled. "Oh! Susan. Hi," she said, looking for escape.

"I know. You're busy. I won't keep you. I'm on a story. Was a little girl brought in shortly after midnight?"

April looked stern. "You know I can't talk about our patients."

"So she's still here!"

"Oh, Susan, you'll get me into trouble!" April started to walk away but Susan caught her arm again. "I can't! I've got to see to my patients!"

"Just one or two questions, all right?"

Finally, April gave in. "Okay," she said. She looked around to see they were alone. "I brought her breakfast and checked her vital signs. She's fine."

Susan glanced around, noticed they were reasonably isolated near the elevators. "April, would you help me sneak into her room? I need to talk to her."

"They'd fire me!" The nurse was shocked. "I can't let you do that. I just absolutely can't. No visitors. None. Not yet."

"Well, then, can you at least tell me her name? Or anything about what she might have said? Please?"

April looked down the corridor toward the nurses' station. One of the nurses was checking charts. No one else was in sight for the moment. She sighed, and said quietly, "The name on her chart is Lily Mae Johnson." She looked around again but still, no one was near. "It's spooky." She drew Susan over to the drinking fountain alcove where they huddled. "I shouldn't be telling you this, but it's so weird, I'm dying to tell someone. But this is not for the paper! Keep it to yourself, okay?"

Susan crossed her heart, held up her hand and said, "My word is my bond. But if it leads to other information—well, I won't mention your name. You're out of it."

April looked dubious, but anxious to talk, nodded. She looked around again and took a breath. "Mrs. Stivik—you know, my supervisor—said when they brought her in, Lily Mae was hysterical, was saying she was supposed to—get this—'be borned from him,' and that if she didn't do what they said, they'd really hurt her." April paused, puzzled. "What did she mean, 'be born from him'? What 'him'? What's it all about?"

Susan stared. "Didn't they tell you where they found her?"

April shook her head. "Just said she was suffering from exposure, possible abuse, and to keep her as quiet as possible. No visitors."

"Didn't you see the *Register* yesterday?"

April's eyes widened. "You mean—that's the girl—" she heard heels clicking. "Sh-h-h." She bent to drink from the fountain. Susan pretended to be waiting for her turn.

The heels clicked without pause to the elevator, disappeared as the doors swished open. April wiped her lips and looked around again. The corridor was clear for several yards. Eyes wide, she finished her question. "She's THAT girl?"

Susan nodded. "Uh-huh. Thanks, April. Listen, if you hear anything else, let me know, will you?"

April vacillated, finally gave in with a small sigh. "Yeah, if possible. I can't promise, though. They're watching her real close."

Susan squeezed April's arm. "Thanks. That's all I'm asking. But don't get into any trouble." April shook her head, and Susan headed for the elevator.

She drove to the Garcia home and found the family preparing to go back to the hospital to be with Karen. The reluctant parents agreed to talk to her briefly.

"No, I really don't know what she's mixed up in," said Mr. Garcia, a man of medium height, dark hair and eyes.

"She was still pretty much out of it last night," said Mrs. Garcia, a small, slender woman with brown hair and gray eyes. "She kept crying, talking about fire, and devils, and punishment. She got real scared when she said 'they,' whoever they are, threatened her with 'the revenge of the black sword.' Weird. You know they killed a man and took that little girl and—well, you know—" She turned her head.

Susan waited a moment for Mrs. Garcia to recover. "Did the doctor say how soon she'd be able to leave the hospital?"

"Maybe tomorrow," said Mr. Garcia. "However long it takes to get the drugs out of her system. They found a mix of blood, urine, heroin, coke, and something else they haven't identified yet in her stomach and bloodstream."

Mrs. Garcia looked at her watch and picked up her purse. "We need to go now. You'll have to excuse us." She opened the door, Susan thanked them and left. She got into her car and sat at the wheel in shock. *What kind of people would do all that? I guess the same kind who would call me in the middle of the night.*

But it seems to be part of the whole thing, she thought, driving toward the paper. *Drugs leading to satanism. I wonder if Matt and Andy have found out anything else?* She decided to go to the Warehouse.

When she got there, she saw a 4x4 at the curb. *Could it be Andy's?* She parked behind it and just as she got out of her Escort, Matt drove past her to park in the rear.

Andy put down the program he was looking at and said "Hi" as she entered the store. Matt waved hello as he came in from the back and told Ricky to take care of everything for awhile, that he could go to lunch when they came back. Ricky nodded and went back to checking stock.

"Where do you want to go for coffee or lunch or whatever, where we can talk in private?" Matt asked as they walked outside.

"Connie's?" Andy suggested.

Matt shook his head. "I'd hate to get her mixed up in this. If we're there too often, they might tie her to us."

Silence. "There's a little Mexican restaurant on Market Street," said Susan. "El Rancho—know the place? The food is good and there's an inner patio that's usually pretty private. Lacey and I have been there."

They went around back to Matt's Chevy and at El Rancho asked to have their lunch on the patio. The hostess picked up three menus and led them through the late lunch crowd to a table under the arched balcony in the quiet, nearly deserted patio. Wordlessly they studied the menus for a few minutes. Andy put his down and handed a sheet of computer paper to Matt. He took it, looking questions at Andy. "Just read. And there's another sheet out in my

Jeep I didn't bring in. Just a list of names. Didn't think it was quite as important. The ones on this are obviously the leaders."

Matt took the paper and started reading. "Wow. This cuts deep," he said in a few moments. "Involves a lot of big names." He finished reading it and handed it to Susan. She read, astonishment growing with every line.

"So," said Matt. "The Chairman has no name. But the district attorney is one of the big honchos, which explains why there have been no arrests. And apparently one of the prosecuting attorneys is in his pocket. I recognize some of the other names. Leaders in computers, industry, businesses from all over the state." He looked at Andy. "But where do the Robinsons and such come in? From what we've learned, they must be in on it, too."

Andy shrugged. "Just a guess. They're financiers. Maybe they don't know what's really going on. I'd guess they're fed some kind of bull about investments which they manipulate, presumably to make everyone rich—or in most cases, richer."

"I still don't understand," said Susan. "Where does the Viking Castle come into it? Surely not all that money is going into purchase and renovation."

"Nope. Don't imagine it is," said Andy. "They're into bazillions from the looks of this. The Castle is probably just one of their meeting places or something. Maybe a hideaway kind of headquarters."

"And they're all satanists?"

Andy shrugged. "I found the list under one of the codes for 'Belial.' What else could they be?"

Just then the same red-skirted waitress who had served Susan and Lacey arrived with chips and salsa. "Are you ready to order?" she asked, and when they nodded, she wrote down their choices. "Tostada for the lady, taco plate, combination burrito, and coffee all around, right?" She smiled her dazzling smile and swished away, her red skirt flouncing.

The three looked at each other. "What about you, Matt?" asked Andy. "Anything?"

Matt shook his head. "Tried to find out who called Susan during the night, but all they could tell me was that it was a call from a pay phone in San Diego." Andy looked surprised, and Susan raised her eyebrows. "San Diego?" she asked, puzzled.

"What call?" asked Andy.

Matt told him, and Andy stared at Susan. "My gosh."

"What about you, Sue?" asked Matt.

"I tried to follow up on that story in yesterday's paper—"

"Yeah. We know which one," said Matt.

"Well, I talked to April at the hospital, and she's going to try to get information if she can do it without being fired. By the way, the little girl's name is Lily Mae Johnson. Anyway—this is crazy—but it seems that—" she shook her head. Taking a deep breath, she plunged on. "That business of being in the body—you know— April talked to one of the nurses who took care of her when they brought her in, and it seems that from what she said, the girl was supposed to be born of that man."

Matt and Andy exchanged glances. "Huh? Born of—" Andy was totally confused.

Red Skirt showed up with a heavy tray, set it on the folding stand, distributed the plates, glasses of ice water, and coffee. She beamed, said "Enjoy your lunch," and left.

Susan shook her head and laid her napkin in her lap. "I don't know for sure." She stared at her plate. "I've read about generational witchcraft—" She looked up. "You know, the whole family for generations back are witches." She stopped and toyed with her fork. "Maybe that's how they were initiating Lily Mae into the coven. Sort of a counterfeit of rebirth in Christ?"

Andy muttered something under his breath. Matt looked grim.

After a moment Susan went on. "I went to the Garcias' home after I left the hospital. They couldn't tell me very much, except that Karen was still woozy last night, crying a lot. Said she babbled about a lot of fire, and devils, and that they killed a man and put Lily Mae—" she looked away. "It's funny. Mrs. Garcia said Karen talked about a black sword. Said she was really scared of it."

"A black sword? Strange—swords are usually kept bright and shining." Matt sat thinking. He shook his head. "Well, whatever. Another piece of the puzzle. Did they say when Karen would be out of the hospital?"

"Maybe tomorrow. Depends."

"You're going to do a story, aren't you?"

Susan picked at her tostada and nodded. "A short one. Just bare outlines. Nothing specific." She looked up at him. "Don't have enough hard facts to back up anything specific."

"Just as well," Matt said. "That phone call scared me, too."

Susan chuckled without mirth. "Did you tell Andy about Lacey and Brother Justin?" she asked Matt. He nodded.

"What about the séance? Does he know?"

"What séance?" asked Andy and Matt in unison.

"Oh, I guess I haven't told either of you." Susan repeated what Lacey had told her the evening before. "And with the healings and all, now she's thoroughly confused. She doesn't know which way is up. Literally."

Matt looked at Andy. "A satanist coven?"

Andy shrugged. "Dunno."

Susan went on. "And she doesn't even know what to think about Gilbert Crozier, since—"

"Wait a minute," said Andy, interrupting. "Did you say Gilbert Crozier?"

"Yes. Why?"

"There's a Gilbert Crozier on the list. The secondary one."

Susan put her fork down. She looked from Andy to Matt and back again. "Who else?"

Andy shook his head. "Your guess is as good as mine."

They toyed with their lunches in silence, eating little.

"The only thing we can do," said Matt, sitting back, "is to keep on digging. We don't have enough yet to get it together."

Susan all but slammed her fork down. "How much are we going to need?" she demanded. "And how are we going to get it?" Her eyes were glinting with anger. "How many other little girls are going to be abused like that?"

Matt shook his head. Andy studied his plate. "All we can do," he said, his voice quiet, "is like Matt said, keep on digging." He looked at Susan. "We've just barely started."

Susan looked at Andy. "You're right. I'm sorry. It's just that it's getting to me." She looked at Andy and Matt. "I hate all this. I think I said that before." She glanced at her watch. "Hey—let's finish up. I've got to get back to work." She forked up another bit of tostada.

2:30 P.M.

Margaret called Lacey at her office. "Miss Lacey," she said, her voice sounding tight. "I don't know what to do. Your mother is awful faint, having awful pains. What should I do?"

Lacey's blood suddenly turned cold. "Have you called Dr. Damron?"

"Yes'm, I did. But the girl who answered said he can't come 'cause he's in surgery, just keep her warm and quiet." She sounded as if she were about to cry.

"All right, Margaret. Thanks for letting me know. I'll talk to Dad, and we'll work it out from here. Just hang on. We'll take care of it." She put the phone down and headed for her father's office.

Frances grabbed her arm as Lacey passed her desk. "You can't go in right now," she said. "Your father is in an important conference, and he isn't even taking phone calls."

Lacey pulled her arm away. "Mom's sick." She strode to the door, opened it, and stood stock still, staring. Her father gasped at her entrance. Four other faces turned to stare at her. Gilbert, Stuart, whom she had met briefly at the séance, and two other men, strangers, gaped at her, motionless.

Jerrod stood up, excused himself, strode to Lacey, took her arm in a tight grip and closed his office door behind them. "I've told you never, ever, to interrupt me in conference!" he hissed at her. He was furious.

Lacey tugged unsuccessfully to get her arm free. "Mom's sick!" she said. "Margaret called. She's faint and having a lot of pain."

Her father's expression changed, and he dropped her arm. He stared at her for a moment, said, "Wait here," and turned back into the office. Lacey heard a faint gabble of voices. Very soon they all came out, Jerrod last.

"Frances," he said, "cancel all the rest of my appointments for the day. Tell Dave he's in charge. Keep the lid on." Frances nodded. He picked up the phone and dialed, ordered an ambulance to be sent immediately to his address, took Lacey's arm, led her to the elevator, and pushed the "down" button.

In short order, they entered the lobby at Richmond General just as they heard the siren of the ambulance coming in the emergency entrance. The lady at the desk picked up the ringing phone, listened a moment, nodded, put it down.

"Mr. Robinson?" she asked, looking at him.

Jerrod nodded.

"Mrs. Robinson is just being brought in," she said. "If you'll be seated, I'll let you know when you can see her."

They sat down in the deeply upholstered blue chairs facing each other in rows along the glass wall overlooking the grounds toward the boulevard. Jerrod picked up a magazine and looked unseeing at one page after another. Lacey fidgeted, watching the clock, which seemed to stand still.

After a blank eternity, Dr. Damron came walking toward them. Jerrod and Lacey hurried to meet him. He looked tired.

"I'm afraid it's serious," he said. "She's on her way to surgery. I hope it's in time. She should have let me set it up long ago."

Lacey and her father looked at each other. This was impossible.

She had been healed! There was nothing the matter with her, nothing serious. There couldn't be!

Lacey's legs gave out, and she plopped down on the nearest chair. The doctor turned to her father.

"Jerrod, we won't know anything for awhile. You can go home if you like. I'll call you the minute we're through in surgery." He put his hand on Jerrod's shoulder for a moment. "Or, if you want, you may wait. It's not as comfortable, but do as you like." He turned, disappeared into an elevator.

Lacey looked at her father. "I want to wait here."

Jerrod stared vacantly out the window. "I do, too." He turned to the woman at the information desk. "Where may we wait for the doctor? He'll be in surgery."

The woman gave them directions. They got off the elevator at the fifth floor. Hospital smells assaulted them. Anxious people sat on couches and chairs along the walls, walked the corridors, or gathered in little knots; nurses, doctors, and aides strolled by; an orderly pushed a cart of bundles of laundry past them; a thin woman in high heels and a business suit carried a clipboard, clacking swiftly toward the nurses' station.

Jerrod turned to a gray-haired woman in a pink uniform who was sitting behind the desk. "Where's the best place to wait? Mrs. Amelia Robinson, Dr. Damron—"

The Pink Lady looked at her notebook, up and down the columns. "Oh, here she is." She pointed down the near corridor. "Right along there, wherever." She pointed in the other direction. "And there's a little waiting room. I think it's full now, but there's coffee there, if you like."

Lacey found an unoccupied molded plastic chair and sat down. Her face epitomized the word "bleak." "Susan was right—she was right—" she muttered. Jerrod went to the crowded waiting room, found two clean styrofoam cups, and filled them with coffee. The chair next to Lacey became vacant just as Jerrod started back. Lacey put her purse in it to save it for her father.

An hour went by. And another. They said things to each other, but they were just words. The coffee was long gone, and Jerrod went to get more. They sipped, sat, waited. People continued to drift by, their voices blending into the cacophony of hospital sounds. A group of nurses pushed an unconscious patient on a gurney past them. A strong smell of anesthetic surrounded them. Jerrod craned his neck to see who it was—an old man, a tube up his nose.

A nervous looking woman came in holding a little girl about three by the hand. The shy girl looked at Lacey and put her thumb in her mouth. The Pink Lady told the mother that her doctor would be coming out soon to let her know.

Dr. Damron, wearing rumpled surgical greens, appeared, his face haggard. Jerrod and Lacey stood. The doctor shook his head.

Lacey turned pale. "What happened? How is she?"

Dr. Damron's weary gaze turned to her. "We lost her," he said. Jerrod, stunned, put his arms around Lacey. She stared at the doctor.

"I don't believe it," she said, a note of hysteria in her voice. "She can't be—!"

Dr. Damron looked from Jerrod to her. "The tumor was very large. What we didn't know before was that it involved a blood vessel. She bled heavily, went into shock. We did all we could, everything possible." He was desolate.

Lacey stared blankly. A searing rage started inside her, grew, welled up, and she lunged, hands clawlike, toward Dr. Damron, shrieking "*no!*"

Jerrod tightened his arms around her, holding her until she stopped struggling and dissolved in tears on his shoulder. He stared over her head at the doctor, a world of grief in his eyes. Dr. Damron put his hand on Jerrod's shoulder. "I can't tell you how sorry I am." Jerrod nodded, tears beginning to spill.

The Pink Lady looked up at them, shaking her head in sympathy. A young man came hesitantly to her desk, asked about a Mrs. Delfina Orozco. The Pink Lady turned toward him, looked up the name, nodded, and pointed toward the row of molded plastic chairs along the wall.

SIXTEEN

Saturday, October 26, 8:45 A.M.

Lacey, dazed, stared straight ahead, her eyes unfocused. She was numb. She couldn't be dead. Not her mother.

Jerrod sat across the table from her, moving his scrambled egg around his plate, his face blank. The sun shone cold into the funereal atmosphere in the breakfast room.

Margaret, her eyes red, came in from the kitchen. She looked from one to the other. "Aw, come on, now, you'll both wind up sick. You gotta eat something." She looked, pleading, from one to the other.

Lacey pushed her plate away, shaking her head. She got up and went out to the south patio. Dimly she heard her father's voice, and Margaret's. She stood by a scarlet bougainvillea, absently pulling bracts apart. A breeze stirred chrysanthemums and petunias in their beds; bees buzzed for nectar and pollen. A hummingbird investigated the fuschias and hovered, sipping. None of it touched Lacey. She was wrapped in a dark cocoon.

Her father came to stand by her side, put his arm around her shoulders. She stood stiffly, bereft of feeling. Even her father's need for warmth and love did not penetrate the paralysis of shock into which she had fallen. Presently, he went away. After awhile she went into the living room. Funny, how her mother's fragrance persisted. She touched the drapes. Her mother had chosen the fabric herself, supervised their hanging and draping. The Louis XIV chair she loved—

The agony of the way she had behaved toward her mother after the séance. Why hadn't she kept her mother from going to Brother Justin in the first place? Every cross word she had ever spoken to her mother shouted back at her, tore at her.

After awhile, Lacey turned and went upstairs. She looked toward her parents' room. She endured the stab of pain and went into her own room. Margaret had already made up her bed. She lay down on it and stared dry-eyed through numbed anguish at the ceiling.

10:20 A.M.

Downstairs, flowers were coming in. Huge baskets and arrangements, potted cyclamen and azaleas, bouquets of roses. Meaningless voices drifted up to Lacey.

After a timeless time, Margaret came to her door and knocked. "Miss Lacey," she said, opening the door, "Susan is here. Will you see her?"

Lacey turned and saw Susan, somber, standing behind Margaret. She nodded and sat up. Susan came in and sat beside her. Margaret closed the door and left.

Susan put an arm gently around Lacey. Suddenly, the protective wall of shock broke and all the searing agony of loss engulfed her. "Oh, Susan!" she wailed. Her despair poured out in wrenching sobs. Susan turned so she could hold Lacey in her arms and let her weep on her shoulder.

"I'm so sorry, so terribly sorry," Susan murmured, stroking her friend's hair. Lacey continued to weep.

Finally, Lacey sat back and reached for a tissue. Her teary eyes red and swollen, she blew her nose, took a deep, shuddering breath. She had to say something. "Thank you." She took another tissue and wiped her eyes.

They looked at each other in silence. "I'm not going to say I know how you feel," Susan said finally, "but I feel awful. I can't tell you how sorry I am."

Lacey nodded. She blew her nose again.

Susan took her hand. "Margaret made some tea. Why don't we go downstairs and have some?"

Why not? Why anything? "All right," Lacey said. She stood up and went obediently to the door, Susan following.

1:45 P.M.

When Susan left the Robinson home, she went to the Warehouse to see Matt. Leaving Ricky in charge, they drove to the beach and strolled barefoot just away from the breakers, eating hamburgers. Matt finished and put his wrapper into a trash container.

"Just what happened?" he asked after they had gone on a short distance. "I mean with Mrs. Robinson?"

Susan swallowed her last bite and crumpled up the wrapper. "It probably would have been all right—" she threw the paper into another trash container, "except they couldn't stop the bleeding." She stared unseeing at the container. "The tumor was so big—and Mrs. Robinson was never very strong, you know."

Matt took her into his arms. They stood there, the wind tossing their hair, waves breaking and hissing down the sands, cool and slithery around their toes. They were oblivious to everything—the people sunning, playing ball, tossing frisbees—voices muffled by their pain. The strident calls of swooping gulls went unheard. Presently Susan pulled away, wiped her eyes, and they continued to plod along the windswept beach.

2:35 P.M.

Raymond had escaped. Sure, he was grounded, but he just had to see Alan. His mom and dad wouldn't even let him use the phone. What was he to do, anyway? He took back-alley shortcuts and made it to the Baxter house in record time. Alan was nowhere in sight, and he didn't dare go up to the door. Maybe Alan was in his room, grounded, too.

Raymond found some pebbles, went around to the back, and hiding behind some bushes, threw one at Alan's bedroom window. Nothing. He tried again. This time Alan raised the sash.

"Hey, quiet!" he hissed. "I'm grounded!"

"So'm I," Raymond said in a stage whisper. "But I sneaked out."

Alan looked around. "I can't get out. They're all downstairs."

"Tie your bedsheets together. That's what I did."

Alan looked at Raymond. "Okay." He disappeared. In awhile, the corner of a sheet snaked out of the window, and Raymond could see Alan feeding it out carefully. It didn't reach all the way down to the ground, but it came close enough that Alan could drop off without damage.

"Did you tie it tight?"

Alan nodded, and straddled the window sill. He lowered himself carefully, hand over hand to the end of the sheets, and dropped. Picking himself up, he brushed off the dirt as he hurried to join Raymond behind the bushes.

"Now what?" he asked.

"Let's go to Chuck's. His folks don't care what he does."

"Okay." The two boys looked all around to see that they hadn't been discovered and fled down the alley and across town to where Chuck lived. They stepped up on the sagging, paint-peeling porch and knocked on the door. His mother, a thin, sallow woman in a faded T-shirt and jeans, opened the door and called out, "Chuck, it's for you." She held the door open for them.

The living room was barely furnished. A brown Naugahyde-covered couch, the principal item of furniture, was accompanied by several unmatched garage-sale chairs. Opposite the couch was a television perched hazardously on a rickety stand.

A thin, brown-haired boy about fifteen came from the kitchen, eating a peanut-butter-and-jelly sandwich. "Hi," he said. "I figured you guys were outta circulation."

Alan nodded. "We escaped." All three sat on the couch and looked indifferently at the cartoon antics on the TV screen.

"What about Eddie and Ralph?" asked Raymond.

Chuck shrugged. "Ain't heard." He swallowed the last of the sandwich and licked jelly off his fingers.

"Wanna go see them? Ralph's got D.C., too," said Alan.

"Okay," said Chuck, getting up. "I'll go talk to my mom."

They heard his voice pleading, his mother backing down. He came back, grinning. "It's okay. I can go."

The boys let themselves out the front door and headed back toward the center of town until they came to a large old apartment house. Chuck pressed the button next to the name Cappello. The speaker buzzed, and they entered.

The dim hallway smelled old and musty, with mixed odors of dust, foods, and human occupation. Steep stairs were on the left. Just as they started climbing, a dark head showed over the railing on the third floor. "Hey, guys!"

They looked up at Eddie. "Hi," they answered, and galloped to the third floor. They stopped a moment to catch their breath. "Whatcha doin', Eddie?" asked Chuck.

"Nothin'. You guys doin' anything?"

"Figured we'd go to Ralph's and play D.C. Wanna go?" asked Alan.

Eddie looked back at his apartment door. "Sure. Mom won't care."

The four rocketed down the stairs and burst into the afternoon sunlight. Turning toward the fringes of the Atterbury district, they ambled along sidewalks, climbed over fences to take shortcuts, and cut across vacant lots until they came to Vernon Street.

The houses on the street were the kind that had gone up by the thousands during the '50s in tracts all over southern California. A handkerchief of a lawn big enough for a single tree in front of a picture window was bounded on the second side by the Knudsens' driveway, sidewalk on the third, and the opposite edge of the neighbor's identical driveway on the fourth, completing the rectangle. Some yards were well-kept, others weedy.

The boys stopped in front of one of the well-kept houses. Ralph Knudsen's father was in the garage, scrabbling around in a tool chest, looking for something.

"Hi, Mr. Knudsen," said Chuck. "Is Ralph at home?"

Mr. Knudsen turned his head, looked at the boys, and nodded. "He's in the house, I guess," he said, and went back to his search.

"Thanks, Mr. Knudsen," said Eddie. The boys went to the door, but Ralph had heard them and was on his way out. "Hi, guys," he said.

"Hi," they answered. "We come over to play D.C. Okay?"

"Sure. C'mon in."

They disappeared into the house, and Mr. Knudsen came out of the garage, carrying a large pipe wrench. He walked around to the back of the house, muttering in disgust over plumbing chores.

4:15 P.M.

Elizabeth Walker ran down the stairs, calling "Don! Don!"

Donovan came into the hall from the living room. "Here, Liz. What's the matter?"

"Raymond's gone! He tied sheets together and went out the window!"

Don's jaw and his newspaper dropped. He brushed past Elizabeth as she came to the bottom step and taking two steps at a time, rushed upstairs to see for himself. "That kid—" he growled, looking blankly into the empty room. "That's it. When I get my hands on him, I'll tan his hide!" He started downstairs, a look of thunder in his eyes.

"We have to find him first," said Elizabeth grimly. She reached for the phone.

In a short time, they had learned that Alan, too, had gone out the window just as Raymond had. Mrs. Cappello didn't know where Eddie was.

"Who else is there?" asked Don. "What about that Chuck kid?"

"Ah—LeGarde. That's the name." Elizabeth looked up the number and learned that Mrs. LeGarde had given Chuck permission to go with Alan and Raymond to Ralph Knudsen's house.

"Knudsen?" asked Elizabeth.

"Yeah," said Mrs. LeGarde. "Otto Knudsen's place, on Vernon Street. The boys sometimes hang out there. Didn't you know?"

"No," said Elizabeth. "Ray never mentioned a Ralph. Was he one of the boys picked up by the police the other night?"

"Uh-huh. They're in the book. Otto Knudsen. Well, listen, if you get in touch, tell Chuck he should come home, too, will ya?"

Elizabeth scribbled the name on the pad. "I will. And thank you, Mrs. LeGarde." She hung up and reached for the phone book. "She thinks they're at Ralph Knudsen's," she said as she looked for the listing.

"Who's he?" asked Don.

"Seems to be a friend of the boys'. Here it is—" She wrote down the address, looked defiantly at Don. "I'm not going to call. We're going to go get him!" Her eyes sparked with anger as she turned away from the phone. "Wait. The Baxters might want to go, too." She punched the familiar number and suggested they come along. Putting down the phone, she looked grimly at her husband. "They're on the way. Well, we'll probably need both cars to haul them off."

They got into their car, met the Baxters' car at the corner, and both drove off toward Vernon Street.

5:05 P.M.

Matt walked up the outside stairs with Susan to her door as the sun disappeared into the fogbank collecting over the ocean. "Are you going to be all right? You sure you don't want to go somewhere for dinner?" he asked anxiously.

Susan, her key in the lock, turned to look at him. She gave him a small smile. "I'm okay. Just not hungry. But thanks." The lock snapped open. Her hand still on the doorknob, she leaned toward Matt and kissed him. "I'll see you tomorrow at church," she said.

Matt sighed, raised his eyebrows. "Okay. I love you." He turned and went down the stairs to his car.

"Me, too," Susan called after him and closed the door behind her. She glanced toward her phone. The message light blinked at her. Putting her purse down, she touched the button.

The voice was her mother's. "Raymond tied his sheets together," the tinny recording reported, "and got out the window. We found him playing Demon Crypt at a friend's house. Call back when you get in."

Susan sat down, drained. This was just too much. The machine clicked off, and she sighed. Might as well get it over with. She picked up the phone and returned the call.

Presently she put down the phone, thinking. Her mother had said the Knudsens seemed like decent, hard-working, likeable people. They could have bought D.C. as innocently for Ralph as the Baxters had for Alan. A lot of people thought Demon Crypt was like any other game. Maybe the Knudsens didn't know the dangers built into the game. But she didn't know that for sure. After what had been happening, she was worried.

Well, Mom and Dad were taking care of Raymond. There was nothing she could do right now, except get a little something to eat, then to bed. It had been a long, joyless, wearisome day.

SEVENTEEN

Sunday, October 27, 8:20 A.M.

Breakfast at the Robinsons was dismal. Everything was hollow, a gray, timeless emptiness. Lacey had scarcely slept since her mother died and had no appetite. Jerrod managed to swallow about a third of his cereal. Margaret fussed over them. Neither seemed to notice.

"I think I'll go to church," said Jerrod, rising from the table. "Come on, Lacey, come with me."

Lacey shook her head. "I'm not going to church anymore."

Robinson stared at her. "Why not?"

Lacey looked down at her untouched breakfast. "You wouldn't understand."

"Try me."

Lacey looked up at him. He could see tears were imminent, held back just out of sight. "All right," she said. "I phoned Pastor Drane last night. I asked how come Jesus let Mom die, although He healed other people, and Pastor Drane's a minister, for heaven's sake! He should know! But trying to get a straight answer from him is like trying to hold a handful of water. Daddy, he doesn't have any answers. The way he talks, I think he doesn't believe anything in the Bible. I'm not sure I believe anything he says, either." She looked back down at her dish, unseeing. "I don't believe in God anymore."

"Lacey!"

She looked back up. "Well, I don't. He let Mother die, didn't He? We all prayed for her, and Brother Justin said he healed her, and still she died!" Tears rolled down her cheeks. "I don't believe anything anymore." She stood up and walked to the window, staring outside. "All Pastor Drane talks about is how you can pray and visualize and get rich." She turned back and looked angrily at her father, wiping tears from her face. "Did you see his new car? A Mercedes, for heaven's sake! From praying for prosperity! Just money. And he can't help people who need help. He thinks he knows all the answers, but when I asked him, he had nothing to say except that tired old 'everything will be all right'!"

Jerrod walked over to her and put his arms around her. She hugged her father and wept on his shoulder. "I should have been nicer to her," she sobbed. "I hurt her feelings so often!"

Jerrod patted her shoulder and kissed her hair. "I know how you feel. I hurt her, too. I neglected her. There was always too much to do. I was too busy. Too busy making money." Tears brimmed in his eyes.

Margaret stopped in the doorway with the pot of fresh coffee, looked at them for a moment, turned, and left them alone.

Sunday, 1:10 P.M.

Susan accompanied the Walkers and a truculent Raymond after church to Randy's Chicken Palace. They were ushered to a corner booth, giving them as much privacy as they could get. The din of conversation in the crowded family restaurant assured them that no one would pay any attention to anything they said.

Susan put a bare chicken bone down on her plate and wiped her mouth with her napkin after she'd heard the details. "So what will you do?"

Elizabeth looked at Don. "Well," he said, "the obvious. Like Alan, he's *really* grounded. He comes straight home from school and stays home weekends. Also, we lucked out and managed to get hold of a counselor late yesterday afternoon, and both he and Alan will see him twice a week."

"What about the other three? Won't they see him, too?"

Don shook his head. "We talked to the parents yesterday. One of the kids has no father. That's Eddie Cappello. The mother doesn't seem to care much what he does. The parents of the other two think they can handle it themselves."

"It's too serious for that," Elizabeth said. "Parents need help as much as the kids. I don't know—ever since Ray started public high school, everything's been different. I wish our school had grades ten through twelve."

Don mopped up some gravy with a piece of bread. "I remember when I was in school, we opened with prayer, the pledge to the flag, and sang 'America' or 'Star Spangled Banner'. God and country. Seems like a totally different world."

"I know what you mean," said Elizabeth. "There's such an anti-Christian atmosphere at public schools, Christian kids have a rough time. And kids don't get any moral training at all if they don't get it at home."

Susan pushed her plate away. "A lot of schools teach religions like witchcraft, Eastern beliefs, and stuff under 'Cultural Differences.' Put that together with Demon Crypt, alcohol, and drugs and it's trouble. Like a doorway into the occult."

Raymond looked up, his expression sullen. "They don't teach religion at school," he said.

"Don't they?" asked his mother. "Christianity is just about the only religion they don't teach at your school. What about the paper you had to write about Navajo and Hopi religions a couple of months ago? And before that, Hindu beliefs. Aren't those religions?"

Raymond scowled and looked down.

"You said it was a 'doorway into the occult'," said Don. "How?"

"Well, from what I understand, they're taught that nothing is absolutely right, and nothing absolutely wrong, and that only they can decide what's right for them. Depends on the situation. But kids don't have the experience to know if something's right for them. So since for Ray and his friends playing Demon Crypt is fun, it's right for them. They don't understand that the philosophy and violence in the game are wrong because the teacher tells them 'nothing is absolutely wrong.' Far as the kids are concerned, it's just a lot of fun." She looked at Raymond. "That right?"

Raymond nodded.

"But where does the occult come in?" asked Don.

Susan sipped some water. "I just read an article about this. Some kids—probably not most of them—form gangs based on these games, and get in so deep they get into drugs. Seems to make it more exciting, I guess. Before they know it, they're hooked." She paused, looked around the table. "I know this sounds wild, but the article said that at that point, in some instances, in some towns, someone introduces them to witchcraft, demonism, satanism. Again, that's something different and exciting, and the kids think that's fun, too."

Elizabeth looked up from her plate. "You think what Lacey ran into on Washington last week and all this other stuff might have something to do with satanism?" Her blue eyes were dark with anxiety.

"Could be. No real proof yet." The three adults looked at Raymond.

"Hey, don't look at me!" he said. "I'm not into anything like that!"

"That's why you're grounded," said his father, looking hard at Raymond. "You're not going to get into it."

Raymond squirmed. "I tell you I'm not into that!"

Susan put her hand over her brother's. "I know you're not. But I've been reading a lot about it. For some players, it's only a short step from D.C. to drugs, to free drugs-and-sex parties, to witchcraft and satanism."

"Hold on," said her father. "What do you mean, 'free drugs-and-sex parties'? And how do you know about such things?" He looked with alarm at his daughter.

"Police files, for one thing," she answered. "Books and articles, for another. I read that there are recruiters who look for kids who are deep into D.C., especially if they drink, or do drugs. A recruiter will invite kids to a party. There, they pick out a few they think are susceptible, take them into a room all set up for them. They get the kids to take cocaine, or to get into bed with a woman, while a hidden camera takes pictures of them. Then later, they try to get them to sign a contract with Satan, or to deal drugs for them, whatever. If the kids refuse, they threaten to give the photos or video to their parents or the police."

Shocked silence followed. "But surely," said Elizabeth, "Ray and his friends wouldn't fall for anything like that! They've got more sense than to get in with such people in the first place."

Susan shook her head. "The problem is that usually the recruiters look like ordinary, normal adults." She looked at Raymond. "There are doctors, lawyers, teachers, even ministers, involved in satanism."

Raymond scowled and looked defiantly at her.

"Don't you look at me like that," she said sharply. "I'm not kidding. These things happen, and we don't want them happening to you!"

Donovan looked at Raymond. "The only reason we're leaning on you is that we don't want to see you in trouble."

Raymond said nothing.

"You know we love you and want the best for you, don't you?" Elizabeth asked.

Raymond nodded.

"Then promise you'll not play Demon Crypt anymore. And stay away from drugs! All right?"

Raymond tightened his lips, but nodded. "Okay."

Elizabeth looked at Raymond, only half-believing him. "Say it," she insisted.

"Okay, I'll stay away from them!" Raymond said loudly, and turned away, glaring. People at nearby tables turned to stare.

As they left, Susan put her arm around her brother's shoulder while their parents headed for the car. "If you like, I'll lend you one of my books that tells about what happened to a good kid who got caught up in it without realizing it."

"Okay." He looked down at his feet. "But the game—you know, like you said, it's fun and it gets you all excited about power and winning, and sometimes, when you get it, you have to think up all sorts of things to keep it and to get more—"

"Ray, I read something that impressed me. A psychiatrist said— just a minute—here—" she dug in her purse and unfolded a piece of paper. "He told about a couple of brothers, fourteen and seventeen, who had played so much D.C., they got bored with it and went on to astral projection and other weird things. One day, a police detective found them both dead, their arms and legs wrapped around each other. The older brother had shot the younger one, then himself."

Raymond finally looked shocked. "That's a lot of bull—" He caught himself and reddened.

"No, it isn't. Police figured out from talking to their friends that they thought they could keep demons from coming here from the spirit world if they went there as a team to hold them back. And they think they got that idea from D.C."

Raymond looked at her, wide-eyed. "For real?"

"For real."

Raymond shook his head slowly. "But it's just a game, like Monopoly or something. And it's a lot more fun."

"It isn't like Monopoly. It's a lot different. Quite a few who've gotten into it got so messed up, they committed suicide. Or killed other people."

Raymond looked at her doubtfully.

"It's true. I wouldn't tell you all this if it weren't true." She put her hands on his shoulders and looked hard at him. "Promise. No more D.C., no more marijuana, no more beer. Promise?"

Raymond glowered. "Yeah." He turned and headed for the car where Elizabeth and Donovan waited for him.

Susan slid behind the wheel of her car and headed home. She wondered what else she could do to help Raymond get his head back on straight. He had not seemed to be much impressed with what she had told him.

Sunday, 3:45 P.M.

Margaret went to Jerrod's door and tapped. "Mr. Robinson, Mr. John Merkel is here. Will you see him?"

Jerrod's impulse was to tell Margaret to get him out of there. He was a pill.

He sighed. "I'll be right there, Margaret," he said, and pushed himself up out of his chair, tapping the tobacco out of his pipe.

John was, as usual, theatrical. He looked down briefly, and as he looked back, his face wore an expression of extreme sorrow. He extended his hand. "Mr. Robinson, I cannot tell you how sorry I am. Mrs. Robinson was perhaps the finest lady I ever knew."

Jerrod took the hand and dropped it. "Thank you, John. Will you sit down? Bring us a drink, Margaret. What will you have?" he asked, turning to John.

"Coffee, please, black," said John.

Jerrod nodded to Margaret, then continued. She nodded. "Here, sit down," he told John. "We haven't seen you lately. How've you been?" He didn't really care, but social niceties demanded conversation.

"Fine, sir, just fine, thank you." John sat down. "This must be deucedly hard on you and Lacey." Margaret came by and offered John a cup of coffee. John sipped from the delicate porcelain cup. "Is she up to receiving guests?"

Jerrod sighed. "Perhaps so." He called Margaret back. "Would you please ask Miss Lacey if she'd like to see Mr. Merkel?" She nodded and started up the stairs.

An awkward silence followed before Margaret came down the stairs. "She'll be down directly, sir," she said.

In just a few moments Lacey appeared. John stood up. "Lacey, dearest." He came toward her, his hand extended.

"Hullo, John," she said, her expression dull.

"I just came over to tell you how sorry, how devastatingly sorry I am," he said, taking her hand. "I really cared for your mother."

"Thank you, John," she said, dropping his hand as soon as she came off the first stair. She sat down in the Louis XIV chair her mother had favored. She looked at her father. He raised his eyebrows as if to say, what could I do?

John sat down again. "Is there anything I can do?"

Father and daughter shook their heads. "Short of bringing Mother back to life, I can't think of a thing," said Lacey.

John sighed and leaned back. "I can't do that, of course," he said, "but there is something."

Jerrod stifled a yawn. "I'm not sure I know what you mean."

"I know a woman, a very fine woman, a trance channeller. It's possible you might be able to get through to Mrs. Robinson's spirit."

Jerrod looked up. "To Amelia? You mean, I might be able to speak to her?"

John shrugged. "It's happened. This trance channeller I'm acquainted with has been able to contact those who have gone beyond."

Jerrod stood up and walked over to the window. After a moment, he turned back to John. "You mean, this woman might actually be able to get in touch with Amelia, and we could talk to her?"

John lounged in the deeply upholstered chair. "That's exactly what I mean. She's been doing this for several years now."

Jerrod walked back to his chair and sat down, deep in thought. "How do we know she's not faking?"

John shrugged again. "It's worked for quite a few people now."

Jerrod gazed, his eyes unfocused, and finally said, "Who is she? Where does she live?"

"Her name is Cynthia Crawford, and she lives in Playa Linda, top of the hill here in Tres Encinos. Actually, I went to high school with her, but her talent hadn't developed then. It's only recently that she's been able to contact the beyond."

"How?"

"She has a control—a disembodied spirit. Her control, Nathaniel, is one who left the mortal sphere some fifteen hundred years ago. He can find others in the great beyond and bring them to her when someone cares very deeply and calls for them."

Lacey had finally begun to hear what John was saying. She studied him. He seemed so sure. This was a person who had been in school with him right here in Playa Linda. Other people would know her, be her friends. And her name, Cynthia Crawford, was so ordinary. So different from Brother Justin and his mumbo jumbo.

"John," she said suddenly, "how did this happen? How did she get in touch with this Nathaniel in the first place?"

. John turned toward Lacey. "It was a strange thing. Cynthia used to ride—the Crawfords kept several horses. Well, one day, she tried to ride her father's horse, he threw her, she bumped her head hard on a fencepost and was unconscious for several hours."

"So?"

"Well, a little while after that, she began to hear a man's voice talking to her in her head from time to time. At first, she couldn't make out what he was saying, but later on, she began to understand him."

"Go on, go on," said Jerrod. "What was the voice saying?"

"She heard him say, 'There is someone here who wants to talk to you, Cynthia.' That was the beginning of it. It turned out to be a friend of Cynthia's who had been killed in a terrible automobile accident on graduation night. Seemed she wanted to tell Cynthia how glad she was that Cynthia had not gone with them that night, although they had asked her."

Jerrod and Lacey sat staring. Lacey was reminded of Sharleena.

"Then once when I was at her house, she suddenly got very quiet, her eyes closed, and this man's voice came out of her. He said, 'John Merkel, your mother wants to talk to you.' That's what he said."

Lacey was all attention. Color had drained from Jerrod's face. "What—what happened next?"

"The voice that spoke then was my mother's. She told me to look into the false bottom of her top righthand desk drawer for a stock certificate she'd taken out for me. Turned out it was worth a lot of money. Financial freedom, in fact."

Silence. Jerrod paced. Lacey pondered. Could Cynthia be different from Sharleena? Could this be real?

"You said she might be able to contact Amelia—or rather, that Nathaniel—?" asked Jerrod.

John nodded. "She's done it for quite a few of her friends now."

Jerrod inhaled sharply. "Make an appointment for us," he said. His voice was decisive. "I want to meet this woman."

Lacey looked half excited, half uncertain. She had decided she wouldn't believe in anything ever again, but what if she could really talk to her mother? Could she risk half-believing this? And what would Susan say about it?

"It's all right, Lacey," her father said. "We'll go see her, talk to her, and if she seems straight, well, we'll take it from there." He stood staring, his eyes misty. "If I could just tell Amelia how much I really loved her. I don't think she ever really knew—"

John stood up. "I'd better be on my way. I'll phone her and set it up. Would next Tuesday evening suit you?"

Jerrod nodded, eyes misted. The funeral was to be Monday.

"Well, then, I'll pick you up at about seven." He shook Jerrod's hand, took Lacey's and kissed it, and headed for the door.

"I'll see you out," said Jerrod, swallowing hard. He closed the door behind John and turned to Lacey.

"I don't know. Maybe this woman can do it, maybe not, but I want to give her a chance. I've so much to say to your mother I never said—" he choked with emotion.

Lacey came to him and hugged him. "I know how you feel, Daddy. It's the same with me."

They stood there together, each hoping and dreading, believing and disbelieving, but each determined to try to rend the barrier between life and death.

EIGHTEEN

Monday, October 28, 7:40 A.M.

"Remember, Ray, you come straight home from school." Elizabeth picked up her books and folders from the table and urged her son out the door. "I'll drop you there on my way."

"Oh, Mother!" Raymond wailed.

"Don't you 'Oh, Mother' me! This time you'll do as we say. Get in." She opened the passenger door with her free hand and went around to get in on the other side.

They were both silent as Elizabeth maneuvered through morning rush traffic to Sherman High School. When she stopped at the curb, Raymond looked peevish. "How long is this gonna go on?" he asked.

"Depends on you."

He scowled. "Sure," he said, his expression sour. "'Bye."

He slung his book pack over his shoulder, exited the car, and, without a backward look, sullenly joined the increasing numbers of noisy, chattering students on their way up the walk toward the entrance.

Elizabeth was uneasy as she watched him go. She shook her head and went on to the Christian school, feeling utterly helpless. *Well,* she thought, *tomorrow we'll see the counselor. Maybe he can help.*

7:55 A.M.

Raymond walked down the corridor toward his locker, his expression glum. "Hi, Chuck," he said, seeing his friend. "What's new?"

"Nothin' much. Goin' to play D.C.?"

"Can't. Gotta go straight home. So does Alan."

"Alan and Eddie and Ralph—we're all cuttin' classes and goin' to a place Eddie knows. You comin' with us?"

Raymond looked at him. "You're all goin'?"

"Yeah."

Raymond leaned against his locker. D.C. It had become his life's passion. Did he dare?

Chuck looked around to see if any of the thickening stream of jostling, jabbering students might overhear. He edged closer to Raymond. "Eddie got some—you know—"

Raymond looked blank for a moment. Then realization hit him. He was startled. "My folks would kill me."

"They don't hafta know."

Raymond opened his locker and stuffed his books into it, thinking fast. If he did, it would be a way to get his folks to notice he was not a kid anymore, and at the same time show them what they could do with their bleepin' rules. A chill settled around him, but defiant, he made his decision. "Okay. What's the deal?"

Chuck grinned. "The rest are out back. I was waitin' for ya. We'll sorta wander out the back door and ease off toward Pine Street. We hop the Washington Avenue bus. Eddie knows an abandoned house where we can play. He'll let us know where we should get off."

A feeble voice inside Raymond insisted "No! Don't!" but he nodded anyway. Resentment rankled at him. No way would he let his parents keep pushing him around. Besides, they were never around anymore anyway, with Mom teaching and Dad always at the store. Even his sister had her own apartment now. Heck, he was going to be sixteen in a few months, practically grown-up. He'd show them. He was going to do what he wanted. Chuck's parents and Eddie's mother never got after them. They always did what they wanted when they wanted.

Chuck headed toward the back of the school, and Raymond hurried to catch up.

Ralph and Chuck sat in the back of the bus. Eddie sat near the front, so the rest could see when he got up to get off. Alan sat by himself a couple of seats in front of Raymond.

The diesel-reeking bus bounced over manhole covers and into chuckholes, squealing to a stop now and then with a whoosh of the doors to pick up or let off passengers. A big nervous knot built up inside Raymond. Should he have stayed at school after all? *Well, it's done now,* he thought. He should be feeling free, but it didn't feel good at all. His stomach was fidgety, sorta heavy, sorta queasy. He looked out the window as the bus wound up Washington Avenue. What a crummy neighborhood.

Eddie stood up. Raymond looked around at the dilapidated houses, almost lost his nerve. Chuck and Ralph passed him on their way to the front of the bus. Alan, standing up, looked back and beckoned impatiently. "Come on, Ray," he said. "This is our stop! Move it!"

Raymond stood up and followed Alan off the bus, watching it as it pulled away from the curb. The world looked bleak as it went out of sight. He had never felt so alone and vulnerable.

8:25 A.M.

Susan checked her IN basket. Only two small items had come in. She picked up the one on top. As she scanned it, her eyes and mouth tightened. Police had gone to arrest Brother Justin for questioning, but he had vanished. *I'll have to tell Matt,* she thought, setting down the fax. The other concerned a robbery in nearby Cromwell which resembled several robberies committed recently in Playa Linda. No real evidence, but the M.O. was similar. She replaced both faxes. They could wait. Mrs. Robinson's funeral would be at 1 P.M., so she had time for at least one interview, maybe even two. She headed for the hospital, identified herself at the desk, and asked if she could interview Lily Mae Johnson.

"Just a moment," the receptionist said, looking it up. "Lily Mae—she's in room 623. Sixth floor." She turned back to her papers.

Susan stopped at the sixth floor nurses' station, showed her press card, and asked how Lily Mae was.

"Physically, she's fine," said the nurse, studying the press card. "But still pretty badly upset."

"May I see her?" Susan asked.

The nurse hesitated, nodded. "She's allowed visitors now." She paused. "Actually, she hasn't had any." Troubled, she looked up at Susan. "We haven't been able to reach her parents," she admitted in a low voice, "and I think a visitor might be good for her. She needs positive reinforcement, so don't come on like a reporter, okay? Just visit and keep her calm."

Susan agreed, and the nurse directed her down the hall.

Lily Mae, small and thin for seven years old, was in a private room, sitting in bed, playing with a little beeping video game. She looked up when Susan came in, and smiled a self-conscious front-tooth-growing-in smile. "Hi," she said. Her straight brown shoulder length hair framed an oval face. Large hazel eyes fringed with long black lashes held mystery in their depths.

"Hi, yourself," said Susan, smiling back. She sat down beside the bed. "What's that you've got?"

"A game. It's dumb. What's your name?"

"Susan. I know yours. It's Lily Mae."

"Are you a nurse?"

"No. I work for the *Register*."

"Oh. I'm a witch."

Susan was startled. "Well. How about that." She tried to keep her voice even. "You mean, you're really a witch?"

"Uh-huh. I am now." Suddenly her cheerful expression crumpled. She squeezed her eyes shut and turned away. "It's a secret. I can't tell."

Susan didn't know what to say, so she put her hand on the little girl's arm. "It's all right, honey. I won't tell anyone."

Lily Mae looked up, her eyes deep wells of pain. "They did something awful to my uncle Billy Joe," she said. "He was a witch, too. And they said—they said—" her chest started heaving, and she began to cry. Susan reached over and picked her up. Lily Mae's arms went around her neck, and they clung to each other. Susan rocked her, murmuring soft endearments.

Soon Lily Mae drew back and wiped her eyes. Susan handed her a tissue from the box on the bedside stand.

"What did they say?" Susan asked gently.

Lily Mae wiped her eyes and blew her nose. Then, gulping, she struggled to stop crying. "They said Uncle Billy Joe did a bad thing, he was going to tell that we were all witches, and they had to kill him so he couldn't tell. And then, so's I could be a witch like all the rest of the family, I had to be borned from him—" Tears rolled and she whimpered, her lip quivering.

"It's okay," said Susan, horrified that a child must endure what would unhinge an adult. "You don't have to talk about it." She cuddled the little girl, murmuring softly to her.

Lily Mae suddenly pulled away, her body rigid, questioning Susan with her eyes, dark with terror. "Will they have to kill me now?"

Susan, shocked, put her arms around the child and held her close. "No, no, honey. Even if they wanted to, and they wouldn't, we won't let them."

Lily Mae's body began to shake. Uttering a tremulous wail, she clutched Susan around the neck and wept hysterically. "I told! I told! The nurse, and the doctor, and now I told you—and nobody tells about being a witch except they get killed, like Uncle Billy Joe," she cried. She wrenched away, and burrowed, howling, in the bed.

The nurse shoved open the door and ran to the bed. "What did you do to her?" she demanded, flashing an angry look at Susan, uncovering, examining Lily Mae.

Astonished, Susan stammered "Nothing—I didn't—"

"I warned you she was badly upset!"

A young nurse rushed in with a syringe. "Here, Mrs. Norton." she said.

"Thanks." Mrs. Norton expelled the air from the needle and injected the liquid into Lily Mae's thin arm. She watched the sedative begin to take effect. "Thank you, Gardiner. You may go." The young nurse left.

Mrs. Norton looked angrily at Susan. "What did you say to her?"

Susan repeated the conversation word for word. "Then she started talking about what had happened, and—" Susan spread her hands. "She fell apart. It sort of poured out of her."

Mrs. Norton's expression softened. She nodded, and watched Lily Mae as she gradually stopped crying and began to relax. "I see. But you'd better go now. She needs quiet."

"Mrs. Norton," Lily Mae said sleepily, "don't send Susan away—"

The nurse looked at Susan. "Well. All right. She can stay. But only a minute." She stepped back and waited.

"I really have to go now," said Susan, stroking Lily Mae's hair. "But I'll try to come back tomorrow. Would you like me to bring you something?"

Lily Mae smiled a sleepy smile. "Uh-huh. Will you bring me my witching doll?"

Susan was stymied. "I—uh—don't know where it is. Maybe I could bring you a new doll? Or a game?"

"No. I only want my witching doll. But I wish you'd come back anyway."

Susan looked at Mrs. Norton. "Okay. I'll be back. Just don't be afraid anymore." Susan looked at Lily Mae, so like any other little seven-year-old, yet so very different. "Go to sleep now. I'll see you tomorrow, okay?"

Lily Mae sighed. "See you—" She was sound asleep. The door closed behind Susan and Mrs. Norton as they left.

"Do you have an address or a phone number for the parents?" Susan asked as they walked toward the desk.

"Just General Delivery. We've asked the police to locate them.

There's very little we can do without the parents' permission. Not that she needs much beyond TLC and security. And counseling."

Mrs. Norton looked curiously at Susan. "How will you write this up?"

Susan bit her lip. "I'll say the child found in the area is under medical care, and that police are trying to locate the parents. Not much detail. That's not necessary."

Mrs. Norton nodded. "As long as you protect Lily Mae. Well, then, I guess we'll see you tomorrow."

8:35 A.M.

Raymond turned from watching the bus out of sight to look at the others. He felt cold even in the bright sunlight. Eddie and Chuck were grinning, punching each other on the arm. Alan looked at Raymond.

"Well, let's go!" Raymond said, trying to look eager.

Eddie led them to a boarded-up house. "We can get in by the cellar door," he said. "No one'll bother us there."

Alan looked around. "I dunno about this—"

Chuck snorted. "What's the matter? Ya scared?"

"Ya crazy? 'Course not! But maybe someone owns this place."

Eddie sneered. "Hey, this place has been empty for years! It's okay, I tell ya!"

"Alan and I have to be home the same time as if we'd been at school," Raymond said. "Our folks will cream us if we don't."

"Don't worry. We'll be outta here by then," Eddie said.

He led them around to the back, went to the cellar door, picked at the lock, lifted it, and descended the stairs to the basement. The rest followed into the dark. Eddie took a flashlight from his pocket, pointed it at the stairs to the kitchen, and, with the others following, went up and pushed the door open. The kitchen was dark except for streaks of light that came in through cracks and knotholes in the boards over the windows.

"This way," said Eddie, going into what must have once been the living room. Here, too, the windows were boarded. Floating dust motes sparkled in streaks of sunlight. The room was bare except for a table surrounded by chairs. "We can set up here." He went over to a corner, picked up a battery-powered lantern, turned it on, and set it on the table.

Once everyone else was seated, Eddie brought out a six-pack of beer from a dark corner and took two packets out of his pocket, one small and one large.

Eddie looked around at the others, who were staring blankly at him and his packets. "What's the matter? Don'tcha know nothin'? This," he said crooning at the smaller one, "is crystal!"

"Wow!" said Chuck. "Totally awesome!"

"The other is pot. We'll mix 'em in a joint."

Chuck looked puzzled. "Hey, man, with crystal ya do lines."

"Yeah, I know," Eddie said. He distributed papers, marijuana, and a small pile of crystal to each. "But Alan and Ray, here, they never done that. This time we make joints like before, but mix in some meth. Okay?"

Chuck shrugged. "Okay."

Wide-eyed, scared, Raymond looked around at the rest. Alan looked worried. Ralph was grinning. So was Chuck. What had he gotten himself into this time?

Ralph reached for the small packet. Eddie slapped at his hand. "Not so fast!"

"Hey Ed, howdja get hold of that?" asked Chuck.

"My uncle Tony's a dealer. I sneaked this last night." Ceremoniously, he opened the packet, displayed the prepowdered crystal, opened the packet of marijuana and chortled. "Crystal meth. Boy, are we gonna have fun!"

Beer cans crackled open. Chuck, Eddie, and Ralph rolled their joints expertly. Slowly, Alan and Raymond followed suit. Raymond didn't dare look ahead to the next few hours. Nervous, he lit his joint, looked at it, dragged, inhaled, coughed, and swallowed some beer. And another big gulp.

As Crypt Master Ralph set up the screen and laid out the map of the game, Alan picked up the ten-sided dice and rolled them several times. He grinned, "I'm a gnome, a fighter," he said. As the rest determined their characters by the dice, Ralph pulled at his beer. Wisps of smoke rose above the table, and the game was on. Raymond was a Magic User. Somehow, today everything was suddenly taking on sharper edges.

Raymond, immersed in his character, was impatient. The game wasn't moving fast enough for him. Fidgeting, he bumped into the table, knocked dice, accumulated treasure slips and all manner of notes to the floor, ducked underneath to retrieve them, and nearly overturned the table. Chuck glared at him and yelled.

"Watch it! We'll burn you!" Ralph snarled.

"Oh, yeah?" Raymond sneered. "Get on with the game!"

Imaginations soared into never-could-be-lands. With Alan directing the game from his map, living game-lives which were more vivid than their own, the boys lost all sense of time, of where and who they were, throwing dice, killing monsters, accumulating treasures, finding their way through dank tunnels to dungeons and mazes, killing monsters and dragons, gaining or losing experience points, drawing new maps, doing all they could to survive and gain more and more power. Power! That's what it was all about!

NINETEEN

Monday, 10:30 A.M.

On the way to the Garcia's, Susan thought over what little she had learned about Karen, beginning with her disappearance from school. Drugs could account for the change in her habits and drop in grades. Was that what had happened to the other two?

Mrs. Garcia came to the door when she rang the bell. "Oh! It's you," she said, starting to close the door.

"Just a minute, please!" Susan begged, putting out her hand to hold the door open. "If I promise not to upset Karen, will you let me talk to her?"

Mr. Garcia had come to the door and stood behind his wife. He spoke softly in her ear. "What do you want from her?" Mrs. Garcia asked.

"I need to know what happened to her when she disappeared from school, and how she came to be at that scene Wednesday about midnight. And how she is now."

"I don't know. She's pretty disturbed, and we don't want to upset her any more."

"Mrs. Garcia," Susan said, "if I can write a story to show how easy it is for kids to get caught up in something like this, maybe it will help keep others from being roped in. But if no one knows about it, this sort of thing will go on and on."

Mrs. Garcia stared at her, thinking. "All right," she said. "But you promised not to upset her."

Susan let her breath out quietly. "Thank you."

Karen was in the living room, watching television. When Susan came in, she turned it off and stood up, nervous as a colt about to flee. The elder Garcias stood in the doorway.

Susan stood still. "Hi. I'm Susan Walker. May we talk? Your mother said it would be all right."

Karen stared at her, then looked to her parents. "I don't know you."

"No. I'm with the *Register*." Karen made a sudden move as if to leave. "No, wait! I'm not here to give you a bad time. All I want is to ask you a few questions. You can answer if you want."

"It'll be all right, Karen," said Mrs. Garcia.

Karen looked long at her mother, and sat down on the edge of the couch. "Well, okay. Go ahead." She drew a breath. "What do you want to know?"

Susan sat in a chair across the room from her. "Your parents were really worried when you disappeared from school. Will you tell me why you didn't come home, and where you went?"

Karen looked steadily at Susan, heaved a big sigh, and looked out the window. "Okay," she said in a small voice. "The whole scene was a bummer." She looked at Susan, nodded. "I already told my folks," she said. "You see, it was this guy in the senior class. He was real cool. Seniors never date juniors. But this guy—he came on to about five of us, 'specially June and me. We really got along real good. Then one afternoon he brought joints, and the five of us cut classes and got stoned. We thought that was cool." She looked at her hands.

Susan scribbled. "It happens more often than a lot of people think."

"I know. But that don't make it right. Anyway, for awhile, that's all it was, a day or so a week. Then he asked us out on a date with some other guys, and this other dude, he was older—not old-old, about twenty-one—he had some coke and later, some other stuff."

She paused. "It went on like that for awhile. Like during lunch and after school, y'know? Then one day at lunch, he told us about this bunch of people who really had it made. They had all the good stuff, and it didn't cost them anything. They said we could be members of a group like that. They called it a coven." Karen's mouth twisted wryly. "They gave us a big line about how joining, we could, like, have all kinds of power over other people."

"Was that what you wanted?"

Karen looked down, thinking. "No, not really. But they also said we could be real popular, and I've never been popular—"

"I see. They promised all the things you didn't have."

"Yeah. And then, when we didn't go for it, they dared us. They asked us if we had the guts to go for it, or were we chicken?" She shrugged. "It was a challenge." She looked at Susan. "And I wanted to be popular.

"June and me, we were the only ones dumb enough to fall for it. The others chickened out. They had to swear in their own blood never to tell what they'd heard or seen or done, or else they'd get hurt real bad."

Karen looked away and was silent for a minute. "But they said we'd have to leave home and stay with them," she continued. "So I took the satanic bible they gave me—June had to go home for hers—and left school with them. Another guy picked June up later. And then we had to do this ritual thing, y'know?"

Susan looked up from her notes. "What kind of a ritual?"

"Well, first, when we got to this place and got good and stoned, we had to sign an agreement in blood—" she looked up in appeal at Susan. "—you know, sort of a pact with the devil—"

Susan kept her face expressionless. "Go on," she said.

"That first night, there were kids from other schools who were new. We all got real wasted. We went out into a field and had kind of a séance, y' know, and one of the guys was the medium. He got into a trance, like, and this voice—it was awful."

"One of the other new ones—was her name Ellen?"

Karen thought. "Yeah, I think so. Yeah, there was an Ellen." She continued. "Then some of the guys, they went up to a cow, knocked it down, and opened it up." She choked up. Susan waited. Karen looked out the window again. "Then one of the men made a big circle on the ground and drew a five-pointed star—he called it a pentagram—inside it. We all stood around the circle and swore loyalty to Satan. The leader said a lot of things I couldn't understand, and they passed around a cup of—" Karen put her head down. "I got real sick. I puked."

After a minute she continued. "The leader said some more stuff I couldn't understand, and we all went to a big bare barn of a house, where everybody lived." She looked up at Susan. "It was a whole family, kids and all, and why we were there was they wanted another coven. That was us." She looked away and shuddered a sigh. "I'd give anything if I could go back and not do it again."

Susan fought to be objective. "You're out of it now," she said. "But what led up to the night when you were caught?"

Karen looked away. "That was even worse. What started it was this older member of the family, I think his name was Billy Joe—Johnson, that was it, he was talking about quitting the coven." She turned back to Susan. "You can't do that!" she said, her dark eyes frightened. "No one quits a coven! But he said he was quitting and threatened to go to the police. Anyway, that's what I heard. So—" Karen gulped, "so they set up this circle with the bonfires." She stopped.

"It's okay," said Susan, crossing over to her. "Take your time. If you don't feel up to it, I'll come back tomorrow."

Karen looked up. "No. If I'm going to tell it, I have to do it now, or later I'll be too scared." Susan sat down on a chair near her. "Well," Karen said, with another deep breath, "those of us who were new, we had to drink from the cup again and take several kinds of drugs, because of what they were going to do, so we could stand it. When we were really out of it, we all got into the circle, and the leader, he got Billy Joe so doped he was almost out, and laid him down near that cross, you know, the upside-down one near the grave?"

Susan nodded.

"Then they—they—" she struggled to get the words out, but couldn't. Karen stared out the window. She was pale as paper. She looked up at Susan, her eyes brimming with tears. Susan took a tissue from her purse and gave it to Karen.

"Anyway," Karen finally went on after wiping her eyes and blowing her nose, "we circled the area for awhile, chanting." Tears welled again. "That's about all I remember, and I don't remember anything real well, except the headlights coming, and I ran, and then I don't remember anything until I woke up in the hospital." She drew a shuddery breath and looked at Susan. "If that man hadn't driven up, no one would ever have known. Whenever there's a ceremony like that, at the end, they bury everything, even the ashes, and put it all back the way it was. No one ever knows. Only this time, the headlights came, and we all ran—"

Susan was silent, scribbling notes.

Karen looked startled suddenly. "You're going to put this in the paper, aren't you?"

Susan nodded. "But don't worry. We won't name you."

"It won't make any difference. They'll know it was me. Because I'm not going back. And all the rest will be there." She was terrified. "You don't know the power they have! They can call demons—they kill—they're *evil*! I'm so scared—" She hung her head, wiped at her eyes with the damp tissue.

Susan put a hand on her arm, felt her quivering. "Look," she said, "when I write it, I'll tell about how Mr. Alvarado broke up the meeting. And I'll tell what he saw, about satanic rituals in general, this one in particular, but I won't mention any names, nor say that I got information from anyone in the group. I'll refer to some books I read. And I'll warn kids how dangerous it is to get mixed up with drugs and witchcraft. That's all. What I really want to do is warn other kids about the whole scene. Okay?"

Karen looked up, her eyes red, face wet with tears. "I guess so—"

Susan picked up her purse. She turned back to Karen. "Hang in there," she said with what she hoped was a reassuring smile. Here was another person in desperate need of prayer, and she would have it!

She got into her car, stopped off at the *Register*, and drove to Connie's for lunch with Matt. They sat in a booth, ordered, and looked at each other silently for a moment.

"Hon—"

"Matt—"

They laughed. "You first," said Matt.

"Brother Justin's disappeared," Susan said. "There was a fax from the police. They're looking for him to question him about Mrs. Robinson's death. Mr. Robinson called them."

Matt sat back. "Can't blame him, really. Just imagine what he's feeling."

"Yeah. And the strange thing is that from what Andy said, the case in England is so much like what happened to Mrs. Robinson that it's spooky. At least, Dr. Damron wasn't on drugs."

"Yeah."

Susan nodded, and after a brief silence, went on to tell what she had learned from Lily Mae and Karen.

Matt sat silent, toying with his beef pie.

Susan continued. "Now Lily Mae is afraid she'll be killed, and Karen is scared stiff, expecting almost anything to happen. These people get rid of any threat to them."

They toyed with their food silently for a few minutes, pushed away their dishes, and stared at each other. "So where do we go from here?" Susan asked.

Matt looked out the window. "Guess we'll just keep on. It's beginning to come together, except at the top." He looked back at Susan. "I'll fill Andy in on what you found out. Maybe that'll give him more to go on."

Susan nodded and glanced at her watch. "Oops. Gotta go." She got up, dropped a hasty kiss on Matt's cheek and hurried to be in time for Mrs. Robinson's funeral. She found a place to park half a block away and arrived just as the service was starting. Afterward she spoke briefly to Lacey and her father and then headed for the *Register*.

2:15 P.M.

"Hey, Susie," called Pete, waving fax papers at her as she came in. "Here. Jackson was looking for you to do this." He handed them to her.

She looked them over and looked up at Pete, a puzzled expression on her face. "What's happening in this town?" she asked. "This sort of stuff goes on in L.A. and New York. Not here," she said. A chill rippled down her back.

Pete shrugged. "So a gang got together and hit a jewelry store in the mall for easy money. What's new about that?"

"Stuff like that just doesn't happen here," she repeated. She read the fax over again as she walked toward her work station. Four youths had smashed the jewelry store windows and counters, scooped expensive rings, necklaces, and bracelets into a sack, shot the jeweler, and lost themselves in the crowd of shoppers. Descriptions from eyewitnesses were conflicting. The police were still looking for them. The jeweler was in critical condition in the hospital. Susan sighed, sat down, pencilled in edits, typeset the edited story, and sent it to makeup.

Just as she reached for her notes on her interviews, Bernie Little, Vanda Rios, and Kay Matsumoto burst into the newsroom, disheveled and excited. Bernie put down his camera equipment and called out to Pete that Vanda had been hurt. Kay was already running to the washroom for wet towels. Bernie's shirt was torn, and Kay's jeans were covered with wet mud.

Pete stared for a moment. "What happened?" he asked. Kay was running back with wet towels and bandages to apply to a cut on Vanda's forehead. The news crew left their stations and followed, asking unheard questions, gathering around Vanda.

"That jewelry store robbery?" Bernie asked, rubbing his head. "We followed the getaway car—Kay spotted it. They stopped in the Atterbury district, and a whole gang of guys was waiting for them with a van." He paused, watching Kay put Band-Aids on Vanda. The bleeding had stopped.

"Those bums," Kay said, peering at Vanda's eyes. "They saw our van, pulled me out into the gutter, hit Vanda with a club, and tried to wreck Bernie's camera. Maybe you should see a doctor, Vanda."

Vanda ignored the suggestion. "Yeah," she said. "Bernie started shooting pix the minute we got there, and if the kids hadn't heard sirens when they did, they'd have gotten the film. As it was, they scattered like rats and got away in the other van." She looked up. "They had guns. They could have killed us. It's a wonder they didn't use them."

The newsroom crew was trying to help, getting in the way and offering suggestions no one heard. Pete held up his hands. "Hey, quiet, you guys!" In the sudden silence, he picked up Bernie's camera. "It looks okay," he said. "You got pictures?"

Bernie half-shrugged. "I hope so. It all happened so fast, I'm not sure I had it focused or what the shutter speed was. I'll have to take it to the darkroom to find out."

Pete handed the camera back to Bernie and waved him off. "What about you, Vanda? You okay?"

Vanda nodded. "Got a peach of a headache, but I'm okay." She got up from the chair she'd stumbled into when she came in. "Better get some of this down." She headed for her work station, and the crew began to break up.

"Me, too," said Kay. "We'll work on this together."

Pete nodded. "If you hurry, we'll make this edition." He turned and called out to Bernie as he opened the darkroom door. "Let me know soon's you get them developed," he said.

Susan sat down at her work station, trying to put it together. Was this also part of everything she'd been working on? *Maybe in a way,* she mused. *Evil does breed evil.* She sat still, thinking. *Our folks taught us the difference between right and wrong; teachers at school used to reinforce what our parents taught us. They're not teaching anything like that anymore.* Her hands went to the keyboard, typed "Girl recovering" as her slug. Her mind continued analyzing. *Kids are taught "comparative truth," "shifting absolutes," "situation ethics," and none of the old-fashioned values. Lack of values can even lead to killing. Like this robbery. What for? To get money for drugs?* She shook her head. *Playa Linda used to be such a nice place to live. But now—everything's upside down.* A deep anxiety sat in the pit of her stomach.

Susan picked up her notes and wrote the lead for her interview with Karen. When she finished, she added the story about Lily Mae and sent them to makeup. She had named no names; just produced an objective description of events and stated the danger to young people. And now there was this gang stuff. There was definitely something evil going on.

Pete came out of the darkroom, headed for his office.

"Pete," she called, "did Bernie get any good pictures?"

"They're good action pictures," Pete said, "but I don't know if any of the faces show well enough for the police to make identifications. We're using a couple. Rest go to the cops."

"That'll be a great story," she said. He nodded, went on. She reached into her IN basket, picked up her blue pencil, and started editing stories for Tuesday's paper. Her articles about Karen and Lily Mae had just made the deadline.

5:14 P.M.

Elizabeth put down the phone. "Alan hasn't come home, either," she said. "Neither has Chuck, nor any of the others, from what Alice Baxter could find out. She called Ralph's mother and that's what Mrs. Knudsen said." She was as angry as worried.

Donovan stopped pacing and looked at his wife. "I don't know what we're going to do. We warned Raymond—he promised and promised—" He stood, deep in thought. "Since no one seems to know anything, we'll just have to call the police."

Elizabeth sighed. "That won't do much good. They haven't been gone long enough. What is it—they have to be gone more than twenty-four hours?"

Don grunted. "I think that's for adults, not kids." He looked out at the fading light. "It's getting dark out there. Didn't anyone have any idea of where they might have gone?"

Elizabeth shook her head.

"Well, we better call the police anyway. They might just accidentally spot one of the boys." He picked up the phone, dialed, waited, and when the officer on duty answered, gave names, descriptions, and phone numbers.

Putting down the phone, he went over to Elizabeth and put his arm around her. "There's one really important thing we can do, Liz. We can pray."

Elizabeth nodded. They fell to their knees, heads bowed, lost to the world in their worship and petition.

5:17 P.M.

Susan yawned and turned off her computer. Setting her desk to rights, she remembered the phone call in the middle of the night. A chill chased down her spine. *Well,* she thought, *I've really done it now. He warned me, but I did it anyway. Whatever happens, I guess it's on my own head.*

For a moment, she considered going to spend the next few days with her own family. *No,* she thought, *that would only drag them into trouble. What about Matt? He would gladly have me stay at his apartment.*

She grinned a little sardonically. *No way. Not for me. Home, Susan,* she decided.

She waved good night at the few who were left in the newsroom and left the building, studying the lot in all directions before she closed the door behind her. Nothing menacing in the sparsely occupied but brightly lit parking lot. She pulled her keys out of her purse, walked swiftly to her car, looked around quickly as she unlocked the door, got in, and locked it again. Suddenly she laughed. The paper wasn't even out yet!

She sighed with relief and started the engine, drove out, tooled along the boulevard, made her turn on Campion Avenue, turned again on Beach, drove the short distance to her apartment house. All was normal. She climbed her stairs, unlocked the door, left her purse and papers on a chair, and dropped onto the sofa with a deep sigh. Maybe now she could relax.

TWENTY

Monday, 5:50 P.M.

The phone rang just as Susan kicked off her shoes. She sighed and reached for the phone. Lacey sounded breathless, eager.

"Oh, Sue, I've got something really wild to tell you. Are you busy for dinner?"

She was tired. But obviously something was happening with Lacey. "No plans. Why don't you come here? I have one of Mom's casseroles in the freezer." She smothered a yawn.

"Great. See you soon, then, okay?"

"Right. 'Bye." Susan put down the phone, wondering. She had expected Lacey to still be depressed, not excited. She was, as usual, dependably unpredictable. She sighed and hauled herself up and into the kitchen.

Susan just finished setting the table when the doorbell rang. Lacey bounced in with a cheery "Hi! How'ya doin'?" Her cheeks glowed pink, her eyes sparkled. They made small talk while Susan, glancing often at Lacey, added the last of the seasonings to the salad and took the steaming casserole out of the microwave. Filling their plates, they headed for the dining nook by the window.

"All right, Lacey, what's going on?" Susan finally asked, tearing off a piece from her roll and putting a tiny bit of butter on it.

Lacey put down her fork. "Okay." She drew a breath. "Honest, I don't know whether to be excited or scared. John Merkel came over last night. He knows a trance channeller—"

Susan interrupted, nearly choking on a mouthful. "Whoa! Did you say trance channeller?" Her eyes were wide with astonishment.

Lacey looked at Susan in surprise. "Why, yes. An old friend of his from high school. Are you all right?" Susan nodded, coughing. Lacey went on. "You see, she bumped her head hard falling off a horse, and after awhile she began to hear voices—"

Susan touched her lips and put down her napkin. "Lacey, that's a medical problem. Something must be pressing on a part of her brain. She should see a doctor before—"

Lacey's veneer of delight vanished. She interrupted. "Do you want to hear about this or not?" she asked.

"Of course. Only—"

"Only don't interrupt," Lacey said sharply. "If you want to hear what I have to say, just let me talk." She drew a deep breath, settled herself, and began again, talking fast. "This trance channeller, her name is Cynthia Crawford, she has this control—you know, a disembodied spirit—called Nathaniel, and he can bring the spirits of those who have gone on to the next world to her, and they tell people things—like John's mother told him about a stock certificate in the false bottom of her desk drawer, and when he looked for it, there it was, and it was worth a lot of money." She looked at Susan in triumph, despite pain still visible deep in her eyes.

Susan stared at Lacey. "Do you really believe that?"

Lacey shrugged a shoulder. "Why should John lie?"

Susan looked dubious.

Lacey, irritated at Susan's skepticism, tried again, her enthusiasm rebuilding as she spoke. "Well, anyway, tomorrow evening, he'll pick up Dad and me to go see Cynthia, and maybe we'll get a chance to talk to Mom, or anyway her spirit. Oh, Susan, it's so wonderful! I can tell her how sorry I am about the way I treated her sometimes!" She leaned forward in her eagerness to draw Susan into her own excitement.

Susan's expression was solemn. She said the first thing that came to her mind. "Don't you remember what happened to King Saul when he went to the Witch of Endor to get her to call up the spirit of Samuel to get some advice from him? The very next day he and his sons were killed in a battle."

Lacey's eager warmth turned off as with the flick of a switch. She sat back. "I thought you'd be glad for me." Her voice was cold. "I didn't come here for a lecture. And I don't care what the Bible says. I don't believe in God anymore."

"Oh, Lacey—" Suddenly remorseful, Susan reached over to put her hand on Lacey's. She had come on too strong, too suddenly. "I'm sorry. This is a rough time for you. Don't be quick to make decisions or judgments—"

"But that's what you're doing!" Lacey snatched her hand away. "You're judging John and Cynthia—you don't even know them— and you're judging me!" She stopped, looked angrily at Susan. Her pain and rage at her mother's death surfaced like a volcano and burned at her as it spilled out. "I don't need your pious, hypocritical religion!" Her eyes sparkled with unshed tears. She stood up, her dinner untouched. "Your prayers didn't help my mother, Brother Justin didn't help her, Pastor Drane didn't help her, Dr. Damron didn't help her, so I'm going to see Cynthia Crawford and maybe get a chance to talk to her!" She picked up her purse. "If you're interested, I'll let you know what happens." She stalked out, leaving Susan gaping and bewildered.

"Of course I'm interested!" Susan called out as the door slammed behind Lacey. She looked at the food on her plate and pushed it away. She wasn't hungry anymore. She kicked at the leg of the table. *You really handled that well, didn't you!* she scolded herself. *Now Lacey's so turned off, maybe I can never reach her. My best friend—what can I do now to help her?* She picked up the dishes, set them on the counter, put the casserole and the leftover salad in the refrigerator, and sat down in the living room staring at the wall. *What in the world can I do about Lacey?* She picked up a cushion and threw it hard across the room. It knocked a candlestand off a small table.

No easy answers came. Not even any hard ones. She scowled.

7:40 P.M.

The Mage called Raymond was completely lost in his own fantasy world. He plowed through perilous passages and shadowy tunnels on his rough map. He killed dragons, monsters, shadowy half-human and inhuman enemies with swords, strokes of lightning, or hideous magic. With each victory he gained power, experience points, treasure, fame! He rolled the dice, only half aware of what came up, then rolled again and again for something he liked better.

"Hey," said Alan, rousing from his fog. "Watch it, Ray. That was stupid! You can't do that. You're dead! You fell into a trap and the Swamp Monster ate you! This isn't Chutes and Ladders, you know!"

"I don't care. I've got magic powers now nobody knows about. I got away from that Slime Monster! I'm gonna scorch all of you!"

"You airhead, that's stupid!" Alan shouted, his voice echoing strangely in his head. "You're dead!" He stood up suddenly and swung a wild punch. Raymond ducked and stood unsteadily to face Alan.

"Beetlebrain! You ready?" He swung, connected. Alan recovered, put his head down, and butted him in the stomach. The two fell on the table, spilling beer and empty cans, knocking down the screen, scattering joints, maps, scraps of paper, and dice all over the room. They rolled and wrestled until the old table top split, dropping them to the floor, knocking over the chairs, breaking the lantern, leaving them in darkness.

Chuck yelled, "Stop that!"

Eddie screamed, "You spoiled everything!"

Ralph, knocked down, dizzy, feeling sick, slid into a corner and put his head between his knees. A cut on the forehead was bleeding into Raymond's eyes. Alan pulled away, panting. Feeling muzzy, Raymond leaned back on his elbows.

"What happened?" he asked. His tongue felt thick.

"You wrecked everything," Eddie yelled. "Look at this place!" He pointed his flashlight at the destruction around them.

Ralph looked up at the windows. No daylight shone through the chinks. "Hey—guys—" he said in a scared little voice. "Look. It's dark outside."

Alan stood still, mouth slack, arms hanging limp. Dark. There was something about before dark, but he couldn't remember.

With an icy shock, a sobering flash of the reality of the situation flooded Raymond. A cold fury shook him. "We were gonna be outta here before dark!" He struggled to his feet and swung at Eddie. Eddie ducked under Raymond's arm, grabbed him from behind, held tight as Raymond flailed the darkness.

Chuck looked around, dismayed. "He's right, guys. It's dark. Hey, Alan, Ray, it's dark. You shoulda been home."

The stupefied boys looked at the darkness beyond the cracks in the boarded windows. Dread, anxiety, fear washed through them. Raymond stopped struggling. When Eddie let go, he slumped to the floor.

Eddie shook his head trying to clear it. "We gotta get outta here. The last bus goes by here at eight. What time is it?" he demanded. Nobody had any idea. "Come on, guys, we hafta go!" he said, panic in his voice. "Alan, help Ray up. Come on, Chuck, Ralph, we gotta go."

Staggering, they left the mess as it was and Eddie led them through the kitchen to the still-open cellar door. He shone his flashlight down the stairs. Chuck went first, then Ralph. Raymond started down, leaning on Alan. Raymond missed a step, fell, and like a bowling ball hitting pins, knocked Chuck and Ralph down. Alan fell on top of the others.

Eddie cursed, coming down fast. "Get up, you bleepin' dopes! Come on! We gotta get outta here!" He hauled them up, shoved them toward the cellar steps.

"What's the matter, Eddie?" asked Chuck, his voice thick. "How come you're in such a bleepin' hurry to get out? You said no one lives here."

"Are you totally crazy?" said Eddie, a frantic note in his voice. "My uncle and his friends come here for meetings three times a week! They'll be here at eight! We gotta be outta here before then. Now GO!" He shoved at Ralph.

Just then, the cellar door lifted.

Eddie cursed softly, fluently, turning off his flashlight. "They're here. We gotta find a place to hide." He scrambled but found nothing.

"There's someone here," a man's voice growled from the top of the stairs. "Y'hear it? Wait. I'll find out."

A bright light shone from the top of the steps. Big feet thumped down, and a shape above the light loomed in the lesser darkness at the opening. The boys shrank away from the light. Only Alan had found a barrel behind which to hide.

The shape stood in front of them, splashing the bright beam from one frightened face to another. Raymond thought his heart would burst. "Hey, Tony," the shape called, "ain't this your cousin?" shining the light on Eddie.

Another shape came partway down the steps and bent over to look. "Nah, that's my nephew Eddie."

Eddie's numbed fingers dropped his flashlight clattering to the floor. Tony came down all the way into the circle of light, his shadow towering over the boys. "How come you're still here, Eddie?"

No answer. Tony held his nephew's shoulder in a viselike grip. "I asked nice. Now, how come you're still here?"

"I dunno, Tony, we was playin' and it got dark and we didn't notice." Eddie's voice became a squeak as Tony put pressure on his grip and shook him.

"I tol' ya, if you ever come here, you be sure you get out before dark!" Tony backhanded the boy's face and turned. "Tell the High Priest to come down."

Eddie whimpered and put his hand up to his stinging cheek.

The shape moved up the stairs, lighting big feet as it went out of sight. The boys heard voices. The light came back. Descending in front of it was a silhouette in the tall black shape of a robe, a cowl over the head, spreading an aura of menace. The boys stood as if rooted to the spot, terrified, silent, pathetically vulnerable.

"Take them upstairs," the silhouette said in a hollow voice. Tony and the man with the big feet herded them up to the kitchen. Raymond was too frightened to do anything but obey. Eddie whined as Tony shoved him along. Chuck snuffled, scuffing his feet. Ralph stumbled on, silent, in front of the men who had followed down the stairs.

8:20 P.M.

Alan waited awhile after the kitchen door closed. Then, muscles stiff from holding still so long and sobered by shock, he crept from behind the barrel. *What am I going to do?* he wondered, trying to focus beyond his fear. I gotta get outta here. *But the guys—they're in big trouble—what about them? I gotta do something!* His skin prickled with terror.

He heard footsteps above, men's voices cursing the mess. A sharp slap, a thump, and Eddie cried, "Ow! Tony, quit it! Lemme alone!" Tony answered with a string of extraordinarily descriptive curses. Then, sounds of more slapping, thumping, Eddie crying, shuffling feet, men's voices cursing, complaining, scraping noises of chairs pushed around.

Alan hesitated. What should he do? *My folks will kill me*, he thought, *but these guys will really kill Ray and Chuck and Ralph and Eddie. I gotta help. But how?*

Moving as quietly as he could in the darkness, he headed for the cellar door. He stumbled over something and stopped, his heart pounding. He listened. Above, nothing changed. In a few minutes, he started again toward the stairs, groping forward. He touched a rail, felt for the step with his foot, found it, and feeling overhead with his hands, started up.

Quiet, now, he thought. *Don't squeak!* he ordered the hinge on the cellar door. He lifted slightly. Silence. He raised the door enough so he could squirm out and let it down silently. Crouching, he fled toward the street, grateful that the windows were boarded.

Oh gosh. The last bus goes by at eight—Tony's uncle and his gang were to be there at eight—the bus must have gone! There would be a bus on the boulevard, but that was almost a mile away. He'd better hurry.

He looked around and saw no one. In the darkness of Washington Avenue, weaving in fright, he half-ran, half-walked toward the boulevard.

Alan's thinking became clearer as the lighting got better and there was more traffic. Washington Avenue after dark was weird. More so with what had happened.

He saw the bus stop and started running. A huge hand landed on his shoulder in mid-stride. Struggling not to fall, he looked around to see brass buttons and a shiny badge on a big blue uniform. Above that, a solemn face stared at him.

"Here, now, son, what's the rush?" the officer said.

Alarmed, Alan stuttered. "I—I—ah—I gotta catch a bus!" He was suddenly aware of how he must look—dusty and disheveled.

The officer put a finger under Alan's chin, lifted his face and squinted at his eyes. "What're you on, kid?" he asked.

"Nothin'!" Alan looked down, squirmed, trying to get away from the officer's grasp.

The officer looked thoughtful. "You just hold still a minute," he said. "What's your name?"

Silence.

"I'll have to take you down to the station if you don't tell me." The officer's voice was mild.

Alan wilted. "Alan Baxter."

The officer raised an eyebrow. "Just a doggone minute, Alan." Without letting go the boy's shoulder, he pulled a notebook out of his pocket and flipped it open. "I thought so. We have an APB out on you and four other kids."

Alan closed his eyes and breathed a deep sigh. An incredible wave of relief went through him. He started talking fast, stumbling over words. The whole story came out in a rush.

TWENTY-ONE

Monday, 8:23 P.M.

Never had Raymond been so scared. The boys had been tossed into a heap in a corner where they still lay. Tony came for Eddie, picked him up by an arm and slapped him around. Profanities fractured the atmosphere as the men moved the broken table away, and, using flashlights for illumination, shoveled off the rest of the mess with skeletal brooms into a dark corner.

Two men carried in another table from somewhere else and placed it in the middle of the room. They laid a cloth on it and put down a flashlight to light up their task. They added two candelabra fitted with black candles, an incense burner, a small bell, cups and vials, some filled with strange-looking substances, and a curious black-handled dagger. Tony picked up the knife and another flashlight and walked over to Eddie. He leaned down, and pointing one by one to the arcane symbols etched into the curved blade, spoke slowly and clearly the terrible, eerie words they represented. He straightened, looked threats at his terrified nephew, and returned the knife to the table. With a warning glance over his shoulder at the boys, he followed Big Feet into another room, into which all but the high priest had disappeared.

At no time was Raymond able to see the face of the high priest, shadowed as it was within the deep cowl. Left alone beside the table, he lit the candles ceremoniously, crossed his arms in his wide sleeves, bent his head down, and muttered unintelligibly. One by one the other men came in. They turned off the flashlights and put them away.

As preparations concluded, malevolent silence shrouded the dimly lit room. Raymond wanted to scream, but his throat was paralyzed into silence. Ralph huddled half on top of him. Chuck was partly under him on the other side. Eddie, trembling all over, slid toward the floor from where he landed on top of Ralph when Tony finally discarded him.

All thirteen men of the coven now wore black robes. The high priest took the black-handled knife into his hand, caressing it. Muttering and chanting, he drew a large chalk circle on the floor around the table. The coven took their places around the circle and began a slow, silent march around the table. As they stopped, the high priest took his place at the center behind the table.

He set the knife down reverently, rang the bell, and intoned, "Hail, Satan!" The twelve answered "Hail, Satan!" Each took a black candle from some deep pocket in his robe, lit it from the candelabra, and resumed the slow march. As they walked, they chanted in strange assonances. The sounds made the hairs on Raymond's arms and at the back of his neck bristle as if in an electrostatic field.

Slowly, as the men walked around, they raised their flickering candles. As the flames rose, so did their voices. "Ave Lucifer excelsi!" they shouted and thrust their candles high above the middle of the table.

The candles smoked, and for a moment, Raymond imagined he saw a loathsome, mocking face in the vapors as they rose and mingled. He closed his eyes, feeling nauseated, detached, adrift. When he dared open them again, the only candles in sight were those in the candelabra, and the misty face was gone.

The members of the coven stood in the circle, nearly invisible except for the gleam of candlelight reflecting from their eyes. Raymond tried hard to concentrate on what was happening, but his mind kept slipping away from him. He had to reach out into unimaginable distance to grasp it again. He wanted to go home.

Tony stepped around to the front of the table and picked up the sacred knife, running his thumb lightly over the razor edges on both sides, almost caressing the curved needle tip.

"Our Father who art in Hell," he said in a quiet, sinister voice, "we bring to you for punishment one who has defiled your sanctuary, one who promised according to his satanic duty to reveal nothing of this place to the unworthy." His voice seemed to Raymond to come echoing through a huge pipe from a great distance, magnifying the menace.

He set the knife down and picked up an empty vial. From the circle came one of the other men. He picked up a cup. "The draught," he said, pouring thick red liquid into the vial.

The man who stood next to Tony stepped forward and picked up a vial filled with a clear liquid. "The facilitator," he said, pouring in a small amount, and returned to his place.

A fourth picked up another cup, poured an amber liquid into the vial, and said, "The completion." He took his place again.

Tony took a thin wand, stirred the fluids together, held the vial up, and spoke an intonation in the same strange syllables. Eddie screamed "No!" and shrank toward Ralph. Raymond imagined he could see in the dim light a vapor arising from the vial in Tony's hand. If he let himself think about it, it became a huge, menacing, living gargoyle. But maybe that was hallucination. He closed his eyes, and it went away.

The high priest raised a cross, spat on it, turned it upside down, and touched the vial with it. At this signal, the men resumed their walk around the table, chanting in the unimaginable language. Tony carried the vial aloft as they walked. He came to stand in front of Eddie, who cowered in terror against Ralph.

At the table, the high priest picked up the knife and directed that the center of the table be cleared. Tony, his face impassive, stared at Eddie.

"Tony, don't!" Eddie said in a small voice, terrified. He clutched at Ralph, who grabbed Raymond around his neck, nearly strangling him. "No-o-o-o! Don't!" Eddie shrieked, as Tony grabbed his arm and dragged him toward the table. Eddie, screaming, tried vainly to pull away.

Two men held Eddie as Tony forced open his mouth and poured some of the liquid from the vial into it. Eddie gagged, but Tony held his mouth and nose closed. He had to swallow. He gasped and sputtered. A thin line of red liquid ran from the corner of his mouth. Again Tony forced him to swallow, and again, until the potion was gone.

Eddie sagged, limp, a dazed look in his eyes. Tony laid Eddie on the table, pulled the front of his shirt up and pants partway down to expose his abdomen. Half-conscious but unable to move, the boy moaned piteously.

Raymond had gone beyond fright into absolute horror. They were going to kill Eddie right in front of him! What could he do? He dared try nothing. Even if he dared, he couldn't move. His head—what was the matter with his head? He couldn't think—he kept seeing demons in candle smoke.

The high priest held the knife over Eddie. "Lucifer, god of this world and the underworld, to your glory and in praise of your power, we hereby rebuke the desecration committed by this youngling. As a small sample of what might happen to him—" He turned to look straight at Raymond, Ralph, and Chuck, "—or any other younglings who would similarly desecrate our holy meeting place—" he looked back at the knife. "We follow your teaching."

Slowly he lifted the knife and slowly brought it down, its needle-sharp point lowering toward Eddie's bared abdomen. "Your malevolent Majesty," the priest intoned, "according to your instructions—"

Eddie tried to scream, but it came out a pathetic wail. Raymond stared in dread.

"—we now—"

A rending crash made every head turn toward the noise. The High Priest froze, the knife halfway to Eddie's skin, his mouth half-open with the next word unspoken.

The front door had slammed down flat. Suddenly, the room was filled to bursting with police officers in a half-crouch, pointing guns at the High Priest. Voices shouted, shades and shadows roiled, and Raymond, his heart pounding with panic and relief all at once, felt himself fade and sink into black unconsciousness.

Raymond came to slowly, realized he was outdoors, lying on dry grass. He tried to sit up, wobbled.

"Not yet, boy. Take it easy." An officer glanced impersonally at Raymond and looked around again at the scene.

Squad cars were parked so their headlights illuminated the house and the grounds. Lights flashed, splashing scarlet and blue on the boys, the prisoners, police, and curious bystanders. Radios in patrol cars spoke in their metallic voices. Police officers read rights, handcuffed and searched the black-robed figures, and led them off into patrol cars. The handcuffed High Priest was brought out, his cowl thrown back, exposing a pasty, undistinguished face topped by thin brown hair. He shouted curses and obscenities at the officers, promising a fiery doom to all who interfered with their religious ceremony. He suddenly became aware of the patrol cars, and his pasty face whitened to chalk.

"Hey, listen," he said, suddenly apprehensive. "All I was gonna do was take a small patch of skin off'n him. Like a postage stamp. That's all! I wouldn't hurt the kid, I swear!" Without ceremony an officer pushed him down and into the back seat. Raymond heard him still shouting protests as the car drove off toward the boulevard.

Eddie lay on the ground, unconscious. A paramedic checked his pulse, respiration, and pupil reaction. He glanced up, disgusted and compassionate, at the other paramedic. Chuck sat, obviously uncomfortable, a short distance away. Ralph came hesitantly toward Raymond. The officer standing by Raymond reached down to help him sit up. Ralph sat down nearby and put his head in his hands. Raymond looked at the young officer. "What will you do with us?" he asked.

"We've called your parents," the officer said. "They should be here soon." He seemed to Raymond to drift off like thistledown as he went to help take the coven members away.

Raymond looked at Ralph. "Where's Alan?"

"Dunno. Haven't seen him. I think he got away. Must've." He looked at Eddie, a thin, unmoving form, bracketed by paramedics. "What was that guy gonna do to Eddie?"

Raymond moistened his lips. "I dunno. I thought he was gonna kill him," he said. He tried to get up, thought better of it, and sat down again. He felt sick.

A car pulled up, and a man and woman rushed out. "Oh, Raymond! Thank God!" the woman called. "Thank God!" Anger replaced relief. "Just wait 'til we get you home. You've really done it this time!" Her voice tightened with determination.

Raymond looked around, saw his mother, tried to get up, but suddenly more ashamed than he could bear, started to crawl off. His father caught him by his waistband.

"Whoa," he said, put his arm around Raymond, pulled him back. "Not so fast!" He held him tightly by the shoulders and stared at him. "You smell like a brewery."

"Ray, you're really going to get it—" His mother was standing beside his father, her face white. Lights flashed all around, headlights and rotating colored lights stabbed into his eyes. Raymond's head seemed to explode.

Elizabeth Walker softened, looked at her husband. "I think he's just about had it," she said, as Raymond's eyes rolled up into his head, and he slumped against his father's chest.

"Phew. He smells awful," Don said.

She looked around at the police. "They have our name and phone number. I don't suppose they'll mind too much if we take him home. He can't tell them anything right now anyway."

Donovan picked Raymond up and slid the unconscious boy into

the back seat. He looked at Chuck and Ralph as he prepared to sit down in the driver's seat. "Your parents will be along soon to pick you up," he said. The boys nodded. The Walker car drove off.

Patrol cars were pulling away, sirens wailing, lights flashing. Paramedics took Eddie to a hospital. Soon only one patrol car was left. The two officers talked to Ralph and Chuck while they waited for the boys' parents to come pick them up.

Otto Knudsen arrived, apologized to the officers, took Ralph angrily by the collar, shoved him into the back seat. The Knudsen car burned rubber taking off.

One of the officers glanced at his watch, looked around, squatted down beside the other officer. "The kid's folks said they'd come pick him up, didn't they?" he asked softly. The other officer nodded. They both stood up to stretch and looked at Chuck sitting alone on the ground.

Ten more minutes went by, and one of the officers went to the patrol car. "I think we'd better take him to the station," he said, and opened the rear door. Chuck got up, stumbled to the patrol car, and sagged into the backseat.

The patrol car headed for the boulevard. The wounded old house was left alone, a gaping maw where the front door had been. All was finally quiet again on Washington Avenue. The rumble of traffic carried from the boulevard, a dog barked. Sounds of televisions drifted from several houses nearby, tuned to different channels. Headlights flashed as a car drove from the boulevard toward Cutler Way. A man and a woman walked by deep in conversation, her heels making sharp clicks on the pavement. Somewhere a baby started crying. A car drove past, stopped, turned in a driveway, came back, parked in front of the house. A thin woman in a faded T-shirt and jeans got out, looked around.

"There's nobody here," she said into the car. "They musta taken him to the police station." She got back in, and the car drove away.

TWENTY-TWO

Tuesday, October 29, 8:15 A.M.

Susan's expression was grim as she drove toward the *Register* Tuesday morning. Her father had phoned and told her about Raymond's escapade. Helpless to do anything about it, she forced a different train of thought.

Passing St. John's Center, one of Playa Linda's Christian shelters for the homeless, she glanced at the long line of people queued up for a hot breakfast. Nothing new; it happened every morning. As she slowed down for pedestrian traffic, one of the men crossing the street caught Susan's attention. Something familiar about his build, his carriage, his walk, nagged at the back of her mind. She stopped at the curb and looked curiously toward him as he took his place at the end of the line.

The man noticed her, turned his head slightly and pulled up his collar to hide as much of his face as possible. Several more people, including women and children, now stood behind him. He kept glancing toward her car as the line moved slowly toward the door, nervously turning to face the wall.

Suddenly he broke from the line. As he walked rapidly away, she recognized him. A fierce anger flamed through her. She flung open her car door, cried "Mr. Yadush!" and ran toward him.

The man hesitated and broke into a run. Susan sprinted and caught him by the arm. "Brother Justin! I want to talk to you!"

The man turned and looked at Susan. The dapper Brother Justin of the faith-healing clinic was gone. Isham Yadush wore a three-days' growth of dark whiskers, and his eyes had the haunted look of a fugitive. He stood as if coiled, ready to flee, glanced toward the line, and wilted. "You know who I am, then."

Susan did not acknowledge his statement. "I think you should know Mrs. Robinson died." Her voice accused.

Yadush closed his eyes and nodded. "I knew she would," he said finally, and drew a ragged breath. "I could feel it," he said. "The tumor, I mean. I was almost certain nothing could be done to help her." He looked away. "I know I should have told Mr. Robinson, but—" he turned to Susan with pain in his eyes. "I needed the money so badly. And she needed hope. But there was none." His brown eyes held defeat, infinite sadness.

Susan was confused. She stared at him. "I don't understand. You knew she would die? How?"

"I was a doctor once. I had a case much like hers years ago." He looked into her eyes, pleading for understanding. "Seeing her brought back painful memories I thought I had buried."

Her anger moderated, remembering what Andy had learned about him. Suddenly she was scarcely aware of people pushing to get into the line for food. There was more here than a case of faith-healing or practicing medicine without a license. What was the rest of the story? More important, was he telling the truth? Or was he a consummate actor, a con man? Could she trust him? Gazing at him intently, trying to see through him, she decided to risk it.

"Mr. Yadush," she said, "come with me. I'll get you breakfast. Maybe we'll try to help you, on one condition."

Yadush's expression was a mix of alarm, panic, and a touch of hope. "And that is?"

"I know quite a bit about you. So do a couple of friends of mine. Something evil is going on in Playa Linda. Maybe we can do something to get rid of it. If you will tell us what you know, we'll tell you what we know. And if you help us, maybe we can help you. I can't promise anything, though. Depends."

Yadush looked startled, distrustful, about to break away. He stopped, thought, slumped. "I should have known I'd never get away." He sighed. "What do you want me to do?"

Susan led him to her car. They drove in silence to the Computer Warehouse. "My friend owns this place," Susan said. "Come in with me."

Yadush followed.

Invoice in hand, Matt was checking new programs that had arrived that morning. Ricky was already putting those checked off on the shelves. Matt turned when Susan opened the door.

"Matt," she said, "I'd like you to meet Isham Yadush, aka Brother Justin. Mr. Yadush, my friend Matt."

Matt whistled through his teeth and stared. Yadush, nervous, gazed at Matt. "Well," Matt said. "I've been hearing about you." He became aware of Ricky standing beside him. "Oh, and this is Ricky Martinez, friend and assistant."

"A great pleasure." Yadush started to offer his hand, then pulled it back, fearing rejection.

"I promised him breakfast," said Susan. "I thought maybe we could go to Dennison's, the cafeteria over on Main Street?"

Matt nodded vaguely, still staring at Yadush.

"I also promised that if he'd tell us what he knew, we'd try to help him."

Matt turned to Susan as if suddenly coming to. "You did what?"

Susan's lips parted. "Well, it's a long story, Matt. Let's talk about it over breakfast for him. And coffee for us, okay?"

Matt looked at her as if she had purple hair and green spots. "That's crazy! The police are looking for him!"

"I know. But I think we should talk to him. He knows things we should know. Remember the lists?" Yadush's eyes widened.

Matt looked at Ricky. Ricky shrugged his shoulders, spread his hands, and went back to putting programs on the shelves. "You're serious." Matt looked back at Susan in disbelief.

She nodded. "Matt, this can be a real breakthrough! Come on, let's talk to him, and after we've heard him out, we can decide what we should do." Her eyes pleaded.

Matt stood and stared at her, at war with himself. "But—but—" he paced, came back to face Susan, shaking an index finger at her. "But what if he—or if he's—well, I just—" He stopped. "What are you getting me into? I won't promise a thing!" He stared angrily at Yadush. "Listen, you, you've got to understand one thing. If we do this, you've got to come clean. Absolutely clean! Understand? You tell us everything! I don't care how it makes you look." He glared at Yadush. Intimidated, Yadush nodded.

Matt reddened, embarrassed. "Sorry. I don't usually get so worked up." His eyebrows angled upward. "I mean, all I want, really, is that you tell us the truth."

Susan grinned.

Yadush exhaled, then nodded. "The truth."

"Honest. That's all we want." Matt turned to Ricky, who waved them off before he could say a word.

Dennison's was a cafeteria where, for a set price, you could eat as much as you wanted. Matt paid at the entrance for one breakfast and three coffees. Yadush glanced at Matt, then piled eggs, pancakes, bacon, sausages, hash browns, fruit, muffins, and preserves high on his plate, and picked up a mug of coffee. As Susan and Matt set their mugs on the table, Yadush looked at his mountain of food and at them. "I'm a doctor. I know this stuff can kill me. But I'm very hungry, and I thank you from the depths of my stomach." He studied Susan and Matt for a long moment. He was hesitant at first, then a look of trust, and of peace, came into his eyes. He picked up his fork and dug into the hash browns. As he ate, he told his story.

"To begin with," he said around a mouthful, "in England, I had a terrible accident in which I almost lost a leg." He described painful treatments, which, although leading to recovery of function, registered high on a scale ranging from painful to unbearable.

He studied the coffee in his cup as he spoke. "They gave me Demerol for the pain, which lasted a long time. It still bothers me. Drugs were easy for me to get, so after my therapist took me off Demerol, I, ah, I wrote fake prescriptions. Never got caught, but I got hooked." After a pause, he swallowed some coffee.

During that period, a young duchess, cousin of the queen, came to him with long-neglected abdominal pains. "We scheduled surgery," he said. "The tumor was large, and I was nervous. She belonged to the nobility, after all. Demerol usually calmed me." He shrugged. "The tumor had grown almost completely around a blood vessel, constricting it. I was—the knife slipped just a micrometer—" He looked down at his hands and said with a catch in his voice, "We couldn't stop the bleeding—"

He stared into his coffee cup for a long moment. Matt and Susan could almost feel the shame of the scandal and the public outcry.

Yadush inhaled deeply and went on. "After the Royal British Medical Society fined me of all I owned and revoked my license, I took whatever work was available. It wasn't easy. Not all the jobs were, well, decent. But it was a matter of survival. And there was nothing else at the time. Besides, I was used to living pretty well." He paused.

"One of my better jobs was driving a taxi." The haunted look on his face faded. "At least it was honest. Mostly. Then, once when I was driving a taxi from Heathrow to a London hotel, I overheard the conversation between my passengers. A messenger they had hired had disappeared on assignment to deliver a package to New York, and they were arguing over whom they could find to replace him."

He looked from Susan to Matt. "I'm a gentleman, after all," he said defiantly. "I was perfectly familiar with the rules, you know, but I just had to break in. I brought the cab to the curb half a mile away from the hotel. One just doesn't do that kind of thing," he said. "I begged pardon for listening to their conversation and offered to be their courier."

The passengers stopped ranting at him when he told them he would do anything they wanted. "They looked at each other as if they had found a rat to sneak into a bedroom," Yadush said, his voice bitter. "I should have known right then that I was making another mistake, but I was desperate to get out of the country, never mind anything else. I needed a fresh start someplace where I was not considered a pariah."

After probing mercilessly into his background, they struck a bargain. On the following Wednesday Yadush would board a commercial flight to New York to deliver a package. He asked about papers. One of his passengers smiled smugly and assured him there would be no problem getting a passport and visa in such a short time.

He interrupted his story to get another cup of coffee. "That's how it began," he said as he sat down, putting preserves on a muffin. "They were satisfied with the way I handled the delivery and offered me steady work. I carried parcels, briefcases, suitcases all over the world. They never told me what was in them, and I didn't ask. I convinced myself it had to do with honest business practices, but—" He shook his head. "I guess down deep I really knew the whole thing was illegal."

He continued, his voice flat. His last trip was a total disaster. In Chicago to deliver a briefcase to a certain room in a nearby hotel, he paid off the taxi several blocks away from the hotel, a normal precaution. He suspected later that someone had informed rivals about the contents of the case. As he walked toward the hotel past an alley, three men suddenly attacked him, bashed him over the head. He came to in the alley on a heap of rubbish near the back door of a retail clothing store, the briefcase nowhere in sight. Staggering out to the street, he felt in his pockets, found his wallet intact, hailed a taxi and went to a small apartment he maintained in Chicago.

There, he swallowed aspirin, *never Demerol again!* drew a bath, and soaked away some of the ache. When the expected pounding at the door started, he pulled a robe around him and opened the door about an inch. His employers shoved the door inward, knocking him down. They were livid. Two million dollars had been in the case, and they held Yadush responsible.

Yadush sighed, leaned back, and sipped his coffee. "It might just as well have been two billion. I had only a few thousand. After they knocked me around awhile, they suggested a way I could repay them. It went against everything I had ever believed. But the alternative was—" He stopped, shivering.

In fear for his life, he became what he hated: a drug pusher, keeping just enough of the profit to pay his own expenses. The bulk would go to his employers against his two million dollar debt.

"Why didn't you go to the police?" Matt asked.

Yadush shrugged. "All my papers were forged. Even my fake visa had expired, and charges were pending in Britain. I couldn't take a chance."

When drug sales slowed down or DEA agents got too close, his employers would move him to another area, then another, and finally to Playa Linda.

"All this time," he said, "I had burned with a deep hunger to be a doctor again, but that was, of course, impossible. So, in addition to distributing drugs, I became Brother Justin. I studied the town, found a spot where people couldn't afford decent medical care." He set up shop near the Atterbury district, where the poor, desperate, and unschooled would come to a healer. "I managed to help many of them," he said, a note of pride creeping into his voice. "I sent those who had real, curable diseases to licensed physicians. I gave them a little money to pay for some treatment. But the majority were mostly just poor, tired out, stressed, lonely, eaten with despair. I was able to help many of them psychologically or with plain, old-fashioned encouragement and advice. Some just needed education in sanitation, nutrition, that sort of thing."

He sipped coffee. "A large percentage of them responded best to mumbo-jumbo of various kinds. These people came out of societies where such practices are the norm." He looked curiously at Matt. "It's interesting. Quite a few people with lots of money came to me when they heard I sometimes did voodoo, magic, and psychic surgery. I'd studied them in connection with the psychology behind them, you see." He paused. "Some of them weren't even sick. I guess they just wanted a taste of something different from their everyday lives. Maybe they were bored, and what I did excited them." Matt and Susan exchanged glances.

Yadush drew a deep breath. "But then, the lovely Amelia, Mrs. Robinson, came in." He was silent a moment. "I felt it, you know," he said, looking up at Susan and Matt. "The size and location of the tumor, that is, and I knew it was all but inoperable. It felt just like the one in England. I think no one could have saved her. So I did what I could." He inhaled, exhaled. "I playacted removing the tumor to give her hope for a short time." He appealed to Susan. "She was happy for awhile, wasn't she?"

Susan nodded. She put both hands around her coffee cup and swirled the cooling dark brown liquid.

"You know the rest. Robinson went to the authorities. I ran. And here I am, with the police and my employers hunting for me." He sat staring at his empty plate. "I had very little cash on hand and didn't dare use plastic or go to the bank." He looked at Susan. "The very first time I went for charity, you recognized me."

Susan became aware of the cafeteria sounds: voices chattering, blending, intertwining, dishes and silverware clattering, chairs scraping against the floor, the shuffling of feet. The aromas of food surrounded them, clung to them. Two overweight men in greasy overalls slid past them to a nearby table, muttering roughly at each other, carrying heavily loaded plates.

Matt cleared his throat. "That's quite a story."

"Every word is true. I will swear to it."

After a brief silence, Matt leaned on his elbows. "Tell me. What do you know about the Viking Castle?"

Startled, Yadush stared wide-eyed. "You know about that, too?" He inhaled. His face became blank.

"There's more to your story, isn't there?" said Susan. "Maybe we believe what you've told us so far. But what about the rest?"

Yadush looked down tight-lipped, staring at the floor tiles. Matt pushed his chair back and stood. "Okay. That's it. Come on, Susan."

Yadush looked up, alarmed. "Wait! I'll tell," he said, agony in his eyes. He looked down again. "I needed the money."

Matt scowled. "You promised the truth, remember?"

Yadush nodded. "I know." He looked up at Matt. "It's just that I'm ashamed." Matt lowered himself slowly into the chair.

Yadush slumped. "To pay back two million dollars—that isn't easy! I had already paid back a little over a million." He sat silent, as if pondering. He fished in a pocket. "Here." He handed Matt a card. "One of my employers became impatient, so he told me about this." His face twisted in disgust. "My job would be to find young people and recruit them for this organization—this Pagan Order of the Black Sword of Belial. For this, they would triple my pay. I could pay my debt that much sooner."

Matt nodded. "Drugs to witchcraft and satanism." He looked with repugnance at the black design on the red card: an ornately carved sword, hilt like the face of a demon, bordered with arcane symbols. "The Pagan Order of the Black Sword of Belial" was printed across the card in an ornate script. Runes stated an indecipherable motto underneath. He flipped it back to Yadush.

"I am deeply ashamed," Yadush said, pocketing the card. "The castle is headquarters for this devilish outfit, and they hired me to work with the architect. I had a bit of training in that, too." He looked at Matt. "Recruiting kids for this goes against everything I have ever believed." He spread his hands in helplessness. "But what else could I do? These people kill."

"We know," said Susan.

"If they find me now, they'll kill me. If you go to the police, they'll imprison me, and there, someone planted by my employers will kill me. Or the police would send me back to Britain, where they'd make sure I'd never see anything but the inside of a tiny cell in Old Bailey. The moldy old prison, you know."

Matt and Susan exchanged glances. Susan raised her eyebrows. Matt looked troubled and shook his head slightly. Susan went ahead anyway.

"We just might have an idea," said Susan. Matt, startled, opened his mouth, put out his hand to stop her. She looked sharply at him and continued. "You see, we need information," she said to Yadush. "You know more than you've told, right?"

Yadush, startled, nodded slowly.

Matt's nostrils flared as he inhaled. "We'd be harboring a fugitive," he said to Susan. "That would make us guilty of a felony. We can't do that!"

Susan stared at him, seeking some alternative. She could see none. "What else can we do? How else do we get in? Who else do we know?" She turned to Yadush, ignoring Matt's objections. "If we do this, and if we get the ones who are doing all this mucking around in our town, will you turn yourself over to the DEA? We'd testify in your behalf, wouldn't we, Matt?" she asked, looking into his eyes.

"Honey, there are so many things that could go wrong!" Matt said. He sighed, looked at Yadush. "You'd have to cooperate without question."

Yadush nodded, a spark of hope in his gloom-darkened eyes.

"We'd have to keep you under wraps, you understand," Matt continued. "We'd milk you for every bit of information you have, and some you don't think you do. But if you could help stop the horrible things going on in Playa Linda—" He paused, turned to Susan with one last plea. "We really ought to go to the police!" he burst out, and suddenly remembered the district attorney was on the list. "Oh, blast it, no." He sighed, finally resigned. He turned to Yadush. "Will you do it?"

"Yes! Most certainly! I might even be able to redeem myself. Cleanse myself. Live like a human again. Yes, I'll do whatever you say." Hope finally danced golden in his dark eyes. His smile was a dazzle of joy.

On impulse, Susan reached across the table and put her hand over Yadush's. Matt stared, incredulous for a moment, sighed, put his on top of Susan's. "I guess we have a pact," Matt said. "First off, we have to stash you somewhere. We'll take it from there, one thing at a time."

They stood up. Yadush put one hand on Matt's shoulder, the other on Susan's. "I can't thank you enough for listening, even if I don't get out of this." Matt was still skeptical. Was this guy real? Could someone make up a story like his?

Outside, they got in Matt's car. Susan sat quietly, thinking how wrong one can be about another person. *Judge not, that you be not judged*, her Master had said. She bowed her head to silently ask forgiveness for her hasty, faulty discernment about Yadush. How can anyone know what's going on inside someone else's head or what burdens they must carry?

TWENTY-THREE

Tuesday, 11:15 A.M.

Matt left Susan at her car outside the Warehouse and took Yadush away to "stash him somewhere." Susan sped to the *Register*, parked, and hurried in.

Heads turned with greetings and good-natured questions as she walked to her work station. "Some rookie!" John Beloit, senior sports reporter, called out. "What a time to get in. When I started out in this business thirty years ago—" A voice in the back of the room interrupted him, "We had to come in early to sharpen the quill pens we used!"

The laughter quieted down. Blushing, smiling, Susan riffled through the papers in her nearly full IN basket to find something interesting to typeset. Yadush was not for publication yet. Just as she selected one, her phone rang.

"Susan? Susan Walker?" The girl's voice was hesitant. "This is Karen Garcia."

Karen's voice was tight. "Karen? Are you all right?" Susan asked. A man's voice, muffled in the background, growled something unintelligible.

"Susan, I'm in tr—" she squealed as if in pain. "Uh—I need help. Will you help me? Please?" Her voice shook.

Susan felt a prickling at the back of her neck. "What's the matter, Karen? What can I do?"

"Come to—ah—do you know the warehouse on Pacific Coast Highway at Main?"

Alarm crawled coldly up Susan's spine. She was familiar with the empty building with the "Condemned. Unsafe. Do Not Enter." sign on the wide front door. Not the best possible environment. "Yes, I know it."

"The door in the middle of the north side is open. Please, come get me and bring—Owwww!" She yelped as if someone had prodded her. "Uh—you *gotta* come alone!" Karen's voice broke off in an aborted cry and so did the connection.

Susan, shocked, stood holding the phone. Images of what might be happening raced through her head. She replaced the handset, thinking fast. This was an obvious trap, probably set by the same person who phoned her in the middle of the night. "Oh, my write-up!" she moaned. "Karen needs help because of my write-up!" Many in the newsroom were looking curiously at her.

Karen said she had to come alone. Emphasis on "gotta." Karen could not have sounded more scared if someone were holding a gun to her head. If Karen's abductors saw someone besides her, they might just shoot Karen, and Susan could never forgive herself. She looked at the items in her IN basket. What could she tell Jackson? That she had a hot tip and had to run with it?

She dialed the Warehouse and told Matt what happened to Karen.

"No! You can't! You absolutely can't go alone!" he almost shouted. "I'm coming with you."

"No, Matt. They were already beating up on her. I'm afraid they'll kill her if they see anyone with me. It's my fault they got to her." She paused, went on as if musing. "But if you just accidentally happened to be going by there and just happened to stop somewhere along the street to watch the world go by, who'd know the difference?" By now nearly everyone was staring. She waved off all the questions coming at her.

She could visualize Matt, mentally thrashing around for a better idea. "Well, all right," he said finally. "Get going. I'll be there soon as I can. Don't worry, I won't be in sight. And I'll call Andy. Just be careful!"

Matt hung up the phone, his brow furrowed. Ricky was standing by, listening. Matt picked up the phone again.

Ricky asked. "Can I do anything from here?"

"Pray!" Matt dialed Andy's number. When he answered, Matt repeated what Susan had told him.

Andy said "Gotcha!" and put down the phone. He was out the door in less than two minutes. Just as Matt was driving out, he pulled up in front of the Warehouse.

"Hey, Matt!" he yelled. Matt looked around and waved at Andy to follow. They sped to the Coast Highway, then turned toward the old warehouse. Approaching Main Street, they slowed down, studying the decaying building across the street. Matt parked a block short of the building. Andy went on another two blocks, parked, walked back, and slipped in beside Matt, closing the door quietly. The morning fog had become a heavy overcast.

Matt indicated the parking area beside the building. "There's Susan's car," he said, his face grim.

"Wonder how long she's been in there?"

"Can't say." He looked pained. "I should have been keeping a closer watch on her. Especially after this morning."

"What happened?"

Matt told about breakfast with Yadush.

Andy stared in silence, absorbing it all. "But what more could you have done? I think you did the right thing. Or do you think this has something to do with what's-his-name, Yadush?"

Matt shook his head. "More likely her story in the paper." His expression was hard with his teeth clenched and his eyes like agates. He grunted. "Lord, how long?" Looked at his watch. 12:10 P.M. "I'm not going to wait any longer." He reached for the ignition.

"Wait!" Andy put his hand on Matt's arm to stop him. "Look."

A car was backing out of the north driveway. Matt made out two men in the front seat, a girl sitting up in the back, and another head leaning on the girl's shoulder. The car turned south in their direction. Matt and Andy scrunched down out of sight. When they were sure it had gone a couple of blocks, they sat up to look. The car turned left on the county road connecting the Coast Highway to I-15.

Burning rubber as he skidded around in a U-turn, Matt followed. Andy, clinging to the door for support, called out, "Hey! Not so fast! They'll spot us!" He clutched at the dashboard as Matt made the left turn. His eyes widened. "Matt, I'll bet I know where they're going."

Matt kept his eyes on the car ahead. "Where?"

"The Viking Castle!"

Matt glanced at Andy and his face lit up. "Gotta be. Listen, I'll let you off. You phone Susan's folks, and the paper, and—Oh, sorry. Your car is way back."

"That's okay. I'll catch a cab and pick it up. I'll make some calls and get more help. You get a look at what we're up against, and when you get back, call me at home, okay?"

Matt nodded, pulled over where he could see well ahead, let Andy out, and was on his way again almost before Andy had both feet on the curb.

Andy sprinted for the public phone on the corner and called the paper. Alison listened, promising to tell Jackson. Andy picked up the phone book, found the Walkers' number, dialed, and left a message on the answering machine.

He looked up another number in the ragged phone book, wondering what he was going to say. How do you tell a stranger his daughter has been kidnapped? He punched in the number. A voice said "The Lamb's Bookstore, Don Walker."

Andy identified himself, told what had happened, and waited for response. It was awhile before Donovan cleared his throat.

"Susan was afraid that article would—" He seemed to be thinking out loud. "Thank you for calling me. You're Matt's friend? Andy? Right?"

"Yeah."

"I've got an idea—"

1:05 P.M.

Matt had followed the car at a distance great enough that twice he thought he had lost them. The road wound past meadows, harvested vegetable fields, through avocado and citrus groves, past a small city and back into brush-covered, deeply folded live oak and eucalyptus studded hills and canyons. Just as he was easing around a bend, he saw the car turn in at the end of a long hedge. "Whoa!" he muttered, stopped, backed up, and pulled off the road close to the bushes, out of sight. He got out, and, keeping close to the tall hedge growing right up to meet the stone wall curving around to the gate, walked to the end where he could study the entrance unseen.

A push button beside a speaker in the wall suggested that the ornate wrought-iron gate was operated from the castle. No access. He parted the branches to look behind them. A six-foot chain-link fence backed the hedge. At the top, he saw barbed wire and insulators at intervals. Electrified. He walked back to the other end of the hedge. The fence continued at a right angle up the hill.

He went back to his car and sat down behind the wheel to think. The girl sitting up in the back of the car had hair darker than Susan's. Must've been Karen. In that case, the head lolling on her shoulder had to be Susan's, and it looked as if she were unconscious. He gritted his teeth. *If they've harmed her in any way—I'll—*For the only time in his life, he wished that, like an Old Testament prophet, he could call down fire upon them.

But wishing didn't help. What he had to do now was find a way to get in there and get Susan and Karen out. How? He stared straight ahead, trying to think of some way to get past the electrified fence. And assuming he could, once in there, what could he do? He admitted it. Alone, nothing. He needed to talk to Andy and Mr. Walker and the others.

Just as he reached to start his engine, another car came up behind him and stopped. This was enemy territory. His stomach turned to ice. He did not recognize the burly man who came walking toward him.

"Hi," the man said, bending down to look in the window. "You must be Matt Reiley. I'm Buck Soderberg, a friend of the Walkers'. Don said you'd probably be here." He thrust a hand at Matt.

Matt let out his breath in a soft sigh and took Buck's hand. "You spooked me!" he said, feeling weak. "I had no idea who you were. You could have been one of the guys who snatched the girls."

Buck chuckled and looked around. "Looks like a fortress. Did you go around to the back?"

Matt shook his head. "Guess we'd better do that, now that you're here." He grinned. "Well, don't just stand there. Let's go explore."

2:05 P.M.

Andy sat in his Jeep, wondering where to go to make the rest of his calls. There were comfortable sit-down public phone booths in the lobby at the Hilton, much closer than his apartment. And safer, in case his apartment was bugged, which he doubted. He turned the Jeep around and headed for the hotel.

Settled in a booth, he opened his notebook and began. The first call was to Gordon Booth, a close friend, an electrician who worked at a security alarm systems company. He told Gordon what he needed.

"Hey, stuff like that is confidential, you know!" Gordon was resolute.

Andy explained what was going on. Gordon hesitated only a moment, then agreed to meet him right after work. "I'll have some drawings for you," he volunteered.

Vern Hunemiller, a volunteer fireman, was next. Andy convinced him of the necessity, and Vern promised to do whatever was possible.

Andy sat a moment, thinking. Laura Neubauer had performed with the "Glory of Christmas" at the Crystal Cathedral. He called and told her what had happened. "Just in case we can get in there to get the girls out, here's what I'd like you to do—" He described a possibility. "It may not come to that."

"Oh, good heavens," she said. "What's the world coming to?"

"You're the only person I know who can do it," Andy said.

"Well, I don't know. It's been some time, but I guess I can manage. Just in case, I'll call some old friends to help."

Andy called all the prayer chains of which he was aware, and finally a Roman Catholic priest. No police. Didn't dare. Not after what he'd seen in the list he broke into a week ago.

He turned to leave and looked at his watch. 2:25. Time for a sandwich and coffee, he decided. He slid the phone booth door open and walked into the hotel coffee shop.

2:30 P.M.

Most of the twenty people Donovan called had come to the church. "I won't waste time," he said. "Susan and Karen Garcia have been kidnapped. We think we know where they are. The place seems to be a fortress, and we'll need all the help we can get to break in. Those of you who can't take part are free to leave now, with no bad feelings. We'll understand."

Several people stood up, and making various excuses, left. A dozen or so stayed.

Don outlined the problem and a possible solution. "We need to separate into, well, I guess you'd call them task forces." He asked for volunteers for the various groups. People looked at each other, grim with concern, but hands went up at each call, and small teams formed.

When they were loosely organized, Don told them the most important thing they could do would be to pray. "We'll be dealing with 'the rulers of the darkness of this age, against spiritual hosts of wickedness in the heavenly places.' Dorothy Webb has organized a prayer vigil, so you'll have help. We'll get together later to tie down a specific plan."

Heads nodded with thoughtful expressions, and the groups left. Don and Pastor Wayman found a table, spread out sheets of paper, and began working out the plan of action. They bent over the papers, and the plan of attack began to take shape.

3:20 P.M.

Andy drove into his parking space, locked the Jeep, and loped up the stairs to his door, two at a time. Coming into the spartanly furnished, book-and-paper-stacked rooms, he heard the phone ringing.

Matt's voice was hurried. "Listen. I'm going to the Walkers' to talk to Don. Do me a favor. Go to the Bedside Manor and get Yadush to draw a layout of the Castle."

Andy scrawled Yadush's room number and the address of the motel on a pad, set the phone back on its cradle, raced down the stairs, and hopped into the Jeep.

At the motel, he knocked on Yadush's door. Finally, he heard a small rustle. "Who is it?" The voice was muffled.

"Andy Bergstrom. I'm a friend of Matt Reiley and Susan Walker."

"What do you want?"

"Susan's in trouble. Let me in, and I'll tell you about it."

The door opened on a chain, and a dark eye peered out. "How do I know you're telling me the truth?"

"Matt told me Susan picked you up near St. John's Center, and they bought you breakfast at Dennison's."

The door closed, the chain rattled, and the door opened all the way. "Come in."

Andy stepped in, and Yadush invited him to sit down in the only armchair. Yadush sat in the chair at the small desk. The dusky room was no larger than necessary, done in practical brown tones.

Yadush leaned back, appearing professional in spite of the situation. "How can I help?" he asked.

"You can draw a layout of the Viking Castle," Andy said. "Matt said you'd helped renovate it. Susan and a high school girl have been kidnapped. We think that's where they're being held."

Yadush's eyes widened.

"And you want to get them out of there." He twisted his interlaced fingers. "You have no idea of what you're getting into."

"Doesn't really matter. We've got to get them out. Anything you can tell me might help. Even if you don't think it would. I need to know everything you know, and everything you know that you don't think you know."

Yadush looked curiously at Andy. "I like the way your mind works, young man. You sound just like your friend Matt." He turned to open the desk drawer and took out a couple of sheets of paper. "All right. I don't know how much I can help, but I'll try." He laid the papers down on the desk and started to draw a meticulous plan of the interior of the castle, describing minutely the details as he sketched.

TWENTY-FOUR

Tuesday, 2:35 P.M.

Karen faced the black-robed High Priest in silence. Guards dressed in jeans and dingy flannel shirts had brought her down a bleak, door-studded hallway, then up in an elevator. The huge, dimly lit meeting hall was draped in gloomy fabrics, leaving a vault of unfinished emptiness in the middle. There was a circular dullness in the center of the parquet floor.

The priest fixed a stony gaze on her and reminded her of the penalty for disobeying coven regulations. "You saw what happened to one who did," he said. Two other black-robed priests were standing solemnly just behind him.

"You're not my High Priest," she said, lifting her chin in defiance. "I never saw you before."

He laughed, an unpleasant sound. "Young lady, I am everyone's High Priest! The man you think of as your high priest is only one of my subordinates. Almost all the covens in the county belong to my Order."

Karen stared. "There are other covens?"

"Several. But we're talking about you. I'm about to decide what to do with you." He turned to confer with the other two priests, occasionally glancing over his shoulder to look at her.

His eyes frightened Karen, reminding her of a snake about to strike. She tightened her lips to keep them from trembling and made fists to keep her hands from shaking.

The High Priest nodded, then turned back to face her.

"We've decided to give you one more chance. On one condition." He paused, and Karen felt like a mouse facing a hungry hawk. She stared back, insolent on the surface, scared inside.

"You're a feisty one, aren't you," he said. "That's good. You'll need spirit for your assignment. Because you're going to enlist Susan Walker into your coven. And you know the penalty for failure."

Karen's jaw dropped in disbelief. With a look of withering scorn, he turned to leave. Two guards bracketed her and took her back to the room to which they had brought her and Susan.

Susan stopped pacing when she heard the key rasp in the lock. Karen was pushed, stumbling, into the room, and the door slammed behind her. She turned and glared at the closed door. Susan had both hands at her head, rubbing her temples.

"They made me do it," Karen sputtered, turning to face Susan. "I didn't want to call you, but they made me!" She took a deep breath. "Oh, I'm glad to see you up. You were still out cold when the guards came for me. Are you feeling all right?"

Susan moaned. "No! What did they do to give me such a headache?"

"Some sort of knockout drug. Shot you in the arm when you grabbed me and tried to get away. You went out like a light. It's my fault! I'm sorry!" Tears welled in her dark eyes.

"Not your fault. Mine. They warned me, told me not to write any more articles." She looked around. "Where are we, anyway?"

Karen shook her head. "Dunno. Inland someplace. We came through fields and groves and a town and more stuff and up in the hills. When we got here, I had to help drag you in so I didn't get a real good look, but the place looks sorta like a castle. Big, gray stone, with a tower at one end, tall skinny windows."

Susan stared, still groggy. "A castle?" Oooo, her head. A castle. That should mean something, but she couldn't think.

Karen went on. "I was so scared. They even had a gun. That's why I called. They came and took me from home early this morning. I don't know how they got in. I guess my folks must be going nuts by now."

"Who are 'they'?" Susan stopped massaging her head.

Karen shrugged. "One of them is the High Priest of the coven—I mean, the family—"

"Okay. I know what you mean. That bunch you got mixed up with." A castle? Her eyes widened. The Viking Castle! If this was the Viking Castle Matt had described as looking like a nucleus of medieval abominations, their future suddenly looked less than dim. She looked around the room and shuddered. Matt had said that the things they had ordered sounded "as if Dracula had been the interior decorator." He was right.

Single beds stood on each side of a gray chest of drawers. Nightmare beings in black were woven into the flaming blood red and purple background of the spreads. Black decals of Satan and versions of the mark of the beast decorated the drawers. A large church of Satan symbol was woven into the center of the gray carpet, surrounded by other satanic emblems—the eye of Lucifer, the lightning bolt, and the seven satanic statements token. The gray walls were generously sprinkled with a confusing variety of occult signs. Hanging over the single tall window at the end of the room was a terrifying sculptured black bird, eyes cruel, talons spread as if diving for a kill, beak open as if about to tear flesh. There was no question in Susan's mind about what kind of place it was.

She swallowed. "Do you have any idea of what they're going to do with us?"

Karen shook her head. "They didn't say anything, only dumped us here and went away. That must've been an hour ago, anyway. Maybe longer." She gazed at Susan, deliberating. "They took me to talk to the High Priest. I'm supposed to recruit you into the coven."

Susan was startled. "What if you don't?"

Karen shivered, then shook her head. She looked through the window at the ragged clouds. "They don't want any outsiders to know what's going on. Like with Billy Joe." Treetops bent and swayed in an eerie, moaning wind. "They're crazy, you know."

Susan heard the words, laughed nervously, her rational mind refusing the thought. "You're kidding, right?" She was suddenly afraid it wasn't a joke.

Karen stared at the treetops. "You know what they did."

Susan paled. "We've got to get out of here!" She looked around. "That door. I suppose it's locked."

Karen nodded.

Susan went to the window, looked down at the cement sidewalk two stories below. She pushed frantically at the immovable sash anyway. "No way out there, either." Panic nibbled at her mind.

"Karen, think of something! We've got to get out of here." Where was Matt? What was he doing? Planning to break in to rescue them, if she knew him. But what could she and Karen do to help? They *had* to do something!

3:32 P.M.

Elizabeth slowed her little blue economy compact as she approached Sherman High School. Traffic was heavy. Scores of cars congregated to pick up youngsters in the extra lanes in front of the school. Students who owned cars gunned their engines as they drove out of the parking lot and into traffic. Many were overflowing with noisy youngsters exuberantly celebrating their release from another day of classes.

A parent drove away, and Elizabeth parked in the vacant spot. *How was Raymond taking all this?* she wondered. What impact had the events of last night made on him? A little worry frown crinkled between her eyebrows.

Before long, Raymond appeared on the sidewalk with an armload of books, dragging his feet. He looked pale, depressed. Furrowed brows implied a fierce headache. Elizabeth touched the horn, and Raymond turned toward the car.

"Hi, honey," Elizabeth said, pushing the passenger side door open. "Get in." He scarcely glanced at his mother as he sat down. "How'd it go today?" she asked, maneuvering into traffic.

"Okay, I guess." He hesitated. Then desperately, he turned and looked at his mother. "Wrong! It's been awful today. Alan won't talk to me, or Chuck, or Ralph, and they don't even talk to each other. The rest of the kids all look at us funny."

Elizabeth made no comment.

He examined the books in his lap, struggling with himself. "Mom, I've been trying to figure out all day how to say this." He took a breath and exhaled. "I've been such a dope!" He looked back at his mother, his eyes deep wells of pain and guilt, then dropped his gaze. The words tumbled out mechanically. "I—ah—I shouldn't have gone with the guys yesterday." There. It was out.

Elizabeth was silent a moment as she guided the car through heavy traffic. "So why did you?"

Raymond hung his head and muttered something unintelligible.

"I didn't catch that. What did you say?"

"I said I wanted to play Demon Crypt." His raised voice was just short of defiant.

Elizabeth shot a glance at him. He was looking out the side window. "Was that the only reason?" She signalled a lane change, slid into the left-turn pocket, and waited for a green arrow.

Raymond fidgeted. "No, I guess not."

Elizabeth waited, but he was silent. "Tell me some of the others."

He shrugged. "Well, Eddie and Chuck don't have to stay home all the time. Like, they can do what they want."

The signal at Carson Avenue turned red, and Elizabeth stopped. A heavy silence surrounded them. The light turned to green, and traffic moved on.

"Besides," Raymond went on, "I'm fifteen now, almost sixteen. But sometimes you treat me like a kid."

Elizabeth tightened her lips. "Seems to me they put voting age at something like eighteen," she said as if to herself. Then glancing at Raymond, "Anything else?"

His brow furrowed. "I dunno. I was mad, I guess."

"Why? Because you were on restriction?"

"I guess so."

"You know why you're on restriction, don't you?"

"Yeah. 'Cause I cut classes, went to play D.C. when you told me not to, drank beer, and did drugs." He slouched farther.

"And that's why we're supposed to treat you as if you were an adult?"

Raymond looked at his mother in surprise. He hadn't thought of it that way. "I—" He fell silent, thinking. "No," he said, pensive. He pushed himself up into a sitting position and fumbled for words. "I guess I was really acting like a kid, like trying to get even with you for putting me on restriction."

Elizabeth glanced at his profile. She was silent for about half a block. "What about Chuck and Eddie? Are they being punished?"

Momentary silence. "No."

"Why not? Isn't it the same thing with them?"

Raymond stared for awhile at the dashboard in front of him, thinking. "I guess—yeah—it should be, but y'know—" The sudden glow of realization nearly wiped away all his resentment. His expression was a study in reflection. "I think their folks don't care much what happens to them." With a touch of wonder in his eyes, he looked at his mother. "I think you do."

Elizabeth, surprised at how far his thinking had taken him, felt her love for her son overwhelming her. She put her right arm around his shoulder for a quick hug. "I'm glad to hear you say that." She swallowed a huge lump, blinked, and turned left on Nutmeg Street. "That's the absolute truth." She glanced at him. "Seems to me you've grown up a lot these past couple of days. Takes a man to admit the things you've just admitted to me."

For a moment, love, appreciation, even understanding washed through Raymond. It was as if a warm blanket had gone around him. "But I made such mess of everything." He sighed, his face screwed with worry again. "What will they do with me?"

"I don't know. We'll have to wait until the hearing next week." She turned onto Cutler Way. "But your attitude will affect their decision. I think maybe they won't be too rough on you."

Raymond shook his head. "Sure hope not. I'd hate my mom and dad to have a jailbird for a son."

Elizabeth chuckled and looked at him. He almost grinned. "By the way, we have another problem. It's serious. I think you could help."

"Would that count in court?" He looked up anxiously.

"Oh, Ray, for heaven's sake!" Elizabeth said sharply. "It might. But I think you'll want to help even if it didn't. It's about Susan. She's been kidnapped."

Ray's eyes bulged. "When?"

"This morning. Matt's friend Andy left a message on our machine and called Dad at the store. He, Dad, and a lot of other people are getting together—kind of a council of war—to figure a way to get her out of there. Looks like we're going to have to do this ourselves." A block later she added, "There's a good reason why we can't call in the police."

"Why?" Raymond was wide-eyed.

Elizabeth weighed how much she should tell him. "We think some of them may be involved in some way." She looked at him sharply. "Not a word to anyone! We're not absolutely sure. *Not a word!*"

Raymond's eyes were wide with unspoken questions. "Okay." He stared out the window. "But what can I do?"

"We'll figure that out tonight when everyone gets together. Dad's talking it over now with Pastor Wayman, Matt, and his friend Andy."

Raymond sat back and glowered. "I'll kill those ba—bums if they've hurt my sister," he said, his young voice grim.

Elizabeth guided the car into the driveway. Perhaps things were not as bad as they had looked at first. Raymond's attitude gave her hope. He appeared to be on the right track again. She was proud of him.

TWENTY-FIVE

Tuesday, 3:45 P.M.

Andy drove home, collected the mail from his box, let himself into his apartment, and plopped down in his recliner, looking aimlessly at the junk flyers. Since he'd called everyone he could think of, what could he do now? He stared blankly at the electric bill envelope and dropped a handful of colorful, glossy papers into a wastebasket. His phone rang.

The gruff voice on the other end said, "This is Hobart Jackson at the *Register*. I've been calling ever since I got your message. What happened? Is Susan—"

Andy interrupted. "Oh, yes, Mr. Jackson. Why don't I come down to the paper? We can talk there."

Slight pause. "Okay. About fifteen minutes?"

"Just about. See you then."

At the paper, Alison jerked a thumb toward Jackson's door. "He's waiting for you. By the way, his bark is a lot worse than his bite."

Andy grinned, flashed "OK," and rapped on the editor's door.

A roar vibrated through the panels. "Well, don't just stand there, come on in!"

Andy turned to Alison, right eyebrow aloft, and entered. Jackson's mustache bristled more than usual, a clear signal he was agitated. He stood, stuck his hand out to Andy, and pointed toward the only other chair in the room. "Let's not waste time. What's been done? Where's Susan?"

Andy told him they thought she was at the Castle and about the calls he'd made. "I don't know what Mr. Walker has done yet," he added. "Have you been able to get anything going?"

"One of my best investigative reporters found some old plans of the original castle. Might help. You can have 'em."

He dug in a drawer and handed Andy a manila envelope stuffed with a much-folded pack of old papers. Andy nodded thanks, and set the envelope in his lap. Jackson continued. "Another just handed me a list of wants and warrants against some of the people named in the list Susan gave me a few days ago."

Alarm bells went off in Andy's mind. "You haven't called the police yet, have you?" He leaned forward in anxiety.

"Not yet. Got it just before you came in. Why?" Jackson's shaggy eyebrows lifted in surprise.

Andy hesitated. "We got hold of some information—don't ask me how." He paused. "This has to be off the record." He sat back, waited for Jackson to comment.

Jackson's chair creaked as he leaned back to study Andy. "This is a *news*paper." The statement hung in the air.

"Susan's life might depend on it." Andy returned Jackson's gaze. "Also the lives of several other people."

Jackson continued to study him, his eyes squinted in contemplation. "That's only your opinion."

"These are the same people who killed that Johnson guy last Wednesday and stuffed the kid in the hole."

"How can you be sure?"

"Can't. But the phone call Susan got warned her not to write any more articles just before she was kidnapped. I can't see that as a coincidence."

Jackson's eyes burrowed deeply into Andy's. "Seems to me the police would be the first to be called to get the girls out of there. I know the chief. He's what we used to call a straight arrow."

Andy sat silent as a rock.

Jackson's beetling brows came together. "I thought you said they were in a dangerous situation. Why shouldn't the police be called?"

"Your word first."

Jackson's eyes narrowed. He wasn't getting very far with this young man. "What about after Susan's out of there?"

Andy breathed. "We'll give you the whole story. Exclusive."

Jackson considered Andy for a moment and sat forward. The chair creaked again. "Okay. My word and hand on it."

Andy leaned forward, gripped Jackson's hand, and sat back. "The district attorney, a prosecutor, and a number of other prominent local and county residents are involved," he said. "We figure that's why there have been no arrests on anything in connection with this and some other strange things that are going on."

"Oh?" Jackson's eyes gleamed. "You didn't say it went so high—" His mustache seemed to quiver.

"Mr. Jackson, you promised. That's not for publication yet. You'll have the whole story just as soon as the girls are safe." He paused for effect. "There's more to it, too." He dangled the statement as bait.

Jackson thrust out his lower lip. He stood up and paced in the crowded area behind his desk. "This could be a prizewinner," he muttered, looking out the grimy window. Finally, he heaved a great sigh and turned back to Andy. "All right. Just for Susan. But I want the story as soon as she's safe. An exclusive, you understand. This will be a blockbuster!" He was already looking toward that Press Club award.

Andy became aware that his muscles were locked in nervous tension and relaxed.

"Keep in touch, Andy." Jackson reached into a drawer and took out a card, scribbling on the back. "That's my home phone, just in case. Thanks for coming. Good luck. And bring Susan back!"

Andy stepped out of the office into a brisk, chilly wind under gray skies, heaved a sigh of relief, and actually opened the door to get into his Jeep. *Wow*, he thought. *One for our team.* He paused with his hand reaching for the ignition. *The Garcias!* He started the engine, drove fast as he dared to a phone, called information for the number and dialed, but there was no answer. He put the phone down, troubled, wondering what should be done. By now they must have gone to the police.

3:58 P.M.

Susan and Karen prowled the room, poking and examining every corner and cranny for the sixteenth time, cold with apprehension.

"Right. No way out of here," Karen muttered, looking out the window. Susan nodded. The drawers in the nightstands held only pamphlets of directions for spells, curses, and potions. The single small closet and the drawers in the chest were stuffed with black and white robes. Nothing else. Nothing sharp, nothing with which to pick a lock. There was nowhere else to look. Susan swallowed hard, trying to purge the sour taste of desperation.

Karen sighed. "Guess we're stuck here until they come get us."

She looked at Susan. "I don't suppose you'd like to join the coven, would you?"

Susan made a wry face. "I'd rather jump off the Coronado Bridge." She glanced at the menacing black bird and shuddered.

"Didn't think you would. I wish I hadn't." Karen scowled. "Little late for that. Wonder what they'll do to us?"

"Don't think about that. Hey, my friends and family are probably working on getting us out right now. Yours, too." She put her arm around Karen's shoulder and squeezed. "Don't worry. They'll think of something. Especially Matt. He always does." She smiled. "You'll like him. When he prays, God listens 'specially well." She tried to feel as confident as she sounded.

Karen studied Susan. She seemed so sure God paid attention to people's prayers, and answered them. Karen fell silent, deep in thought. Would God really help them when they were faced with satanism? Her eyes widened in sudden heartfelt realization of the depth to which she had fallen in the last few weeks. She had actually signed a pact with the devil! In blood! Drugged into a stupor, unconscious that she was turning away from God to Satan, she had made an eternal pact to follow the devil! In complete disobedience to God! Icy cold spread outward from her stomach. The dark enormity of separation from God engulfed her.

Susan saw Karen turn pale. "What is it? What's wrong?"

Karen turned slowly to Susan, her face a mirror of devastation. "Oh, Susan, I just realized what I've done!" She groped for words. "I don't know how to say it—It was the drugs! I wasn't thinking about anything else. It was just words, just something to get more drugs. I really, truly signed a pact with the devil!" she wailed. "But I didn't mean it! Honest!" Her mouth moved silently, reaching for words to say the unsayable.

Susan's mouth opened, but nothing came out. Was it actually possible for her to sign a pact with Satan and not realize what she was doing? What do you say in a situation like this?

Karen paced the length of the room, feeling caught in a net that was closing relentlessly around her. A covenant with the devil was a big sin! She'd go to hell! Forever! Horror engulfed her.

She turned back to Susan, terrified, her eyes fearful. "Do you think I'll go straight to hell?" Her hands covered her mouth.

Susan's eyes widened. "Huh?"

"For joining the coven. For signing a covenant in blood with the devil. For drinking blood. For not going to confession for absolution." The words tumbled out.

Susan's knees gave way and she sat down on the bed. "Wow." She stared at Karen, reaching for answers, finding too many blanks. "I'm not a minister," she said finally, "not a teacher. Don't even go to your church. I don't know how to answer you."

"But you know so much more than I do. I don't know much about the Bible. Do you think there's any chance that God would forgive me instead of sending me straight to hell? Maybe if I said a hundred Hail Marys and Our Fathers?"

Susan stared. "How can I tell you anything? I don't even believe in penances."

Karen looked surprised. "You don't?" She dropped down in astonishment on the other bed opposite Susan.

"No." Susan paused, thinking fast. "The Bible teaches that the Lord forgives when we ask because He loves us—not because of something we do."

Karen was puzzled. "But what about all your sins? Don't your family and friends have to pray for your forgiveness so you can get into heaven?"

"We don't believe that. But we do pray for others for blessings."

Karen scarcely heard. "I haven't done half enough good deeds—haven't gone to confession every week—" Karen turned, anguished, to Susan. "What I did was a real big sin and that means hell forever! Oh, Susan, I'm scared!" Her eyes were dark, bottomless pools of fear.

Susan searched for words. How to begin? She took a breath. "Listen. We study the Bible a lot, and it tells us that when Jesus went to the cross at Calvary, He took on Himself all our sins—past, present, and future. If we believe that His sacrifice saved us, we belong to Him. He *bought* us, paid for us with His blood. He *owns* us. We ask Him to forgive our sins, and He does. *All* of them. No matter how bad. Then when we die, we'll go straight to be with Him. Just simply because we believe Him. Just on faith."

Karen stared at Susan. "You don't have to work for salvation? The Bible says that? For sure?"

"Uh-huh."

Karen continued to stare. There was no priest here to ask about it. Only Susan. And satanists. She was in the worst quandary of her life. "Susan, if I were to ask God to forgive me for joining a coven and all that other stuff, would He do it? With all the terrible things I did?"

"Saul persecuted Christians," Susan said, "and even held the coats of the people who stoned Stephen to death. God forgave him, and he became Apostle Paul, the greatest missionary of all."

She studied Karen. "But this is a different situation." What should she do or say? How should she handle this? "Karen, you'd better think about this. And about what the priest at your church might say. Wouldn't he—uh—absolve you?" She hoped that was the right word.

Karen shot a look of misery at Susan. "I don't know. He said there are some unforgivable sins, and maybe this is one of them. And even if I did go to confession, I don't know—And besides, there's no time now!" She looked up at Susan in panic. "They'll probably kill us! Can you absolve me? Right now?"

Susan was startled. "Only Jesus can forgive sin," she said. "He did that at the cross. Just as the Bible says. Our pastor teaches that you just need to go to Him and ask Him to forgive you." She thought of Lacey, of the many people who had little, if any, real conviction of the tremendous need everyone has for Jesus. "If you're not just 'playing church'," she said, "if you're not simply going to church because it's what a person does on Sunday, but because you really love and need Him and want Him to forgive you now, He will."

"Oh, I do!" Karen shuddered. "If I had really known what I was getting into right off at first, I'd have run like a rabbit to get away! I want to get out of this! Will you help me, please?" Her voice nearly cracked with urgency.

Susan considered. She looked at Karen and paused. "I'm not talking about 'religion'—the business of going through rituals and prayers. Heck, a person can brush his teeth 'religiously.' We're talking about something that is more like—oh, how can I say this?" She paused, studying Karen. "Look. If you can think of your First Communion as a dedication to the Lord, then what you need to do now is more like—well, person to Person. You offer Him your heart, and He takes up residence there."

Karen looked a bit puzzled, and then the light seemed to go on. "Oh! You mean, like a friendship!"

Susan bit her lip. "Sort of. But more. Kind of like really getting engaged to be the bride of Christ. You don't have to become a nun, or anything, just give your whole heart to the Lord. In any Christian church. Yours or mine. Either one. Purely on a spiritual basis."

"Oh. Yeah. Uh-huh, I see—I think—"

"But you have to be sure that more than anything, you need Jesus in your heart and in charge of your life. Are you sure?"

"Susan, I've never been so sure!"

Susan saw anguish, appeal, and conviction in Karen's eyes. "I think you really mean it." She bit her lip. This was an enormous step for both of them. "Perhaps we could use a form of the sinner's prayer to confess what you've done, ask forgiveness, and put you right with God again. Then we could pray for help in getting out. And promise me that when we're out, you'll talk to your priest about this, tell him what we did. Okay?"

Karen's smile was eager, full of hope. "I will. Okay! Let's do it!"

They reached for each others' hands and fell to their knees between the beds. As Susan prayed, a soft, golden radiance seemed to envelop them, overshadowing all the demonic influences surrounding them, setting them apart from all that was evil.

5:58 P.M.

Andy was at his computer when the phone rang.

"Hi, Matt! Everything going okay?" Andy said when Matt spoke.

"Yeah, except it looks like a major demolition job just to get by the fence. Hey, day after tomorrow's Halloween, isn't it?"

"Yeah. Why?"

"Great. It's all coming together. What did you find out?"

"Yadush is sketching the interior of the castle. One of Jackson's reporters got old blueprints of the original plans. We can compare them. Maybe that'll help some, maybe not. Depends on whether or not they demolished the whole interior before they did their renovations. Matt, I wonder if the Garcias have gone to the police. I tried to call, but there was no answer."

Andy heard air hissing between teeth. "Oh, rats. The Garcias—I should have thought of that. Well, I guess there's nothing to be done about it now. If they've talked to the police, all they've been able to tell them is that Karen's been kidnapped. That's all they know, so the police won't connect them to anything else that's going on. I hope!"

"Thank God for small mercies!" Andy sighed with relief.

"Amen! Oh, by the way, while I was at the castle, another guy came up to look the place over, Buck Soderberg, a friend of the Walkers'. He took some pictures. Might help. Mr. Walker and Pastor Wayman said we'd all get together to plan something."

"When? Can I help? I feel kinda useless with nothing to do."

"Now. And yes, you can help. We're all going to the Walkers' to work it out. Mr. Walker has called a bunch of other guys, too. Can you get over there about six-thirty? And bring Yadush along too, will you?"

"Sure, except I don't know where the Walkers live."

He scribbled the address Matt gave him, took the packet of old blueprints, and snatched a warm jacket from his closet as he went past on the way to the door. He stopped at the Bedside Manor to pick up Yadush, and zoomed off to Cutler Way.

TWENTY-SIX

Tuesday, 7 P.M.

Eight people sat around the dining table at the Walker home, most of them craning their necks to see the blueprints and drawings. Don sat at the head. Andy, Matt, and Yadush sat together at his left. Pastor Wayman, Buck Soderberg, Stanley Raisbeck, Jessica Fairchild, and Dorothy Webb completed the circle. Elizabeth and Raymond sat apart, listening, occasionally asking questions and making suggestions. Elizabeth frequently refilled the iced tea pitcher and brought more cookies.

The layout of the original castle had been compared to the drawings Yadush brought with him. Some discrepancies showed up immediately.

"If they didn't tear this down when they put up the new wall," said Yadush, pointing, "we might be able to use that space and those stairs. There are some other places—we'll have to compare the two sets of plans more closely before we can get a handle on anything, though."

Matt's brow furrowed. "Even if we get in past the fence, there's no place to hide. That could be a problem."

"Yeah," said Buck Soderberg. "It's mostly bare ground, without even weeds. Just a few bushes and a lot of rocks. Some of them are pretty big. Boulders. Thin soil. The rock underneath comes through. And there aren't any neighbors anywhere near. It's spooky." Buck rummaged in the briefcase he had brought with him.

Don looked thoughtful. "Wonder if they'll have outside lights after dark?"

Stan Raisbeck was chief engineer with the county electric company. "Yeah, they have lights. Real sophisticated setup. I hope we can play a few tricks. I'll examine the layout more closely and talk to the boss."

Buck laid a large map on the table. "This is an enlargement of the area around the castle," he said. "Using my pictures for reference, Aaron Mapes drew in the building, the fencing, shrubbery, all the stuff we could see." He pointed. "The gate is here, on the west side. As Matt said, there's practically no cover anywhere around the castle. They've also cleared a path all around the fence, about four feet wide. See here in the back." The drawings showed a slope covered with shrubbery. The fence came closer to the building there than at any other point.

"What are these things?" asked Stanley, pointing at circles.

"Rocks, man, rocks!" Buck said. "Some of them are actually boulders. These big ones here and here."

"Are they big enough to provide cover?" Don asked.

"I think so. But that there's electrified fence. Need to get around or over that."

"I'll see what I can do," said Stanley. "Depends on the actual electrical layout. Like I said, I'll talk to the boss."

"I spoke to the mothers," Jessica said. "Most of them are anxious to help. Everything will be ready Thursday."

Dorothy's vigil was solid, and like her prayer chain, already operating.

"I called a Roman Catholic priest I know," said Andy. "Father Anthony of St. Joseph's. I hope that's all right." Pastor Wayman shot a startled look toward Andy. "Tony's two years older than me. We got to be friends in computer class in high school, and I still see him now and then. He's had some experience in exorcisms." He grinned sheepishly. "Don't know how much that might help, but it can't hurt."

Pastor Wayman looked askance. "You say he's a friend?"

"Yeah. Real neat guy. Loves mystery stories. Sorta like that priest in the Father Brown books, only younger."

Pastor Wayman looked around at the others. There was some chuckling about exorcisms, but no apparent objection. He was silent a moment. "Well, all right. He's welcome."

"Good," said Don. "Any other thoughts, ideas, before we leave?" No one spoke. "Let's pray." They bowed their heads, asking the unseen angels gathered around to strengthen them. As the guests left, the peace surrounding them seemed almost palpable.

Andy turned at the door and thrust his hand out to Don.

"Mr. Walker," he began, but Donovan interrupted.

"Call me Don," he said. "Everyone does."

Andy smiled. "Thanks, Don. You know, for the first time, I feel as if we're going to get the girls back. These people here tonight—they're super."

7:05 P.M.

Lacey put the finishing touches on her makeup, looked one last time in the mirror, and ran downstairs. "I'm ready," she announced to John and her father.

They got up to leave. "Margaret," Jerrod called out. "We're going now."

Margaret appeared at the dining room door. "When should I expect you back?"

"When we get here." Jerrod put on his hat, offered his arm to his daughter, and the three left.

"Let's take my car," John said. "I know the way."

The Robinson limousine stood waiting. Jerrod waved the driver away and walked with Lacey to the luxury sedan.

"Just what can we expect tonight?" asked Jerrod, seated in back. "Should we be ready for ghosts or anything like that?"

"Oh, it won't be anything spectacular. She just sits quietly and speaks. That's about it."

"No guests sitting in the dark around a table, holding hands, mysterious taps, apparitions?"

John chuckled. "Nothing like that." He turned off on one of the streets that climbed steeply up to the top of the range of hills. At a gated driveway, glowing in the light of a lamppost on each side, he pressed a button, spoke his name, and the gate opened. As the driveway curved toward the pillared mansion, the car's headlights illuminated beds of asters and chrysanthemums bordering the emerald lawn. Liquidambers showed a touch of gold in their leaves. John stopped at the porte-cochére, where a butler appeared to show them in.

A crystal chandelier, blazing with the light of dozens of small bulbs hung high over an intricate cinnamon-colored circular design set into the large white tile-floored entry. A curved stairway on the left led up past abstract paintings. Lacey stared appreciatively at the tasteful appointments.

"This way, please." The butler's voice brought her back to the reason she was here. He took Jerrod's hat and Lacey's jacket, and led them to a sitting room at the right of the entry.

Lacey gazed around, enjoying the decor. The walls were a muted rose, paintings were by French Impressionists, the carpet a warm earth tone. Accent pillows on the beige furniture were in lavender, blue, and green with touches of rose. A tall young woman with long ash blonde hair and eyes somewhere between green and blue stood to greet them. She wore a simple aquamarine dress, highlighted by an unusual pendant, a two-inch, five-pointed silver star, the points extending slightly past the circle upon which it was mounted. Something about the design looked familiar to Lacey.

"Thank you for letting us come," John said, kissing her hand. "Cynthia, these are my friends, Lacey and her father, Jerrod Robinson. Miss Crawford." He gestured theatrically.

"What a pleasure," said Cynthia, extending her hand to Lacey, then to Jerrod. "Won't you sit down?" She indicated the upholstered seats placed in an informal circle.

A clear turquoise-colored crystal globe on an iridescent base glowed with subtle shadings on a small table in front of one of the seats. Cynthia took her place behind the crystal. John looked at the sphere and raised his eyebrows.

"I got this crystal a couple of weeks ago," she explained. "It helps me to concentrate."

John sat back, elbows on the arms, fingers tented. "Interesting," he said. "I didn't know you needed external aids."

Cynthia blushed. "I don't, not really. But it's a gorgeous color." She turned to Lacey and Jerrod. "John told me you were anxious to get in touch with the spirit of Mrs. Robinson?"

"That's right," said Jerrod, embarrassed. "That is, if it's possible." Lacey nodded.

"It seems to be a favorable night," Cynthia said. "But first, tell me something about her."

Lacey told about Brother Justin, the healing ceremony, the operation, and her death.

Jerrod added, "She was always somewhat fragile. Always a fine lady—" His voice broke.

Cynthia appeared sympathetic. "One more thing. Would you tell me the dates of her birth and her death?"

Lacey answered.

Cynthia nodded. She reached up to the pendant on her necklace, closed her hand over it and leaned back, staring into the depths of the crystal.

Lacey turned from Cynthia to watch the sphere. It seemed as if she were gazing into a deep pool on some mysterious mountain.

For an instant she felt as if she were being drawn into the slowly swirling heart of the crystal. She tore away, alarmed.

Cynthia's eyes were closing. Her breathing slowed and became shallow. The room was absolutely quiet, the silence uncanny, mystic. Lacey felt the little hairs on her arms and at the back of her neck stirring.

Cynthia drew a deep breath, opened her eyes, and sat tall. Lacey had the same queer perception as at the séance—of someone else looking through Cynthia's large eyes.

The voice was deep, masculine, kindly. "Good evening, Cynthia. I'm happy to see you. Amelia is here beside me. She wishes to speak to Lacey and Jerrod."

Lacey's heart turned over when she heard the next voice. She was certain it was her mother's. "Lacey, Jerrod, my darlings," the familiar voice said. "Don't grieve for me. I'm very happy here, and there's no more pain."

"Amelia!" Jerrod's voice was hoarse with emotion. "Oh, Amelia, there's so much I want to tell you—so much I never said because I was always too busy—"

"Jerrod, my dear, I know what you want to say. Didn't you realize I knew all along that you loved me?"

Jerrod groaned and put his face in his hands. Tears trickled between his fingers.

"Mother," Lacey finally managed to whisper. "Mother, I miss you so much!" Her eyes filled with tears. "I hurt you so often, especially that night after the séance, and I'm so, so sorry for the awful way I behaved! I love you, Mom. I miss you."

"Lacey darling, it's all right. I knew what you were feeling, and remember, I was your age once." Her voice began to fade as if into an unimaginable distance. "Don't feel bad any more. I never blamed you. I love you." Then the voice was gone.

"Mother, come back!"

"Amelia, don't leave us—"

Lacey and Jerrod called to her as one, reaching out as if to hold her.

"I'm sorry, but it was necessary for her to leave," said the masculine voice. "This is tiring for one so recently arrived. Cynthia, as usual, it was good to be with you. Good night."

Heavy silence. Cynthia's eyes closed again, and she relaxed against the back of the chair. She inhaled deeply, exhaled, and her eyes flicked open. "Well," she said, stretching her back as if she were waking up. "Tell me about it."

"Don't you know what happened?" Jerrod was incredulous.

Cynthia shook her head. "Not this time. I heard nothing but Nathaniel's greeting. It happens that way sometimes."

Jerrod, wiping his eyes, repeated what Amelia had said. "You've no idea how much better I feel, now that I know she knew I loved her," said Jerrod.

Lacey, unable to talk, looked down, shaking her head slowly. Finally, she blew her nose and looked up, lips curving in a tremulous smile. Her eyes were shining, wet with tears.

John turned the conversation toward the crystal sphere. "This is fascinating, you know?" he said, touching it gently. "That pendant. I never saw that before, either."

Cynthia held it away from herself so she could look at it. "Isn't it pretty? I bought it at the same time I got the crystal. It's a pentacle. It also helps me get in touch with Nathaniel."

"A pentacle?" Lacey wiped her eyes on a tissue and looked at Cynthia wide-eyed, remembering where she had seen the design before. There had been pentacles for sale at Brother Justin's. "But doesn't that have something to do with witchcraft?"

"Why, I don't know," Cynthia said. "I don't know anything about witchcraft." She half-laughed apologetically. "As a matter of fact, I don't even know much about what I do. I've never looked into it. I've been in touch with Nathaniel only since I fell off my father's horse, and I haven't taken time to study it. John, do you know if it does?"

He pursed his lips and lifted a shoulder. "Well, I've heard, that is, some have said that it does. But does that mean anything if you don't believe in witchcraft? Isn't it just a clever design under such circumstances?"

Cynthia examined her pendant curiously. "I wonder. All I know is that when I wear it, I feel confident that I can reach Nathaniel." She reached back, unfastened the clasp and turned the pendant over. "Oh, look, here on the back of the circle!" she said, running her finger over the silver, holding it out to John. "There's something written here."

John looked closely. Lacey and Jerrod clustered near, trying to see. "It's hard to make out," John said, squinting. "O happy soul—" John brought the pendant closer—"of Wicca's mark—with learning bright—and knowledge dark!" He pointed it out to Cynthia. "There. Right around the back of the circle. See?" He handed it back to her.

"Funny, I never noticed that before," she said, studying it, puzzled. "I wonder what it means." She read it over and looked back at John. "That doesn't make sense."

John cast a quick glance at Jerrod and Lacey. "Cynthia, I think I know someone who can tell you about this. A group of my friends is meeting Thursday evening. They know about things like this. Would you like to go?"

Cynthia looked at the pentacle. "I don't know. Something about that verse makes me feel a little uneasy."

"If they could decipher it and tell you what it meant, you'd understand, and it wouldn't be mysterious. You might not feel uneasy any more."

Cynthia looked doubtful. "'Learning bright and knowledge dark'—" She set the necklace down on the table. "Well, if you're sure they wouldn't mind. All right, I'll go."

John turned to Lacey and Jerrod. "What about you two? Would you like to come?"

"Sorry, John, but I have a meeting Thursday at the Viking Castle," Jerrod said. "Can't make it."

John appeared to be amazed. "I can't believe it. At the Viking Castle? That's where my friends are meeting!"

Their eyes met for a moment in silence. "That's a coincidence," said Jerrod. "Well, of course, it's a large building, lots of rooms."

"Maybe another time, then? What about you, Lacey? Would you like to come with Cynthia and me?"

Lacey looked toward Cynthia. "Well—"

Cynthia's eyes pleaded.

"Oh, all right. What time?"

John was delighted. "I'll pick you up. Eight-thirty?"

Lacey's eyebrows drew together in a tiny frown. "So late?" The whole thing seemed bizarre. "Well, all right. I'll be ready. What's the dress code?"

John hesitated. "Anything you like, I think. It'll be Halloween. Whatever's comfortable. Wear a sweater. Or a jacket. It will probably be cool."

Lacey nodded. Cynthia had picked up the pendant and was studying it. Lacey went to see. Cynthia looked up at her.

"Funny I never noticed that before." She ran a finger around the raised letters. "All I saw was that it was unusual and pretty. I guess I really should find out more about what I'm doing." She fastened it around her neck. "Well, as far as I'm concerned, it's just another pendant." She smiled.

Lacey smiled back. "Thank you for letting us come, Cynthia," she said. "I feel a lot better about Mother now." She hesitated. "Cynthia, would you like to come over to our house some afternoon for a swim? Our pool's heated."

"Thanks! I'd love that. Well, I guess I'll see you Thursday anyway. Let's plan it then." She giggled. "Halloween! What fun! Costumes, of course." She put out her hand. Lacey took it.

"Deal." She looked around for her father. He and John were deep in conversation. "Daddy?"

Jerrod looked at his watch, then came to Cynthia and took her hand. "Thank you, my dear. Tonight has meant more to me than I can say." He reached into an inside pocket, took out a check, and handed it to Cynthia. "Please take this. It's just a little token of appreciation from us both."

Cynthia shook her head. "I don't ever take anything for this," she said. "I do it for friends. If you wish, you might give it to the New Age Center on Oak Street. I got this pendant and the crystal there. They seem to be very nice people."

Jerrod nodded and put the check back in his pocket.

John kissed Cynthia on the cheek, and as if by magic, the butler appeared to escort them to the door. He handed Jerrod his hat, Lacey her jacket, and opened the car door.

On the way back, Jerrod asked John about his meeting. "It's just a group of acquaintances," he said. "A bit on the weird side, but they're nice people. They're into the occult."

"Hmmm," Jerrod hmmmmd. "I'm meeting with a group of financial consultants. Obviously one has nothing to do with the other. Well, a large building like that can accommodate a good many meetings at a time, I suppose."

"You said they're into the occult?" asked Lacey. "I don't know about that. I don't feel right about it."

John glanced briefly toward her. "But you've already promised Cynthia. She'd be very disappointed if you let her down. You may not realize it, but she's a very sensitive person, sort of delicate emotionally. Especially since that accident. Besides, all we're really going for is to get a better understanding of the verse on her pendant."

Lacey studied her hands. Unbidden, Susan and what she had said about Saul and the Witch of Endor came back to her. She shouldn't have been so sharp with Susan the last time she'd seen her. But she was such a goose sometimes. And what about tonight? That absolutely was her mother's voice! She decided she'd call Susan in the morning, apologize, and talk to her about Cynthia.

John seemed to be waiting for her to respond. "Oh, I guess it'll be all right," she said finally. "Do you think we could leave right after Cynthia finds out what that verse means?"

He kept his eyes on the road. "We'll see," he said.

Lacey looked at him. Funny. She'd never before noticed how in profile he somehow gave the impression of a hungry hawk. She quickly dismissed the resemblance as an effect of the dashboard lights. But why, for the first time since she met him several years ago, did she suddenly feel edgy? *Oh, don't be ridiculous,* she scolded herself. She shifted a little away from him anyway, and watched the road changing in the headlights as they wound down the hill.

TWENTY-SEVEN

Wednesday, October 30, 9:05 A.M.

Controlled chaos ruled in the church parish hall. The large table in the middle of the room was heaped with donated fabrics, edgings, tape measures, patterns, scissors—everything necessary for creating costumes. A galaxy of women pawed through the materials, gabbling, arguing. Jessica Fairchild raised her voice over the hubbub.

"Have you taken measurements?" she called out. A chorus of yesses and a few noes arose. "All right. Those of you who didn't, go buy whatever costumes are left at the store. Just get the right sizes of whatever you can find. We'll have a final planning meeting at three tomorrow afternoon. Then be back here by seven, in costume!" Several women left in a clatter of heels and chattering confusion of voices.

A clamor arose again over who was to have which patterns, what fabrics. "Hold it!" Jessica shouted over the din. "I'll start with the patterns. Who wants this clown pattern?" She held up the envelope with the illustration on the front. "It's size medium adult." Three hands went up. "All right, you three work it out among yourselves. Now, this pumpkin. Fits all sizes." Only one hand went up. "It's yours, Marian."

Ultimately all the fabrics and patterns from frogs to fairy princesses were distributed. No ghouls, ghosts, skeletons, devils, or witches. "Now," said Jessica, "remember the three o'clock planning meeting. Deadline for costumes is seven tomorrow at the latest, so get with it! Cut, pin, sew, and everyone be here by seven, in costume! In case I forgot to tell you: in costumes, here, at *seven!*" She looked mock sternly at the giggling, grinning women. "We'll have a light supper here before we go out. And most important, pray!"

Women clustered in noisy, chattering groups over the table where some trim was still unclaimed, asking questions, making suggestions and holding fabrics up next to their own and others' bodies.

"Get with it, ladies," Jessica called out. She turned to Marian, the short brunette who had the pumpkin pattern, patiently waiting to ask her question. Anxiety was written all over her face.

"Where can I get something to hold the pumpkin shape?" Her manner said she thought it would be impossible.

"Chicken wire at the hardware store," Jessica said, and enormously relieved, Marian scurried off. Jessica called out, "Be sure to bind the edges with heavy fabric so it won't scratch." She shook her head, sighed, and turned to the next question.

9:35 A.M.

The grating of a key in the lock signalled the return of the High Priest. Karen clutched at Susan, but as the door swung open, they stood stiffly apart. Both knew the question the priest would ask, and both knew the answer. What they did not know was the result.

"Well?" The High Priest stood, dangling keys on a large ring from his index finger. Two black-clad men stood behind him. "Well? What about it?" His eyes were fixed on Karen. "Did you persuade her?"

Her chin lifted slightly. "I didn't even try."

The High Priest's face clouded with outrage, and his hand gripped the iron key ring tightly. He controlled himself with perceptible effort. His voice became silky, and his eyes narrowed as he looked at Karen. "In that case, you will come with us."

Susan mumbled quickly to Karen, "Remember, greater is He that is in you than he that is in the world!"

"What's that you're mumbling?" demanded the priest, staring at Susan, an edge of alarm in his voice.

"I just told her you're not so much." She stared back boldly, continuing to pray silently, calling on the name of the Lord.

For a moment, the High Priest faltered. Quickly he regained arrogance. "So you think not, do you!" He flared in fury at Susan. "Young lady, before tomorrow night is over, you'll learn! You'll learn!" His voice rose in pitch as he pointed his index finger at her. With a peremptory gesture, he ordered the guards to take Karen out. As each took an arm, Karen turned to Susan, and winked. But her face was pale.

As the door closed, isolation, anxiety, and an urgent need to do something, *anything* descended on Susan. She stood desolate in the dismal room, hearing the rasp in the lock as the key turned. What would they do to Karen? *It's my fault!* she cried silently, despairing.

10:50 A.M.

Lacey felt guilty about the argument she and Susan had on Monday evening. She should have listened to Susan, then explained her own position calmly, rationally. But she hadn't. She'd blown up instead.

For the third time that morning, first at nine-thirty, again at ten-fifteen, and now, she pulled back her hand from the telephone. She yearned to tell Susan all about Cynthia, and that they had contacted her mother. Yet the quarrel still rankled.

Susan hadn't called either. But then, it wasn't really up to her. It had not been Susan who got mad. *I lost it,* Lacey thought. *I said a lot of rotten things to her, things I didn't really mean. But,* Lacey rationalized, *Susan had started quoting the Bible again, and she didn't even give Cynthia the benefit of the doubt.* Still, Lacey was afraid that if she didn't call Susan and apologize, she'd lose her best friend. And best friends—since kindergarten, yet!—are pretty hard to find.

Setting her jaw, she reached for the phone. "Frances, put me through to the paper." There! She had done it. She drummed her fingers on her desk as the call went through.

"This is Lacey Robinson," she said when Alison answered. "I'd like to speak to Susan."

Alison hesitated, then said quietly, "She's out on a story." Expectation splintered and crashed flat. "Do you expect her later?" Lacey felt abandoned.

Pause. "It's hard to know. Would you like to leave a message?"

"Uh—no, I guess not. I'll call back this afternoon." She put down the phone and stared at it. Would she call? Would she have the same determination to mend fences later that she had now? She didn't know.

Strange. She was both relieved and disappointed that Susan wasn't in. *Well, maybe Alison will tell her anyway that I called, and she'll call back. If not, maybe I'll call tomorrow. Or will I?* She didn't understand her mixed emotions. They made her irritable. Annoyed, she picked up the next file, read from the open law book, and started making notes.

1:50 P.M.

Susan heard footsteps stop at the door. She stuffed the pamphlet on spells and hexes back in the drawer and sat down on one of the beds. She walked quickly to stand with her back to the window, wanting to be only a silhouette, able to see, and not be seen clearly by whoever came in.

As the High Priest came into the room alone, she noticed his expression was mild, his manner conciliatory, and his voice carefully modulated. Very different from his behavior earlier.

"Ah, Miss Walker," he said, "won't you sit down?"

"Thank you, no. I'd rather stand."

"Then you'll excuse me if I sit?" Susan inclined her head slightly. "It's been a tiring morning, getting ready for our celebration tomorrow. It'll be something of a housewarming. We've just moved in here. But I came to apologize for that little scene earlier." He paused, as if waiting for comment. Susan was silent. He continued. "Forgive me for my outburst. It was totally uncalled for. And you must understand, little Karen was disobedient. She needed to be disciplined. Our organization is a large one, and each member must do what is expected, or discipline breaks down. You do understand, don't you?" He raised his eyebrows in question.

"No."

His voice was like cream. "Miss Walker, I apologize for my—well, I'll admit it—my harsh behavior. I slept poorly last night, lost my temper and was, perhaps, unnecessarily hard on the girl, but discipline must be administered when rules are broken. Now she's forgiven, and is among her friends again." He smiled engagingly. "Please, Miss Walker, do sit down."

Susan frowned, reached out for the straight chair near the winow, pulled it over and perched gingerly on the edge. *What's going on? Why is he being so—nice?* she wondered.

The High Priest sighed, shook his head. "I feel as if you don't trust me," he said, his voice sad.

"I don't. Your people abducted us, and drugged me."

He looked wounded. "That was a mistake. There's no reason to distrust me. Look. Why don't you just stay with us overnight, enjoy our little celebration with us tomorrow, and you'll see we're just another group of ordinary people, perhaps more fond of the dramatic than most, but basically harmless. I don't know what you've heard, but don't you agree that staying with us for the day will show you the kind of people we really are? Then your mind will be at ease, and you can trust us. Isn't that so?"

Susan studied him carefully, knowing her face was shadowed. "I don't think so. And I don't think Karen is with friends." She stopped, studied him a moment, stood up. "If you really want me to trust you, let Karen and me go, now. Right now."

He shook his head slightly. "I'm sorry. I really can't do that. In Karen's case, she's made a commitment, and she should keep it. In your case, as a reporter, you should become familiar with this entire group before you leave, lest you give your readers a misconception of what we are. Miss Walker, I invite you again to stay through our celebration, and then, you may leave. Perhaps, after getting to know our organization, you might even want to stay with us. The choice will be yours." His smile was ingratiating.

Cold shivers raced up and down inside her. If she hadn't learned as much as she had in the last few weeks, she might accept this too-gracious invitation. Silently calling on the Lord, she chose her words carefully. "Thank you, but no, thank you. I have work to do, people are depending on me to be at my job, so I need to leave. Now. And since Karen was abducted just as I was, I insist that you allow us to leave together."

The High Priest's eyes flashed fire for an instant. He sat rock still, then looked down. "As I said, I'm sorry. I can't do that." His hard eyes looked up at her. "You may wish you had accepted my invitation before much longer." He stood. "Servants will take care of your needs." He studied her, top to toe. "You would have made a striking addition to our organization," he said. "Margo will prepare you for Samhain," he added, his voice cold, and left, locking the door behind him.

Susan sat down hard. Samhain. Named for the satanic god of the dead. All Hallow's Eve. Of course. How could it have slipped her mind? A shiver ran through her, as she thought of the news reports of weird activities on Halloween in recent years. Devil's Night in—where was it? Detroit? Cincinnati? Destruction and burning buildings. Animal shelters refusing to sell black cats for a month before Halloween, because so many had been sacrificed, dismembered in past years. She remembered a story from the previous Halloween, when on a tip, police had broken into a coven that was preparing to sacrifice a live baby boy. Her expression was bleak. So was her future, if she didn't get out of there.

There had to be a way out of that castle.

3:20 P.M.

Gilbert Crozier stepped out of the elevator and went to Frances' desk. "Could I speak to Lacey, please?" he said. He looked apologetic.

Frances looked up at him. "Is something wrong?"

"No. Not really—I just found out something she should know."

Frances pushed a button, her eyes still on Gilbert. "Miss Robinson?" she said, "Gilbert Crozier is here to see you."

The voice from the speaker was tinny. "I'm busy right now."

"I'll wait," Gilbert said.

"He'll—" Frances started to say.

"I heard him." Pause. "Okay. Send him in."

Frances indicated the office.

Gilbert nodded thanks and opened the door. Lacey acknowledged him with a slight nod and waved a hand at a chair. "You wanted to see me?" Her manner was cool. She continued to study the papers on her desk.

Gilbert looked questions at her. "What's the matter? Have I done something to offend you?"

"No. I'm just busy. You wanted to see me?" Lacey looked up and really saw him. His manner was uncertain. He seemed vulnerable, which was totally uncharacteristic for Gilbert. She stared.

"Yes. I've found out something you should know. Could we have dinner when you get done here?"

"What's it about?" She continued to study him.

"Come have dinner with me. I'll tell you then."

Lacey tapped a tooth with a pen. "All right," she said. "Pick me up here at five." Deliberately, she turned to her work, made notes. Gilbert still sat. She looked up at him. "I said I'd have dinner with you. Is there something else?"

"Uh—no." Gilbert shook his head. "I'll pick you up at five." He stood up, held out his hand to her, but she turned back to the papers. He withdrew it, embarrassed, and left.

When the door had closed behind him, Lacey stared at the paneling. *That was mean,* a little voice in her mind said. *Maybe it was. But you don't really trust Gilbert, do you, Lacey? No, I don't,* she thought. *But he seems so different today. He's always been so sure of himself before. Why is everything so different today? Something strange seems to be going on.* She frowned, glanced at the law book, turned back to the brief, made more notes, and turned the page.

5:12 P.M.

Gilbert had been waiting for her in the office since five. He stood up and offered his arm to Lacey. She walked past him.

When she reached the elevator she turned back to Gilbert. "Are you coming?"

Gilbert reddened and moved up beside her. When the elevator door opened, they entered.

"Tell me something," he said. "Are you angry at me for some reason?"

Lacey looked down. "No. Yes. I dunno. It's just that—" Her expression hardened. "At the séance, your precious Sharleena said my mother was healed. It was all a fake. I don't trust you anymore."

Gilbert's mouth tightened slightly. "I know it now," he said. "That it was a fake, I mean." The elevator stopped, and the door opened. Taking her by the elbow, he escorted her to his car. "I'm trying to tell you how sorry I am about the whole thing. How about dinner at The Continental?"

Lacey nodded. They rode in silence to the edge of town and stopped in front of the discreetly elegant restaurant. A valet took Gilbert's keys and drove off with the car as the doorman ushered them in.

Seated comfortably in a curtained alcove, Lacey watched Gilbert as he studied the menu. He *had* changed. No longer was there the sense of command, of certainty. It was as if foundation blocks had been knocked out from under him. She wondered what had happened.

"Green salad, beef Wellington, baked potatoes," he told the waiter. The waiter scribbled and left.

Gilbert looked earnestly at Lacey and leaned forward. "Please believe me when I say I've changed. I've learned a lot since I saw you last time." He paused. "And what I really want to tell to you is that I've learned something disturbing—well, shocking is a better word—about the financial deal your father and I have been working on. You must warn him."

Lacey was surprised. This was not what she had expected. "The financial deal?" She remembered listening in on the phone call when her father was talking. Suddenly interested, she leaned forward on her elbows. "Do you think that's what he's been so upset about recently?"

Gilbert nodded. "I expect so." He played with his fork. "You see, the way it works is that our Corporation matches whatever funds we invest in something. The profit is split between us and the Corporation according to a rigid formula, based on the size of the profit. But what we didn't know—what no one in the group knew, except probably the Chairman—is that much of what goes to the

Corporation goes to—" he paused and turned away. "I feel like such an idiot." He looked back, his face set. "Most of it goes to buying influence with state and national legislators."

"Influence? What kind?"

"Anything that will make us more money, so we can pay the legislators more money. The Corporation pays them to pass laws, grant contracts, anything, that will benefit us—and them."

"But that's dirty! Daddy hates that!"

"I know. And the Corporation makes sure the money is carefully made to look legal—with our names on it. The Corporation stays clean." He scowled at the tablecloth. "I hate the whole thing. I like making money, and I don't mind a flatout swindle. But this—this is monstrous."

Lacey stared at him.

"It gets worse." He looked almost apologetic. "It's associated with another scheme to push drugs to get kids and young people hooked. Just to get more money."

Lacey's jaw dropped. "And Daddy doesn't know?"

"I don't think so. I wouldn't have known either, except I was considering an investment, checking the financial records of the—" He caught himself before naming the firm. "Well, I stumbled on something that seemed odd to me, and I followed the trail." He inhaled and let his breath out sharply. "It blew the whole thing open for me." He looked hard at Lacey. "I think your father suspects in some way the whole thing's illegal, but I doubt he knows what. He needs to be told. And I don't know how to do it."

He was silent for a moment of misery. "You see," he continued, "the rotten truth is that I've been feeling superior. My investments have brought in more than his have, so my cuts have been more generous. I think he's envious, and I've been, well, unkind about it. I don't know how he'd take this coming from me."

One of Lacey's eyebrows went up, the other down. "Was that what you two were quarreling about last Wednesday evening?"

"Well, something like that. I told him I suspected he was about to be put out of the Corporation because he wasn't earning enough." He tented his fingers, embarrassed to the point of a deep flush up his neck. "And I hardly know how to tell you—"

Just then the curtains parted. The waiter brought the salad, then left.

Gilbert continued. "You mentioned the séance at Laurelyn's. Your mother asked how Sharleena knew about her condition?"

She nodded.

He sighed. "I told Laurelyn about Brother Justin when I found out Amelia had been to him. But only because I knew she would be glad for your mother. I had no idea she'd tell Sharleena." He paused. "I hate to admit it, but I had believed Brother Justin could cure her, too." His eyes were mournful. "I've been a fool."

Lacey stared unspoken questions at him.

He hesitated. "I was such a nothing in school. No one liked me. Especially you." He looked at her with longing. "I just worshiped you. You were always so beautiful and so popular—" He tore his gaze away, became businesslike again. "So when I began to make money, I let myself be influenced by a lot of nonsense, wanting to be accepted as one of the bunch."

Lacey was beginning to understand. "I never knew that," she said softly. "I'm sorry. I guess I wasn't very kind."

A wry grin touched Gilbert's lips. "Forget it. It's past." He picked up his fork. "But the Corporation. That's here and now, and I'm afraid for your father and all the others who think this is an honest business operation."

Lacey studied Gilbert. Could she believe him? Did she dare not to? "You're absolutely sure about what you said about the Corporation?"

Gilbert nodded. "The trail I was following? I found one of that company's private ledgers, the private accounts, mixed in accidentally with the public ones. That was a bad mistake on their part. The names and numbers were totally different. And the more I dug, the worse it got, until I came to the real program."

Susan stared. "What are you going to do? What *can* you do?"

"I don't know. Your father's just had one shock. How can I hit him with another?"

"But he has to know." Lacey finally understood the change in Gilbert. If all this was true, of course he would feel hurt, angry, resentful, dirty, used. "How can you not tell him?" Lacey paused, thought. "And then again, how can you? It might kill him—he's been—Oh, I don't know how he's been." Lacey sat back, drained. "Oh, gosh. He has a meeting tomorrow night at eight-thirty at the Viking Castle. Is that the Corporation meeting?"

Gilbert nodded.

"Are you going?"

"Yes." Gilbert's brow furrowed. "Maybe it's time all of them knew about it. I don't know them very well, but I hope most of them are decent people who would never knowingly do anything like this, any more than your father would. Or I would. I mean, I wouldn't. I hope you know what I mean."

Lacey pushed her fork around in the salad. "Are you saying you'd tell everyone at the meeting where the money's going? To legislators to buy favors, and to deal drugs?"

Gilbert was silent a moment. "I'm not sure I have the courage. But something has to be done, and I guess it's up to me. Yes. I'll tell them. Then I'll tell the law."

Lacey nodded. "By the way, I'm going to a meeting tomorrow night. You know, it's funny. It's at the Viking Castle, too. John's picking me up at quarter to nine. Maybe I'll see you there."

Gilbert looked up from his salad, a strange expression on his face. "What kind of a meeting?"

"Something to do with the occult. You see, Cynthia Crawford has a pendant with a strange inscription on it. John—do you know John Merkel?"

Gilbert shook his head. "I don't know—what's her name?—Cynthia, either."

"Well, anyway, he said these people he knows might be able to explain the inscription to her, and she wanted me to come along. I didn't really want to after all I've been through, but I said I would. That's all."

Gilbert studied Lacey. "Be careful, please. I have a bad feeling about tomorrow."

Lacey nodded and forked another bite of her salad, although she had no appetite. She did not tell him that she felt uneasy, too.

TWENTY-EIGHT

Wednesday, 9:45 P.M.

Donovan said good night to Buck Soderberg and Stanley Raisbeck, who had arrived about eight-thirty. He couldn't believe how well the evening had gone.

Stanley had come in grinning. "I don't know how they got it through the department," he had told them, "but these guys are on a separate line all by themselves. Bet it took more money than all of us could put together. Not only that, but once the line gets to the property, most of the important functions are separated where I can get at them. I think we can manage some surprises."

Now Don grinned despite his concern about his daughter. "Yadush said he's going to get Laura and her crew into the castle tomorrow morning while it's still dark. There won't be any chance to get them in later. You might pray about that," he added as he walked out with them.

Stanley nodded. "And at about ten, electricians will be working around there. Nobody notices electricians or telephone repair or meter readers. But you might keep us in mind."

"Sure will." Don extended his hand to each of them.

"See you tomorrow, then," said Buck, getting in his car.

"Right. At three for the planning meeting, and at seven for supper." Don waved good night and contemplated the shredded clouds in the moonlight. The weather report had predicted rain for Thursday. *Hope it'll hold off until after we're done*, he mused, and went back into the house.

9:30 P.M.

Preparations continued in the shadowy Great Hall on the third floor of the Castle. The altar, a large oak table, was carried by six men into position near one end of the room.

When the table had been placed, two workmen came in, struggling with a huge, nether-worldly looking black sword. The jet-black blade gleamed with a brilliant gloss. The hilt shone with jewels. A pair of large hooks had been set into the wall behind the table. The workmen, wearing heavy gloves, heaved the sword into position. The quillons, fashioned vaguely like batwings, kept the sword from settling on the hooks.

"No, no," screamed the High Priest, "not that way! Face it around the other way!"

The workmen wrestled the heavy sword to reverse it. With a final "U-u-gg-hhhh!" the workmen let the sword down into place as ordered, where it glimmered and shone, loathsome and monstrous.

"Face" the room it did, indeed. Carved into the large ebony hilt was the image of the demon Belial. His diabolic features leered into the hall. The faceted ruby eyes reflected intense rays of scarlet from the light of the many candles, delegating a kind of depraved life to the face. Scribed in red on the black double-edged blade were runes and symbols that appeared in the uncertain light to scamper and run into each other in a dance of evil.

"All right, all right," grumbled the High Priest, the epitome of impatience. "Now move the table this way about a foot." He watched critically as they obeyed until the table was just where he wanted it. He dismissed them with a contemptuous wave of his hand.

Gazing in adoration at the sword, the priest stood before it, spread his arms wide, and spoke words that made abominable shadows in the oddly turbulent air. Presently he bowed his head in worship. Hearing a disturbance, he turned to see several workmen retrieving dropped black and purple draperies, struggling clumsily to put them up. Others were setting huge black candles on massive candlestands. One stumbled, bumping into a stand, catching the mammoth candle just before it fell. The High Priest's temper exploded. Too much had been going wrong all day.

"Enough!" he cried in high dudgeon. "Finish it in the morning. Get to it first thing!" Like automatons, the workmen set down whatever they were doing and left.

He scowled after them, and turned back to see a dark-haired woman in a jewel-studded black gown emerge from his private quarters. She came gliding across the floor to the priest.

"Lilith!" the High Priest said with obvious pleasure. "See? There it is," he said, pointing at the sword. "I shall stand in front of it, drawing its strength into myself. Nothing will stop us now. Doesn't it look magnificent?"

"Oh, it does!" the High Priestess purred.

"That wonderful sword," he said, gazing at it. "You know its history, don't you?"

"Of course. I *am* the High Priestess, after all!" She swayed and caressed him as she recited. "It was forged by a famous alchemist/blacksmith in the twelfth century. Sorry, can't remember his name right now. Was he the one who fashioned *Nothung*? I forget. He used a meteorite, several metals he never identified, some of his own mysterious potions, ancient spells, a dozen or so curses, and wrought them by his magic with the finest steel from Damascus. There was never another like it. Never will be either."

The priest's eyes were half-closed in the rapture her hands aroused. "And we're the ones who have it!" he crooned.

"Of course!" Her silken voice caressed his ego. "Naturally."

He looked at her covetously, then turned to the Great Hall, studying it. "Everything will be as it should, if those bumbling workmen ever get things straight. By this time tomorrow, Playa Linda will be ours!" He laughed unpleasantly, and the High Priest carried her through a scarcely noticeable doorway beside the tower elevator into his own private chambers. He gazed lasciviously at her as he set her down on his bed.

"Tomorrow will be our first full Samhain in our new headquarters. The blood collected will carry us through to our own Black Sabbath while the world is celebrating Christmas!"

Lilith raised her brows at him. "Is there a young man, a King of the Feast, for me?" She liked young men, especially teenagers. They were best at bringing success and fertility from the other side after the feasts were over.

A frown crossed the High Priest's face. "Not yet." He contemplated Lilith. "But there will be, I promise. There will be!"

He suddenly looked up and around, startled, alarmed. "Did you hear that?" He shivered.

"What?"

"That—those awful voices."

"I didn't hear anything. Forget it. Come on!" She reached up and tried to pull him down to her. He resisted, listening.

"There! like voices, like—who would be singing?" He brushed his hand in front of his face as if to brush away an insect. He sniffed.

"Are you sure you didn't hear it?" He sniffed again. "I smell something—"

Lilith wound her arms around his neck. "My perfume. Special for you. And I didn't hear a thing. You've been working too hard." Her voice was sultry, beguiling.

"Doesn't smell like perfume—" the priest muttered. Then he forgot everything else but her fragrance and her passion.

11 P.M.

Dorothy sighed with weariness as her turn in the prayer vigil ended. Praying was usually as natural and as easy for her as talking to her best friend, which was really what she was doing. But tonight it had been different. There was resistance of some kind. For the first time in years, her mind had wandered. In spite of her determination, other inconsequential things intruded. Forcing her thoughts back to prayer was difficult.

She turned her wheelchair toward her bedroom. *Am I getting too old?* she wondered, then dismissed the thought. Many older people were great prayer warriors. It wasn't that she was not praying wholeheartedly. She had been praying earnestly. It had to be something else. With a little shock, she realized that the only other thing it could be was the Enemy.

As she rolled through the hallway, she became aware of an odor, something foul, musty. *That's not coming from my house,* she thought. Her face was grim, her trust complete. "In the name of Jesus Christ, I command you to be gone!" She spoke the words loudly, and feeling a disorienting rush, realized the odor and the creeping sense of oppression had both vanished.

"Thank you, Lord Jesus," she murmured, a smile on her lips. She prepared happily for bed, praising God. She knew which side would win.

11:45 P.M.

Lights in several houses which ordinarily would be dark bore witness that members of the prayer chain and vigil continued the battle. Some warriors experienced the same difficulties that had beset Dorothy and redoubled their prayers, singing hymns and praising God just as Dorothy had done. Lorraine Kesterson had been praying in her home since two in the afternoon. She was not the only one continuing past her allotted time, reinforcing others' prayers, the power to free Susan.

Outside, eerie tendrils of a noxious darkness kept reaching out to these houses. Although they faded like early morning mist in the face of the rising sun as they came near, new tendrils continued to appear to replace those that had vanished. Faint wailings of defeated darknesses were felt more than heard, and they spurred increasingly earnest prayers.

━━◆━━

Matt paced in his apartment, going over what he had to do in the morning. His undergirding thought was of Susan. Was she all right? Could he get to her before something appalling happened? Erase the thought. Of course he could, with God's help. He went to the window and stared unseeing as ragged clouds scudded across the moon, driven by an intensifying wind.

━━◆━━

Andy lay in bed, restless. Sleep eluded him. What could he do to help? Susan seemed like such a decent person. He liked her. She was just right for Matt. Finally, he sat up, counting off on his fingers the various duties assigned to different people. There wasn't much for him to do, and he felt left out. Even irritated. He decided on sudden impulse to go to the Castle first thing in the morning to see the layout for himself. Pictures and drawings were fine, but no substitute for seeing the place for himself. Then perhaps he could be more help. He lay back down, and soon was asleep.

━━◆━━

At the Garcias, lights were on in the living room, where Karen's parents paced, restless and worried. Neither Henry nor Carla was able to sleep, wondering if the police would be able to do anything. Carla's voice caught as she wound her arms around Henry's waist and laid her head on his chest. "The police sergeant didn't seem to think Karen's disappearance was all that serious," she murmured. "Wonder what he'd say if it was his daughter." Henry stroked her hair as he held her in silence.

━━◆━━

Don and Elizabeth sat at the kitchen table over the drawings, sipping hot chocolate and going over the plans. A tear slipped down Elizabeth's cheek as she set her cup down. "I don't know, Don," she said. "That's such a fortress. Maybe they're too strong for us."

Don glanced up. "Don't even think that!" he said, looking back at the map. "It's a good plan—" But his voice trailed off.

Raymond was sitting up in his bed, his eyes closed, lips moving as he prayed intensely, not only for forgiveness, but that his sister would come back home unharmed. But would God hear him, let alone answer his prayer? He had been so rotten, done such awful things. Would He even listen? He opened his eyes, gazed into the darkness, and burrowed under his covers, choking back a frightened sob.

Susan lay wide awake, thinking of her family, of Matt. Surely by now they would have something planned, some way to get into the grounds, into the Castle. Andy, too. He was just what Matt had said, a really exceptional person.

Worry gnawed at her. What about Karen? What have they done with her? Is she all right, or have they filled her with drugs again? She shook off the thought. Worry won't help a bit, she told herself sternly. Her stomach reminded her of the food and the pills the servant Margo had brought. She had flushed them down the toilet. Deliberately turning her thoughts away, she continued to pray. In moments she was lost in praise and petition, spreading a soft radiance in the Castle's horrid darkness.

A peculiar uneasiness permeated the Castle. The High Priest was propped up on his elbow, looking perplexed at Lilith. She had turned her back to him angrily. For the first time he had been unable to satisfy her. Something was making him jittery. He felt as if little creatures were crawling all over him. And those voices! Where were they coming from? Why didn't Lilith hear them? He fussed, fumed, cursed, yet he could not relax.

Lilith was furious. What if he did feel uneasy? It shouldn't affect his performance! She had expected him to satiate her, as he had always done before, but tonight it seemed as if he wasn't really there at all. *What's more important than me?* she demanded of the night. *He's here to serve me, High Priestess Lilith!*

A sudden chill went through her. An almost imperceptible presence seemed to hover over them, watching them. An unfamiliar feeling crept like ice through her. Could this be *guilt?* Was something, someone actually *judging* them? No! Who would dare judge *them*? They were accountable to no one but Belial! She turned suddenly and jabbed the High Priest in the stomach with her elbow.

He doubled up, gasping. "What did you do that for?" he wheezed. She turned away from him again without a word and lay silently in the dark. For awhile she nursed her spite. As the minutes passed, she grew increasingly fidgety. Vague shimmers, nearly invisible at first, seemed to loom before her, then suddenly behind her, near the ceiling, at the door. Never had she seen anything like this! Fear grew like a monstrous devouring beast within her. She screamed, turned to the High Priest, and terrified, wound her arms around his neck, nearly strangling him.

Like the poisonous tendrils attacking homes of Dorothy's vigil members, patches of darkness surrounded certain churches where larger groups were deep in prayer. Sections of the evil black shadows seemed to break off in inhuman shapes to batter and destroy themselves on roofs, impervious windows, or doors. Horrid wailings were answered with songs of praise to God, anthems and psalms. But the vain buffeting went on.

Most of the city slept, read books, watched late TV, played poker, danced to frenzied rhythms, or worked at night jobs. Mothers wakened and staggered to warm milk and to change a diaper for crying infants. Addicts swallowed more pills or prepared more shots of cocaine. Felons committed crimes, unaware, uncaring, unconscious that there was a war going on. Yet the world itself seemed to be hushed, waiting, as the battle continued.

The winter storm track from Alaska down the Pacific coast had started early, October rather than November. San Francisco had been lashed with torrential rain. Heavy winds had torn power lines loose, causing fires, or a chilly darkness in many areas of the city, an accidental electrocution, confusion in the streets, traffic collisions, heavy runoff. The Golden Gate Bridge swayed in the gale, paralyzing motorists with dread.

Rain had started in Santa Barbara about ten o'clock. In the expectation of heavy drainage from the mountains, homeowners sandbagged their buildings by flashlight, and prayed there would be no landslides resulting from extensive wildfires during the previous summer, which had robbed the hills of soil-holding vegetation. People in low-lying areas in Ventura, remembering the disastrous flooding of the previous year, looked apprehensively at the rapidly rising streams and the drainage from the hills.

The leading edge of the storm was making itself known in Los Angeles. Sprinkles dampened the streets just enough to loosen oils and grease, causing fender benders, twisted tempers, and a few serious accidents. A truck jackknifed against a power pole, cutting off power from brilliantly lit Hollywood. Police fought vainly to prevent looting in downtown stores. Partying celebrities merrily continued their Halloween celebrations by candlelight.

A howling wind tore huge, ragged veils from the massive black cloud approaching Playa Linda from the north. A restless police captain stepped outside to the sidewalk, sniffed the stormy wind, studied the threatening sky, and shook his head. *Halloween,* he thought. *What kinds of mischief will we have to deal with tomorrow?* A small shiver shook his shoulders, and scowling, he went back in, sat down at his desk, and added several names to the duty roster.

TWENTY-NINE

Thursday, Halloween, 5:32 A.M.

The gusty northwest wind howled. Yadush, dressed in jeans and a shirt like the work crews at the Viking Castle, led Laura Neubauer and her assistants from the van eastward up the hill at wide intervals. Most of her crew were burdened with equipment, and all were dressed like Yadush.

Although the eastern sky showed a faint opalescent glow under storm clouds, darkness still shrouded their path. Each in turn sprinted up the hill, stooping, occasionally stopping to see if they had been discovered, then made another brief rush, hugging the brush at the edge of the south walkway. Short of breath, they turned north through the scrub oaks, toward the cellar door at the back of the building. In the first faint light of dawn major obstacles, such as brush, rocks, and trees, were only blacker darknesses along the way. The only light in the Castle came from the kitchen.

At the fence separating them from the cellar door, Yadush took a small radio from his pocket and spoke a few quiet words. The radio squawked a reply, and Yadush nodded at Laura. With unexpected agility Laura and her crew climbed quickly over the briefly neutralized fence. The crouching run to the Castle was an exercise in disciplined panic. Buffeted by gusts which drove dry leaves, dust, and other small particles against their faces, they slipped one by one from boulder to boulder. Finally in a rush, they arrived breathless at the cellar door.

Yadush knew the combination to the lock. "I helped in the renovation," he said, his voice hushed, and briefed them on the layout. "Most of the workmen used to be—I guess they still are—under the influence of an exotic drug. It makes them incapable of individual thought or decision. For all practical purposes, they're temporarily zombies. So don't forget," he warned. "If you have to come down for any reason, you have no minds of your own. If, God forbid, one of the coven should order you to do something, drop whatever you're doing and *do* it! Do just as you're told and nothing else."

He led them down the cellar stairs, along the empty corridor to the elevator, and up to the Great Hall on the third floor. As the elevator doors swished open, they assumed blank expressions and stepped out into the dim immensity of the deserted room just as if they belonged there and knew where they were to go. They looked around, saw heaps of fabrics near the tall windows, large candles as if dropped here and there on the floor, and huge candlestands set about apparently at random. All looked unfinished.

"By the way," Laura whispered, "where are these coven people? I don't see anyone." She shivered involuntarily.

"Witches and satanists are night people," said Yadush. "They get up late in the morning. The workmen will get here about eight."

Laura and the five men nodded, looking around. "Good thing no one's here yet," Manny, her foreman, said. He pointed to the ceiling beams. "We can get up there and string the lines." He looked from place to place, mentally mapping his strategy, tugging at his lines to make sure the pulleys and nylon ropes worked smoothly. He faded into the shadows, barely clanking.

Laura sighed. "It's going to be a long day," she said. Her long blonde hair was tucked into a bulging cap. At thirty-five, her figure was as slim as it had been ten years ago, but was now hidden under a loose flannel shirt. Her costume was in the bundle she carried. "Isn't there any other place I could stay until it's my turn?" Her voice was wistful.

Yadush shook his head sympathetically. "A pretty broad ledge runs around near the top of the room. Maybe I can find some cushions so you'll have a place to relax, at least."

She made a wry face. "Guess that'll have to do." She turned to one of the two who had not yet disappeared. "Chris, hang around down here until this turkey brings the cushions, and bring them up to me, willya?" Yadush grinned. No one had ever called him a turkey before. Somehow it made him feel as if he belonged. Laura looked at him skeptically. "You know something? You're nuts. We'll never bring this thing off."

Yadush lifted a shoulder. "We've got to try."

Laura tightened her lips, nodded, and gestured to Chris. He

faded into the draperies. She turned to the other. "Better get up top, Kevin."

Kevin picked up the last of the cloth-covered loudspeakers and went to find a place to put it. Yadush looked around once more to make sure no one else had arrived. In a short time the hall would be a beehive of activity. Oh, yes. Cushions. There would be cushions on the first floor. He stepped into the elevator and emerged a short time later nearly hidden behind a mass of cushions. Chris took them from him, wondering how he'd ever manage to get up to the ledge with all of them.

Leaving the way he had come in, Yadush sorted out what else he needed to do before showing up at the Walkers'.

6:45 A.M.

Andy looked back to see if his vehicle was visible. He had parked close to the hedge, just around the bend. Nothing. It was satisfactorily out of sight. The wind was growing stronger, he noticed as he squinted at the roiling dark clouds.

He put his back to the hedge and sidled against the wind toward the gate to see it for himself. Matt's description was explicit, but he wanted to see for himself. Feeling a little let down, he could see Matt had been absolutely complete and accurate. So why was he here? The brick entrance curved into a heavy wrought iron gate. Just like Matt said. Most likely only a switch inside the Castle would cause the gate to swing open. Or a general power outage. Or a short.

Seemed for a moment there that he had an idea. But only for a moment. It was a long way to the building. Even if he could get past the gate, he wouldn't get very far. Gusts of cold wind flung gouts of dust and pebbles from the bare ground. Andy shivered with the chill.

He turned and started back to his 4X4. Glancing at his watch, he saw there was time enough to explore a little before the meeting at Walkers'. He walked uphill for a better look at the other end of the hedge and gazed up the slope of the hill south of the fence. If he went up that way, he'd be in plain view to anyone at a window on the east side of the west-facing Castle. The chaparral had been cleared from inside the fence, just as Matt and Buck Soderberg said. Outside the fence, except for the four-foot wide path, the bushes grew thick and practically impenetrable except to a rabbit.

Straight ahead on the east, where the hill rose more steeply beyond the fence, live oaks scattered among the shrubs might provide cover, but how would he get there? He had noticed the north side looked much like the south, except there were almost no windows. But he saw poison oak growing under what looked to him like poison sumac along the walkway. Good place to stay away from.

He heaved a sigh and went back downhill to the Jeep. He reached into the glove box for a copy of the Castle layout, spread it out over his steering wheel, studied it, trying to decide what, if anything, he could do. The tap on his shoulder startled him. So did the ham-handed individual dressed in black sweatshirt and jeans who yanked him out of his vehicle.

A big red-haired wrestler-type slugged him in the stomach before he could adjust to the sudden change in position. A hard right to the jaw put him down on the blacktop, and all six and a half feet of Ham-hands stood straddled above him. Dazed, Andy struggled to one elbow, gently feeling the left side of his jaw.

"We seen ya prowlin' around. Ain't nobody does that 'round here." Ham-hands reached down, grabbed Andy by the collar and hauled him toward the gate. Red-head drove off in Andy's Jeep. Andy was too groggy to protest. Ham-hands pushed the button beside the speaker, said "Scanlon," and in moments the gates opened. Head throbbing, feet stumbling, Andy finally found himself inside the fence, although not quite in the way he had planned it.

9:00 A.M.

Lacey was worried about Susan. There had been no answer at her apartment the night before, nor at eight this morning. Susan didn't usually leave for work until about eight-fifteen. Maybe she had misdialed. She called the *Register*.

Alison answered.

"This is Lacey Robinson. Could I speak to Susan?"

"Susan? Just a moment." Alison put Lacey on hold while she pondered what to say. Jackson's only instructions were still to tell people she was out. She punched the button. "I'm sorry," she said. "She's not in right now. Can I take a message?"

Maybe she's on the way, Lacey thought. "Would you ask her to call me when she gets in? I'm at my office at Robinson, Beckman, and Stolt."

"Sure thing. Thank you for calling the *Register*." Alison punched the button to cut the connection before Lacey could say anything else.

Strange, Lacey thought, turning on her desk lamp. *Susan's usually at work on time. Oh, well, she'll call when she can. Susan will call.* But uneasiness gathered like threatening clouds on her horizon, intensified by the dark, rolling storm clouds she could see out the window.

9:20 A.M.

Donovan, Pastor Wayman, Buck Soderberg, Stanley Raisbeck, Jessica Fairchild, and Dorothy Webb sat around the freshly cleared table in the Walkers' dining room, comparing notes. The fragrance of coffee still hung in the air.

"Hasn't anyone heard from Andy?" asked Donovan, looking around the group. No one had. "He was supposed to be here for breakfast. Hope everything's all right," he muttered.

The doorbell rang. "Maybe that's Andy," Don said. He came back with Yadush in tow. "He hasn't seen Andy either," he said, indicating Yadush. "But he got Laura and her crew into the Castle already. Here, sit by me. Will someone try Andy's phone again?"

Jessica went to the phone, stood listening, put down the instrument, shook her head, and shrugged her shoulders. "Not even his answering machine."

Buck got his map out again and laid it on the table. Everyone studied it silently. "Okay," said Matt. "So Stan turns off the juice, and we get through the gate. What's to keep the guards from yelling to alarm the Castle?"

Pastor Wayman held up several slender cylinders. "Don't ask. When I told a friend what was going on, he gave them to me. They're harmless. They'll put the guards to sleep for a couple of hours. When we figure out who's going to use them, I'll tell them how. Just don't get near enough to breathe any of the stuff. Won't hurt you, but you'll be awfully sleepy."

"Gordon Booth got the drawings of the alarm system his company set up for the Castle," Matt said. "Andy turned them over to me, and Stan knows a guy who can disable it in no time."

"That's great. How many stories in the Castle?" Don asked. "Five at the tower?"

"Right," Yadush said. "The rest is three stories high. And there are two elevators, one for the tower, and one in the entry for the first three floors. Plus stairways."

"And the Great Hall. You said that's on the third floor?"

"That's right. The first floor is like an ordinary house: living room, dining room, huge kitchen, bedrooms. There's a big meeting room on the second floor, several smaller ones, and bedrooms. A dumb waiter connects the kitchen to the second floor meeting room. Of course the Samhain ritual will be in the Great Hall on the third floor. Besides the Great Hall, there are three conference rooms. Oh, and the High Priest's quarters. The tower rooms on the fourth and fifth floors are reserved for special participants in the rituals, and a locked room that no one but the High Priest uses."

Matt nodded. "Vern Hunemiller promised to do his stuff. I hope this wind won't mess him up." He looked around. "So Laura Neubauer and her associates are the first ones in place. Thanks, Isham." He nodded toward Yadush. "It'll be a long day for them, but it can't be helped."

Don smiled. "It should be quite a spectacle when it's time."

Jessica shivered. "Is it cold in here?" she asked, rubbing her arms.

"Wasn't," Matt said, "but I feel a chill now, too."

"I'll bet the Enemy's working overtime," Dorothy said. "I had a rough time praying last night, and I think one of his representatives was in my house. I ordered it out."

Pastor Wayman nodded. "I'd guess what we're feeling now is only a shadow of what the people in the Castle have planned for tonight." He looked grim. "I've an idea it won't be a picnic."

"Oh, by the way," said Matt, "remember Father Anthony at St. Joseph's? Andy said he's really anxious to be part of this."

Don looked dismayed. "Oh, I forgot. He could have joined us here." Don thought a moment. "Why don't you call and ask him to come over? We'll go over what we've planned, and maybe he'll think of something we haven't." He looked around at everyone. "Meantime, I think we're entitled to a coffee break."

"Thanks," said Jessica, "but I have to get back to the costumes. They've got to be ready. Coming, Dorothy?" Jessica had driven her to the Walkers' and would take her home.

"Right." Dorothy turned and wheeled her chair toward the door. Buck leaped to help her get into Jessica's car. "I can stay," Buck called over his shoulder. "The boys can keep the garage going for awhile."

"I'll have to go, too," said Stanley. "And thank Andy for the alarm system layout. George will come with me later."

As Matt spoke with Father Anthony on the phone, Don and Pastor Wayman put their heads together, planning.

9:35 A.M.

Andy sat up, swung his legs off the edge of the bed to the floor, looked around, and put his head in his hands. Where was he? What in the world had happened? Little by little, it came back to him through the pain. *Man, what a dumb move it had been to come to the Castle alone.* His head ached beyond description, his jaw was sore, he was bruised all over from the pounding Scanlon and Rusty had given him when they had dragged him into the building.

Looking around the dismal room to which he had been brought and shuddering at the representations of devils and their symbols, he hoped he had been missed by now. He prayed no one would be foolish enough to try to be a Lone Ranger like he had and come for him without an army.

He pushed himself to his feet, wincing with pain. Muttering and groaning, he limped to the window and looked down. A large prickly pear cactus covered the ground two stories below. Nevertheless, he shoved at the narrow double-hung sash. It was immovable. He scowled, turned to see if anything else looked as if it might promise escape.

He jumped nervously as the doorlock scraped. Backing up, he stood in the center of the room, wild-eyed, fighting to appear calm.

The door opened. He stared. She looked like a school girl, dressed in a simple white dress. Her lustrous brown hair hung in soft waves to her shoulders. Her gray eyes looked innocent.

"Please don't be alarmed," she said in a gentle voice, closing the door behind her. "I'm Lorena. The High Priest wanted me to explain the situation to you." She smiled and sat down in one of the chairs. Andy backed off a step. She laughed. "I'm not going to eat you! Why don't you sit down and relax?" Her head tilted slightly, and, more than ever, she looked young and vulnerable.

Andy glanced around for a chair and sat, continuing to stare.

Lorena looked sympathetically at his bruises. "Rusty and Scanlon got mashed for treating you so rough. They thought you were a thief, and the High Priest asked me to apologize for him. We've had some break-ins recently, and the boys went way too far. They should only have questioned you. We want to make it up to you."

What's going on here? Andy wondered. His eyes narrowed slightly as he looked at Lorena. "He does? Then how about you show me the door, and let me go home?"

Lorena's light laugh rippled. "How would it look to your friends if you went home looking like that? You're invited to stay here as our guest and have our nurse take care of you and your bruises while you rest up. By the way, we have some special medications that can help heal them very quickly." She smiled archly. "And you're invited to be our special honored guest at our celebration tonight."

Uh-oh, Andy thought. "Thank you very much," he said, his voice cracking like a teenager's, "but I'm due at a very important meeting—uh—right about now. As a matter of fact," he added hastily, "I'm late. I need to go now."

"Oh, but you mustn't! We really want you to stay and enjoy our little party. It's our very first celebration since we've moved in here, and it'll be very special. You'll stay, won't you? Please?" Her eyes implored as she stood up and came over, taking Andy's hands.

Andy shuddered. Her hands were cold as she exerted small pressure for him to stand. He pulled his hands away, but stood. "No, miss, I really have to go now."

Lorena sighed, looked into his eyes sorrowfully. "I wish you'd stay," she said wistfully. "I'll have to tell the High Priest you want to go." Her softness seemed to diminish as he watched. "But it's up to him, of course." She turned and glided out.

Just as she turned, Andy felt a chill. He had seen her eyes narrow, her soft lips thin into a tight, hard line, and the school-girl look vanish like smoke. *What's it all about, Andy?* he wondered. *Was she for real? And what was all that about being an "honored guest"?*

9:50 A.M.

Buck was just folding up his maps again when the doorbell rang. Don went to open the door and saw a young man in Levi's, a red plaid flannel shirt, and a navy wool jacket.

"I'm Father Anthony from St. Joseph's. Are you Don Walker?" He smiled broadly, showing toothpaste-ad-white teeth and dancing blue eyes. Rosy cheeks accented fair skin and wavy light brown hair.

"Uh—ah—yes, I'm Don Walker. Come in, come in!" Don said, extending his hand, his face showing his surprise. "I—mm—"

"Expected to see me in a black suit and backward collar?"

Don closed the door behind him and chuckled. "Right. But you aren't, are you? Here," he said, ushering him into the dining room. "Father Anthony," he said, introducing him to the others.

"Call me Tony. I'm not on duty right now." He repeated the names as Don spoke them, memorizing them. He looked around. "I don't see Andy."

"He hasn't shown up yet," said Matt. "Hope he'll get here soon. I'm about to start worrying."

Father Tony's eyebrow rose. "Wonder what happened? He's always been johnny-on-the-spot, long as I've known him."

"Well, sit down," Don said. "He'll probably show up soon." Yadush came in, set the coffee pot back on the table. The aroma of fresh coffee followed him into the dining room. Buck brought in a fresh tray loaded with cookies and mugs.

While they helped themselves to the goodies, Don, searching for something to say to this surprising stranger, asked Father Tony if he thought exorcism would be appropriate.

The priest shook his head. "Not under the circumstances. There will be a mob there, so I can't use the direct approach, one on one, you know. I'll try to generalize, improvise, and pray the devil out of them, but I can't guarantee a thing as far as exorcising demons is concerned. But I do want to help, and I'm game for anything."

Don's eyes twinkled as his smile finally welcomed Father Tony into the meeting. "That's probably just about what we'll have to deal with there at the Castle. I like your attitude." He sipped his coffee, approving this young man.

THIRTY

Thursday, Halloween, 10:45 A.M.

The young mother cringed as one of the coven priests came into the little tower room assigned her. She drew back as deeply into the bed as she could force her body, cradling her newborn son, desperate to protect him.

"Now, Elsa, you know better, don't you?" he said in his most soothing tone. "Just think of the honor, the greatness that is about to be bestowed on you both." He reached for the child. Elsa fought him, beating at him with one hand, screaming epithets at him, scrambling to get away from him.

"No! You can't! I won't let you!" she screeched, clutching her baby tightly.

She shrieked as he tore the infant from her grasp. The door opened, and two guards came in and took her by the arms, wrestling her down on the bed as she screamed for her baby. They held her while the priest set the howling baby down in an easy chair, took a syringe from a deep pocket, and jabbed it into Elsa's arm.

"You know what to do," the priest said, picking up the infant and slamming the door behind him.

A table in another room was covered with towels. Various oils and ointments stood by, ready for use. The priest set the wailing child down and began his litany. He poured a bit of oil on the baby's body and rubbed it all over the child as he chanted, dedicating him to Satan. He then took another towel and wiped the baby clean. The infant had stopped crying. Now he was ready for the special unguents which would be applied during the service. The priest laid the newborn down in a prepared bassinet and left the room. The baby whimpered, then fell asleep.

11:00 A.M.

Leaving Lilith, the High Priest assumed a properly haughty manner as he approached his subordinate priests. "Now, have you assigned someone to bring in the infant?" He looked at Karen's priest.

"Yes. The one who wanted to quit."

"Fine. Good choice. Be sure she's properly prepared."

The man nodded. "The chalice is ready and so is the knife."

One of the lesser priests coughed. "What's the matter, Sternfeld?" The High Priest stared forbiddingly.

Sternfeld looked anxious, frightened. "It's just that—Well, my four recruits don't want to participate." He looked down, worried. Failure was unacceptable.

The High Priest seemed to tower over the others. "You know that does not matter, not with us. Are their physical capabilities up to requirements?" His voice was icy.

"Yes." Sternfeld looked at his feet.

"Then do whatever you must to see to it that they will perform their sacrifice tonight." His voice had risen from cold to shrill. He turned away from Sternfeld to the rest.

He straightened as if to smooth his ruffled feathers. "Any questions?" He looked from one intimidated priest to another. "None? All right. Just be sure everyone is ready. Right, Sternfeld?"

"Right." Sternfeld looked glum.

The High Priest faltered, appeared to test the atmosphere, sniffed, scowled, his air of command somehow diminished. He looked around with a distrustful expression. "I don't like this. Too many things going wrong."

Sternfeld became apologetic, fearful. "I'll take care of them at once!" he assured his superior. "No matter what I have to do."

The High Priest looked at the distraught Sternfeld. "Not you specifically, Sternfeld!" he said with withering scorn. Sternfeld shrank within himself.

"Anything else?" His sense of authority was firmly reestablished. Silence. "In that case, you are dismissed." The High Priest stalked off to his private quarters, and the rest dispersed. Sternfeld stopped to look daggers after the High Priest as he disappeared. He muttered something under his breath and joined the others.

2:10 P.M.

Jerrod Robinson was wearing a path in his rug, churning over and over again the Chairman's reaction to his government securities plan. *What was the matter with it?* he wondered. *Money's money, the plan would have made lots of it, and that's what we're in this for, isn't it? Or is it? Is there something I'm not seeing here? Something about the setup that stinks?*

He gazed out the window at the wind-whipped whitecaps, the angry breakers, the wildly tossing eucalypti, the traffic on the boulevard below. He had half a mind to resign at the meeting. The more he thought about resignation, the lighter the weight on his back. *I'll do it,* he decided, then turned on his heel and sat down at his desk.

3:10 P.M.

Andy paced the small room, becoming angrier and more frightened by the minute. The High Priest had come in after lunch with the High Priestess, she who had dared assume the name of the ancient sorceress Lilith. The woman had prodded, questioned, and rubbed up against him, all the while studying him as if he were a side of beef hanging in a meat locker. Finally, with an enigmatic smile and a sidelong glance at him from her mysterious eyes, she turned to the High Priest and announced, "Lorena's right. He'll do."

"Do what?" he had demanded.

The priest had looked disdainful as he turned to Andy. "The High Priestess has approved of you as King of the Feast."

Icy chill rippled through Andy as he remembered tales from his distant pagan Scandinavian past. And as he had stood transfixed, Lilith had let him know that unless she had her way with him, she'd plan a less desirable—and less alive—role for him that evening. "Better change your mind and cooperate," she had snarled.

Hah! he thought. He'd be dead anyway if he couldn't get out. He had shouted defiance, flung open the door, and actually put his hands on them, shoving the struggling pair out of the room. Their angry threats, obscenities, and blasphemies still rung in his ears.

I've got to get out of here before they come back with more muscle, he thought. He had studied every corner, every latch. Nothing. What about the closet? That was one place he hadn't really explored.

A few empty hangers hung on the rod. With cold, shaking hands, he pushed at the back of the closet experimentally. Was he dreaming? Did it really yield a bit? Hope soared as he explored the edges and the moldings.

4:20 P.M.

Matt waved the truck to a stop before it came near the gate. "Park here," he yelled. Some fifteen men jumped down and clustered around Matt, asking questions and pulling equipment down from the truck, which had water district signs stuck magnetically to the doors. The men all wore orange vests and hard hats, and some carried shovels.

"George and Stan have already done their thing to the alarm system," Matt said. "Just make it look as if you're working and get things set. When everything's ready, come back here and we'll see what has to be done then."

They scattered, each to his assigned location. Matt looked at his watch, then up and down the road, waiting for the next arrivals.

4:30 P.M.

Voices, footfalls, the scraping of moved furniture, sounds of energetic preparation, and the clatter of pots and pans from the kitchen filtered through to Yadush, standing alert in front of the door to the deserted office on the ground floor. He peered both ways down the vacant hall, opened the door, slipped in, and closed it silently behind him.

It was an ordinary office: a desk, several chairs, a bookshelf, and a row of files set up against the rear wall.

The files, he thought. Hoping they were not locked, he headed for them. Not sure which one held the information he needed, he started at one end, pulled open a drawer, looked over a few folders, then moved over to the next stack. He paused over a list, replaced it, closed the drawer, and pulled out the one below it. He shook his head, skipped a row, opened a drawer, flipped through several file folders, stopped, took out a sheet, read, nodded, and closed the drawer. He reached into his pocket, took out a folded floor plan, and spread it on the desk. He turned on the lamp and referred to the file sheet and back to the sketch. He smiled grimly in satisfaction.

From another pocket he took another plan, compared the two, folded both layouts and the sheet of paper, turned off the light, and eased out of the office. The corridor was still empty.

He headed for a seldom-noticed door at the end of the hall, opened it, and disappeared into the dark.

4:30 P.M.

The tall, expressionless woman had been helping coven members prepare for the evening ceremonies. She was dressed in a long, sleeveless white sheath with a low neckline, which emphasized her wraithlike frame. At the end of the room Karen sat still and quiet; she had been injected with sedatives. Now the woman headed for Karen, carrying a filmy white garment.

"Stand up," she said in a thin, expressionless voice. "Take off your clothes and put this on."

Karen, light-headed and foggy from the drugs, took the garment from the woman's hand and looked at it. There was almost nothing to it. "All my clothes?" she murmured as the woman turned away. She didn't want to do this, but her new-found strength and resolve had drained away, leaving only skin-prickles of anticipated horror.

The woman stopped. "All." She looked coldly at Karen, then was gone. Karen wanted to scream her defiance, but her vocal cords seemed paralyzed.

She looked around at the twelve other girls in her coven. They all wore simple black floor-length gowns with cap sleeves, except for June Parkhurst and Ellen Rodzinsky, whose knee-length, low-cut gowns were white. The tall blonde seemed groggy, a ghost of a smile occasionally touching her lips.

Karen turned her back to the room, and, snuffling in misery, removed her clothes and slipped the flimsy garment over her head. She pulled it down as far as she could, but it came just to the tops of her thighs. It was so sheer as to be almost transparent, and, although it was gathered here and there and flared below the waist, she felt as exposed as if she were totally naked. She could feel blood rushing to her face in embarrassment. "Lord," she whispered, "give me strength!" But she felt only terrifying weakness.

Her coven priest came into the room to check progress. Nodding to the others, he came toward her, staring. "You'll do," he said, his voice hoarse. "Come with me." He took her hand and dragged her, protesting, through the clusters of girls staring curiously at her. Outside the door, he pulled her toward the tower elevator at the end of the hall, gripping her hand so tightly she could not pull away.

"Don't! Don't!" Karen begged tearfully, dragging back, dreading what must come next. "Let me go!"

He said nothing. Karen sobbed and struggled to pull free. The elevator doors slid open and the priest dragged Karen in. Still fighting, Karen cried, "No, no, no!" The doors slid shut, and the hallway fell silent.

4:32 P.M.

Yadush turned on his flashlight, which illuminated the old staircase and reflected off little piles and scatterings of sawdust and construction litter on the floor and the risers. Warily, he mounted the stairs to the second floor. They had been used recently, even though the stairwell had been boarded up. Not long ago, someone had left footprints, now covered with a thin film of dust. Who? When? Why?

But there was no time to wonder. At the top, he shone the light around the landing. The stairs continued up to the third floor, but there on the landing was what he was searching for. A panel in the otherwise solid wall. He hesitated. What would he find on the other side? The drawings indicated a small cubicle, most likely a closet. But would there be someone in the room on the other side of the closet?

It didn't matter. He had to try it. Susan's life might be at stake, and he owed her at least this much. He pushed. The panel seemed to be stuck. He pushed a little harder. It refused to budge. He stopped, thought, and tentatively pried at an edge with his knife. A portion came loose. He pulled the panel, creaking, partially away from the nails that held it.

His flashlight showed a rod just above eye level from which hung a few empty wire clothes hangers. Good. Maybe no one was in the room. He left the panel hanging from the moldings inside the closet and put his ear to the door. No sound but the thump and rush of blood coursing through his own veins, and the heavy breathing he was trying to control.

Gently he turned the knob, grateful there was one on the inside, and opened the door a crack. He could see a corner of a bare mattress on an iron bedstead. He pushed the door open farther and stepped into the empty room. He walked to the window to orient himself relative to the room the list told him Susan would be in. Silently, he let himself out into the hall, listening for any sounds that might indicate the arrival of one of the guards.

There. That was the room. He reached for the keys he had appropriated from a desk drawer and found the master. He inserted it in the lock and turned it as quietly as possible. He opened the door partway, then he relaxed. Susan was standing in the middle of the room, a strange expression on her face. He stepped in, opening his mouth to speak. Then the lights went out.

Andy looked in astonishment from Yadush's prone figure to

Susan, then put down the remains of the chair which he had smashed on Isham's head. "That's not a guard."

Susan rushed to Yadush. "Close the door, quick!" she whispered to Andy, feeling Yadush's head to see if the skin was broken. There was no blood, only a growing bump.

Andy brought a moist towel from the tiny bathroom. "Here. Maybe that will help." He knelt down, turned Yadush over on his back, and held him up by the shoulders.

Yadush moaned and his eyelids fluttered. Susan blotted his forehead with the damp towel, and moved it to the top of his head. His eyes flew open and reacting, he pulled away, landing on the floor. "What—oh, my God—Susan!" He looked up at her. "Why did you wallop me? But you were in the middle—" he looked around perplexed, and his eyes bulged. There, hunkered down on the other side, looking painfully apologetic, was Andy.

"I thought you were a guard, and I was going to take your keys and get Susan out of here," he said contritely.

Yadush struggled to sit up. He put his hand up to his head. "Aaaagh!" he groaned, touched the growing knot. "Never mind that now. I was coming to get her out myself." He winced, struggled to his feet, and looked curiously at Andy. "What are you doing here?"

Andy shrugged in embarrassment. "Trying to make up for my stupidity. I came out alone this morning to look over the place. Couple of goons caught me and put me in a little room like this one."

"But how did you get in here with Susan?"

Andy told how he had found the loose panel in his closet, removed it, and stepped into the empty closet of the adjoining room. He had listened; no sounds. He opened the door to an empty room, went to the closet on the other side of the room, took the panel down, and stepped into Susan's closet. "So here I am. We were just figuring how to get out, when we heard the key."

"And I was never happier to see anyone in my life!" Susan said. She stared at Yadush. "How in the world did you—Never mind. Tell me later. Let's get out of here!"

Yadush's broad smile transformed his solemn face. "Right! The sooner the better." He opened the door a crack and peered out.

Suddenly distressed, Susan reached past him and pushed the door closed, shaking her head. "I can't! Karen's still here. I can't leave without her!"

Yadush looked with compassion at Susan. "I'm sorry, but the

three of us cannot get her out." He hated to say it. "She's scheduled for something special—I don't know what—and they've taken her to the tower. We'll have to wait for the others, then do what we can."

Susan wavered. "I don't know. We came here together, and we should leave together." She turned back to Yadush. "Isn't there any way we can get her from the tower?"

Yadush shook his head again. "The elevator is the only way to get there, and you have to know the combination to get in. I don't."

Susan could not let go of the urgent need to do something to get Karen out of there. Karen had trusted her. "What can we do?" She turned anxiously to Andy.

"What Isham said. Wait for the others and pray God will lead us." Andy looked at Yadush. "What's going on outside?"

"They're working on the attack tonight. You'd be surprised at the number of people involved. Even your friend Tony. I honestly think our best bet for getting Karen out is to come in with the troops. They're planning to put the fear of your God into these—" he bit off the epithet. "Well, these people."

Susan bit her lip, then nodded reluctantly. "All right. Let's go. The sooner we let Matt know what's happened to Karen, the better. Lead the way!"

Yadush opened the door slightly, peered out in both directions, and beckoned them to follow into the empty room at the end of the hall, into the closet, and down the old stairway.

THIRTY-ONE

Thursday, Halloween, 5:27 P.M.

Yadush cracked open the cellar door to the outside and peeked. He could see only bare ground and rocks, although the dim evening light could have hidden a troop behind the boulders. Turning back to Susan and Andy, he said, "I think there's enough light so you can see to get to the fence." He described the routine of dashing from one rock to the next boulder, waiting a bit, and making short run after run.

"Wait there for me. I'll call to get the power shut off, and we'll climb out. Then I'll lead the way from there." Susan and Andy nodded in unison.

Yadush opened the door, stepped out, and flattened himself against the wall. Susan followed, Andy joined them, and at Yadush's nod, Andy ran in a crouch for the nearest rock, melting into it in the dim light. By the time he reached the fence, Susan was ready. When Yadush joined them at the fence, he spoke into his little radio, waited a moment, and nodded to Susan. Clambering up the links, she arched her body over the barbed wire and dropped on the other side, followed by the men.

"Okay," Yadush said softly. "It's not full dark yet." He looked at Susan's gray dress and the dark blue shirt over Andy's jeans. "But I think if we're careful, we can make it down to the road unless someone is watching out of the east windows. But I doubt it. They're all too busy getting ready."

Yadush went first and was almost immediately lost to sight. Andy cocked an eyebrow at Susan. She slithered along the bushes, making use of every bit of cover she could find. Andy finished the slow dance with shadows, and at the road, hastily rounded the chaparral beyond the south end of the hedge where Susan and Yadush waited for him.

"The car is just out of sight behind a small bunch of young scrub oaks," Yadush said. "Better stay close to the brush along the road just in case someone from the Castle comes along." They walked the quarter mile to the car in silence.

Opening the door, Yadush said, "I wonder if you know how happy your friends will be to see you. They've really been worried. And they'll be grateful for anything you can tell them about what's happening. He got in and started the engine. All three smiles were so bright the headlights seemed superfluous as Yadush made a U-turn and skidded around the bends toward Playa Linda.

5:48 P.M.

The High Priest supervised the preparation and mixing of the potions for the ceremony, praising a man here, urging more care there. The elevator door in the hall dinged open. Sudden footsteps, angry female voices, and general tumult approached the laboratory. He looked up angrily. "What is the matter with you?" He shouted, pulling open the door to reveal Lilith, Lorena, and several other witches.

"He's gone!" Lilith shrieked, throwing her arms up and open. "He took down the panel at the back of the closet and escaped! My King of the Feast!"

The High Priest's eyes flamed with fury. "I *told* them to make those walls solid!" he thundered. "But no, 'It's costing too much,' they complained, and—" He stopped, thinking smugly to himself, *except, of course, for my own private passage.* Suddenly, his eyes widened. "What about that Walker girl?" he demanded, clutching Lilith's arm.

"Ow! You're hurting me!" She pulled away, sullen. "What Walker girl?"

"*You know* what Walker girl!" he shouted. "The one from the paper who wrote about us! Publicized us!"

Lilith smoothed down her hair and her gown. "Oh. Her. I don't know. How should I know? I've nothing to do with her. But my King—"

The High Priest pushed her aside and strode angrily from the room. Lilith and her coven of witches watched in astonishment as he disappeared toward the elevator. She muttered fluent, extraordinary curses, and herded her retinue urgently after him.

The priests and assistants left behind had stopped their work, staring. When all were out of sight, they looked at each other perplexed, then went back to their pouring, measuring, and mixing.

6:05 P.M.

A cold, eerie feeling pervaded Karen's tower room. Black velvet draperies covered the walls, swallowing much of the light from the black candles placed around the room. A table covered in purple velvet at the end of the cubicle held a chalice and several vials.

The priest pushed her, shaking with fear, down onto a chair. "Listen closely, little one. There's time to say this only once. Tonight I will give you to Belial. Our lord will either bestow his gifts or his punishment on you, depending on your obedience. Now drink this." He took a vial filled with a brownish-red liquid from the table and extended it toward Karen.

"No!" Karen exploded with anger. Fear had cleared her mind. "I won't! I don't care what you do to me." She was astonished at her own words.

The priest's expression did not change. He quickly slipped his left arm around her head, pinched her nose, forced the vial between her lips, her teeth, and poured, tipping her head back in the same movement. Karen struggled but he held her in a savagely powerful grip. Finally, dizzy for lack of oxygen, Karen swallowed, coughed, gasped, and sputtered. The nauseating liquid slid sickeningly down her throat in spite of all she could do. She tried to stand, to run from the room, but her legs betrayed her.

The priest turned back to the table, picked up another vial, and set it aside. Turning back to her, he said, "You will play an important part in the ritual tonight. Did you ever meet Elsa? No? She just had a baby this morning. You, my dear, will offer to Belial the purest, most pleasing sacrifice of all, a newborn baby." He chuckled. "A newborn baby is pure. He belongs to God, and you will give him to the devil! How fitting!" He looked fiendishly at Karen. "You, a child of God, will sacrifice the purest of all beings to Belial!" His wicked laughter echoed and re-echoed in her head as she felt herself growing faint.

"Oh, no, you don't! Not yet!" the priest said, slapping her sharply, bringing her back to consciousness. *Oh, dear God*, she prayed silently, *help me! Help me!* But it seemed to her the prayer was absorbed by the black velvet, and the priest's evil laughter was her only answer.

He took up the vial he had set aside and turned back to Karen.

"Now. You will drink this. It will calm you, and you won't be afraid any more. Here." He extended it to Karen.

"No! I won't, I won't, I won't!" she cried, slapping the vial from his hand to the floor, where the liquid puddled, a faint vapor rising from the spilled draught. She stared in horror as her priest seemed to expand in his rage, to tower over her.

"Yes, you will, you will, you will!" he whispered sibilantly, his face close to hers. He reached back for another vial. "You will drink this one, then," he said. Again he reached around her head to pinch her nose and force the liquid between her clenched teeth.

As the fluid slipped down her throat, a peculiar numbness came over her. Then, before she faded into unconsciousness, she suddenly felt a warm, glowing Presence enveloping her. A gentle voice said, "My child, do not be afraid, for I am with you. I am always with you. Whatever happens, do not fear. I will care for you." The words echoed and re-echoed into the eternity out of which they came, and Karen slumped unconscious into the priest's arms. He picked her up, carried her into an adjoining cubicle, and dumped her on the cot.

We'll see, little one, we'll see, he said to himself. *You'll do as you're told. You'll see. And you'll belong to Satan.* Smiling grimly, he left the room.

6:10 P.M.

Lilith and the High Priest, starting at opposite ends of the corridor, ran from room to room, banging doors, searching for the missing King of the Feast and the Designated Sacrifice, one Susan Walker.

All the rooms had been searched to no avail. The High Priest met Lilith, scowling, at the end of the corridor. She turned viciously to him, screaming obscenities. "You finally found me a decent King of the Feast and what did you do, you bumbling third-class idiot? You let him get away! Now what will we do for a king?"

The High Priest's eyes narrowed as he looked at the fuming witch. "Don't be any more of an imbecile than you need to be," he hissed. "That Walker woman is the real problem, not your young plaything. We can assign any coven member you want, but Susan Walker is a reporter!"

Lilith, her rage diminishing, glanced up at the priest through her lashes. "*Any* coven member? From *any* coven?"

His voice was acid. "Yes. Go! Find yourself a playmate!" He turned away in pique, presenting his back to her. When he heard the elevator doors close behind her, he looked around. The corridor was empty. Swiftly, he moved to the last door on his right, opened it, entered, and closed it quietly behind him. He opened the closet door, examined the back panel, which had been hastily, clumsily, re-fastened. He touched a spot six inches to the right of the panel, three feet above the floor. The panel swung open, and he took a flashlight from a pocket in his voluminous robe and pointed it at the floor. His eyes glittered like shards of ice as he gazed at the three pairs of footprints on the landing and the stairs.

Straightening his back, his face a mask of demonic wrath, he slipped the flashlight back into his pocket. In the dark, he spoke in massive Ogygian phrases, pronouncing doom for those who dared to violate his private passages, who defied his will, who dared threaten the very heart of his sanctuary. As he uttered the terrible words, luminosities in grotesque forms appeared at the very edge of vision, adding their gibbering to the rending disharmonies stirring the very dust of the Castle.

7:22 P.M.

Jessica Fairchild was supervising the fitting of the last of the costumes to the latecomers. They had eaten stew and homemade bread as soon as they arrived. The ones who were ready earlier were still at the long dining tables.

Raymond and Alan looked at each other and burst out laughing. Raymond, as Robin Hood, had stuck his beard and mustache on crookedly. Alan reached out to straighten it.

"Hey, careful!" Raymond said. "That sticky stuff makes it sting when you pull it off!"

"Cry baby," Will Scarlet teased. "There. That's better. So what's so funny about me?"

"You've got your hat on backward!" Raymond doubled up laughing. Alan went to Jessica to ask how it should be and had it reversed.

A five-foot-tall green elf spoke out in a baritone voice. "It's too tight across the shoulders. Can I have some more room?" The woman adjusting it nodded, her lips holding pins. Jessica fled to guide a short fairy princess who was backing up too closely to a wall, crushing her wings. Another mother was struggling to turn up the hem of the skirt.

"Oh," the princess said in a boy voice. "Sorry. Didn't see that back there."

"It's okay," Jessica said. "The wings weren't hurt this time. But be careful not to back into anything again." She looked at him, a brown-belt karate student, amazed that he looked so soft, so pretty.

Pastor Wayman, touching a paper napkin to the corner of his mouth, came from the tables to look over the bustling scene. He nodded in satisfaction, standing beside Jessica as she pointed out several of the strongest, some of them among the shortest, characters. "Especially this young man, who came in this morning from the Lutheran church to volunteer," said Jessica. "He's right over there." She pointed at a merry pointy-faced clown wearing an orange fright wig and a baggy costume and brandishing a huge red water pistol.

The pastor grinned, nodded appreciation at the young man, and glanced out the window. "I hope the weather holds off," he said. "It's getting cold outside. Be sure they all have something warm to wear when they start out."

"Oh! By the way, when are we supposed to be at the Castle?"

"From what Mr. Yadush says, they start the ceremonies about nine-thirty. I think we should be there soon after eight-thirty. We probably should leave here at—oh, nine at the latest."

"Fine. We'll be ready. Oh, no!" Jessica took off, hurrying across the room where a young pilgrim was struggling out of his freshly basted costume, nearly ripping the seams. "Careful!" she cried. "I'll help you!"

Pastor Wayman grinned, watching Jessica maneuver elbows and knees past strained seams. He looked out the window again. The sky was heavy with dark, scudding clouds. A stiff wind blew dust and dry leaves against the glass. Not a good night for kids to be out, but what else could they do?

8:50 P.M.

Jerrod, sitting at the impressive teak conference table in the Castle's second floor meeting room with the twenty-three other members of the Corporation stifled a yawn. The room was dimly lit by copper-shaded desk lamps at each place, which illuminated whatever papers members had brought. Their faces were distorted by the reflected light, which cast eerie shadows, making caricatures of their faces. So far the meeting had been just report after report. Numbers, numbers, numbers. None of them made any real sense.

Jerrod glanced toward Gilbert and wondered briefly what was the matter with him. The young man fidgeted and seemed nervous. His fingers went to his mouth frequently. Jerrod's eyes went to the Chairman. As usual, his lamp was dark, making it impossible to see his face even as vaguely as those of the others. He sighed quietly as the voice droned on and fingered his own report. Would he have the courage he'd felt that afternoon? Would he actually resign? He bit his lip.

Gilbert struggled against weakening resolve. The problem was that he was making a lot of money. He liked money. He liked being important in other people's eyes. But the way this bunch was doing it—how could he go on with it? His house of cards had been tumbling ever since he found out where the money was going. Never had he imagined that conscience would prod him the way it did. He had never thought he even *had* a conscience!

People he swindled deserved to lose. They wanted something for nothing. It was on their own heads. They should know there's no free lunch. But paying legislators to cheat, to twist laws to benefit themselves and the Corporation rather than the country—and making drug addicts of kids. Who knew what terrible things might happen to them? Something inside him rebelled. No. He couldn't do it any more. He paused in his contemplations.

Suddenly, an unfamiliar thought came out of nowhere. People talked about God giving strength in tough situations. Did He? *Was* He? Gilbert was desperate, ready to try anything.

Well, God, he thought, *if You're there, if You're real, I need to know it. I need more courage than I have. When it's my turn to give my report, if You're really there, will You stand with me and give me the guts to say what I really think? I don't know what will happen when I do, but it's at the point now where I don't really care. God, if You are, I really need You.* He hesitated and nearly stopped, then went on. *If You'll help me, I'll know You're real, 'cause I can't do this myself. And if I can do it, I'll believe in You. I'll have to!*

He wouldn't have called it a prayer, only a deal.

THIRTY-TWO

Thursday, Halloween, 8:32 P.M.

Lacey was ready. She had studied every line, every touch of makeup in the picture of Elizabeth Taylor, and had copied it exactly. It was the eye makeup and violet contact lenses that finally did it, she decided. She put away the diamond-dusted purple mask, which would have obscured her eyes. Standing in front of her mirror, she looked from her reflection to the photo and back again. She adjusted the augmentation of her bustline, pulled her hair into loose curls as much as possible, and approved the general appearance of the Liz Taylor look-alike that gazed back at her. The dress wasn't exact, but it was near enough to the violet spangled bodice and flowing skirt in the photo to emphasize the likeness. She looked great.

So why did she feel so edgy? So nervous?

She closed her bedroom door behind her, imitated the characteristic Taylor descent of the curving staircase, a gloved hand on the balustrade, a soft fox jacket held in the other hand following down the stairs.

John, dressed head to toe in black as a cat burglar, stared, astonished. "My dear," he said, "if I didn't know it was you, I would ask for an autograph. I may just do that anyway." He took her hand and kissed the glove, bowing more deeply than usual.

"Silly! Help me with this jacket. It's cold out there." John helped her shrug into it, and they left as the wind wailed eerily around the house. Margaret stood in the shadows, wringing her hands, a prayer on her lips. *'Tain't right, it ain't*, she thought. *Something's wrong. 'Twas a banshee I heard just now, for certain."* Shaking her head, she went back into the kitchen.

8:40 P.M.

At the Crawford home, Cynthia was ready. Her pale hair was arranged in a lofty jeweled mass, and she swung a long, extravagantly embroidered black velvet cape around a sleek, full-skirted red satin gown. As a final touch, she added a small black mask over her eyes, smiling in mischief as she hooked it behind her ears.

"Cynthia, you look wonderful!" Lacey said. "Who're you supposed to be?"

"Nobody special. I just let my imagination make me into something I'm really not. If this weren't Halloween, I'd feel foolish!"

John stared appreciatively. "Never feel foolish, darling. That outfit brings out a Cynthia I never knew before. You're simply gorgeous."

Cynthia blushed and spoke hesitantly. "Ah—could we go now, please?" She turned to Lacey, taking her by the arm as they hurried toward the car. "Incidentally, you fooled me. I actually thought I was looking at Liz."

Lacey beamed. "Oh, you're kidding. But thanks!" She was enormously pleased.

Arriving just before nine, their lights showed a work truck parked by the road a short distance from the curved Castle entrance. Several limousines were parked near the gates. John pressed the button, spoke his name, and the gates swung open.

"I'll have to leave you for a few minutes with the group," he said as they passed through the iron gates. "I hope you don't mind. There are a couple of people I need to talk to, but I'll get back to you soon. Of course, I'll introduce you and get you started. Okay?"

Cynthia and Lacey looked dubiously at each other. "Must you?" Lacey asked.

"I'm really sorry, but it won't take long. You'll like these people, I'm sure."

Lacey studied the forbidding-looking Castle. "Are you sure this place isn't haunted or occupied by Frankenstein?" The car stopped at the entrance.

John laughed. "I'm sure. Come on. They're expecting you." He opened the door, and they scrambled out, fighting the wind. A large, rough-looking guard let them in and indicated the arched living room entrance.

Lacey looked back at the guard as they crossed the hallway. "What goes on here that they need a bouncer?" she asked, smoothing her windblown hair back into place.

"I heard they've had some break-ins lately," John said. "These people own valuable artifacts and art objects, so they've hired extra help."

A group of variously dressed young people sat in a circle near the fireplace. Three thick candles stood on the round table in the middle of the circle. Except for the fireplace, they were the only source of light in that cavernous, shadowy room. Lacey suppressed a shudder. The wind was blowing a gale, making eerie sounds in the fireplace chimney and around corners. Heads turned as the three newcomers entered, some smiling, some curious.

A man, sporting a tie-dyed boat-necked T-shirt, ragged jeans, long hair, and mustache, stood up and extended a hand. "John!"

"Good to see you, Eric," John said, taking his hand. "How's business?"

"You know how it is with stocks. Up and down. Mostly up this week. But these young ladies must be Cynthia and Lacey!" He stared at them, struggling to control the amused grin twitching at the corner of his mouth.

Lacey struggled to smother her embarrassment. *Liz Taylor*, at Height-Ashbury? She put her hand up and spoke in John's ear. "Why didn't you tell us?" she whispered. She glanced at Cynthia, who was similarly chagrined.

John spoke softly from the corner of his mouth. "Remember? I said 'something comfortable'." He greeted several others and turned to a tall woman in orange.

"Tasha, this is Cynthia, the one with the pentacle. I'm sure you can help her. Now if you'll excuse me?" He disappeared without another word.

9:10 P.M.

Vern Hunemiller parked his pickup well east of the hedge, his headlights illuminating the dusty night. "I dunno, Ralph," he said to the man sitting beside him. "This wind makes me nervous."

"Maybe we better go on to the north side." Ralph said. The men back in the pickup bed were moving restlessly, rocking the pickup. "Wind coming from the northwest, it could be dangerous here, unless it rains a lot and soon."

Vern sat silent, started his engine, and moved on to a dim light by the side of the road. The headlamps shone on Matt, huddled deep in his jacket against the wind. He held a flashlight, his hand nearly covering the lens.

"Hey, where'd you park your car?" Vern asked out his window.

"'Bout a mile down the road," Matt answered, shivering. "Sorry about the wind. Can you still manage something? S'posed to rain later."

"We wondered about setting up on the north side instead. That do it?"

Matt nodded. "Okay by me. The effect will be the same. Guess you can control it easier from there."

Vern glanced at Ralph. "Think so?"

Ralph strained to see, took out a map and a flashlight, studied, then nodded. "Yeah, I think so. Better than on the south. It's well cleared, and we'll watch it. Sure hope it will rain. I'd feel a lot better about it."

Matt nodded. "Go ahead. Set it up for about quarter to ten. The Trick or Treat gang should be here a little after nine-thirty."

The pickup switched to parking lights, rolled ahead, and Vern guided it slowly past the curve beyond the far end of the hedge. Parked, it was nearly invisible, as were the eighteen men who unloaded equipment and quietly walked back to the fence.

9:12 P.M.

Tasha, the tall girl in the loose-fitting, dropped-waist orange print dress, studied the inscription on the pentacle by the light of the candles, then looked up at Cynthia. "You'll find a similar inscription on a lot of these," she said. "This one's nice."

Several of the group left their chairs and clustered around Tasha, shoving between the two, crowding Cynthia toward Lacey, who had moved back away from the group. Lacey's eyes met Cynthia's. She scowled in disapproval at their lack of consideration. Cynthia shrugged.

"Cynthia!" Tasha called. "Come here." She shoved an opening for her. Cynthia and Lacey pushed through the knot of people toward Tasha.

"See?" Tasha said when both were standing beside her. The others went back to their seats. "What it means is that the soul who is involved with Wicca—that's an ancient art and religion, you know, probably the original religion in the world—anyway, as it says here, the soul who lives in the heart of Wicca is always happy. That soul knows good from evil, knows them both intimately. Consequently, she's always able to choose the good. See?"

Cynthia looked up, frowning. "Wicca. I've been wondering about that. Does it have anything to do with witchcraft?"

"It's another name for witchcraft," Tasha said. "Actually, it's an old word for witch. But there are good witches and evil witches, and we do only white magic, good magic."

Lacey shivered unaccountably, pulled her fur jacket closely around her. Where had John gone? Why had he left them with these people? Where was the party? There had to be a party. Cynthia still stared at Tasha, who spoke in her cultured voice about the wonderful things they'd been able to do with their white magic. Lacey wished she hadn't come. Why didn't John come back?

"So you see," said Tasha, "it's what you have in your mind. You think on good things, and with this pentacle to help, good things happen." She returned the pendant. Cynthia hesitated, but finally fastened it around her neck again, biting her lip in indecision.

"Thank you," she said. "I appreciate your explanation. Do you know where John went?" She tried to keep the strain she felt from her voice.

"He'll be back in a little while," Tasha said. "Why don't you sit down with us and join in? We're calling on the forces of nature to heal our world."

Cynthia looked toward Lacey. Lacey looked anxious, almost jittery. But what choice did they have? Eric rose and fetched two more chairs. He made room in the circle for them and invited them to sit down.

"Come on," he said. "The more people we have calling, the stronger the forces to heal." He smiled, stood invitingly behind the chairs.

Just as Lacey and Cynthia started toward the circle, John appeared in the doorway and beckoned to them, looking harried.

"Cynthia, Lacey," he said, "something's come up. I think you can help me." He turned to the others. "Eric, bring your group up at the regular time. About twenty minutes." Eric nodded and moved the extra chairs away. When he had resumed his seat, they all took hands, closed their eyes, and hummed, "Ommmmm." Lacey shivered again, and followed Cynthia and John to the elevator.

"Where are we going?" Lacey asked. "What's going on, anyway?" The doors closed behind them. "I know it's Halloween, but how come the whole place is so dark?"

John's expression was solemn. "There's another meeting upstairs, but a couple of the people who were supposed to be present aren't there. They need a certain number—it's kind of a long story, but if you'll help out by just being there as substitutes, they'll be very grateful!" He ignored her question.

"What would we have to do?"

"Nothing. Just stand. Just be there. And—well—whatever you see, don't take it seriously. Actually, try not to notice anything." He spoke rapidly, obviously trying to make it sound innocuous.

Lacey looked uneasily at Cynthia. She looked only annoyed. The elevator came to a stop and the doors opened, John took them both by the elbow and led them across an immense dimly lit hall through a wide, open doorway, to what looked like a dressing room.

"It isn't that you don't look wonderful, both of you," John said, "but this group wears simple robes. I hate to ask you, but would you change? There are white robes in the closet there, and after the meeting, you can dress in your own clothes, and we'll have a party. All right?"

As Lacey thought through the confusing explanation he'd given, something screamed "No!" inside her, but some other, stronger force made her nod her head. Cynthia also nodded grudgingly.

"I can't thank you enough," said John with a grim smile. He stepped out, closing the door behind him.

Lacey turned to Cynthia. "What's going on? I don't like any of this," she said.

"Neither do I," Cynthia answered, but she began to change her clothes.

9:15 P.M.

"Mr. Crozier, your report." The Chairman had not appeared to move at all during the meeting. The wind howled at the windows, under the eaves.

Gilbert shuffled his papers nervously with shaking hands, his breathing ragged. He looked around the table from one face to another, shivering as ice gathered around his stomach. Suddenly, unable to bear more, he stood and glared at the Chairman.

"No! No longer! This—this *gentlemen's club*," he said scornfully, "is nothing by a pack of wolves!"

In confusion and astonishment, several men stood up at their places and shook their papers at him, shouting about money. The Chairman gaveled them into silence.

"Mr. Crozier," he said in his icy, dry voice, "I will accept an apology on behalf of the Corporation and an explanation after the meeting."

"No apology." Gilbert was suddenly calm and in charge. "I know where the profits go. I know how they influence certain people. I know about the drugs." He looked around at the shocked Corporation members, and noted that only Jerrod Robinson wore an expression compounded equally of astonishment, awe, and even appreciation.

Gilbert continued. "A large percentage of the profits that go to the Corporation are used to pay state and national legislators to influence the passage of laws that will benefit them and us!"

The gavel started pounding again and cries of protest arose. "And that's not all," Gilbert shouted over the noise. "Much of the rest goes to buy drugs to sell to kids! School kids! Your kids!" Men rose to their feet, shouting, and the Chairman pounded his gavel, shouted "Guards! Order! Order! Guards!"

"And that's not the worst of it," Gilbert went on. "Then they get their addicts into witchcraft—"

A large guard dressed in black rushed into the room and pinned Gilbert's arms behind him.

"—and satanism!" he shouted, as the guard dragged him toward the door. "And that's with the money *you* bring into the organization!" he bellowed, his voice fading as he was dragged down the hall.

The pounding continued, little by little the voices fell silent and one by one the men sat down.

All but Jerrod Robinson. He looked around with an expression of contempt, scorn, and pity. Fixing his gaze on the Chairman, he began. "I cannot tell you how grateful I am for what Mr. Crozier has done here this evening." He turned to face the men at the table. "I came here ready to retire from the group, not because of what he said, since I knew nothing about that, but because your *dis*honorable Chairman not only turned down my indisputably profitable plan dealing with government securities, but violated my trust by opening my briefcase." A murmur of disapproval and cries of "I don't believe it!" went around the table. The Chairman gaveled for silence.

With his voice dripping contempt, Jerrod went on. "Now that Gilbert has exposed the rotten heart of this organization, I understand why the Chairman had to turn down my plan. Investing in government securities would eventually have uncovered this whole corrupt scheme. It is with the greatest of pleasure that I resign!" He picked up his papers and scattered them over the heads of the men seated by him and turned to leave the room. He was met at the door by two black-clothed guards. He went quietly.

Had they been there to see it, both Jerrod and Gilbert would have been pleased to see eleven others gather up their papers and leave the room. The Chairman slouched back in his chair. The others looked nervously around at each other, and a twelfth finally re-moved himself. A heavy silence shrouded the room.

＊＊＊

"Hey, Vince, what's going on?" The guards at the gate were stamping their feet and blowing on their hands, trying to keep warm.

"Whaddaya mean, Artie?" Vince asked, turning his back to the wind.

"Those guys." Artie pointed at a group of about a dozen well-dressed men carrying briefcases, walking swiftly toward the gate. "It ain't time for the meeting to be over yet."

Artie shrugged. "Who knows. All we gotta do is let them out." He pressed a button, the gates swung open, and the small group of cohorts disappeared into their limousines.

9:25 P.M.

Chill gusts leaked around the windows and billowed the drap-eries. Wailing winds hooted and howled around the building, whining and weeping like a soul in anguish. The High Priest looked around in satisfaction. A heavy storm was forecast for later in the evening. Perfect. Even the forces of nature were cooperating. If only Susan and whatzizname had not gotten away. Some wretch had obviously helped them. Even used his own, secret, private stair-way! Who could it be? Nobody knew about it. He scowled. Never mind. He'd find out, then, they would *all* go to Satan! A distant rolling reverberation of thunder promised a brilliant, pounding storm later. He laughed wickedly. "Ah, Belial," he crooned, "you make it so easy!"

THIRTY-THREE

Thursday, Halloween, 9:30 P.M.

The Great Hall was ready, empty, and silent, lit only by tall free-standing candles, and the illuminated pentacle set into the center of the floor. It was scarcely visible unless lighted from below, as it was now. Glowing with an unearthly light, it infused the room with an aura of malevolence. A black painted circle surrounded the pentacle three feet away. Within the encircled area were painted occultic, alchemic, and satanic symbols.

Into the silence crept a faint murmuring as the satanists arrived one by one in flickering black lines from opposite sides, each carrying a candle and chanting in an unintelligible, rumbling, macabre gabble. Their voices grew louder as they arrayed themselves on either side of the hall.

The room settled into an eerie hush. Even the candle flames stood erect and still before silent, half-lit faces. After a moment, without a signal, a strong chant started: "All hail to the father, Satan! All hail to the father, Satan." As the chanting continued, the High Priest entered from his private chamber, a goat's head mask covering him down to his shoulders. Arcane symbols in gold glittered on his black velvet robe. As he walked, he held a large, intricately sculpted silver chalice before him.

His measured tread carried him to the altar, where he set the vessel down at one end. Heavy carving on its sides showed disturbing designs of men and women with animals, centaurs and Pans cavorting, and vines bearing not only oddly malformed fruit and flowers, but also wicked instruments of torment. The purple altar cloth, which was decorated with a black upside-down cross outlined in silver on the front, fell to the floor on all sides. Satanic symbols in gold bordered the edges.

The chanting continued as Lilith followed in a robe of scarlet and purple, emblazoned with satanic symbols formed of pearls and gemstones. In her hand was a smaller silver goblet, filled with reddish fluid. Curious symbols, embroidered in gold, decorated the scarlet headband that restrained her hair, which fell down her back like ebony serpents. Her makeup was heavy, almost grotesque, but her small, self-indulgent smile marked her obvious pleasure in her appearance. Joining the High Priest, she set the goblet on the opposite end of the altar.

Lilith and the High Priest lifted high their hands toward each other, touched fingertips, and in a loud voice proclaimed, "Hail, Satan, god of the world. Hail, Satan, god of the world. Fill us with your power!"

Turning slowly toward the thirteen-stemmed candelabra at the ends of the table, they touched one finger at a time to the wick of each unlit black candle, flaring them into flame. The covens answered with a shout, "Hail, Satan!" thrusting high their own candles. After a timeless moment, they lowered, extinguished, and put them away into hidden pockets in their robes.

The ceremony had begun.

9:32 P.M.

In a basement room Jerrod paced and Gilbert sat at the table, drumming his fingers.

"So what do we do now?" Jerrod asked.

Gilbert looked miserably at him. "Honest, I didn't mean to get you into trouble. I just couldn't go along with this thing anymore."

"I wasn't criticizing you, believe me," Jerrod said. "I was never more happy to hear anyone speak out like that in my life. My hat's off to you, my boy. You didn't get me in trouble at all. It was my own doing. I told them off, too, and resigned, only it doesn't look as if they took me seriously." He looked with obvious distaste around the little cell.

"You actually resigned, Mr. Robinson?" Gilbert looked surprised, pleased. "You agree with me?"

"Call me Jerrod. I didn't know anything of what you said tonight. I was just upset because the Chairman got into my briefcase."

Gilbert stood up and paced, ruddy with embarrassment. "Jerrod, there's something I have to get off my chest."

"Oh? More?"

Gilbert shook his head. They sat on one of the cots as Gilbert told him what he had discussed with Lacey the evening before, with emphasis and apologies for feeling superior because he had been more successful with the Corporation, and for many of the things he had said.

"Forget it," Jerrod said. "That's all behind us. Now our problem is—how do we get out of here?"

9:35 P.M.

Coasting to a stop at Matt's signal, three station wagons unloaded clowns, frogs, princesses, and other creatures into a stormy wind hurling leaves, rubbish, sand, and pebbles at them. They conferred briefly in front of the hedge where hasty whispers prompted nods. Sorting themselves into three groups, the first started for the gate and stopped just short of entering the curve, holding tight their costumes, masks, and headdresses. The other two collections of fairy-folk stood waiting by the cars.

"What's the holdup?" Robin Hood whispered. Raymond had insisted on going with the first group.

"Pastor Wayman isn't here yet."

"Oh." They held their places. The wind was blowing hard, smelling of rain in the offing. Dirt and rubbish skittered along, sometimes lifted high by little dust devils toward the heavy clouds.

The heights of the hall were deep in shadow. Up on the high ledge, Laura Neubauer shuddered as coven members lined up to a pulsing, repetitive chant. Deliberately turning away, she checked the rigging, the hooks, the fastenings on her harness. Although her stomach still churned from the sight of the vile scene below, she flashed an "OK" sign to Manny.

He turned to Chris. "Won't be long now," he breathed quietly. Chris nodded, and for the sixth time checked the connections on the CD player and made sure he had the right disc. Everyone else was in position.

On the north side, Vern Hunemiller and several of his men placed mounds of combustibles from the large supply on the truck partly inside the fence. All the firemen were positioned strategically to control any unforeseen events. The signal to start would be shouts of "Trick or Treat!" from the Castle entrance.

9:40 P.M.

Pastor Wayman, Don, Andy, Father Tony, Susan, and Yadush arrived in two small cars and stopped behind the station wagons. Everyone, but especially Elizabeth, had been so relieved when they had heard about Susan's escape. And despite protests from the group, Susan had insisted on going along on the mission.

"Is everyone ready?" The pastor asked. Dorothy nodded. Masks, hats, and headdresses nodded with almost too much enthusiasm for stability.

"Good. Now, Buck!" Buck led his group of eight men, including Sean Reiley dressed as a leprechaun complete with shillelagh, to greet the pastor.

"Let's do it!" he said. The pastor slipped a silvery cylinder to each of Buck's men, and gathering the group around him, showed how to trigger them. "Just be careful to stay upwind!" he added.

"Leaders have handy-talkies?" he asked. More nods. "Okay. But before we do anything else, let's pray." He squeezed his eyes shut tightly, and a golden silence fell around the entire company.

As they finished praying, one more car stopped by the motley group. Six men, all wearing clerical collars, joined them.

"Evening," one said. Curious nods acknowledged him. "We heard about this, and we all want to help. What can we do?"

Pastor Wayman drew a deep breath, beamed a glad smile, and took them aside to outline the plan.

9:41 P.M.

"How long has it been now?" Cynthia asked Lacey.

Lacey glanced at her watch. "About fifteen minutes." She scowled again. "This is crazy! Here we sit like warts on a frog, ignored, forgotten, suspended in time, and nothing makes sense! What's going on?"

Cynthia fidgeted. "I'm worried. Something's not right. Why hasn't John come back for us?"

The door opened. A stone-faced woman dressed in a long white robe came into the dressing room. "Do you know what you're to do?" she asked.

Cynthia shook her head, her brow creased with anxiety.

"No one told us anything except to get into these gowns and to wait here until someone came for us to be substitutes," Lacey said.

"What's going on? What are we supposed to do? Who are we substituting for?"

She stopped, looking closely at the woman. Something about her triggered a rush of adrenalin. Fight or flight. She set her jaw. "I've changed my mind. I'm going home. I don't like the feel of this place. Where's the phone? I want to call a taxi." She stared at the woman, her heart pounding, waiting for an answer. Cynthia gazed at Lacey, wondering why she was suddenly so obviously frightened.

The woman's voice became harsh. "You will join a group of young ladies. We're two short of what we need, and you are the substitutes. You will stand in line with the others, and unless someone speaks directly to you, you will do nothing. Is that clear?"

"What—" Cynthia swallowed "—if someone speaks to us?"

"You will do as you are told. Follow me."

Lacey stiffened her shoulders. "I don't know what you're going to do," Lacey said, "but I'm going home." She opened the closet door to get her Liz Taylor costume. "Count me out of this game." Her voice was grim.

The woman snapped "Lacey!" in a sharp voice. Lacey turned. The woman's eyes were the coldest Lacey had ever seen. Separating her words like beads on a chain, she said "You will come with me. Now. No excuses." She added a sinister-sounding phrase in what seemed a rapid alien tongue. A strange power emanated from her, enfolding Lacey in an unpleasant tingle. Suddenly, it became impossible to resist. She closed the closet door and turned like an automaton to follow the woman. Cynthia seemed to be under the same strange spell. The woman led them into the corridor, into an immense, dark hall lit only by candles and a circle of light in the middle of the floor.

As they stepped in, another woman handed each a cup, saying, "Drink." Lacey, struggling against bizarre lethargy, tried to shake her head "no." The woman put the cup to her lips and ordered, "Drink!" Lacey did, gagged, and swallowed. Cynthia followed suit.

A row of nine young women in black stood just inside the entrance. As if they were puppets, Cynthia and Lacey took their places at the end of the row. Lacey felt as if she were floating mindlessly. She was scarcely able even to wonder at the goat-man by an altar at one end of the hall, on either side of which stood double rows of black robes.

The prayer group at Playa Linda Community Church became aware of an interference, an urgency, a need, a foreboding. Lifting their voices in praise to God, they sang hymns, read psalms, and prayed fervently. The rooftop battering multiplied; the prayer group praised God more resolutely still.

———

The High Priest sensed a baffling anomaly in the unseen darkness, a thin fracture in the unison of the covens' purpose. Uneasiness assaulted him as he finished pouring the last of the wine into the chalice. It wasn't possible, of course, but he still felt as if his control was slipping away. Looking around, he saw Lilith holding her hands to her temples, grimacing in pain. He could feel the fabric of evil wearing thin. Restless coven members shuffled their feet. Desperately he moved to restore the iniquitous harmony.

"Ave, Lucifer excelsi!" he began loudly, although it was not the next item in the ritual. The covens took the cue and shouted the response. He took a page from the Black Mass and spoke the first few words of the blasphemous backward Lord's Prayer, the covens joining in a rousing crescendo.

9:45 P.M.

Matt swung his flashlight up and down in the signal to begin the assault. The first group of Trick or Treaters rushed the gate, shouting "Trick or Treat! Trick or Treat!" They grasped the bars and shook the gates, making a clatter that brought guards on the run.

"What the devil do you kids want?" Scanlon growled, reaching the gate first. Rusty and two others closed in quickly.

"Trick or Treat!" the pointy-faced clown cried. "Give us a treat or we'll trick you!" He fired a squirt of water from his red water pistol at Scanlon and laughed. Suddenly, the lights above the gateposts went out. The group surged forward, leaning on the gates. With the power off, they fell open. The costumed youngsters separated to let Buck's men rush in to hold their slim canisters as close as possible to the guards' noses. Others rushed behind them to try to hold them still. Struggling against the powerful sedative, the guards fell back until they collapsed, sound asleep.

The first wave of youngsters raced through wind-scattered dust and debris for the Castle entrance, followed by Buck's contingent, which now included Father Tony and Yadush. The second and third rank of youngsters were hard on their heels, with the pastors bringing up the rear.

Vern Hunemiller nursed the flame, shielding it from the keening wind with his body. The material must become heated to a certain point, or else the fire would not spread. The process was taking too long, or was he just too anxious? He saw several other embryonic fires scattered where they would frighten, rather than harm, if they could be kept blazing. For a moment he worried. The wind let up briefly; the flame brightened, reached out, caught, and roared into life. Vern stepped back, relieved. He saw the others had also been successful. Now when the wind scattered the material, whatever lodged in the sparse brush inside the fence would continue to burn, slowly at first, but then with increasing ferocity. His eyes sparkled as he went back to the truck to bring armloads of more fuel for the fires.

The first wave hit the Castle door, pounding and yelling, "Trick or Treat! Trick or Treat!" Buck and those whose cylinders were still charged were at the ready for the doors to open. Yadush and Father Tony pushed their way through the tangle of costumes. A shuffling sound, and the knob began to turn. Yadush and Tony squeezed themselves hard against the doors, and two men with live canisters moved in beside them as the door opened.

A large black-clad guard scowled at the yelling youngsters. Father Tony and Yadush, squeezing past, muttered, "Excuse me, I'm late" and fled to the elevator, scarcely noticed. A second, smaller guard joined the first.

"Whaddaya kids want?" the large one growled.

With a small hissing sound, two gas canisters unloaded under the guards' noses. They collapsed slowly. Turning toward fresh air, the youngsters exhaled, breathed cold, fresh air, and rocketed over the sleepers. Buck's men retreated into the shadows outside, waiting for the next wave. The youngsters headed for the stairs, then stopped dead in their tracks.

"Well, hello," said a burly guard, a nasty grin exposing stained teeth. "Sorry, but the party upstairs has already started, and they hate latecomers."

The wide-eyed Trick or Treaters fumbled for words. "Hey," Robin Hood said, "all we want is a treat. Got any candy?" He held out a bag, a hopeful smile on his mouth, although there was fright in his eyes. Sounds of peculiar chanting came down from above, reminding him of Washington Avenue. Chills raced down his spine.

The burly one turned to his four companions. "Nervy, ain't they!"

"Yeh," the tall thin one chuckled. "We better put 'em away." He looked at the sleeping guards. "Lou, go see are they dead or what. We'll take these guys downstairs."

As Lou prodded the unconscious guards, Bull, Beanpole, and the other two herded the youngsters down a flight of stairs. Clown edged closer to the so delicate-looking Fairy Princess and murmured, "First chance we get, I'll jump the tall one, and you get big mouth." Princess nodded, a grim expression in his ice-blue eyes. Robin Hood nodded, lips tight.

Crouched outside, Buck's men watched, helpless, as the youngsters disappeared. Don stopped the rush of the second and third Trick or Treat wave. "Something's gone wrong," he hissed at them. "Buck, can you do something to keep the doors open for awhile?"

Buck, his eyes on the doors, nodded. "I'll see," he said, streaking off to one side of the stairs. Aaron hurried to the other side, peering into the entry. A whispered conference across the stoop; the men scrabbled in the dirt, reached up, forcing something into the door jambs.

Buck and Aaron ran back in a crouch. "Aaron fixed it for awhile," Buck said. "What's the plan?"

A frown creased Don's brow. Raymond was in the group that went in first. What had happened to him? He'd never be able to forgive himself if Raymond was hurt—or worse. His stomach shriveled at the thought. "Gotta work something out quick!" he said. He backed into the shadows with his crew, the ministers, and Trick or Treaters surrounding him, planning their next move. They split into two teams, each fading into the shadows at the sides of the entry stairs, lips moving in silent prayer.

9:50 P.M.

The High Priest took down the Black Sword of Belial reverently, grasped it with both hands by the hilt, and held it high. "All hail to Satan!" the covens roared. Stepping toward the center of the room, holding the sword in both hands, he pointed to the north, to the west, to the south, and to the east. "All hail to Satan!" he cried, lifting the sword high above his head.

"We swear allegiance to Belial! Let the sacrifice begin!" The full-throated response made candle flames flicker.

Lacey, her mind gone to mush, quivered inside. Menace grinned at her everywhere out of the darkness. Sliding her glance toward Cynthia, she knew from her pasty skin and wide eyes that Cynthia felt it, too. They had really done it this time, she thought. Susan had been right all the way. Why hadn't she listened to her? Where was Susan? Why hadn't John come back for them? The questions circled helplessly in a fluorescent spiral, nudging something just out of reach, something that she knew, but couldn't quite catch. The High Priest was saying something—"sacrifice." Icy fingers squeezed at her, but no matter how hard she tried, the scream would not come.

THIRTY-FOUR

Halloween, 9:50 P.M.

The rippling undercurrent of murmured responses resonated in the dark atmosphere as one of the priests stepped out of the shadows, followed by Lorena, naked, docile, her lips curving in a faint smile. The priest stopped in front of the altar, picked her up, laid her down on purple velvet. Priests from several covens stepped forward, aligning themselves behind the altar, each awaiting his turn. Lacey turned her head away as the covens roared approval. At the end, Lorena was carried off into the shadows.

Two priests on each side escorted June Parkhurst, dazed, to the altar.

The High Priest, his hands resting on the top of the great sword, its point on the floor, stood watching. "A great privilege has come your way," he said to her. "Akibeel has asked to have you tonight." Lacey thought she saw June's lips curve in a small smile of satisfaction.

Pointing the sword at the lighted pentacle in the center of the hall, the High Priest stepped inside the outer circle. There, in a loud voice, speaking chilling syllables, the goat-headed High Priest called forth Akibeel, servant of Lucifer. A swirling mist appeared just above the light, took shape, solidified into a tall, powerfully-built, quasi-human form with a striking demonic, almost hypnotically fascinating face, distorted by the light from beneath.

"Hail, Akibeel!" The welcoming roar from the priests almost drowned out the sound of thunder rolling around the building.

"Welcome, Akibeel," the High Priest said, bowing deeply. The vertiginously wavering specter in the satanic circle rumbled in what might have been acknowledgment. "We have prepared a young woman for you so she might bring forth a giant for you, as in the days before the Flood."

Lorraine Kesterson gasped. She had finished the dishes, put the children to bed, come back to the living room, and was just about to sit down with Alfred to read until her turn on the prayer vigil.

"What's the matter, honey?" her husband asked, looking around the edge of the newspaper. Lorraine stared; her face was paper white.

"Something's awfully wrong! I *feel* it!" she groaned, as she dropped to her knees. She began intercessory prayer and implored the Lord to intervene.

Simultaneously, the entire vigil experienced the same terrifying premonition, reacting as one. Prayers soared like eagles, seeking prey.

Yadush had led Father Tony, running as if late for the ceremony, up the stairs to the Great Hall. Sidling through the entrance into the shadows, their faces hidden within cowls, Yadush suggested that Tony ease toward the end of the nearer of the black lines, and blend in as best he could. "Perhaps you'd best pray to your God to help," he said. "These lower echelons of priests are drugged, so they might not even notice you. But the leaders don't use drugs, so watch out for them."

Tony nodded and slipped off into the deeper shadows. Yadush pattered down the stairs again, grateful that the one guard who was on duty was apparently mesmerized by what was going on in the Hall and did not notice him. He slipped quietly outside again and like a shadow, joined Don and the others waiting their turn, hidden at the outside stairs.

Laura signalled to Manny and to Chris. Softly, quietly, music from Handel's *Messiah* began to sound from everywhere, nowhere, all around the Great Hall, insinuating itself in a slow crescendo under and into the chanting of the priests. Dim in the lofty heights, a gossamer figure soared like a bird of paradise, swinging and circling lower and lower.

An icy shiver rippled down the High Priest's spine and for a moment the room seemed to spin. He closed his eyes, shook his head sharply, and everything was solidly back in place again. Relieved, he swept his arm toward the altar. "Take your pleasure with her." June was staring eagerly at the demon.

An unearthly flash of lightning shattered the darkness with its brilliance. Thunder crashed and rumbled, and the wind keened, howling around the windows. A sudden change in the murky atmosphere caused Akibeel to cower and look around in dread. He glanced up, saw the shining glory of an angelic figure swooping down toward him, its arm pointing directly at him. His appearance metamorphosed from demonic-attractive to terrified-evil, the golden lustful glow in his eyes to scarlet flame. With a quick sorcerous gesture, the figure dissolved into a mist that flowed down like liquid and disappeared into the pentacle.

"No!" the High Priest shrieked, feeling again the prickly sensation of little creatures crawling all over his skin. Torn by indecision, he shouted, "Take the girl away! Bring the infant!" June screamed as priest assistants led her stumbling off into another room. She demanded in vain to be taken back to the Hall.

Another priest carrying the baby hurried past June and her escorts, and laid the half-conscious infant on the altar. A slight figure in a short, sheer garment followed, her young face gaunt, haunted, groggy. The priest picked up a shining steel knife, the scarlet runes inscribed on the razor-sharp blade glowing, and pressed the handle into Karen's hand. She heard a smothered cry from the north end of the hall.

"Offer your sacrifice," he commanded. "Now!"

Karen choked down a sob and shook her head vigorously.

"Offer your sacrifice to Satan!" The priest's voice was sharp, forceful. He took Karen's hand and lifted it above the baby. She pulled with all her strength and broke his hold. "No! No! Never!" she shrieked. Sobbing, she dropped the knife and ran off. In two steps he caught her and brought her back, screaming, struggling in horror, to the altar.

"Sac-ri-fice! Sac-ri-fice!" The chanting from the rows of covens began slowly and gradually built up in volume and tempo as he picked up the knife and forced it into her hand again, holding her tightly as she fought against him.

The music of *People that Walked in Darkness* increased in volume, soaring above the chanting.

The High Priest shouted at Karen, "Do it! Get on with the

sacrifice!" He shook with anger, with indescribable fury, on the edge of panic. Karen stood rigid, as in a trance, her eyes squinched, shutting out the chanting, listening to the music from above. She held the knife held stiffly by her side, praying, praying. A nervous tremor among the priests fractured the tonal tissue of the chanting. A similar rift brought disarray to the malevolence of the atmosphere.

"Fire!"
The shout echoed from several locations.

Guards rushed out, dashing around in complete disorganization. Some carried blankets or jackets, shouting conflicting orders and running toward isolated blazes scattered everywhere inside the fence. Others searched for anything with which to beat out the flames. Lamps on the gateposts were shining again, lighting the grounds enough that they did not quite run into each other. The bushes inside the fence were blazing furiously, fed by the wind, spreading to weeds that had not been pulled out. Where one hot spot was finally beaten out, sparks driven by the wind ignited another, and another, and yet another.

One of the guards, sooty and dusty from beating out a burning bush, turned to his companion, dragging an arm across his forehead. "Hey, Vince," he said, "how did this ever get started?"

Vince looked around, leaning into the gale-force wind. "I dunno, Artie. Maybe the wind blew wires down, and they sparked and started it."

Artie looked wearily at yet another burning shrub. "Yeah," he said, "coulda bin somethin' like that." They beat viciously at the other bush.

Vern Hunemiller and company dissolved into the shadows, chuckling, watching closely that nothing outside the fence began burning. Seeing how clumsily the guards worked, several firemen ran for a pickup truck and moved to the south and east to prevent fire from escaping the fence into brush. The rest stayed behind, ready with more fuel to keep fires burning, keeping the guards occupied.

The front doors stood wide open. Watching from the shadows by the outside stairs, the rescuers scampered into the building as soon as the guards began, frantically trying to put out the multiplying blazes.

"Get upstairs to the third floor," Pastor Wayman told the ministers, the newest members of the attack force. "Stick to the shadows. Turn right at the top of the stairs, go to the second door on your right. It's a dressing room, and I'll join you there in a minute."

Don gave instructions to the youngsters to search the rooms on the first and second floors. "In groups of three!" he added, as they scattered.

Matt, Andy, Yadush, and Susan had their heads together, wondering about Karen. "She's most likely in the Great Hall about now," Yadush said. Susan bit her lip, her eyes showing her fright.

"What about the kids who went in first?" Matt asked.

"If they were caught, they'd be in the basement in one of the little rooms where they keep unwelcome guests." Yadush glanced at Susan.

"Sh-h-h-h!" Susan said, her head cocked, listening. "Hear it?" Mixed sounds of chanting and a chorus from *The Messiah* floated down to the first floor. The music lifted her, bringing a smile to her lips.

Matt and Yadush nodded. "Right on schedule," Matt said. "Isham, you and Buck see if you can find the kids. I'll go upstairs with Susan to find Karen."

Yadush nodded, called Buck away from where Don spoke to the others.

Matt looked at Susan. "Ready?"

Susan closed her eyes for a moment, her lips moving. "Yes. Let's go!" She put her hand on the balustrade and stepped up toward the music.

The woman who had brought Lacey and Cynthia into the Hall looked nervously toward the altar where Karen, rigid and unresponsive, faced the exposively angry High Priest. "Something's wrong," she said, a quaver in her voice. "We must do something. Follow me. We'll start our sacrifice."

Lacey and Cynthia looked at each other in dismay. "We're only supposed to stand here as substitutes," Lacey protested, her tongue thick.

"As substitutes, you will do as they would do if they were here," the woman said. Lacey looked at her curiously. The woman's voice was still cold, but it trembled. And how come the mixture of chanting and choral-orchestral music that sounded vaguely familiar? Puzzled, she followed the line to the altar.

A large chalice stood on the table next to a small, shining blade, with several young women dressed in black standing around the table, their eyes blank. Cynthia moved close to Lacey, pressing against her back. "I don't like the looks of this!" she breathed. "I want to get out of here!"

"Sh-h-h!" Lacey shushed. "Me, too! We've got to get away!" *Oh, help, someone!* she agonized, wondering what kind of miracle it would take to get them away. If only her eyes would focus and her head would clear!

Father Tony had found a spot in the shadows at the end of a row of priests. Closing his eyes in a brief prayer, he made a subtle sign of the cross, kissed his crucifix, and hid it back inside the robe. He scattered a bit of holy water from a vial and began mumbling his prayers as quietly as possible. "Almighty Father, Lord God of the Universe—" a shiver seemed to ripple through the man at his left "—hear my prayer." He continued his appeal.

"Listen!" Buck said. He and Yadush had just stepped off the stairs into the basement hallway. "Hear it?" A thumping and yelling, muffled by the thickness of the walls and doors, identified two separate rooms. They raced down the stairs, following the sounds. The first one, three doors down on the left, was high pitched, juvenile. Buck grinned at Yadush.

"The kids!" Yadush said, relieved, sorting through the keys he had not returned to the office desk. "This looks like the one," he said, inserting a key and turning it. He kicked the door open, standing well back.

Two of the boys held chairs, two were ready with fists, two poised for a karate kick, and all six were suddenly astonished.

Yadush and Buck grinned. "Well, say something!" Buck said.

Robin Hood was first to recover. "Wow!" he said, dropped his chair, and ran into Buck's arms. "We were ready to pulverize you!" The rest were talking as fast as teenagers can.

"Hey, take it easy," Yadush said. "They'll hear you clear at the top floor, and pulverize all of us." He turned to Buck. "Get them out of here. I'll see who else is climbing the walls."

The fourth door on the right yielded to the same key. Before he opened the door, Yadush said, "Stand back. Way back. I don't want anyone to be hurt."

He pushed the door open an inch and waited, but everything was quiet. He pushed at it again with his foot and stood aside. This time he saw two men, one of whom was Jerrod Robinson, goggle-eyed. His stomach dropped to his knees.

"You're not one of them, are you?" The younger man put his chair down.

"No, he's not!" Jerrod found his voice and stepped forward, florid with rage, raising his chair. "He's the quack who killed my Amelia!" Yadush stood his ground, his pale face a study in sorrow mixed with anxiety.

Gilbert stepped in front of Jerrod, forced the chair down, and looked him in the eye. "Stop it. Maybe he is, but he's our ticket out of here. If you disable him now, we might never get out."

Jerrod stared bitterly at Yadush, gradually gaining control. "You are Brother Justin, aren't you?"

Yadush sighed. "Yes. I was. But if we're to get out of here, we have to move quickly. We're on a rescue mission, and there's no telling what may happen."

Jerrod's eyes still glittered with hate, but he nodded. "All right. For now. But when we're out of here—"

"Jerrod!" Gilbert snapped. "Enough! Let's go!"

Yadush locked the door behind them. "I guess it's best to keep them in the office for now," he said to Buck. "There's a good reason," he said when Buck protested. "I'll tell you about it later," he said, starting up the stairs.

As they passed the open front door, they glimpsed guards still running from blaze to blaze, shouting to each other. Yadush smothered a grin.

Pastor Wayman, dressed in a black, cowled robe, peeked cautiously from the stairs over the edge of the third floor, hoping no one would be in sight. A thin sigh of relief. They must all be in the Hall, he thought. Slipping along the hallway to the third door on the right, he opened it.

Six nervous black-robed ministers waited, two sitting, four pacing.

"Pastor Wayman!" one breathed, reaching out his hands to grasp Wayman's. "We'd begun to think something had happened to you."

Pastor Wayman shook his head. "Just a lot of planning. Father Anthony of St. Joseph's is already in place. If we move out one at a time, I think we can join him. Stand a little behind him and try not to be noticed."

One of the ministers snorted. "Not much chance of that. I've been hearing a lot of stuff going on, and I think things are going haywire."

"Good!" said Wayman. "On my signal, Father Tony will lead, you will arrange yourselves in whatever version of a phalanx you can dream up on the moment, and I'll bring up the rear. Then we'll see God's power, saving His children!"

"You're sure of that?" asked a timid-looking minister, biting his lip.

"Yes. Have you forgotten? 'He that is in you is greater than he that is in the world'? And there are many here who are with us. Don't worry, Keith. It's all in His hands."

Pausing only for one more hasty prayer, the ministers left singly, let themselves into the Great Hall, and disappeared into the shadows.

THIRTY-FIVE

Halloween, 10:03 P.M.

The High Priest stared at Karen, his face twisted with rage. Lifting his hand to strike her, he stopped as if suddenly frozen. Soaring above the instrumental interlude, *Sheep Shall Safely Graze*, a deep bass voice sounded from everywhere, intoning the solemn words, *In the beginning was the Word, and the Word was with God, and the Word was God.*

As the terrible utterances continued, the High Priest stood still in shock. A tremor shivered through the assembled covens. Elsa, distraught and disheveled, took advantage of the momentary confusion to run from the shadows. She dashed to the altar, snatched up her baby from in front of Karen and the High Priest, and streaked for the door. The High Priest started to run after her, then stopped and turned back, perplexed. He stood still, overcome by indecision. He was bewildered, flustered, and frustrated, not knowing why he was so confused.

Half-sensed vortices had formed in the dim atmosphere, whirling and dipping toward coven members, who ducked at their approach even though they weren't sure there was anything there at all. Then suddenly, the graceful form of an angel plummeted toward the High Priestess. Lilith screamed dreadfully, and put up her hands to fend off the fearful being as it swooped away.

Lacey clutched Cynthia's hand, said, "Let's go! Run!" She staggered through the entrance of the Hall, with Cynthia stumbling behind. They followed Elsa and her baby. Lacey stopped stock still, staring, and ran into Susan's arms.

"Susan!" she cried, choking with a giddy mixture of fear and relief. "I'm so glad to see you," she said, fighting against the dizziness overcoming her.

Susan held her close. "I was afraid I'd never see you again!" She smiled at Cynthia over Lacey's shoulder.

Lacey pulled away, looked at Matt, hugged him, burying her face in his chest. Matt's eyebrows raised, but slowly his arms went around her. "It's okay now, Lacey." He pushed her away gently. "Who's this?" he asked, looking at Cynthia.

"Oh!" Lacey wiped her eyes. "Cynthia Crawford—uh—introductions later? Please? Let's get out of here!"

"In a minute. I've got to see this," Susan said, turning back to watch the proceedings in the Hall. Lacey sagged, sat on the top step, leaning against the bannister beside Cynthia.

Father Tony stepped out between the rows of confused priests, a phalanx of ministers behind him, joining their voices to the recorded ones singing *Unto us a Child is born, Unto us a Child is giv'n.* As they advanced toward the altar, the neat rows of black-garbed coven priests crumbled, some running into the shadows, others stumbling, falling over each other in dread. A few fled in panic for the doorway, down the stairs, and out.

Smoke-covered guards, who were still beating out fires, saw the priests escaping and rushed into the Castle and into a mob of costumed rescuers. Stopped as if by a wall, they stared at the surprised mass of youngsters and saw other strangers on the stairs and the landings, staring down at them from the second and third floors. The inexplicable, fearsome, antisatanic Christian music from upstairs shook them to the bone. Most of them turned and ran out, and never turned back.

Scanlon and three of his closest friends leaped at the costumed youngsters on the first floor, expecting childish, weak resistance. To their astonishment, they were hurled back ferociously. More rescuers pounded down the stairs, pulling off masks and ripping away costumes for action. Scanlon, lying on the floor against a wall, looked at Rusty wide-eyed. They picked themselves up and bolted for the door. There, Buck and his men formed a solid wall. Rusty looked back at the young people facing them on the other side, and all of a sudden, the fight went out of all four of them.

"Hang on to them," Buck told his men. "Watch 'em, kids," he added. "I'm going to the truck to get some of those nylon handcuffs

I picked up from a patrolman friend." He started out, then turned. "I'm real proud of you guys!"

⸻⸱⸺

Karen, suddenly aware the High Priest was paying no attention to her, dropped the knife and ran for the door, blundering into Susan and Matt.

"Karen!" Susan cried, as her arms went around her, but Karen pulled away, running in panic for the stairs. Two steps down, Karen jolted to a stop. "I can't go out like this!" she squealed. "My clothes!"

"Wait! Don't you want to see what's going to happen?" Susan reached her hands out to her.

Karen stared in unbelief. "Susan! Aren't we going to get out of here?"

"In just a minute. I want to see the Lord win this one!" Susan beckoned, excited as she peered into the hall. Karen stared, slack-jawed.

"I'll get you a robe," Matt said, ducking into one of the dressing rooms.

Don, Andy, Buck, and Yadush, having stashed the guards in a truck, pounded up the stairs and stopped to stare at the gathering in the Great Hall. Don pulled Susan into his arms to hug and protect her. Andy stared at Karen, Lacey, and Cynthia. Buck and Yadush watched the ceremony fall apart. Matt returned with a robe for Karen. The group in the hall was becoming a crowd.

Fierce, howling winds battered the building. A slashing bolt of lightning was followed by an ear-splitting crash of thunder. Father Tony continued toward the altar, with Pastor Wayman and the other ministers in a wedge behind him. All of them were singing the *Hallelujah Chorus* with great enthusiasm.

Laura, the angel, soared again as the powerful chorus rang out, *The Kingdom of this world is become*—the angel swooped over the evil gathering, producing panic—*the Kingdom of our Lord, and of His Christ and He shall reign for ever and ever!*

The High Priest, in desperate agitation, grasped the Black Sword, held it high, shouting, "Stop or we'll kill you all!"

A shimmering vortex whirled transparent in front of the phalanx of ministers. At the sight, the priest dropped the sword and put his arms up over his eyes to shut out the monstrous sight. Lilith, terrified, picked up the smaller chalice and hurled it toward the vortex. The chalice bounced off and dropped to the floor, spilling blood at the High Priest's feet. Aghast, she turned and ran for the

High Priest's chamber, but rebounded off an invisible barrier. She dissolved in a helpless, weeping heap on the floor.

Tony and the ministers stopped just before they reached the outer circle of the lighted pentacle and sang mightily, their bodies erect, unmoving.

The High Priest gritted his teeth, rekindled his faltering courage, eyes flaming with rage behind the mask. Cautiously, watching Tony, he bent to retrieve the Black Sword. Raising the diabolic blade, his contempt for Christ intensified. Arrogant, he stepped inside the outer circle again, pointed the sword at the pentacle, spoke shattering sounds, evil utterances, vile words like hideous towers and battlements in the air, calling "Belial! Lucifer! Azazyel! Nergal! Beelzebub! Moloch! Lord Satan! To me! To me!"

Vague blue shimmerings surrounded the High Priest and the sword as he pointed it unwaveringly toward the center of the pentacle, repeating his summons. Hearing his abominable words, Lilith stopped crying, and stood up. Black streaks of eye makeup wandered over her cheeks. Swirling mists appeared above the pentacle, grew, began to solidify, melted, arose again. Some of the priests stopped wailing and watched the pentacle.

The music of *The Messiah* built to an electrifying crescendo with *King of Kings, and Lord of Lords*—

The mists wavered, thinned, appearances of faces came and went, appeared and disappeared, evil, horrid, beautiful, and grotesque. Finally, they faded. The High Priest stood bewildered, the sword inadvertently lowering. Why could he not conjure them as before?

"What is it, my lords?" he shouted over the music, the sword hanging limply from his hand, an expression of confused terror in the eyes visible through the openings in the mask.

And He shall reign forever and ever.

With sounds like great waterfalls, roarings like furnaces were shaped into words that seemed to come from an unfathomable distance. "You have failed," the melded voices proclaimed. "Your false promises and feeble efforts condemn you. You are no longer in charge." The sounds re-echoed, diminished, vanished. The pentacle dimmed, darkened, quenched as the music came to a close.

Hallelujah! Hallelujah! Hal-le-lu-jah!

Tony and the ministers suddenly launched into *Onward Christian soldiers, Marching as to war! With the cross of Jesus going on before!* and it seemed as if all the choruses and orchestras in the world accompanied them. The frantic High Priest pleaded into the dark nothingness before him, then turned to his dissolved covens. Wide-eyed, those remaining backed away from him in terror and disgust. Rage building within him, he yelled, "I'm still your High Priest! Hold your positions! Obey me!" His voice cracked in frustration.

Once more the thwarted High Priest pointed the great sword at the pentacle and shouted the awful spells. This time there was no response, no swirling mist, only the darkened, lifeless circle. In his towering rage, the High Priest tore off the goat mask, his eyes blazing hatred.

In the doorway, Lacey and Cynthia gasped in unison, "John!" Lacey stared wide-eyed, her hand to her mouth, disbelieving. She was only peripherally aware of Susan's arm going around her shoulder, squeezing her and trying to steady her, of Cynthia saying softly, "No, no, no." Cynthia's hands were at her cheeks, eyes staring.

Lightning crackled, thunder crashed and rolled, and the wind howled and keened, as rain drummed at the windows and on the metallic roof. The storm seemed to spin around the Viking Castle, almost drowning out the ministers as they sang again, *With the cross of Jesus going on before!*

"Vengeance!" John howled, swinging the sword around his head with both hands. "Vengeance upon all who dare interrupt the sacred magic of Samhain!" He pledged his soul in blasphemous utterances to Satan, and demanded devastation upon all who did not.

The shimmering vortex advanced to whirl directly in front of him, driving him beyond the outer circle of the pentacle, until he was bent backward over the altar, arms up over his face, still holding the sword, terrified by whatever it was that whirled in front of him. The shimmer suddenly materialized, and a tall, magnificent man clothed in a shining white garment stood before him.

Simultaneously, the other vortices solidified into flying angels, swooping closer and closer to the already panicked covens. Defiant, the remaining satanists hurled pathetic bolts of energy from their fingers, which died as they came near the angels. Little by little, as the angels swooped upon them, some of the coven priests, who had given their human spirits over totally, irretrievably to Satan, deformed and shrank visibly, and they became demons hidden beneath the human masks. Begging piteously not to be sent into the abyss, they vanished into mist as the angels' swords touched them.

Laura, about to begin another swooping flight, hissed and signalled to Manny to stop. "No, Chris, keep the music going!" she signalled when he moved to shut it off.

"What's the matter?" Manny asked. "Something wrong with the gear?"

She shook her head. "Look. Real angels." She pointed. "We're not needed now," she said in awe as she unhitched her harness, and led her crew around to a section where they could all sit, overwhelmed, dazzled, watching the salvation of the Lord.

John stared at the shining being before him. His face white with sudden fury, he straightened and raised the Black Sword of Belial over his head, demanding the power of Satan to strike down the angel before him. Gathering his strength, he stepped forward to strike a death blow.

The shining being raised his arm and said quietly, "Now." A blinding bolt of lightning struck the tower with a deafening, sizzling crack, and ran hissing down the metal roofing. A blue flame leaped from a rafter to the point of the upraised sword and through John, engulfing him in a seething maze of blue fire. He writhed in paralyzing torment. The smoking, scarred sword turned as it fell from his hand, pinning him to the floor. The ruby crystal eyes cracked into rubble as the blue flame died.

The simultaneous thunderous crash assaulted eardrums and rattled the building before it rolled off into the distance, and a heavy hail pounded the roof.

Lilith, frenzied, watched in horror as her High Priest died. She picked up a candelabrum from the table and hurled it at the angel, screaming her rage and loss. Blazing, it flew through only space as the angel vanished. It crashed instead against the draperies and in moments they were flaming. Lilith crumpled to the floor, weeping with rage and sorrow.

Up on the ledge, Laura's eyes widened as she saw the fiery drapes. "We've got to get out! Now!" Swiftly, efficiently, leaving equipment behind, they rappelled down ropes and raced for the elevator.

Seeing death and destruction, to say nothing of damnation, coming toward them, a few coven members and even a few of the satanic priests fell to their knees to pray feebly to Christ in the midst of chaos. The ministers rushed to help them, to pray demons out of them. The rest ran blindly in frenzied circles. Unrepentant, angry, defiant, and lost, they met flames everywhere, setting themselves afire, never finding a doorway in shifting walls of smoke and flame. Sean Reiley with Buck and his men used his shillelagh to good advantage, herding the ministers and their helpless repentants like sheep, guiding them downstairs to safety.

Matt shouted over the din, "We've got to get out! Now!" He pushed the group down the stairs. Flames roared behind them as they staggered down.

Karen stopped on the stairs, causing a tangled backup. "Ellen and June! They're still up there!" She shoved upstairs past the others and ran back into the fiery Great Hall, into the dizzying confusion of panicked people. Matt caught Susan and held her tightly as she tried to follow Karen, and forced her, struggling, down the stairs. Flames had spread almost everywhere. The other candelabrum had been knocked off the altar and the velvet table-cloth was blazing. Priestesses and coven members near the table were screaming, beating at their flaming garments. Others ran deranged, not knowing what they were doing. Their robes, coming in contact with others, spread the fires. Karen squinted through the smoke and flame, yelling at the top of her voice, "June! Ellen!" A wail answered her from the darkness behind the altar.

Yadush and Andy turned on the stairs when they heard Karen's call. Andy yelled at Matt, "Get the others out! We'll bring the girls!" They ran back up and into what was becoming an inferno. "Karen!" they called, seeing her racing toward a dark-haired girl in white, who was frozen with fear.

Karen dodged flames surrounding the altar and ran toward the north end of the hall. Yadush followed, calling "Karen! Here! This way!" Andy circled around the other side to reach the girls. Flaming draperies fell on Yadush's shoulder; he brushed them off, unaware that his robe was afire, and struggled toward the girls. Karen had taken Ellen's hand and was coming toward Yadush. A towering candlestand toppled, striking the side of Karen's head. She fell and Ellen screamed. Andy, his clothing scorched, shoved the fallen candlestand aside and bent to examine Karen. She was unconscious. He touched her hair, and his hand came away covered with blood.

Shoving through masses of panicked people, Yadush reached Ellen. Her fists at her mouth, she screamed continually.

Andy looked up at Yadush's burning robe, ripped it off and hurled the flaming cloth away, and beat out the remaining fire with his hands. He took Ellen by the shoulders, shook her hard. "Come out of it!" he shouted. "Run for the door!" She stopped screaming and ran for the doorway, dodging fiery obstacles.

Yadush bent over Karen and felt the side of her head. His hand also came away bloody. Hastily he and Andy lifted her and started toward the door. A wall of flame stood between them and freedom.

Lilith, seeing Yadush carrying Karen, exploded with fury, wrath, and unexpected grief. In her rage, she picked up the knife Karen had dropped and flung it. The blade buried itself in Yadush's back. He fell, dropping Karen. Andy picked her up and ran to the hallway.

Buck and Don had just reached the top of the stairs to look for them. Andy laid Karen in Buck's arms and raced back into the flames after Yadush.

A massive burning rafter fell from the high roof, striking Lilith squarely on the head. She fell back, sprawling lifeless as a broken doll.

Andy, head down and arm shielding his eyes, shoved his way through to where Yadush lay. Dizzy from breathing smoke, Andy slipped his arms under Yadush and stumbled with him around flaming obstacles, wondering if he'd ever make it to the doorway. Then suddenly Don took Yadush's limp figure from him and both started down the stairs.

"Is that everyone now?" Don asked on the way down.

Andy, coughing, sagged against the balustrade, nodded. "I think so," he finally managed to croak. "Let's get out of here!"

THIRTY-SIX

Thursday, Halloween, 10:14 P.M.

Buck stumbled with Karen into the rain outside, yelling, "Is there a doctor here?"

One of the ministers, drenched, his robe singed, hurried to him. "I was a doctor before I came into the ministry. Name's Kendall Mackey. Call me Mac," he said. He touched the side of Karen's head and his face lost all expression. He turned and shouted, "We need a ground cloth! Henry! Get my bag from the car!"

Vern Hunemiller motioned to one of his men. He ran to a nearby truck, raced back, and laid the ground cloth at the doctor's feet. Buck set Karen down gently, and Mac felt her pulse, then put his head down to listen to her heart. He lifted her eyelid, then shouted. "Anyone have a car phone?" Rainwater ran off his hair.

"I have!" a voice answered.

"Call an ambulance! STAT!"

Don stumbled out of the door and down the steps, carrying Yadush. Andy, his face blackened with soot, staggered out behind him and sat down on the steps. He held up his blistered hands to stare incredulously at them. Ellen stood in shock, answering only in monosyllables.

Sean Reiley took Yadush from Don and carried him over to the doctor. He set the wounded man down on the ground cloth, holding up his shoulders. "See what you can do for this one," he said, his voice hoarse with weariness and smoke. Mac's eyes widened as he saw the dagger sticking out of Yadush's back. He studied it, pulled it out, and carefully lay Yadush down next to Karen. Checking for his pulse, breathing, and rate of bleeding, he nodded. "He'll be all right, I think. Can't tell for sure, but it looks as if no vital spots were hit."

Don tottered and dropped down on the wet ground. "Thank God. This man is nothing if not heroic. Oh, and there's Andy over there. Another hero. He'll need you, too." Mac went to check Andy and fastened bandaging around his hands. "See me in the morning to change that," Mac said, hurrying back to Yadush and Karen.

The ministers and their new converts knelt in the mud, rain streaming from them, praising God, their arms uplifted, faces radiant. Someone began singing quietly, "Praise God from whom all blessings flow—" and one by one, voices joined in until by the third repeat, all were singing.

Lacey stood by her father, holding his arm, trying vainly to sort out her chaotic feelings. Rain cascaded over them, plastering her curly hair close to her skull, her robe limp and clinging to her body. She had just had a close brush with death, so why was she still alive? Everything had been a mess since her mother died. She didn't know what to think, what to believe. Susan told her one thing; Pastor Drane something else. Who was right? How could she know? Then there were Sharleena and Cynthia, and they said something else, and now the horror of this night! All she knew was that these people in the Castle and everyone connected with them frightened—terrified—her. She looked around, saw Tasha and Eric and two or three others from the group Cynthia had come to see. They looked toward her, and she turned her back.

And never had her father looked so devastated, not even when her mother died. His whole life had shattered into chaos, and his face was etched with misery, with guilt. He looked down at Lacey, fearing for her, knowing he'd have to answer to charges of insider trading. Would he have to serve a term in prison? And what of Lacey while he was away?

Gilbert, too, stood as if waiting for doom, making no move to escape. He only wondered vaguely what had happened to the rest of the Corporation. He could see none of them anywhere. He hoped they had escaped. His attention turned to Lacey and Jerrod. He wanted to go to them, talk to them, but somehow, he couldn't. His feet seemed rooted.

Cynthia stood alone, staring at the blazing Castle. Her face twisted suddenly in loathing. She grasped her silver pentacle, tore it from her neck, and hurled it with all her strength into the fire. A shiver went through her, and she turned away, sobs wrenching her as she stumbled farther away from the building. Father Tony, standing by with the other ministers, noticed her distress and walked toward her, holding out his hand to her.

"I'm Father Anthony of St. Joseph's Church," he said. "I don't think we've met."

Cynthia gulped, looked up, wiped her eyes hastily, and inhaled with a sharp shudder. "I—I'm Cynthia—Crawford—" She dissolved in tears, and Father Tony folded her gently in his arms.

"That's all right, Cynthia. It's all right to cry."

After awhile Cynthia was able to talk with him as they walked aimlessly around the grounds. It was so easy to tell this nice man all about the voices, the pentacle, the strange people in the Castle. When words began to fail, Father Tony found one of his crumpled cards in a pocket, gave it to her, and assured her that he'd talk to her anytime she wanted. They shook hands solemnly, and he went to talk to Mac and pray for Yadush and Karen.

Pastor Wayman shook hands with Laura as her crew took their places in the truck. "You were magnificent," he said. "You softened up the satanists, I'm sure. And the music—" he kissed his fingers and blew it off into the rain—"it was superb, and superbly done! God bless you!"

"You exaggerate, but thank you," Laura said. "I sort of got the feeling we weren't really needed."

"Oh, you were needed! Every voice, every prayer, every move we made was needed. We faced a tough enemy, and God won our battle for us." He paused, musing. "Thank you again."

Laura felt herself blushing. "In that case, we were in the best possible company. Well, we'd better get on our way." She waved good night, climbed into the truck, and with tires slipping on the wet, muddy pavement, the flying angel went home, praising God.

Matt took charge of Cynthia when he noticed she was alone again. She was shivering as he put his jacket around her rain-drenched robe. He brought her to Susan, who had by that time turned Ellen over to a group of women who toweled her, talked to her, and tucked her into a car among coats and jackets.

While Susan and Cynthia were getting acquainted, Susan kept looking from one group to another. There had been no sign of June Parkhurst, nor any other coven members. The pit of her stomach chilled. How could she tell June's parents? Or was that her responsibility?

Seeing that Susan and Cynthia had responded well to each other, Matt continued taking inventory of the bedraggled mob watching the flames eat the Castle: the costumed invaders, the firemen, Pastor Wayman, Father Tony, the ministers. Yes, they were all accounted for. Even Elsa and her baby. Jessica had taken one look, led them to her car, and somehow found a thermos of coffee for Elsa. She dragged a blanket from her trunk, wrapped it around Elsa and the baby in the back seat, and in almost no time, had Elsa telling her life story.

Don was suddenly surrounded by his crew of rain-wet, bedraggled, half-costumed youngsters. "You were great!" he said. "You really gave those guards what they had coming to them. But you'd better get out of the rain and to the cars, or you're likely to miss your rides home." Thoughtful and unusually silent, they scattered, waving good nights to him.

Don stood watching them go with his arm around Raymond's shoulders. The rain had wilted Robin Hood's jaunty cap, and the feather was sitting on his shoulder. They looked at each other and saw only love.

The electrical storm moved off southeast toward the mountains around Pine Valley, lightning etching clouds in the sky, thunder muttering and rolling off into the distance.

A siren sounded. The ambulance had arrived. Pelting rain continued as paramedics took charge of Karen and Yadush. As the ambulance drove away, another siren announced the arrival of Playa Linda police. When they had listened to the stories and sorted out the various individuals, they took Jerrod, Gilbert, Scanlon, Rusty, a number of guards, and the coven members and priests in tow. The fire department arrived as the officers were reading rights.

The chief stood by Don, looking at the conflagration. He shook his head. "This rain will probably do more than we can," he said. "We'd better see if there is anyone left alive in there." He motioned to his men to take hoses and breathing equipment into what was left of the building.

The remaining rescuers huddled together in the rain, talking sporadically, watching the flames in all the windows of the top floor. Mesmerized, they stood in horror as floors crashed down and down. A huge blazing torch engulfed the tower. The entire building except for the stone walls was being devoured by a sizzling, flaming, roaring monster. The firemen returned, shaking their heads. No one visible anywhere. "We'll have to wait for it to cool," one of them said.

As one by one the watchers fell silent, only the howl of flames from the infernally glowing heap of rubble was to be heard—until a voice arose, praying for the souls of those who had died, blending with the booming rumble and roar of the flames and the crash of falling timbers. Father Tony, on his knees, with his face toward the weeping sky and arms uplifted, prayed mightily that some, at least, might have been saved. One by one, the rest fell to their knees in intercession, gratitude, wonder, and love, aware once again how great was the mercy of God, that He should save them from such a monstrous evil as had come to despoil their city, even at such daunting cost.

The flames began to diminish. Remaining groups piled into cars and drove away. Finally, only Susan, Matt, Andy, Cynthia, and Lacey were left. The rain had settled down to a steady drizzle. They turned toward the two vehicles still waiting behind the hedge.

Susan could not tell if they were tears or raindrops running down Lacey's cheeks. "Lacey," she said, "please come home with me. You shouldn't be alone."

Lacey hung her head, biting her lip. "No, thanks. I better not."

"Whyever not?"

Lacey shrugged, shook her head. "I don't know how I feel. I have to sort things out. Everything's so mixed up. I don't know anything anymore. And I think it would be best for me to be alone. I need to think. Besides, I won't be alone. Margaret's there."

Susan drew a breath and let it out slowly. She thought she understood, but did she? Were they still friends?

Andy spoke up. "I'll take you home if you like," he offered. "It's not much of a car, but it'll go where I want it to. I think." He held up his bandaged hands. "I think I'll be able to handle it."

Lacey turned toward him. "Thanks."

"What about you, Cynthia?" Matt asked. "Could Susan and I take you home?"

Cynthia nodded. "I'd be grateful," she said. "What with John—" her voice caught, and she fell silent.

Plodding, sloshing sodden through the rain, they separated. Andy and Lacey climbed into his wet 4x4; Cynthia and Susan slid into the front seat of Matt's car. Engines started, eyes looked once more at the still incandescent heap, its stone tower a bleak skeleton with the fires of hell glowing inside.

Two vehicles drove around the curve toward Playa Linda, leaving only John Merkel's luxury sedan waiting in the dark near the Castle, in the rain, abandoned.

THIRTY-SEVEN

Friday, November 1, All Saints' Day, 2:35 P.M.

Connie had just refilled the three coffee cups. Susan sat soberly watching the little bubbles breaking around the edge of the dark, steaming liquid. A trick of her mind made her almost see scarlet flames dancing on the surface of the dark brown brew. She closed her eyes. When she opened them, they were gone. Matt, sitting beside her, seemed equally preoccupied. Andy, across from Matt, tried to stick the plaster holding a bandage on his palm back to his hand. His normally perpetual cheer was still in hiding.

Silence wrapped around them like a shroud. Flatware clattering and scraping on dishes, ice tinkling in tall glasses, and voices in conversation filled the little café, but the sounds did not quite reach the last booth on the left.

Matt finally stirred. "Who's going to write the story? You?"

Susan shook her head. "Andy and I talked to Jackson and Pete. They'll both work on it. I don't even want to read it, much less write it."

Silence. Matt scribed circles on the table with the end of his spoon.

"This plaster won't stick anymore," Andy said.

Silence. Susan picked up her cup and sipped.

"Anyone know how Isham and Karen are doing?" Andy asked finally.

Susan looked up from her cup, her eyes dark. "I called the hospital. Karen's in a coma. They don't know much yet—guess they're doing all sorts of tests. Her parents are frantic. The doctors haven't given them much hope. Her skull was fractured, and there's pressure—" Her expression became still more solemn, her eyes sparkled with unshed tears. "If she dies, it'll be my fault. Because of my story."

"No, honey," Matt said. "It's not your fault. Besides, from what you said, no matter what happens, she's safe. Even if, God forbid, she should die. She'd be with Jesus. But I'm betting she'll get well."

Susan turned toward Matt and a tear ran down her cheek. "Thank you for that," she said, her voice breaking. "Maybe after awhile I can think that way, too." She fell silent a moment. "As for June Parkhurst, they've not found anything yet."

Silence. Andy picked up his cup and turned it around and around.

"I wish I could have seen the Rodzinskys when Ellen came home," Susan said. "They had been so worried."

Silence. Susan picked up her spoon and stirred the coffee.

"But Yadush is coming along well," she added. "The knife went through muscle and other soft tissue, so it's painful but not too dangerous. It just missed an artery. One of his lungs was somewhat damaged, though."

"Speaking about serious," Matt began, "I hear the feds are already in town, looking for him."

"So soon?" Susan twisted to look incredulously at Matt. "Can't they even let him get well?"

Matt shrugged. "You know bureaucracies. They either stick like glue to the letter of the law or they ignore it completely."

Susan scowled. "This time they could ignore it! He's a hero, y'know?"

Andy nodded. "Don't you suppose that when they get the whole story, and find out he was responsible in a big way for stopping all this mess and getting some of the leaders, that they'll go easy on him?"

"I sure hope so," Susan said. "Isn't there anything we can do, like start a petition or something?"

"Maybe," said Matt. "Let's wait to see what they do."

Silence. They sipped coffee.

"Anyone know anything about Robinson and Crozier?" Andy asked.

Both Matt and Susan shook their heads. "They're still locked up, waiting for bail. Guess it's up to the courts. But they did expose the scheme. That should help," Matt said.

Silence.

"How're your hands, Andy?" Susan asked.

"Oh, they're okay. They kinda smart. Doctor said to keep these bandages on for a couple days more, then come see him again." He fought a wry grin. "I know there's nothing funny about it. I really feel sorry for the firemen who got into the poison oak." But the vision of them scratching stretched the grin. Matt and Susan nodded.

Silence.

"Have you heard from Lacey?" Matt asked Susan.

"No, not directly. Margaret called and said she's been talking to Pastor Wayman." Susan looked at her hands. "I think she's going to be fine." She paused. "Margaret said she was hit hard when her friend John Merkel turned out the way he did. She thought he was just a businessman. And to see him die like that—" She shuddered. "It was more than just awful. She's having trouble getting over it." Her eyes darkened as her mind played the scene over again. "You know, it's a funny thing. As often as she spoke of him, I'd never met him. I didn't know who he was when he came to talk to me there in the room in the Castle."

"What about that other girl, the pretty one, Cynthia?" Andy asked.

"Cynthia?" Susan put on her bright mask. "Well, Andy, it seems that your friend Tony talked to her last night, helped cheer her up, and she called him this morning. Then she called me, and told me that she was through with her trance channelling and was going to start church at St. Joseph's."

"Not at Community?" Matt looked disappointed.

"Oh, give her a break. It's better for her to be at St. Joseph's than conjuring up that Nathaniel spook!"

Andy grinned. "Say, what about the little girl from that other mess—Lucy May?"

"Lily Mae," Susan said. "Would you believe it? When her parents never came for her nor answered any of the correspondence from the hospital, Pastor and Mrs. Wayman took her home with them. They're talking about adopting her if her parents don't show up to claim her."

"They're not worried that she's a witch?" Andy asked.

"They'll take care of that little problem. They'll have her hooked on Jesus in no time." Susan thought back to the sad little girl she had seen. "I doubt she was really crazy about the idea of being a witch, anyway. She'd seen too much."

Matt glanced at his watch. "Oops, it's 'way past three." He sighed, looked at Susan. "Gotta get back to work." He studied her, noted her pallor and the dullness in her eyes that seemed to return every time she let the bright mask fall. "Are you sure you're all right, Honey?" he asked.

She sat for a moment in silence. "Yeah, I'm all right," she said, her voice as dull as her eyes. "It's just—well, everything that's happened—it's hit me hard. I'll never forget it. I never knew there was such terrible evil, such—awful, filthy, sick, bloody wickedness in the world. You hear about it, but it's different when you actually see it happening. So dreadfully different." Her darkened eyes looked huge in her white face.

Matt slipped his arm around her shoulders. "I know, Sweetheart, I know." She leaned her head on his shoulder.

"Me, too," said Andy, looking up from his bandages. "For awhile there in the Castle, I didn't know for sure if we'd ever get out."

Susan drew a deep breath and put on a smile. "But we did, didn't we? Thanks to Isham." She became serious. "I don't know what we'd have done if Dorothy and Jessica and Pastor Wayman and Tony and all the others hadn't given everything they had in prayer for us." The three looked at each other, identifying with each others' minds and hearts, not daring to contemplate what could have happened. No one mentioned the angels. The experience had touched them too deeply for something as ordinary as speech.

"And wasn't Laura wonderful!" Susan could see her soaring above the—She turned her mind away from the remembrance of what was going on below Laura. But God's angels were truly there, winning their battle for them!

Matt and Andy nodded, unable to speak, the vision of the angels still hovering in their minds as well. God, rather than any of them, had fought and won the battle. All they had done was pray, do all they could possibly do, and, as Paul wrote, "having done all, to stand."

"And the music!" Matt said. "I think that really, really got to them."

Susan nodded. "It gave me chills!" She looked at her watch. "Well, I guess I'd better get back to work." She turned to Matt. "Thanks, Matt. See you for dinner?" Her expression pleaded.

"Sure thing. Soon's we close up shop."

Andy finished his coffee and stood up. "Well, guys, it's been—" he stopped—"I was going to say it's been fun, but I guess that's not the word I wanted." He stepped out of the booth. "But it was sure interesting. Considering we might never have gotten out of there."

He paused, shivered. "Listen, I'll see you later. Thanks for the coffee. Gotta go."

Matt watched him out the door. Susan pawed through her purse, found a lipstick and a small mirror. "There," she said a moment later. "Better?" She smiled and her cheerful mask slipped into place.

Matt appraised her. "Amazing. You paint your mouth and all of a sudden, your whole face comes alive."

She chuckled, and he put his arm back around her shoulders as they left. Matt stopped as they reached her Escort at the curb. "I know it's been hard on you. What can I do to help?"

Susan put her arms around his waist and buried her face in his chest. "Just love me, pray for me, be there when I need you, help me to think about other things, too. Okay?"

"You got it." He looked at the top of her head and thought of how depressed she was. "By the way, I've been thinking. Something you should be thinking about, too." He reached into a pocket. "I was going to give this to you tonight, but I think maybe now's a better time."

He handed her a small dark blue velvet box. "You've had a rough time these last few weeks. It's time you had something good happen. At least, I hope you'll think it's good." His eyes held hope, anxiety, a touch of fear, and a world of love.

Susan looked at it in surprise, looked up at Matt, back at the box. "Well, open it!"

She looked long into his eyes, looked back at the box, lifted the lid slowly. Nestled in satin, a diamond glimmered in a graceful setting, winking in the sunlight that is always so brilliant after the world has been washed clean by rain. Her lower lip quivered, her eyes brimmed with tears, but the smile she turned on Matt put the sunlight to shame. She folded the box in her hand and hugged Matt as if to crush him, leaving her tears on his shirt.

"I love it!" she said, pulling away, looking into his eager eyes. "It's so beautiful! Please, put it on for me?"

"You will marry me, then? For sure? Next month?"

"I should play hard to get, but—Yes! Yes, I'll marry you!"

Matt took the box from her, removed the ring, slipped it on her finger, bent down, and kissed her hand. Susan's face showed her struggle between tears of despairing sorrow, of joy, and a desire to whoop with delight.

Their arms around each other, lost in a world of their own making, they were completely unaware of traffic whizzing past, of people standing on the sidewalk, smiling, and of Connie finally coming out of the café and shooing the pedestrians on their way. When they had gone, Connie stood there another moment, enjoying the sight.

"'Bout time," she muttered, turning to go back to her customers.

-END-

ABOUT THE AUTHOR

Helen DesErmia has worked in music education, art, journalism, and writing. She is active in the San Diego County Christian Writers' Guild and the Palomar Branch, National League of Pen Women. Additional interests include ancient biblical history, sub-tropical horticulture, and photography.

Helen lives with her husband in southern California.